Special Seating: An Illustrated Guide

Revised Edition

Jean Anne Zollars, MA, PT

Prickly Pear Publications

www.seatingzollars.com

2010

ISBN: 978 1 4507 3735 7

Library of Congress Cataloging-in-Publication Data

A catalog record for this book is available from the Library of Congress

Printed in the United States of America

Cover design: Gaye Roth

Prickly Pear Publications
PO Box 35818
Albuquerque, NM 87176
www.seatingzollars.com

Table of Contents

FOREWORD

PREFACE

INTRODUCTION

Part I. ASSESSMENT

Chapter 1   Gathering Background Information

Chapter 2   Physical Assessment: Posture, Movement, and Function

Dedication

This book is dedicated to my true teachers—all the adults and children I have worked with over the years who have gently encouraged me to expand my heart and mind, and share this information with others.

Acknowledgments

The second edition was developed with the input from many people. I wish to thank the following people:

Jamie Noon, who spent countless hours with me discussing seating and sharing his innovative ideas.

Adrienne Bergen, PT, ATP, who meticulously perused the first edition and provided comments, opinions and wisdom in the field of seating and mobility.

Jessica Presperin-Pedersen, MBA, OTR/L, ATP, who inspired me to rewrite the book. Jessica provided valuable input in Chapter 17.

Mark Richter, PhD, who helped rewrite Chapter 15: Wheelchair Considerations.

Betsy McKone, BA, OTR, ATP, who contributed to Chapter 17: sections on osteogenesis imperfecta, muscular dystrophy, and arthrogryposis multiple congenita.

Cindy Smith, PT, ATP, who edited and provided input for Chapter 14: Pressure Relief Cushions, Chapter 17: section on spinal cord injury.

Brenda Canning, OTR/L, and **Debra Pucci, OTR/L,** who contributed to Chapter 17: section on spinal cord injury.

Peter Axelson, MS, ME, David Cooper, M. Sc. Kines, Simon Margolis, ATP, and **Kelly Waugh, PT, MAPT, ATP,** for technical and conceptual assistance.

Guillermo Prado, who initially designed and laid out the book.

Gaye Roth, who modified and created new illustrations, and completed the book design.

Heidi Schulman, who assisted in editing the book.

My husband, **Gerhardt**, and son, **Isaac** for their loving patience.

For the first edition, I wish to thank the following people: **Joyce Knezevich**, who illustrated the book, **Simon Margolis**, who organized the design and production; **Cristine Wright-Ott**, for her editorial and conceptual assistance; **Elsa** and **Bill Zollars** for their loving support; **Aaron Johnson-Benning** for just being himself and for sharing his story; **Monica Mann, Kristin Obrinsky, Bill Bazata, Bonnie Morgan**, and **Anita Feder-Chernila** for their support and friendship.

Twenty years ago at a seating seminar, Jean Anne asked me to help design a molded seating system for a person in rural Mexico. We became a team after our trip to Mexico, brainstorming and working through seating issues. This book illustrates that process, which Jean Anne and I were fortunate to do together. This process occurs when a person who understands the physical and functional needs of the person with disability, can communicate to a designer, and who can translate those needs into equipment. Jean Anne and I understand that if you really take the time to listen to a person, both to the body and what the person expresses, you will be successful in designing and fitting equipment to enhance that person's life. This is the intuitive aspect of seating. With any intuitive practice, one must know the basics of assessment and how to create or choose the appropriate technology.

Jean Anne and I have worked together at the Rehabilitation Engineering Center, Lucile Salter Packard Children's Hospital at Stanford, in New Mexico, Mexico, England, and the former Soviet Union. During our collaboration, we evaluated, created, designed, and taught seating. I went on to work throughout the developed and developing world. My own approach and views have been greatly influenced by hers. The first edition of Jean Anne's book has been used extensively by special seating services around the world, and her name has, most deservedly, been on the tongues of practitioners everywhere.

Over the years, experts from many areas, including physical and occupational therapists, designers, prosthetists, orthotists, and engineers, as well as the parents of children with disabilities, have contributed their perspectives. This expanded edition reflects their valuable contributions. With more than a little excitement, I welcome this revised edition, assured that people around the world will benefit even more from her work. And that is what it is all about, isn't it? Enhancing people's quality of life!

— **Jamie Noon**, *Seating Designer/Trainer*

Foreword

Jean Anne Zollars has revised and expanded her original book, *Special Seating: An Illustrated Guide* (OttoBock, MN, 1996), which has served as a valuable tool for students, therapists, suppliers, and persons with disabilities. This new edition contains updated information and illustrations as well as a new chapter on special considerations for individuals with a variety of diagnoses and conditions. The revised edition retains the same easy-to-read text and clear illustrations demonstrating the evaluation process and design ideas for seating/mobility intervention.

Jean Anne expresses the need to balance seating intervention with the person's physical, functional, psychological, cognitive, and spiritual being. She continues to project a holistic approach, focusing on observation and handling techniques, while recognizing the contribution of higher technology. Jean Anne consistently emphasizes that seating is both an art and a science that involves not only critical thinking and analysis, but an intuitive understanding of the person's needs, motivation, and acceptance of the technology. This book will be a valuable addition to the seating therapist's library and a joy to share with people with disabilities and their families, students, designers, and suppliers.

— **Jessica Presperin-Pedersen**, *MBA, OTR/L, ATP*

Preface

Before we start on this journey through seating, I would like to share my approach as a therapist. I approach each person with a tremendous amount of respect, compassion, and curiosity. I feel honored to partake in a person-to-person partnership, whether in therapy or in the assessment and provision of seating. I believe each person is a surprise, an incredible storehouse of information, who is influenced by many internal systems—physical, intellectual, emotional, spiritual— that vie for balance with the vast array of external systems in the world. Given the wonderful complexities of each human being, I do not pretend to know the answers. I would not be honest if I thought I did. I see myself as a guide, a facilitator, an investigator to help people find their own answers.

I see the seating assessment and design process like a picture frame that provides structure and organization to the process. The emptiness of the frame does not imply nothingness. Instead, beyond the frame lies an unseen canvas awaiting the creative possibilities of the imagination. In order to explore the unknown, I believe we need to have a strong, secure understanding of the basics of seating.

I wrote this book because people who are providing seating and mobility systems throughout the world need to learn more about the seating assessment and design process. My dream is that if people approach seating with greater awareness and understanding, individuals with disabilities will be more appropriately fit with seating and mobility systems.

The first version of this book was based on my experiences in areas of the world where people and projects lack money and resources. Frequently people had inappropriate or no seating/mobility systems. Often professionals and people with disabilities were unaware that specialized seating was a possibility. Most people with spinal cord injuries in these countries die of pressure sores within the first year after injury. Additionally, I realized that those of us in wealthier and more technologically advanced parts of the world need to be better trained. In the United States, where many technological options are available, seating components and systems are often used inappropriately. I am aware, based on my own experience that it is difficult to become educated or trained in seating and mobility because few standardized training programs or methodologies exist.

When I first became involved with seating, I could not find a manual to guide me in the seating assessment and problem-solving process. Literature, seminars, conferences, and most importantly, experiences with persons with disabilities, helped me put the puzzle pieces together to develop my approach to seating.

Seating is difficult to teach because it is an art form, a creative problem-solving process. Biomechanical, ergonomic, and neurodevelopmental principles can provide us with a structure, but logical, analytical thought processes must be integrated with the creative, intuitive mind. This active interchange between the right (creative) and left (analytical) sides of the brain is a challenge if only one person is providing seating. If a team is working together, the people using the intuitive skills (often the therapists) need to communicate clearly with those needing concrete technical information (usually the engineers or technology suppliers). This book provides descriptive questions to bridge the communication gap between the sensing information and the mechanical aspect of seating. Workers in rehabilitation projects in Mexico and Nicaragua strengthened my belief in the power of the intuitive mind. The workers, most of whom had only a third-grade education and none of whom were professionally trained in seating or therapy, relied on their common sense and intuition to create innovative and appropriate seating systems.

Central to these intuitive processes is the use of our hands and body to feel, sense, and observe how the person responds to different types of postural support and relationships to gravity. Listening with our hands and senses is the essence of this book.

Seating is an art enriched by experience and practice. People respond differently to support or pressure, different textures, allowing or restraining their movement. Your best tools are listening with all of your senses and getting in touch with each individual to understand his or her needs. If we always approach seating like beginners, we can remain open to the diverse needs of each individual. There are always a multitude of factors to consider and compromises to make. Seating is challenging, fun, and very, very important work. Take it seriously and laugh a lot. I wish you well on your journey.

Introduction

A Purpose of this Book

Who is this book written for?

This seating book is written for people with disabilities; physical, occupational, and speech therapists; rehabilitation technology suppliers, physicians, parents, teachers, vocational counselors, technologists, engineers, and just about anyone who is involved in the prescription, fabrication, provision, and use of special seating and mobility systems for people with disabilities.

What is special seating?

Many children and adults with disabilities need more postural support than is provided by an ordinary chair or wheelchair. An existing wheelchair or chair can be adapted, or a seating system can be specially designed for that person. A *seating system* can be made with wheels, or designed to fit inside a *mobility system*. A seating system usually consists of a seat cushion, back support, and additional components that give the person more postural support. A mobility system is the base that allows the individual to move from place to place. Examples of mobility systems are wheelchairs, strollers, power wheelchairs, carts, and horses.

Why are seating and mobility important?

Special seating and wheelchairs (mobility) can provide the key to independence for persons with disabilities. An individual who is unable to walk is sitting most of the day, so the seating system should fit like flexible but supportive clothing. Mobility systems should provide an efficient means to move about in indoor and outdoor environments. Mobility directly impacts integration into the community. Children are able to go to school and participate in various activities. Adults have the ability to work, shop, and participate in recreational activities. Integration is not only good for people with disabilities, but wonderful and essential for the society.

Children with disabilities who are unable to walk or sit by themselves are limited to lying on the floor or being carried. Their opportunities to see, play, and learn like other children are further restricted when they become too large or heavy to be carried and are simply left behind. Breathing and eating can become difficult for these children, and contractures and deformities may also develop. Persons who cannot eat, write, play independently, or use their hands fully, may be able to do these things better when seated comfortably and optimally for functioning.

1

Seating and mobility directly impacts the possibility of changing negative societal attitudes. Without seating and mobility, individuals with disabilities cannot easily get out of their homes, become visible, vital members of society, and organize to fight for their rights. They are the very ones who have made, and will make changes in their own lives, attitudes, policies, and laws. These attitudes not only affect those with disabilities personally, but often impact the allocation of resources, funds, and services. In the United States, people with disabilities have struggled long and hard to create and change laws. Worldwide, individuals and communities must continue to raise their levels of awareness and deepen their compassion so that all human beings are respected for their abilities as well as disabilities. Dehumanizing attitudes about disability constantly need to be challenged and changed on both personal and societal levels. Seating and mobility are vehicles to facilitate this process.

What is the purpose of this book?

The intent of this book is to get back to the basics of seating assessment and design of seating systems. The language is clear or clearly defined, and the book is fully illustrated. It can be used by just about anyone interested in the seating process, from beginners or people who consider themselves experts. It is intended to be inclusive, as it has been written for and about people of different disciplines and expertise, people of different socioeconomic status, cultures, religions, ethnicities, and those who live in rural as well as urban environments.

What is included in this seating book?

This book provides assessment guidelines and ideas for appropriate postural supports and modifications. Intervention suggestions are provided in a systematic way in an attempt to organize the thought process and to present a variety of available options; however, please do not limit yourself to the presented options. Each person requiring a seating system has unique and individual needs. Approach each person with an open frame of mind. The person requiring the seating/mobility system is the expert. The professional is one who can help clarify the issues and come up with possible solutions. The design is not created by one person, but by the interaction of all the people involved with the consumer. Use your judgment and creativity to expand and change ideas presented in this book to design an appropriate seating system for the individual. The best way to understand the concepts presented in the book is to practice the techniques on other people with or without disabilities. The best way to learn about seating is to do it, and evaluate whether it achieves the intended outcomes.

How is this book different from other seating books?

The unique aspect of this book is *hand simulation*. This is different than using a simulator, seating evaluation chair, or creating a trial seating system. Hand simulation means supporting or sculpting the person's body with your hands while the person is sitting on a flat firm surface. Take this hand support a step further: use your hands and body to feel, sense, and observe how the individual responds to support in different areas, to different shapes and relationships to gravity. Next, describe very specifically how you are supporting the person with your hands before a single component is discussed. This step is essential. It is very easy to grab pieces and parts of equipment and to want to find quick solutions. We must spend more time with our hands to get really clear about the individual's needs before equipment is considered.

Difficult words

Seating can be complicated and made more confusing by long medical terms. An attempt was made to use understandable language, supported by illustrations. The difficult words are italicized and bolded the first time they are presented (i.e. *contractures*), and explained in the Glossary at the end of the book.

ISO Standards

The technical terminology for seating and mobility has been changed to align with current 2008 ISO Standards created by the RESNA Standards Committee on Wheelchair and Related Seating (see Suggested Reading). Beginning in Chapter 5, the first time an ISO term is used, a world sign (⊕) appears next to the term. For example, the term "back support" (⊕) is used instead of "backrest."

How is the second edition different from the first edition?

This edition is intended to be clearer, and more thorough and accurate than the first edition. Seating experts from around the world clarified existing information and added new ideas. In this field, seating experts' "best practices" guide us to the most effective seating/mobility intervention. Also, the literature and research has been reviewed and included. In this time of evidence-based practice, practitioners aware of the research are more informed on behalf of their clients and will be able to justify their seating decisions for third-party payers.[1,2]

Most research has been focused on pressure measurements in relation to cushion effectiveness, tilt, and function in persons with spinal cord injury and in the elderly; and wheelchair propulsion in the prevention of upper extremity injuries in persons with spinal cord injuries. More research is needed on the effectiveness of seating intervention for children with cerebral palsy and other conditions.[3,4] Keep in mind that research results do not determine seating/mobility decisions. The person with the disability and her team, and clinical judgment of the seating practitioners determine the seating/mobility choices. Research can inform but not determine your decisions.[5]

This edition provides seating considerations for people with a variety of clinical conditions, including *traumatic brain injury, osteogenesis imperfecta, arthrogryposis multiplex congenita, muscular dystrophy, pain, spinal cord injuries, spina bifida, multiple sclerosis*, amputees, the elderly, and hemiplegia. It provides more ideas about simulation with materials. Information about assessing pressure, and developing or choosing cushions from that assessment is included. Also, some assessment considerations have been added. For instance, the term "practical flexibility" is used in addition to the percentage of joint mobility to assess the comfortable flexibility in a person's joint. In addition, hip flexion joint measurement has been changed to be consistent with traditional physical therapy measures.

For therapists and designers: don't be misled by the simplicity of the language in this book. This is not a basic book on seating. This book pushes the edges of seating. It pushes us to take the time to fully and specifically assess what the person needs prior to rushing into a seating/mobility decision. It also encourages us to be creative. Seating assessment, design terminology, and concepts should be made understandable not only to therapists and designers, but also to the person with the disability and to those who know this person. Family members and caregivers really know the child or adult with a disability, her day-to-day needs, what works, and what does not work. In many places in the United States, parents and suppliers are deciding on seating/mobility interventions. Thus, this book is accessible to everyone—it needs to be. The end goal is a seating and mobility system that improves the life for the person with the disability.

Touch

Ask permission before touching a person and their equipment. It is best to explain what you plan to do prior to touching the person. Please be sensitive and respectful when you are touching another person. We all have been touched improperly. People with disabilities often have had negative experiences with health professionals "doing" things to them, whether during medical or therapeutic procedures. In this book you are asked many times to "let your hands guide you" to understand how the seating supports should function. As you simulate with your hands, recognize when you are forcing and not supporting the person's body. Different degrees and amount of support and pressure are appropriate for specific problems. Think about how this would feel to your own body, and whether the seating system should provide this support.

Note: Gender-related pronouns

The illustrations show both men and women requiring seating intervention. However, for clarity and language flow, the text uses only the pronoun *she/her* when referring to the person with a disability. This is true except in the section on Duchenne's muscular dystrophy, which affects only boys.

A special story...

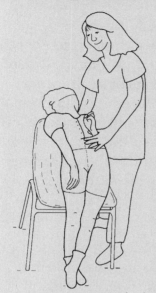

Haslin was 9 years old and had cerebral palsy.* Her mother brought her to a seating program, as Haslin needed a seating/mobility system so that she could to go to school. Because Haslin's muscles were very stiff, her back arched and her legs pushed out straight. In this posture, she had difficulty breathing and could not eat without choking. She did not speak, although she communicated with facial expressions.

The project workers evaluated Haslin and decided to make her a special wheeled chair. A special seat cushion, postural supports and straps were used to support her hips, legs, ankles, and trunk, so that she could hold her head up. Next, the workers and her mother made a headband with a pointer attached to it. They also made a communication board with pictures of Haslin's family, activities in her life and faces showing different emotions.

A whole new life opened up for Haslin with her special wheeled chair. She was finally able to leave her home and play with the other children in the village. The special supports in the chair allowed her to sit by herself so that she could play, learn, and use her head pointer to communicate her needs. A kitten adopted her, as the kitten would snuggle in her lap. Her breathing improved and eating was easier. She felt better about herself, and her friends were beginning to treat her with more respect.

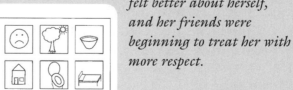

---

* I worked with Haslin (name changed) in 1987 in Malaysia. She was my inspiration for this book.

B | Benefits of Seating

As we can see from Haslin's story, special seating can help a person in many ways. Reasons for special seating will be specific to each person, depending on his or her needs. For instance, a child with *cerebral palsy*, like Haslin, needs support to control her posture and abnormal movements. Other important seating goals for Haslin are to improve her ability to eat, breathe, communicate, socialize, and learn. A person with a spinal cord injury may be unable to feel discomfort and *pressure* under her buttocks when sitting. Without this *sensation*, she does not naturally move to relieve the pressure. Without a cushion to help to relieve pressure under the buttocks, she can quickly develop life-threatening *pressure sores*. Therefore, an important seating goal for a person with a *spinal cord injury* is the prevention of pressure sores.

Special seating can:

- **Improve comfort**. The person must be comfortable in the seating system, particularly if she will be sitting for long periods of time and has difficulty moving her body. If the person is uncomfortable, she may cry, become anxious, not want to sit upright, or move around a lot to try to find comfort. This movement can be a problem if she gets stuck in poor postures that hinder function.[6-8]
- **Relieve pressure**. If a person has no feeling (sensation) under her buttocks or other areas, a cushion should help to relieve or distribute pressure to help prevent *tissue* (skin and muscle) breakdown over *bony prominences* (bony areas that protrude under the muscle and skin).[6-11]
- **Support the body**. If the person has difficulty sitting because parts of her body are weak, the muscles are tight (*spasticity*), or movements are difficult to control, the seating system should provide enough support so that she feels posturally secure and safe. With her body well supported, she may be able to use her arms more effectively. Also, it may be easier for her to hold her head up, so that she will be able to see and interact with people and things in her environment. Too much postural support can be problematic if it hinders a person's function. Supporting the body can also help to reduce the forces that contribute to *contractures* and *deformities*.[6-8]
- **Improve function**. Seating should improve the person's ability to function. This may mean making it easier to toilet, bathe, eat,[12-14] digest,[15,16] dress, work, learn, use her arms or legs,[17-23] communicate,[24] get around in the wheelchair indoors and in the community,[25] and participate in recreational activities. Any device used by the person should help, and never hinder, function.[6,7] Because different sitting postures are required for various functional activities, the seating/mobility system may need to be adjustable.[26] If it cannot be adjusted, the person may need more than one seating system. If the person has limited endurance to the upright position, the seating/mobility system should adjust or tilt to allow the person to rest.

- **Improve bodily functions**. Breathing will be easier if a person is sitting fairly upright in her neutral posture, than if her trunk is curved forward (*kyphosis*) or to the side (*scoliosis*).[27,28] Blood flow and digestion can also be improved if she is supported appropriately.
- **Change/adapt**. A person's first seating system and/or wheelchair may provide a lot of postural support. However, as she gains more internal postural stability, control, and strength, the amount of *postural support* provided by the seating system may be decreased. This can best be determined by reassessing the person and seating system every 6 months. A seating system may also need to be adjustable to allow for various functional requirements during the day, or for seasonal clothing needs. Lastly, it should allow for changes due to weight gain, growth, or progressive health conditions.

C Posture

1. The Relationship Between Posture, Movement, and Function

The terms *position* and *posture* have different meanings. Position is a static, inactive term referring to nonliving things. We will describe the **position** of seating components, but refer to the **posture** of the person. Posture is active and dynamic, meaning that the body is ready to move.[29] Posture is how the body parts are aligned or arranged at any given moment. Normally our posture is constantly shifting and changing so that we can move to function.[30] In order to move one part of our body, we stabilize another part of our body. For instance, if I want to type at the computer, I wrap my ankles around the legrests of my chair to stabilize my legs and pelvis so that I can use my arms to type. But if I want to reach behind and above me for a book on the shelf, I will shift my pelvis, lean my midback against the backrest. I then press my arm into the armrest to stabilize myself so that I can reach behind me. I need *postural options*, or choices of different postures, in order to function in sitting. So, when assessing and providing postural support for a person in a seating system, a variety of postural options should be available to her.

2. Neutral Posture

a. What is *the person's* neutral posture?

It is the posture in which the person's body is well-aligned, stable, and balanced. It is her home base, or the place to come back to between extremes of postural changes. In *the person's* neutral posture, she is more rested, and her muscles do not have to work a lot to maintain this posture. However, she is not collapsed and inactive. It is the starting place for other postures to occur. In this posture, the individual is ready for action.

Where do we start? How do we help the person find her neutral posture? Where is the person's body well-aligned, stable, balanced, rested, but ready for action? How do we determine what postures will allow her to be active, to function, and to move optimally?

b. What is *the* neutral posture?

Before we discuss how to find *the person's* neutral posture, we will describe *the* neutral posture. This will be used as our reference point for a "well-aligned" posture. *The* neutral posture is different than *the person's* neutral posture. Everyone's neutral posture, point of balance and stability (disabled or nondisabled) can be slightly or radically different. For years, researchers and seating experts have had varying opinions about the optimal posture.[29-35] I suggest that each person must be assessed to determine her own optimal neutral posture and range of postural options.

The Neutral Posture

- *Pelvis* upright and level (neutral) or slightly rolled forward
- Trunk upright with the back following its natural curves
- Hips and legs separated (5-8° from midline)
- Knees and ankles bent (usually *right angles* (90°), or more bent than 90°), so that the feet rest on the floor or support surface
- Head upright, in *midline* (center of the body) and balanced over the body, allowing her to look at things in front of her
- Shoulders relaxed, arms free to move and function

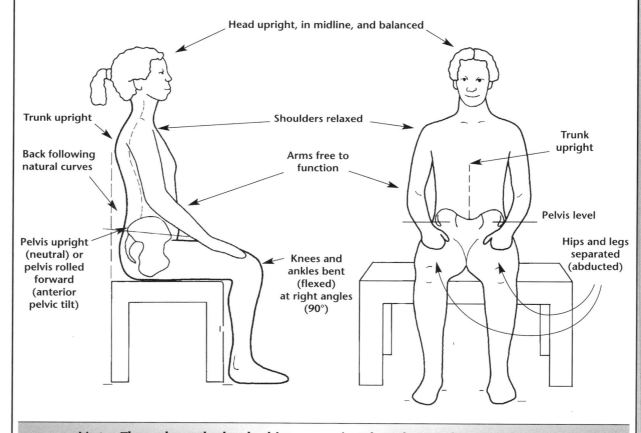

Head upright, in midline, and balanced

Trunk upright

Back following natural curves

Pelvis upright (neutral) or pelvis rolled forward (anterior pelvic tilt)

Shoulders relaxed

Arms free to function

Knees and ankles bent (flexed) at right angles (90°)

Trunk upright

Pelvis level

Hips and legs separated (abducted)

Note: Throughout the book, this posture is referred to as *the* neutral posture.

---

c. **Why do we start with this posture?** *The* neutral posture:

- **Provides a stable *base of support*.** The pelvis, hips, legs, and feet are our foundation in sitting, providing a stable base from which we shift our weight to move. The posture of the pelvis affects the posture of the whole body. If the pelvis is in the neutral posture, the rest of the body has a better chance of being balanced, stable, and active. When the hips and legs are separated so that the knees are wider than the pelvic width, the base of support is more stable. If the hips and legs are in this posture, and the knees and ankles are flexed to 90° or greater so that the feet are behind the knees, the person may be able to move her pelvis forward over her thighs. This movement allows her to reach forward to perform tasks.

- **Puts the body into a "ready" posture.** When the natural curves of the spine are supported, the body will feel more alive and ready to move. The back is not flat. The low back (*lumbar spine*) and neck (*cervical spine*) have a natural arch (*lordosis*). The midback (*thoracic spine*) and *sacrum* naturally curve forward (*kyphosis*).

- **Enhances vision.** The person should be able to see directly in front of and below her, and rotate her head freely to both sides. The posture of the head depends on the posture of the pelvis and trunk. The head is balanced on top of the spine like a bowling ball on a stick. The head is heavy and its point of balance is very sensitive and subtle, so that a slight body movement may affect the head posture. Because of the mobile nature of the bones of the neck (cervical spine), the head can move in many directions. Thus, if a person has weakness or poorly controlled movement, the head and neck are often unstable. The head's neutral or desirable posture is where the head is balanced on top of the spine.

- **Optimizes arm and hand function.** In the neutral posture, with the *shoulder girdles* (shoulder joints, clavicles, shoulder blades [*scapulae*]) relaxed, the arms should be free to move and function.

d. **How do we determine *the person's* neutral posture?**

Starting from *the* neutral posture, the person's joint and muscular flexibility, response to gravity, stiffness (tone), movement patterns, point of stability, and balance will determine *the person's* neutral posture. The assessment section will help you determine the person's neutral posture and postural options required for functional movement.

e. **What posture(s) are we trying to support, assist, and or prevent in the seating system?**

Optimally, the seating system should:
- Support the person in **her neutral posture**
- Allow and support the person in postures that she requires for function, giving her **postural options**

D Understanding the Pelvis—Spine Connection

1. Feeling the Pelvis

The pelvis is commonly referred to as the hip bone. Put your hands on your "hips" (the pelvis). You are feeling the top ridge of the pelvis called the *iliac crest*. Follow this ridge towards the front and you will feel a bony area that sticks out (bony prominence). This is called the *ASIS* (anterior superior iliac spine). Follow the iliac crest towards the back of the body. The crest ends at another bony prominence called the *PSIS* (posterior superior iliac spine). Without moving your shoulders, tilt your pelvis forwards and backwards. This movement is occurring *above the pelvis* between the sacrum and lumbar spine, and between the individual back bones (*vertebrae*) of the lumbar spine. Also, this movement is occurring *below the pelvis*, at the hip joint between the pelvis and the thigh bone (*femur*).

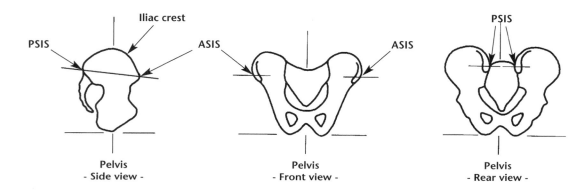

2. A Neutral Pelvis

To feel another person's pelvis, sit to her side, or in front or back. She should be sitting on a flat level surface. Find the person's ASIS, iliac crest, and PSIS as described above. Tilt her pelvis forward and backward. The pelvis is *neutral* when the bony prominences at the top/front of the pelvis (ASIS) are just slightly lower than the bony prominences at the top/back of the pelvis (PSIS). You can also feel the pelvic movements and a neutral pelvis when the person is lying on her back or her side.

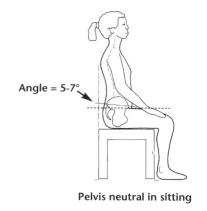

Pelvis neutral in sitting

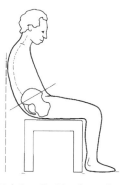

Pelvis rolled backwards
(posterior pelvic tilt)

Pelvis neutral when lying on his back

Pelvis not neutral (posteriorly tilted)
when lying on his back

3. Importance of the Pelvic Posture

Why do you think the posture of the pelvis is important? Close your eyes and *very* slowly, tilt your pelvis side to side and then front to back. Feel how the posture of your back, head, legs, and arms changes as you move your pelvis. Do you feel how you can not change the posture of your pelvis without affecting the posture of the rest of your body? If the pelvis is stuck in a certain posture, the rest of the body will also be stuck in a certain posture. If the pelvis is able to achieve the neutral posture, the rest of the body has a better chance of achieving a neutral posture.

Now, with your pelvis upright, reach forward. Tilt your pelvis backwards and reach again. Again, tilt your pelvis into a neutral, upright posture. Swallow. Now tilt your pelvis to the side and swallow. Notice whether there is any difference in swallowing. Can you feel that when the pelvis is in different postures that your function is affected?

4. The Sacrum

The sacrum is a wedge-shaped bone located between both sides of the back of the pelvis. The sacrum's bottom end is connected to the tailbone (*coccyx*). Its upper end is connected to the bones of the low back (lumbar vertebrae). The sacrum is actually five vertebrae fused together. To find your sacrum, reach to the back of your buttocks. With your middle finger on your tailbone, pointing towards the seat, your palm will be cupping the sacrum. This bone is important in seating because of its shape and the movement between it and the lumbar spine. Sometimes we provide postural support to the sacrum. In people with little fat or inactive buttock muscles, bony prominences (*spinous processes*) of the sacral vertebrae stick out. If the back support does not allow space or cushioning for these areas, the tissue may be at risk for breakdown.

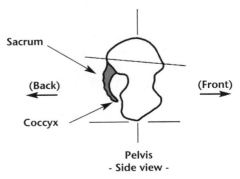

Sacrum

(Back)

Coccyx

Pelvis
- Side view -

(Front)

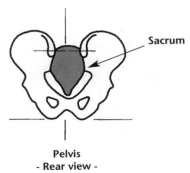

Sacrum

Pelvis
- Rear view -

References

1. Schmeler M, Boninger M, Cooper R, Viteck M. Using peer-reviewed literature and other evidence to justify wheelchair seating and mobility interventions. *Proceedings from the 18th International Seating Symposium.* 2002.

2. Schmeler M, Chovan C. Assessment and provision of wheeled mobility and seating using best practice, evidence-based practice and understanding coverage policy. *Proceedings from the 22nd International Seating Symposium.* 2006:182-5.

3. Roxborough L. Review of the efficacy and effectiveness of adaptive seating for children with cerebral palsy. *Assist Technol.* 1995;7(1):17-25.

4. Minkel J, Harris S. Evidence-based practice in seating and mobility: Can we support what we are doing? *Proceedings from the 12th International Seating Symposium* 1996:195-8.

5. Eng J. Spinal cord injury rehabilitation: What's the evidence telling us? *Proceedings from the 22nd International Seating Symposium.* 2006:31-4.

6. Bergen A, Presperin J, Tallman T. *Positioning for Function: Wheelchairs and Other Assistive Technologies.* Valhalla, NY: Valhalla Rehabilitation Publications, Ltd.; 1990.

7. Trefler E, Hobson D, Taylor SJ, Monahan L, Shaw CG. *Seating and Mobility for Persons with Physical Disabilities.* Tucson, AZ: Therapy Skill Builders; 1993.

8. Presperin J. Seating systems: The therapist and the rehabilitation engineering team. *Phys Occup Ther Pediatr.* Spring 1990.

9. Brienza D, Karg PE, Geyer MJ, Kelsey S, Trefler E. The relationship between pressure ulcer incidence and buttock–seat cushion interface pressure in at-risk elderly wheelchair users. *Arch Phys Med Rehabil.* 2001 April;82(4):529-3.

10. Shaw G. Seat cushion comparison for nursing home wheelchair users. *Assist Technol.* 1993;5(2):92-105.

11. Ferguson-Pell M, Wilkie IC, Reswick JB, Barbenel JC. Pressure sore prevention for the wheelchair-bound spinal injury patient. *Paraplegia.* 1980;18:42-51.

12. Bazata C. Open wide: Eating and seating. *Proceedings from the 7th International Seating Symposium.* 1991:197-9.

13. Bazata C. Positioning for oral motor function. *Proceedings from the 8th International Seating Symposium.* 1992:9-13.

14. Hulme JB, et al. Effects of adaptive seating devices on the eating and drinking of children with multiple handicaps. *Am J Occup Ther.* 1987;41(2):81-9.

15. Hardwick K, Handley R. The use of automated seating and mobility systems for management of dysphagia in individuals with multiple disabilities. *Proceedings from the 9th International Seating Symposium.* 1993:271-3.

16. Hardwick K, The role of seating and positioning in the treatment of dysphagia. *Proceedings from the 12th International Seating Symposium.* 1996:47-8.

17. Porter D, Schindler, K. Does postural support influence ability to perform attention tasks in children with cerebral palsy? *Proceedings from the 24th International Seating Symposium.* 2008:158-9.

18. Staveness C. The effect of positioning for children with cerebral palsy on upper-extremity function: A review of the evidence. *Phys Occup Ther Pediatr.* 2006;26(3):39-53.

19. Myhr U, vonWendt L, Norrlin S, Radell U. Five-year follow-up of functional sitting position in children with cerebral palsy. *Dev Med Child Neurol.* 1995;37(7):587-96.

20. Chung J, Evans J, Lee C, Rabbani Y, Roxborough L, Harris SR. Effectiveness of adaptive seating on sitting posture and postural control in children with cerebral palsy. *Pediatr Phys Ther.* 2008 Winter;20(4):303-17.

21. Reid DT, Sochaaniwskyi A. Effects of anterior-tipped seating on respiratory function of normal children and children with cerebral palsy. *Int J Rehabil Res.* 1991; 14(3):203-12.

22. Sprigle S, Wooten M, Sawacha Z, Thielman G. Relationships among cushion type, backrest height, seated posture, and reach of wheelchair users with spinal cord injury. *J Spinal Cord Med.* 2003 Fall;(3):236-43.

23. Aissaoui R, Boucher C, Bourbonnais D, Lacoste M, Danseareau J. Effect of seat cushion on dynamic stability in sitting during a reaching task in wheelchair users with paraplegia. *Arch Phys Med Rehabil.* 2001 February; 82(2):274-81.

24. Hulme JB, Bain B, Hardin M, McKinnon A, Waldron D. The influences of seating devices on vocalization. *J Commun Disord.* 1989;22(2):137-45.

25. Engstrom B. *Ergonomics Wheelchairs and Positioning.* Hasselby, Sweden: Bromma Tryck AB; 1993.

26. Kangas, K. Seating for task performance. *Proceedings from the 18th International Seating Symposium.* 2002.

27. Lin F, Parthasarathy S, Taylor SJ, Pucci D, Hendrix R, Makhsous M. Effect of different sitting postures on lung capacity, expiratory flow, and lumbar lordosis. *Arch Phys Med Rehabil.* 2006 April ;87:504-9.

28. Nwaobi O, Smith P. Effects of adaptive seating on pulmonary function of children with cerebral palsy. *Dev Med Child Neurol.* 1986;28:351-4.

29. Ward D. *Prescriptive Seating for Wheeled Mobility.* Ft. Lauderdale, FL: HealthWealth International; 1994.

30. Kangas K. Sensory systems and seating for function: The need for both active postural control (use of vestibular system) and passive postural management (use of the tactile system). *Proceedings from the 21st International Seating Symposium.* 2005:47.

31. Andersson GBJ, Murphy RW, Ortengren R, Nachemson AL. The influence of backrest inclination and lumbar support on lumbar lordosis. *Spine.* 1979:52-8.

32. Caillet R. *Soft Tissue Pain and Disability.* Philadelphia, PA: F.A. Davis; 1977.

33. Keegan JJ. Alterations of the lumbar curve related to posture and seating. *J Bone Joint Surg.* 1953;35:589-603.

34. Van Niekerk S-M, Louw Q, Vaughan C, Grimmer-Somers K, Schreve K. Photographic measurement of upper-body sitting posture of high school students: A reliability and validity study. *BMC Musculoskelet Disord.* 2008;9:113-26.

35. Zacharow D. *Posture: Sitting, Standing, Chair Design and Exercise.* Springfield, IL: Charles Thomas; 1988.

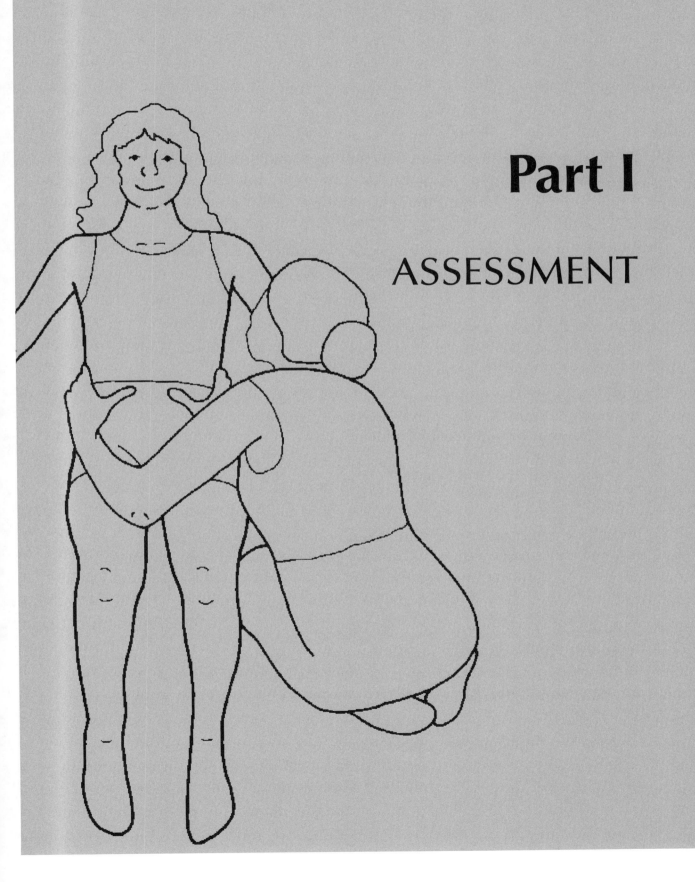

Part I

ASSESSMENT

The following are general assessment guidelines for persons requiring special seating/mobility systems. Remember, *these are only guidelines*. There are always exceptions to the following suggestions. Use these guidelines along with your common sense, observations, and communication with the person being assessed.

Lives of human beings are complex. Seating is complex. It takes time to do a thorough seating assessment. We need to take the time to clearly and completely understand the daily life of the person with the disability. Ideally, everyone who has information about the person's functional, environmental, and health issues impacting the seating assessment should be present at the assessment. If this cannot happen, other members of this "team" need to present the perspectives of the missing team members.

Even though the seating assessment process is an integrative flowing one, for purposes of discussion, we separate it into four parts:
- Gathering background information
- Physical assessment
- Simulation and measurements
- Clarifying objectives

Initially, we **gather background information** about the person's health, environmental, transportation, and funding issues; and current seating/mobility equipment. Next, the person's **physical and functional strengths and limitations** are assessed in relationship to the sitting posture. The next step is to **simulate** or try different postural support options, first with our hands and then with various seating *components* to evaluate what works and what doesn't work. Initial measurements can be taken during hand *simulation*, and then further specified during simulation with materials. After this information is gathered, it is important to clarify and match the **specific objectives** of the person with the objectives of the seating/mobility system.[1-4]

Chapters 1 to 4 will guide you through this process. Refer to the assessment forms in Appendix A (used when learning the assessment process) and Appendix B (which follows the same organization and format as this book). While doing an assessment, take notes on one of these forms.

Chapter 1
Gathering Background Information

A   Reasons for the Seating Assessment

What does the person with the disability want to achieve as a result of obtaining the seating/mobility system? What are the person's objectives, not the objectives of the seating system. Listen carefully, and keep the person's objectives and concerns in mind throughout the assessment process. What are the objectives and concerns of other members of the team? It is important to get everyone's agenda clear from the beginning, as sometimes the agendas are different. The person or team member's goals may be as general as our list on pages 6-7. Become as specific as possible about your objectives right from the beginning. Objectives will be modified and clarified during the assessment.

- The person may communicate "I want to sit better." Ask why. Get specific.
- Is it because she is uncomfortable? Why?
- Is it because she can't comb her hair? Why?
- Is it because she has difficulty working on her computer? Why?
- Is it because she can't see her friend because her head falls down? Why?

Examples of Specific Objectives

Todd wants to "improve his toilet transfers." That objective does not direct us towards seating intervention issues. We ask him, "How specifically?" His answer: "I need to be able to do a sliding board transfer independently onto the toilet." This objective helps us think of factors that will impact our seating/mobility decisions.

Sammy's therapist wants him to "improve his head control." What does that mean? How will it impact the seating system? This objective is more descriptive: "Sammy will be able to visually select choices from his communication board on his laptray." From this objective we know that the seating system will either have to support Sammy's body so that he can independently use his head, and/or his head will be directly supported by a seating component in order to function.

Maggie's mother wants Maggie to "improve her arm function." How? Why can't she do it now? This objective is more descriptive: "Maggie will be able to reach and hit three circular switches placed on her laptray." This objective not only describes what type of arm function, but also where and how we want her arm to function. By understanding the specific functional requirements of her arms, we know that her body must be supported so that her arms can perform that function.

Listen to the person's and team's concerns about comfort, pain, tissue condition, function, transportation, and interaction with the environment and other people. The questions in the assessment will stimulate discussion about additional concerns and objectives.

B Health Issues Related to the Person's Disability

When gathering information about the person's health, think about how these issues may impact the seating/mobility system.

1. **Person's *diagnosis*/disability:** Is the person's condition expected to improve or progressively deteriorate?

2. **Breathing problems:** Does the person have any difficulty breathing? What sitting postures help or hinder breathing? Does tilting the seating system backwards at times improve or aggravate breathing?

3. **Heart and circulatory problems:** Does the person have any heart or circulatory problems that are affected by certain sitting postures? Which postures?

4. ***Seizures:*** If the person stiffens a lot during a seizure, does she push excessively on the seating components? Does she lose consciousness and fall out of the seating/mobility system?

5. **Bladder/bowel control:** Does the person have bowel and bladder control?

6. **Nutrition/digestion:** Does the person have eating, digestion or nutritional problems that may be related to her sitting posture? Describe them.[5]

7. **Medications:** Is the person taking medications that may make her sleepy or change the effect of spasticity on her movement?

8. **Surgeries:** Has the person had any surgeries in the past? Are surgeries planned in the future that may affect her sitting posture?

9. **Orthopedic concerns:** Does the person have any bony deformities, joint *contractures, subluxations* or *dislocations?* Where? Is there a tendency for fractures? *Osteoporosis? Myositis ossificans? Heterotopic ossification?*

10. ***Orthotic* intervention (braces):** Is the person currently using any orthoses for her legs, spine, or arms? Will they be worn while in her seating/mobility system?

11. **Skin condition:** Are there any areas of skin breakdown, areas at risk for breakdown, areas of redness and or scarring from previous skin breakdown? Where? Describe them. If there is *paralysis* (absence of voluntary movement), how will the person relieve pressure under the pelvis?

12. **Sensation:** Is the person able to feel touch? Where is touch sensation absent or less? Does she have a history of tissue breakdown? Is the person extremely sensitive to touch (*tactile sensitivity*) so that certain textures and surfaces may cause discomfort? Does the person require deep pressure (*proprioception*) and

contact to relax and calm the nervous system? Does the person enjoy movement in various directions (*vestibular system*) or is that difficult to tolerate?[6,7]

13. **Pain:** Does the person experience pain? Where in the body? When during the day? What does the person do to relieve the pain? Is it *peripheral nervous system pain* or *central nervous system pain*? If peripheral nervous system pain, can the seating/mobility system be set up to help reduce the pain?[8,9]

14. **Seeing:** Does the person have visual limitations? Do these visual limitations affect the person's sitting posture, balance, and movement? How?[10-12]

15. **Hearing:** Does the person have any hearing problems? Describe them.

16. **Cognitive/perceptual/behavioral status:** Are there cognitive, perceptual, or behavioral issues that might affect seating posture, movement, or safety? Describe them. These may include poor safety awareness, *motor planning difficulties*, or *visual perceptual problems*.

C Environmental Issues

In what environments does the person live her life? At home? At work? At school? During recreation? In each of these environments, assess the problems that the person may have getting around in a seating/mobility system. Record the sizes of doorways, turning space (in hallways, small rooms, etc.), ramp incline, stairs, room sizes, and table heights.

D Transportation Issues

How will the person get around outside her home? Will she use a car, van, pickup truck, schoolbus, public transportation, horse, donkey, or boat? Does the seating/mobility system need to collapse or be taken apart to fit into a car or other vehicle? If the person is sitting in the seating system in the vehicle, what extra postural supports will she require to ensure maximum safety?

E Assessment of Present Seating/Mobility System

What seating/mobility system(s) does the person have now? What is its age and condition? What are the strengths and problems of the system(s)? What equipment has she had in the past and how well did it work? What other equipment is used in conjunction with the seating/mobility system, such as computer, *augmentative communication device*, *environmental control unit*, *respirator*, or *ventilator*.

F Funding Issues

How will the seating/mobility system be paid for? What are the restrictions, guidelines or criteria established by the funding source? Which suppliers will the insurance company work with? What documentation is required by the funding source?

References

1. Bergen A, Presperin J, Tallman T. *Positioning for Function: Wheelchairs and Other Assistive Technologies.* Valhalla, NY: Valhalla Rehabilitation Publications, Ltd.; 1990.

2. Trefler E, Hobson D, Taylor SJ, Monahan L, Shaw CG. *Seating and Mobility for Persons with Physical Disabilities.* Tucson, AZ: Therapy Skill Builders; 1993.

3. Presperin J. Seating systems: The therapist and the rehabilitation engineering team. *Phys Occup Ther Pediatr.* Spring 1990.

4. Ward D. *Prescriptive Seating for Wheeled Mobility.* Ft. Lauderdale, FL: HealthWealth International; 1994.

5. Hardwick K. Best practice in the use of seating and positioning for individuals with dysphagia. *Proceedings from the 14th International Seating Symposium.* 1998:49-50.

6. Kangas K. Sensory systems and seating for function: The need for both active postural control (use of vestibular system) and passive postural management (use of the tactile system). *Proceedings from the 21st International Seating Symposium.* 2005:47.

7. Kangas K. Hyperextension, obligatory reflexes, or the opisthontonic reaction? Facing the seating challenges of children whose seating systems do not recognize this body posture. *Proceedings from the 21st International Seating Symposium.* 2005:163-5.

8. Presperin-Pedersen J, O'Connor A. Pain: Defining, categorizing, and determining its effect on seating. *Proceedings from the 21st International Seating Symposium.* 2005:101-2.

9. Presperin-Pedersen J., O'Connor A. Pain mechanisms and intervention regarding seating. *Proceedings from the 22nd International Seating Symposium.* 2006:118-20.

10. Padula W. Vision affecting posture of the persons seated in a wheelchair. *Proceedings from the 7th International Seating Symposium.* 1991:53-4.

11. Marburger R, Millenbach D, Stewart S. Functional vision and its influence on posture. *Proceedings from the 9th International Seating Symposium.* 1993:51-3.

12. Eastman MJ, Montgomery I. The effect of functional vision on seating interventions. *Proceedings from the 10th International Seating Symposium.* 1994:55-8.

Introducing Aaron

Throughout this book, Aaron's story will illustrate the various aspects of the seating assessment and design process. His filled in assessment form at the end of the book summarizes the assessment and design process and final seating/mobility system.

Background Information

Aaron is a 14-year-old who lives with his family in Richmond, California. He attends high school and is in a special education class. Aaron has spastic quadriplegia and is blind due to brain damage at the age of three. At that time, he had a respiratory arrest caused by a severe asthma attack. Even though Aaron has spastic quadriplegia, he has fairly good function of his left arm. He has normal intelligence, but has not been in school consistently over the years due to his asthma. Aaron enjoys music, cartoon characters, TV shows, the Miami Dolphins, playing the drums, drawing, and telling stories. He loves to move, whether he is in or out of his wheelchair. Over the last few years he has overcome a lot of his fears, so now he wants to do more for himself such as dressing, toileting, transferring, and manipulating the wheelchair components. His feet and head are extremely sensitive to touch. Aaron has some memory problems and difficulties knowing where his body is in space and sometimes confuses left and right.

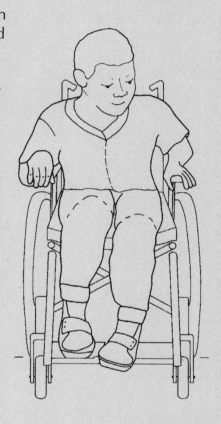

Aaron has had a number of surgeries. In 1989 he underwent a *Nissan fundal plication* for *gastroesophageal reflux*. In 1990 he underwent bilateral *adductor releases*, *Achilles tendon lengthenings*, and a right *derotation osteotomy* because of right hip *subluxation*. He wears plastic *ankle-foot orthoses (AFOs)*, which control the posturing of his ankles and feet.

Aaron and his family have many reasons for wanting a seating assessment. Aaron wants to be able to wheel by himself faster and with more control in his home and school. He wants to be more comfortable. Sometimes he experiences pain around his right hip. He wants to transfer out of the wheelchair onto the toilet more easily, using a stand-pivot transfer. His therapist, teacher, and mother hope that if his body is better supported, his functional abilities such as self-feeding, dressing, drawing, using the computer, and Braille writer will improve.

Aaron spends most of his time either at home, school or church. His classroom has an accessible bathroom with wide doorways, sufficient turning space and a horizontal handrail which allows him to stand to use the urinal. The toilet height is 15″. The undersurface of his desk at school is 25″ high. There are two steps to enter the house. Aaron sleeps in his own bedroom on the first floor of his home. The smallest doorway in his home is 27″ wide. He usually eats at the family dining table, which is 30″ high, undersurface height is 28″. The toilet height is 15″, and bed height is 26″. These measurements are important for the finished seat-surface height at the front edge.

Aaron is transported to school on a special bus that has a lift, tie-downs, and a shoulder strap that attaches to the floor of the vehicle. The family has a van without a lift. His wheelchair needs to fold to be transported. He sits in the front seat using regulation vehicular safety straps.

Aaron is currently using a standard wheelchair with a sling seat and sling back, a seatbelt attached to the wheelchair frame, and a lap tray. The wheelchair is 4 years old and is in good condition. At school, he uses a one-handed Braille writer, which is positioned either on his lap tray or desk. He accesses a computer using a touch-sensitive pad called a Unicorn board.

Aaron's father's private health insurance will pay for a seating system and wheelchair as long as it is medically justifiable.

Chapter 2
Physical Assessment: Posture, Movement, and Function

After the background information is gathered, we focus on the person's physical relationship with the seating/mobility system. We begin by assessing and describing the person's posture(s), movement, and function in her current seating system. Next, we try to figure out *why* the person uses these postures and movements. During this hands-on assessment, we will first assess the person lying down, then sitting up on a firm surface. Parts of the physical assessment are introduced here, and are more thoroughly described later in the book.

A Posture in Present Seating/Mobility System

To assess posture, movement, and function, we start by looking at the person's *resting posture*(s) in her present seating/mobility system, that is when she is not doing a functional activity. Even though we are looking at the whole person, we will focus on and describe the posture of the pelvis and low back, trunk, hips, and legs, knees, ankles and feet, head, shoulder girdles and arms. Section A, page 26 will further describe this process.

Reminder: During the assessment process, explain to the person and to the team what you are doing so that they understand what is going on and what will be happening.

B Functional Abilities in Present Seating/Mobility System

Now that we have an understanding of the person's resting posture in her current seating system, we will assess *what* and *how* activities are performed in or from the seating system. This means observing *how* the person stabilizes and moves her body to perform the functional movement. Always keep in mind *how* functional issues may affect the choice and design of the seating/mobility system. Remember, we want the seating system to improve, not diminish, the person's present function.

---

* In the physical assessment, the identification of typical therapeutic parameters such as "tone, reflexes, and muscle strength" are purposefully not included. I prefer to describe the person's posture, movement, and function, as these will more clearly guide us towards appropriate seating intervention. Definitions and descriptions of tone, reflexes, and so on, are subject to debate. These terms can cause us to think in preconceptions, preventing us from really observing and understanding what is happening with the person.

The following functional activities, among others, should be assessed: walking, transfers, wheelchair propulsion, dressing, bathing, toileting, swallowing, eating, digesting, breathing, communicating, tabletop activities, work, and vocational and homemaking activities. Section B, page 38, will guide you through the process of functional assessment.

Function needs to be assessed at different times during the seating evaluation:
- At the beginning of the assessment with the person in her current seating/mobility system.
- When the person is seated in a simulated or trial seating system.
- When the final seating system is fabricated and fit.
- Every 4-6 months thereafter.

C Joint and Muscular Flexibility

In Sections A and B, we observed and described the person's postural stability, movement, and function in her present seating/mobility system. Now we ask *why* the person may be sitting and moving like this. Many factors can affect a person's seated posture and movement, such as lack of flexibility in the joints, muscle tightness, weakness, discomfort, uncontrolled patterns of movement, or problems with the seating/mobility system. We begin by assessing joint and muscular flexibility with the person lying down on her back (supine) or side (sidelying). Section C, page 41 will further describe this process.

D Balance and Postural Control in Sitting

Before assessing the person's joint flexibility, posture, and movement in sitting, we will get a general idea of the person's balance and *postural control* when sitting on a firm surface with her feet well supported. See Section D, page 63.

E Assessment in Sitting: Flexibility and Postural Support

Muscle tightness, weakness, movement patterns, and gravity may influence a person's sitting posture. In this section, we will assess joint flexibility when the person is sitting on a flat firm surface with her feet well supported. We will also observe and feel the person's muscular activity and movement patterns. Then, with our hands, we will begin to assess where the individual's body needs support to achieve *the person's* neutral posture. Refer to Section E, page 64.

F The Effect of Gravity in Sitting

In Section F, page 89, we will assess the effect of gravity on the person's body when the seating system is upright and tilted at different angles.

G Pressure

Pressure under vulnerable boney prominences must be assessed in people who lack sensation, the elderly and people who lack the ability to move. (Refer to Section G, page 90.)

---

* For additional information on physical assessment, see Bergen, Presperin and Tallman (1990),[1] Trefler et al. (1993),[2] Presperin (1990),[3] Ward (1994),[4] and Minkel (2003).[5]

A | Posture in Present Seating/Mobility System

1. Pelvis/low back
2. Trunk
3. Hips and legs
4. Knees
5. Ankles and feet
6. Head and neck
7. Shoulder girdles
8. Arms
9. Summary

First, we assess the person's posture(s), movement, and postural options in her present seating/mobility system. Our posture is constantly changing and shifting in order to move and function. Persons with disabilities often do not have as many postural options as persons without disabilities.

Where do we start? I suggest we start by looking at the person's *resting posture*, when she is not doing functional activities. The person should be in her typical posture, so it may require some repositioning by a caregiver. In Section B, we will assess *how* the person's posture changes during different activities. Even though we always look at the whole person, to simplify this complex process, we will focus on and describe the posture of the pelvis, trunk, hips and legs, knees, ankles and feet, head and neck, and shoulders and arms. Describe and feel the posture of her body without trying to "correct" or change it. Observe how the movement of one body part affects the posture and movement of other body parts. It is helpful to draw a stick figure of the person's habitual posture(s), or if possible, take a photograph. Even to the well-trained eye, it can be overwhelming to analyze how a person postures or stabilizes her body in order to move.

In the following sections, the questions under letters *a* and *b* refer to the person's ability to actively move and control a certain body part. Letter *a* refers to the person's ability to **attain and maintain the neutral posture** by herself. Letter *b* refers to the person's ability to **actively control** movements of that body part. The statements and questions describe some typical abnormal postures, postures in which a person may or may not get stuck. Unlike *a* and *b* (**active movement**), these postures will need to be corrected **passively** by the evaluator. Again we will begin at the pelvis.

1. Pelvis/Low Back

Note: The posture of the pelvis is critical. It influences the posture of the rest of the body.

a. Is the person able to actively move her pelvis into a neutral posture and maintain that posture? (neutral pelvis)

b. Can she move through different pelvic postures and control that movement? (active pelvic control)

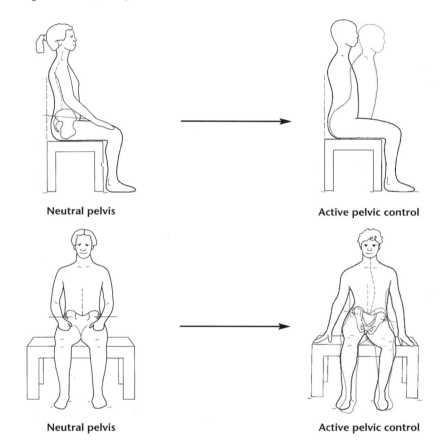

Neutral pelvis

Active pelvic control

Neutral pelvis

Active pelvic control

If not a or b, observe and feel if the person's pelvis is:

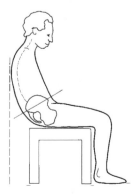

Rolled backward
(posterior pelvic tilt)

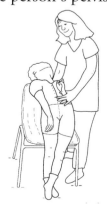

Stiffening and sliding
forward (extensor thrust)

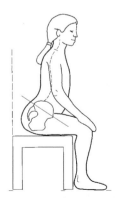

Rolled forward
(anterior pelvic tilt)

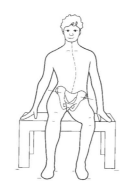

Tilted to the side (lateral pelvic tilt, described by its lower side)

Turned (rotated, described by the side that is backward)

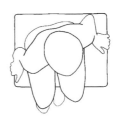

Turned (rotated) - Top view -

2. Trunk

Describe the posture of the person's trunk (mid-back or thoracic spine and chest).

   a. Is the person able to actively move her trunk into a neutral posture and maintain that posture? (neutral trunk)

   b. Can she move her trunk through different postures and control that movement? (active trunk control)

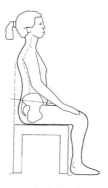

Neutral trunk

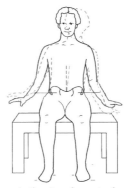

Active trunk control

If not a or b, note if the person's trunk is:

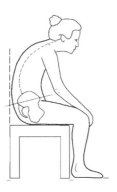

Curved forward (kyphosis)

Curved to one side (scoliosis)

Rotated forward on one side - Top view -

Arched backward (extended)

3. Hips and Legs

When describing the posture(s) of the person's hips and legs, observe how the legs are stabilizing the body.

a. Is the person able to move her hips and legs into a neutral posture (slightly apart, 5-8° of abduction) and use her legs and feet for a stable base of support? (neutral hips)

b. Can she move her hips in and out, up and down, and control each movement? (active hip control)

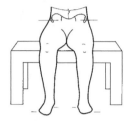

Neutral hips

Active hip control

If not a or b, note if the hips and legs are:

Stiffened out straight (extended)

Bent (flexed)

Turned in (internally rotated)

Moved towards midline (adducted)

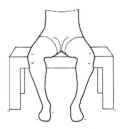

Turned out (externally rotated)

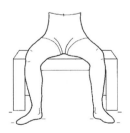

Spread open (abducted)

Both turned to the same side (windswept)

Moving constantly

Note: Usually you will observe a combination of these above postures.

4. Knees

    a. Can the person bend her knees to 90° so that the bottoms of her feet contact the floor/foot rests? (neutral knees)

    b. Can the person control bending and straightening of her knees? (active knee control)

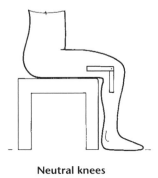

Neutral knees

Active knee control

If not a or b, are the knees:

**Bent so feet are under
the seat (flexed)**

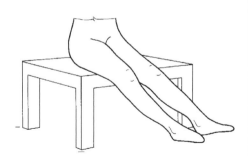

Stiffened out straight (extended)

5. Ankles and Feet

a. Can the person actively bend her ankles to 90° so that her feet rest on the floor or support surface? (neutral ankles)

b. Observe and describe the active movements occurring at the ankles? (bending ankle up, down, in, and out). (active ankle control)

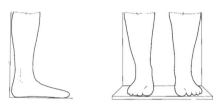

Neutral ankles

Active ankle control

If not a or b, are the ankles/feet:

Bent up excessively (dorsiflexed)

Bent down excessively (plantarflexed)

Turned in (inverted)

Turned out (everted)

6. Head and Neck

    a. Is the person able to hold her head up to see people and things in her environment? (neutral head) How long can she maintain that posture?

    b. Can the person turn her head to either side? (active head control)

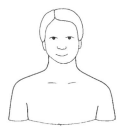 

Neutral head

If the person has difficulty controlling movements of the head, does it tend to:

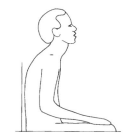  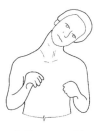 

| **Fall back (extension)** | **Push back (extension with force)** | **Fall to one side (lateral flexion)** | **Turn and push to one side (rotation)** |

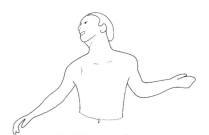 

Push back and turn (extension with rotation)   **Fall forward (flexion)**   **Pull forward (flexion with force)**

If a combination of the above movements occurs, then describe the movements.

7. Shoulder Girdles

The shoulder girdles include the shoulders, the shoulder blades (scapulae), and clavicles. When referring to posture and movement, it is difficult to separate the shoulders/scapulae from the arms. However, for purposes of directing our attention, we will first focus on the person's shoulder girdles.

    a. Is the person able to actively bring her shoulder(s) and arm(s) into a neutral posture? (neutral posture)

    b. Is she able to actively control movement of her arms? (active arm control) (In Section B. Functional Skills, we will further assess the person's shoulder girdle and arm posture, control, and movement during functional activities.)

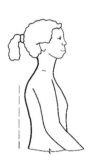
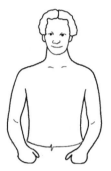

Neutral posture   **Active arm control**

If not a or b, observe if the person's shoulders/scapulae are:

Shrugged upwards (elevated)   **Pulled forward and turned in (protracted and internally rotated)**   **Pulled backward and turned out (retracted and externally rotated)**

8. Arms

We will now focus on the posture, movement, and control of the person's arms. (See 7 above for assessment of active arm control.)

If the person is unable to actively attain a neutral posture, note the posture of the arms:

One arm stiffened straight (extended), the other bent (flexed)

Both arms are stiffly bent (flexed)

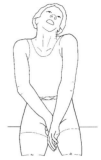

Both arms are stiffly straight (extended)

One arm is strong and the other arm is weak or stiff

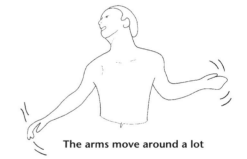

The arms move around a lot

9. Summary

After describing the posture of different parts of the person's body, look at her whole body. It is helpful for us to try to replicate this posture in our own body. Yes, assume the posture(s) of the person with the disability. Feel how the person moves. Where do you feel that you lack or gain stability and movement?

The following are examples of total body resting postures.

    a. **Pelvis**: rolled backward (posterior pelvic tilt)
       Trunk: curved forward (kyphosis)
       Hips and legs: turned out (externally rotated) and spread open (abducted)
       Knees: neutral knees
       Ankles and feet: neutral ankles
       Head: falls forward (flexion)
       Shoulder girdles and arms: active arm control

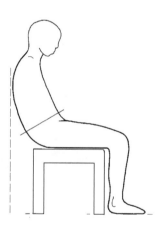 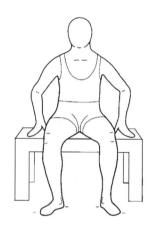

b. **Pelvis**: stiffens and slides forward
(extensor thurst)
Trunk: arched backward (extended)
Hips and legs: stiffened out straight
(extended) and moved towards midline
(adducted)
Knees: stiffened out straight (extended)
Ankles and feet: bent down excessively
(plantarflexed)
Head: pushes back (extension with
force)
Shoulder girdles: pulled backward and
turned out (retracted and externally
rotated)
Arms: one arm stiffly bent (flexed), one
arm stiffly straight (extended)

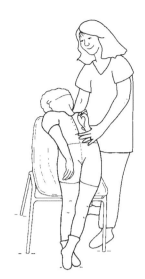

c. **Pelvis**: neutral
Trunk: curved to the side (scoliosis)
Hips and legs: both turned to the same
side (windswept)
Knees: bent under the seat (flexed)
Ankles and feet: bent down excessively
(plantarflexed)
Head: neutral
Shoulder girdles and arms: one arm
stiffened straight (extended), the other
bent (flexed)

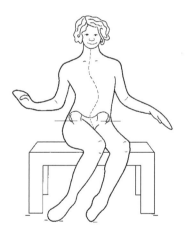

Posture in Present Seating/Mobility System

In his present wheelchair, Aaron's pelvis rolls backward (posterior tilt), tilts down on the right (right lateral pelvic tilt) and rotates backward on the left. His trunk curves forward (kyphosis) and curves to the side with a right-sided **convexity**. His left hip is in a neutral posture; however, his right hip is turned and moved in (internally rotated, adducted). His left knee tends to extend so that his foot is not on the foot support. His right knee tends to bend with some spasticity into flexion. Both of his ankles and feet turn in (invert), but when he is sitting in the wheelchair he usually wears ankle-foot orthoses that control his ankle/foot posturing. He has good head control but tends to rotate his head to the left. His left shoulder girdle tends to shrug (elevate), but he has good active control of his shoulder and arm. His right shoulder can relax in the neutral posture so that his forearm rests on the arm support, but it tends to lift stiffly out to the side (abduct). He has some control of flexion and extension of his right elbow; however, it is very stiff with a lot of spasticity.

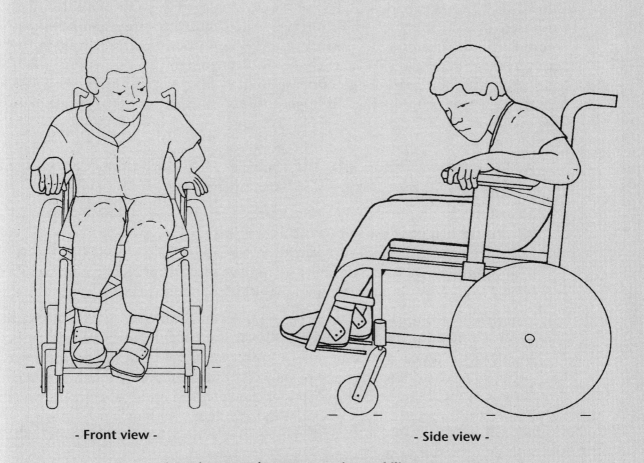

- Front view -

- Side view -

Aaron's posture in present seating/mobility system

B Functional Abilities in Present Seating/Mobility System

1. Walking
2. Transfers
3. Wheelchair propulsion
4. Dressing
5. Bathing
6. Toileting
7. Eating/digesting
8. Breathing
9. Communicating
10. Tabletop activities
11. Work/vocational/homemaking activities

Now that we have an understanding of the person's resting posture, we describe *what* activities she is doing in, or from the seating/mobility system and *how* she does these activities. How does her posture change? How does she stabilize and move her body in order to perform the activity? Always keep in mind how functional issues may affect the choice and design of the seating/mobility system. Assess the following functional activities if the person is doing the activity in or from the seating/mobility system.

1. **Walking**: Can the person walk? If so, how far? How much assistance is needed? What device(s) is used (orthoses, walker, crutches, cane, etc.)?

2. **Transfers** (getting in and out of the wheelchair): How are the transfers done? What is the height of the surfaces (height of bed, toilet, bathtub, car, plane, etc.) If the person needs help from a caregiver, how much help is needed? Is a lift used? Can she independently adjust or remove seating/mobility components (wheel brakes, seat belt, trunk straps, lower leg supports, etc.)?

3. **Wheelchair propulsion**: Can the person independently operate her wheelchair or must it be pushed by someone else? If she is unable to independently push a wheelchair, is it possible for her to use power mobility? If the person is using a power wheelchair, how does she operate it? Observe and describe the change in her posture, stability, and movement when maneuvering the wheelchair, whether it is manual or power. If the person is independently pushing a manual wheelchair, where are her shoulders in relationship to the axle, the center of the rear wheels? (See page 239.)

4. **Dressing**: Does the person dress independently? Is dressing done in the seating/mobility system? If so, observe and describe how it is done.

5. **Bathing**: Does the person bathe independently? Describe how bathing is done.

6. **Toileting**: Does the person use a urinal or catheter while in the seating system?

7. **Eating/digesting**: Does the person eat while in the seating/mobility system? Is the person able to feed herself? What posture(s) and movements of the head, neck, and trunk are optimal for the person to be able to: accept food and liquids into the mouth, to swallow, and to chew? Is the person at risk for *aspiration* or *gastroesophageal reflux*? Does the person use a *gastrostomy* or *naso-gastric tube*? Is rapid weight gain expected? If a person has difficulty digesting food or has a tendency for constipation, is the seating system (like a seat belt) interfering with passage of food through the digestive system?

8. **Breathing**: Is the person comfortably breathing? Can you see the chest rise and fall with the breath? Are there parts of the ribcage that are not moving so well?

9. **Communicating**: How does the person communicate—speaking, sign language, gestures, or by using an assistive device? If the latter, how does she access the device? How do you know when the person is upset, uncomfortable, or happy? Watch the person communicating and observe changes in her posture and movement. Where and how does she stabilize her body in order to function?

10. **Tabletop activities:** What activities does the person do from the seating/mobility system (playing, writing, drawing, using a computer or augmentative communication device, etc.) Observe the changes in her posture and movement. Where and how does she stabilize her body in order to function?

11. **Work/vocational/homemaking activities**: The person needs to be evaluated in her actual or simulated work/vocational environment to understand how she postures, stabilizes, and moves her body in order to function.

Functional Skills in Present Seating/Mobility System

With maximal assistance, Aaron is able to walk about 10 feet. If the transferring surface is not too high, Aaron is able to assist with a stand-pivot transfer. His father still lifts and carries him into bed and into the car. Aaron is able to do and undo the push-button on his seatbelt. He is able to propel his wheelchair with his left hand but the wheelchair goes in circles. When he propels, he leans his trunk more forward and to the right, his right leg flexes up and his left knee extends more. Family members, his teacher, and kids at school push him in his wheelchair. The current push-handle height is 36" (91.4 cm). Aaron assists his mother when she puts on and takes off his shirt. Sometimes this is done while he is sitting in his wheelchair. In order to put on his shirt, he needs to bend his trunk forward and rotate it to the right. He puts on and removes his pants in bed. He feeds himself with a utensil in his left hand. When he eats, his right arm and leg flex up more and his left knee extends. When using the Braille writer, Unicorn board, or when drawing, the tabletop surface needs to be close to his chest. Also, if his right arm is not leaning on a surface, it tends to become stiff, extending and lifting out to the side.

**Aaron's posture in his present
wheelchair when eating**

C Joint and Muscular Flexibility

In Sections A and B, we observed and described the person's postural stability, movement and function in her present seating/mobility system. Now we begin to determine *why* the person may be sitting and moving in this manner. Many factors can affect a person's seated posture and movement: lack of flexibility in the joints, muscle tightness and/or weakness, tone, discomfort, hypersensitivity, insecurity, fear, problems with the existing seating/mobility system, uncoordinated patterns of movement, functional activities such as talking, reaching, and so on. We will begin by assessing joint and muscular flexibility with the person lying down on her back (supine) or side (sidelying). The person should lie on her back on a firm, flat surface (not a soft bed or cot), which we will refer to as a *mat table*. We will determine if the joints are *flexible* (able to attain the neutral posture), *fixed* (stuck and unable to move), or *partially flexible*. In this case, note the *flexible* percentage of the total movement. Sometimes the joints are *flexible*, but are resistant to correction, due possibly to tone or soft tissue tightness. Although, we do not know the cause, we must respect this limitation and take note of the degree of comfortable correction. We will call this *practical flexibility*. In order to clearly assess pelvic mobility, we need to eliminate any factors that might decrease the person's flexibility. You may need more people to help with this process. Thus,

- Create a calm, non-threatening environment with someone familiar to the person helping to soothe her. Be playful.
- Keeping the body bent or flexed with a pillow under the head, and flexing the hips and knees, will help reduce any *spasticity* or excessive stiffness. We are trying to assess the joint mobility underneath the spasticity, so we need to do all we can to reduce spasticity.

In the following sections, we **first** refer to the *typical posture* that the person tends to assume (if the person has a typical posture). Next we describe the movement to be assessed. For example, in 3b (page 51), the person's typical posture is the **hips/legs moved in toward midline** (adducted). The movement to be assessed is **moving the hips out to the side** (abduction).

We will check the flexibility of the pelvis/low back, trunk, hips and legs, knees, ankles/feet, shoulder girdles, and arms. We begin by assessing the pelvis, whose posture affects that of the whole body. What joint, muscular, or tissue limitations may prevent the pelvis from achieving the neutral posture in sitting? The posture(s) of the pelvis is affected by tissues:

- **Behind, in front and above the pelvis:** Tension, contractures, tightness in the spinal joints, muscles and tissues between the pelvis, sacrum and lumbar spine, and from the pelvis to the sternum and ribcage. (Assessed in 1a, 1b and 1d)

- **Under and to the sides of the pelvis:** Tension, contractures, tightness in the spinal joints, muscles and tissues from the sides of the pelvis to the ribs and spine. (Assessed in 1c and 1d)

We determine the flexibility of these areas when we assess the person's hips and pelvis/low back in supine (lying on her back) or sidelying (lying on her side), and later in the sitting position.

1. Pelvic/Low Back Flexibility

First, we will assess the motion between the pelvis and the low back (lumbar and sacral spine), and flexibility of the tissues between the pelvis and the sternum and ribcage. If the person cannot actively move her pelvis, passively move the pelvis to feel if her posture is *fixed* or *flexible*. For example, if a person's pelvis tends to roll backward (posterior pelvic tilt), feel whether you can move the pelvis to the neutral posture (see page 8). If you can move the pelvis to the neutral posture, it is *flexible*. If you cannot move the pelvis and it stays stuck in that rolled back (posteriorly tilted) posture, it is *fixed*. Note the flexible percentage of the total movement. For instance, can you move the pelvis all the way to a neutral posture? Halfway? How easy is it to correct? What is the practical flexibility? Note this in your own language, such as "pelvis flexible to neutral, but tight in posterior tilt," or "pelvis is 75% flexible but pulls strongly down on the left."

Put your hands on the ASIS and PSIS (or if you can't reach the PSIS, the back part of the iliac crest) and move the pelvis first in the direction opposite of the person's preferred or typical posture. Then move it in all other directions. Check the flexibility when the pelvis is:

- Rolled backward (posterior pelvic tilt)
- Rolled forward (anterior pelvic tilt)
- Tilted to the side (lateral pelvic tilt)
- Turned (rotated forward on one side, back on the other side)

- Never force a person's body into painful or unnatural postures. Before designing the seating system we first need to know how much the person's joints can move.
- Always tell the person what you are going to do and why.
- Move the person's limbs and joints slowly. If the limb does not move any more, STOP! Never force a movement.
- Determine how the person will signal you to stop. If the person's speech is difficult to understand, watch her face for any signs of pain or discomfort.

> Note: In the following sections, we first refer to the typical posture that the person tends to assume (if the person has a typical posture).

a. Rolled backward (posterior pelvic tilt)

If holding onto and moving the pelvis directly is difficult, put your hands behind the lumbar spine and slowly move it towards the ceiling. You can also use a strap behind the pelvis to lift it up. Note how much force and pressure are required to move the pelvis. If flexible, how practically flexible?

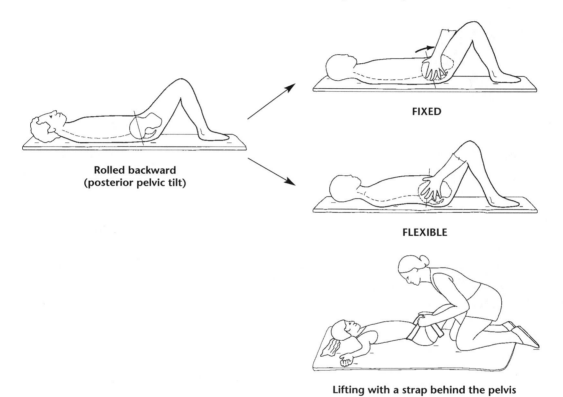

**Rolled backward
(posterior pelvic tilt)**

FIXED

FLEXIBLE

Lifting with a strap behind the pelvis

b. Rolled forward (anterior pelvic tilt)

If flexible, how practically flexible?

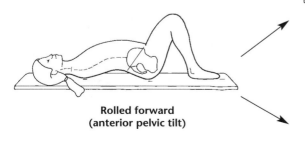

**Rolled forward
(anterior pelvic tilt)**

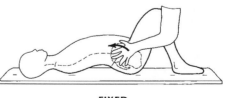

FIXED

FLEXIBLE

43

c. Tilted to the side (oblique)

Describe the tilt, left or right, by the side that is lower. If flexible, how practically flexible?

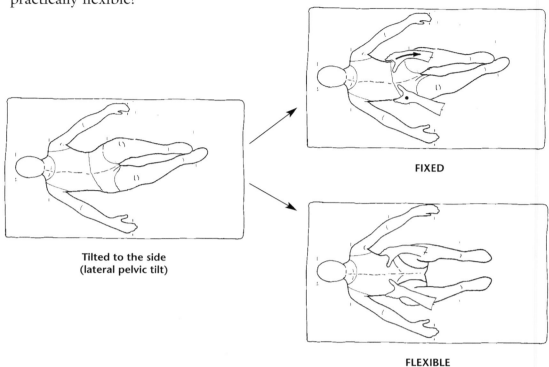

Tilted to the side
(lateral pelvic tilt)

FIXED

FLEXIBLE

d. Turned forward on one side, back on the other side (rotated)

Describe the rotation as the side that is more backward. If flexible, how practically flexible?

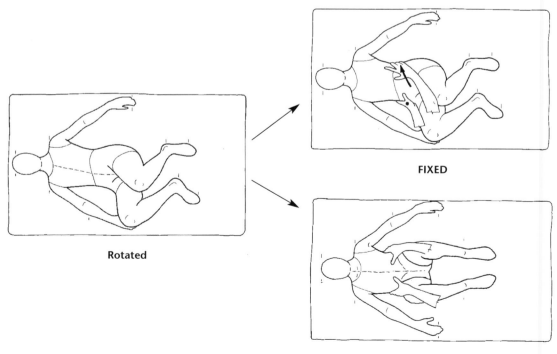

Rotated

FIXED

FLEXIBLE

2. Trunk (Mid-Back, Thoracic Spine and Chest) Flexibility

In Section A (page 26), we observed the posture of the trunk in the person's current seating system. Now we assess trunk flexibility because:

- Joint and tissue limitations need to be respected so that we do not force the trunk beyond its physical limitations.
- Trunk flexibility will affect the posture of the head and the shoulder girdle.

Trunk flexibility can be affected by tightness and limitations in the thoracic spine, the rib cage, and the tissues in the chest. Check whether the trunk can attain the neutral posture, or if it is fixed and inflexible. For example, if the trunk is curved forward, can you or the person move the spine so that it is relatively straight (*flexible*) or does it stay curved (*fixed*)?

The person's hips and knees should be bent up (flexed) so that the feet are resting on the mat table. Your helper holds the pelvis in the neutral position (or the limit of the person's flexibility) and prevents it from moving. The pelvis is held at the ASIS and the PSIS (or the back of the iliac crest, described on page 42). Move the trunk first in the direction opposite of the person's preferred or typical posture. Then move it in all other directions. The hand placement will vary, please refer to the illustrations. Observe and record precisely where the trunk and midback are flexible or fixed. Note the percentage of *flexibility* and *practical flexibility*.

Check the flexibility when the trunk is:

- Curved forward (kyphosis)
- Curved to one side (scoliosis)
- Rotated forward on one side (rotated)
- Arched backward (extended)

a. Curved forward (kyphosis)

If flexible, how practically flexible?

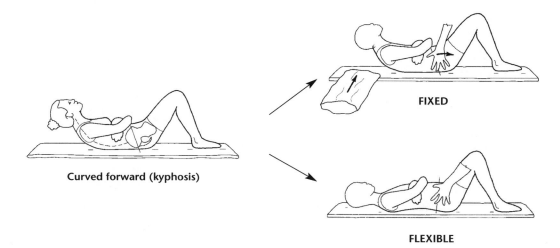

Curved forward (kyphosis)

FIXED

FLEXIBLE

b. Curved to one side (scoliosis)

If flexible, how practically flexible?

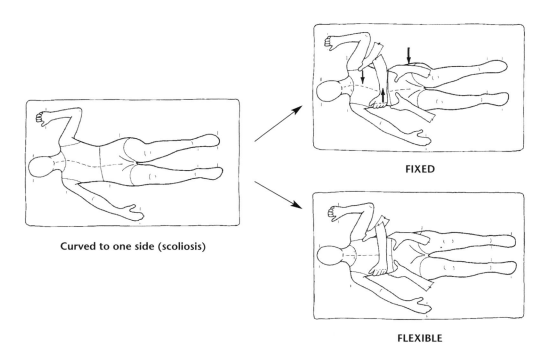

Curved to one side (scoliosis)

FIXED

FLEXIBLE

c. Rotated forward on one side (rotated)

If flexible, how practically flexible?

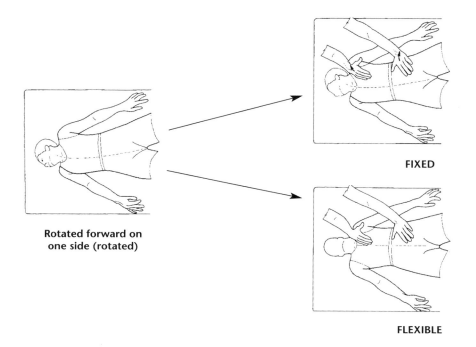

**Rotated forward on
one side (rotated)**

FIXED

FLEXIBLE

d. Arched backward (extended)

If flexible, how practically flexible?

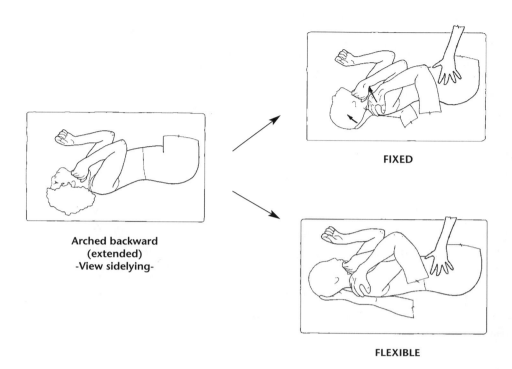

Arched backward
(extended)
-View sidelying-

FIXED

FLEXIBLE

Measuring angles

Therapists typically measure angles using goniometers. If you do not have a goniometer, make an *angle measure* by using two tongue depressors, wide popsicle sticks, cardboard, or flat pieces of wood or plastic. A brad (flexible metal) is used to connect these sticks, through holes at the end of the sticks. The sticks pivot around the brad. Hold the angle measure so that the brad pivot is lined up with the joint you are measuring. The sticks line up with the length of the bones. The brad or joint of the goniometer lines up with the joint. Remember to mark which side of the stick was against the person's body. Trace the angle on your assessment form to use later for reference.

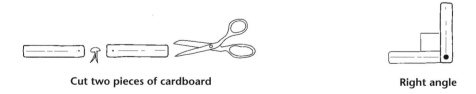

Cut two pieces of cardboard

Right angle

3. Hip Flexibility

While the person is still supine or sidelying, we assess the flexibility of the hip joints and surrounding tissues. Why is it important to assess hip flexibility?

- Tension, contractures, and or tightness in the hip joint and/or muscles and tissues under and to the sides of the pelvis can affect the pelvic posture. As mentioned before, the pelvic posture affects the entire body.
- In our seating system, we do not want to force the hip and leg into postures that are beyond the person's joint limitations.

Hip flexibility in five postures is assessed:

- Bending each hip separately (flexion)
- Hips/legs moved towards midline (adducted)
- Hips turned in (internally rotated)
- Hips/legs spread open (abducted)
- Hips turned out (externally rotated)

> **Note: Instead of first describing a typical posture as we do in the other sections, we are describing the movement of hip flexion.**

a. Bending each hip separately (flexion):

Starting position: First bend the hip up that you are *not* going to test, so that the foot is resting on the surface. This reduces the tension in the hip. Your helper feels the ASIS and PSIS (or iliac crest) and holds the pelvis in a neutral position, preventing it from moving (described on page 42).

Step 1: Bend (flex) the hip and leg up. Keep the knee bent (flexed) more than 90° to decrease the tension of the hamstrings (muscles behind the thigh). When your helper feels the pelvis starting to roll backward (posterior tilt), STOP lifting the leg.

Step 2: Measure the person's *hip flexion angle* with the *angle measure*. This angle will help to determine the seating system's ***seat-to-back support angle***. (If the person is obese, it may be difficult to get an accurate measurement in supine position. Get an idea in the supine postion, then measure the angle again in sitting.)

Step 3: Using the same technique, measure the hip flexion of the other leg. Is there a difference between the person's left and right hip flexion angles? If yes, re-measure to verify the difference.

Starting position   Measuring hip flexion

 Can you think of how the person's hip flexion angle might affect the seating system?

If the person's hip flexion angle is *90° or greater* (as in the above example), the person can probably sit in a chair with a seat-to-back support angle set at 90° or greater.

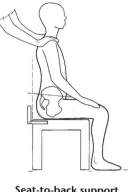

**Seat-to-back support
angle = 90°**

If the person's hip flexion is less than 90°, the seat-to-back support angle needs to be set to match the person's hip flexion angle.

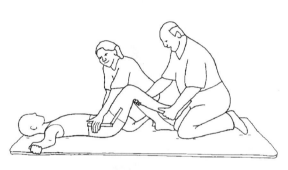

Hip flexion less than 90°

**Seat-to-back support
angle greater than 90°**

If this is not done, the person will be sitting on a pelvis that is rolled backward (posterior pelvic tilt).

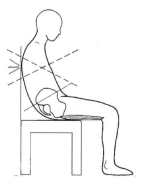

Posterior pelvic tilt

Is there a difference between the person's left and right hip flexion angles?

If there is, the seat cushion may need to be split, so that the tighter hip can drop down, and the looser hip can be supported. The amount that the seat drops down depends on the difference found in hip flexion.

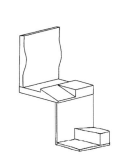

Split-seat cushion

b. Hips/legs moved towards midline (adducted): Typical posture (lying down)

Movement to assess: Move the hip and leg out to the side (abduction).

Starting position: The hip being assessed should be supported at 90°, or at the limit of hip flexion. The other leg should be bent with the foot supported on the table, and held stable so that it does not move. Your helper holds onto the ASIS and PSIS (or back part of the iliac crest) aligned in the person's neutral posture, preventing the pelvis from moving.

Step 1: Move the thigh and leg away from the midline of the body. Stop when the pelvis begins to move (rotate).

Step 2: Looking down at the person from above: If the thigh and leg are in line with the pelvis before the pelvis moves (rotates), the hip is *flexible*. If the pelvis moves before the thigh and leg line up with the pelvis, that hip is *fixed*. If the hip is *fixed* or partially fixed, record the number of inches or centimeters that the hip moves from midline. Note the practical flexibility.

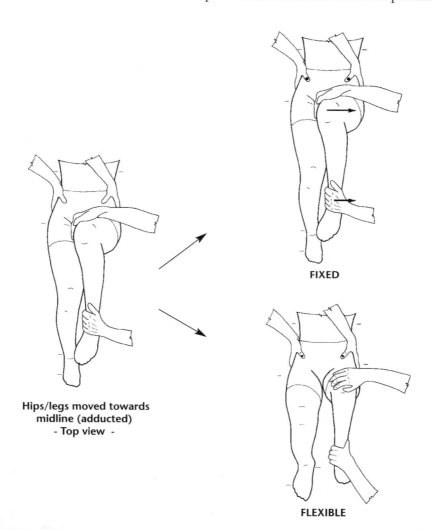

Hips/legs moved towards midline (adducted)
- Top view -

FIXED

FLEXIBLE

✋ **CAUTION!**

If a hip moves and turns in excessively, is not very *flexible*, and is painful, the hip could be dislocated (out of the socket) or subluxed (partly out of the socket). If this is the case, an X-ray, if available, will clarify the status of the hip. If the hip is dislocated, DO NOT force it out to the side (abduct).

c. **Hips turned in (internally rotated):** Typical posture

Movement to assess: Turn the hip and thigh out (external rotation) so that the foot moves in towards midline.

Starting position: (Refer to b above.)

Step 1: Externally rotate the hip and thigh so that the foot moves in towards the midline.

Step 2: Looking down at the person from above: If the hip moves so that the foot and lower leg are in line with the pelvis before the pelvis moves (rotates), the hip is *flexible*. If the pelvis moves before the foot and lower leg are in line with the pelvis, that hip is *fixed*. What is the practical flexibility?

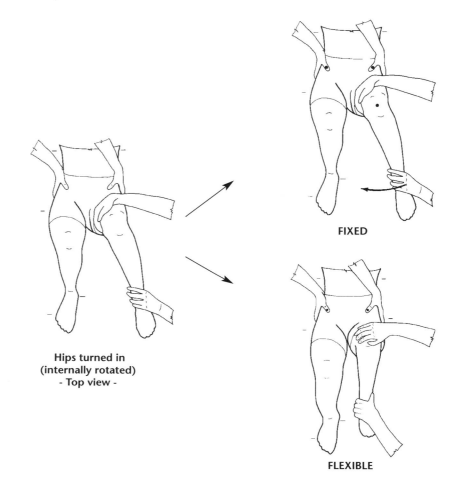

**Hips turned in
(internally rotated)
- Top view -**

FIXED

FLEXIBLE

Feeling the effect of a hip joint limitation on your posture:
Squeeze your knees together to pretend you have tightness in your hip adductor muscles. Keep squeezing your knees together and ask a friend to pull one of your knees out to the side (to abduct your hip). Resist the force of the pull. What happens to your pelvis and trunk? Do you feel your body rotating? That's what would happen if we placed a knee block between the knees and the hip joint was not flexible. As you can feel, this causes pain and additional postural problems.

d. Hips/legs spread open (abducted): Typical posture

Movement to assess: Move the thigh and leg in (adduction)

Starting position: (Refer to b above.)

Step 1: Move the thigh and leg toward midline.

Step 2: (Refer to b above to assess *flexible* vs. *fixed*.)

What is the practical flexibility?

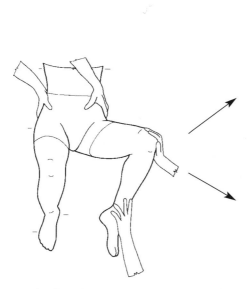

Hips/legs spread open
(abducted)
- Top view -

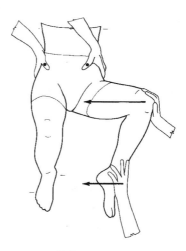

FIXED

FLEXIBLE

Why is it important to differentiate abduction from external rotation? Hint: Look at the difference in the position of the knees and ankles.

(See Chapter 8, Section B for answers.)

e. **Hips turned out (externally rotated):** Typical posture

Movement to assess: Similar to letter d. Instead of moving the leg towards the middle in a straight plane, turn the hip in (internal rotation) so the foot moves away from midline of the body.

Starting position: (Refer to b above.)

Step 1: Rotate the thigh in so that the foot moves away from the body.

Step 2: (Refer to c above to assess *flexible* vs. *fixed*)

What is the practical flexibility?

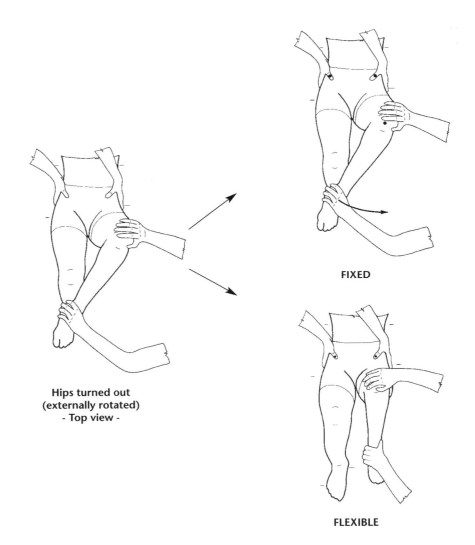

**Hips turned out
(externally rotated)
- Top view -**

FIXED

FLEXIBLE

 If a hip is fixed in external rotation and abduction, what happens if feet are tied into shoeholders that are located on typical wheelchair foot supports? Yes, this will cause hip pain and the person will shift and move the pelvis to try to find some comfort.

4. Knee Flexibility

We will assume the same starting position as in 3a (page 48). The helper needs to stabilize the pelvis in neutral and prevent it from moving. For the knee being assessed, the hip should be flexed to 90° or to its limit of flexion. Evaluate one knee at a time. Assess knee flexibility if the person's knee(s) tend to be:

- Bent (flexed)
- Straightened (extended)

a. Bent (flexed): Typical posture

Movement to assess: Straightening (extending) the knee. With one hand on the thigh above the knee and the other hand behind the lower leg above the ankle, begin to straighten the leg at the knee. When the helper feels the pelvis start to roll under (posterior tilt), stop straightening the knee. Measure that angle. If the knee straightens to 90°, it is considered flexible. (If the person wants to use elevating lower leg supports (elevating legrests), assess the person's full knee flexibility, past 90°.)

 Why is it important to measure the knee flexion angle?

If the knees extend (straighten) to at least 90°, the person can sit with the leg-to-seat surface angle set at 90° or less.

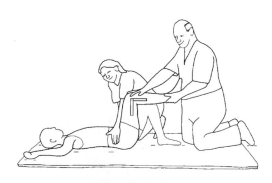

Knee(s) straighten to 90°

Leg-to-seat surface support angle set at 90°

 Why is it important to stabilize the pelvis? The muscles that bend the knees (the hamstrings) are also connected to the underside of the pelvis at the ischial tuberosities. If the hamstrings are tight, straightening the knees may cause the pelvis to roll backwards (posteriorly tilt).

If the knees do not extend to 90°, the seat cushion and lower leg support must allow the legs to go under the seat.

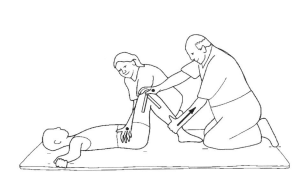

Knees do not straighten to 90°

Leg-to-seat surface angle less than 90°

If not, the muscles in the back of the knees (hamstrings) will roll the pelvis backward (posterior tilt).

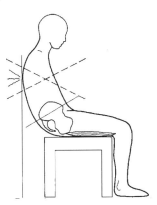

Posterior pelvic tilt

Feeling the effect of tight hamstrings:

Sit on a chair. Bend your knees more than 90° so that your feet are behind your knees. Imagine that there is a wide, taut rubber band connected from your butt bones (ischial tuberosities) of your pelvis to just below the back of your knee joint. The rubber band does not allow your knees to straighten (extend) to 90°. Pull your legs into more flexion. Ask a friend to try to straighten your knees. Resist the pull. What happens to your pelvis? Do you feel it rolling backward into a posterior pelvic tilt?

b. Straight (extended): Typical posture

Movement to assess: Bending (flexing) the knees. As with the hamstrings, the muscles in the front of the thigh can also be tight. Position the person as in 4a. With one hand on the thigh above the knee and the other hand in front of the lower leg above the ankle, bend the knee(s). Measure that angle. If the knee bends to at least 90°, it is considered flexible.

If the knee does not flex (bend) to 90°, the lower leg support will have to support the lower leg at the available angle.

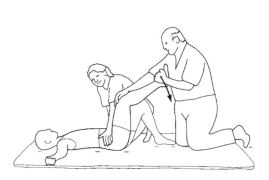

Bending (flexing) the knees

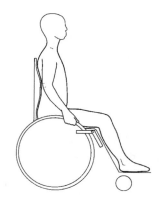

Leg-to-seat surface
angle greater than 90°

5. Ankle and Foot Flexibility

With the hip and knee flexed, move the ankle up and down, in and out. Note the degree of flexibility. The ankle is in the neutral posture if it is bent up (dorsiflexed) to 90°, and neither turned in (inverted) nor out (everted). Checking the ankle/foot flexibility is important for determining if the foot supports need to be angled down/up, out/in.

Check the flexibility if the ankle/foot tends to assume one of the following postures:

- Bent up excessively (dorsiflexed)
- Bent down excessively (plantarflexed)
- Turned in (inverted)
- Turned out (everted)

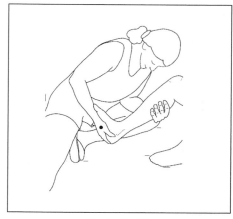

Neutral ankle

a. Bent up excessively (dorsiflexed)

Movement to assess: Move the ankle/foot down (plantarflexion). Support the back of the lower calf. Grasp onto the top part of the foot and try to move it down. Does it bend down to 90°? If not, measure the angle.

Move the ankle/foot down (plantarflexion)

b. Bent down excessively (plantarflexed)

Movement to assess: Move the ankle/foot up (dorsiflexion). Hold on to the lower leg with one hand, and grasp the heel and foot with your other hand. The ankle and forefoot should be in a neutral position (between inversion and eversion). Bend it up slowly to allow any spasticity to relax. Does it bend up to 90°? If not, measure the angle.

Move the ankle/foot up (dorsiflexion)

c. Turned in (inverted)

Movement to assess: Turn the ankle/foot out (evert). Hold as in 5a and turn the foot out. Does it come to a middle/neutral position?

Turn the ankle/foot out (evert)

d. Turned out (everted)

Movement to assess: Turn the ankle/foot in (invert). Hold as in 5a and turn the foot in. Does it come to a middle/neutral position?

Turn the ankle/foot in (invert)

6. Head and Neck

The head and neck region is very complex and sensitive. Many movements and postures of the neck (cervical spine) are combined postures (such as extension with rotation). Assess the posture of the head and neck, and its balance over the pelvis and spine in the seated posture. Special care should be taken if you decide to assess cervical flexibility.

7. Shoulder Girdle Flexibility

Assess if you can reduce or correct the posture of the person's shoulder girdle. Remember to reduce any *spasticity* by flexing the knees and hips and placing a pillow under the head. Why is it important to assess the flexibility of this area? We do not want to force the shoulder girdle into postures that will cause discomfort or pain. Assess the practical flexibility if the shoulder girdle is:

- Shrugged upwards (elevated)
- Pulled forward and turned in (protracted and internally rotated)
- Pulled backward and turned out (retracted and externally rotated)

a. Shrugged upwards (elevated)

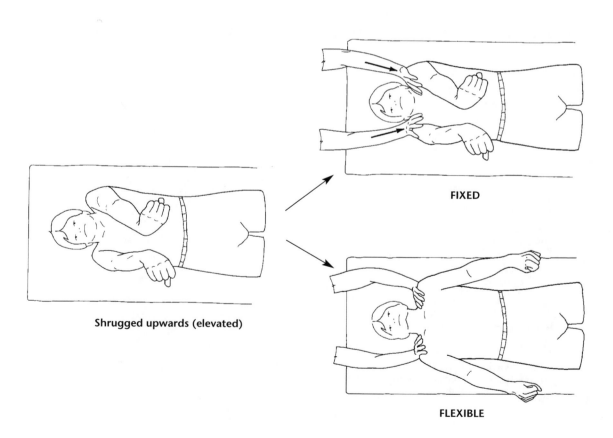

Shrugged upwards (elevated)

FIXED

FLEXIBLE

b. **Pulled forward and turned in (protracted and internally rotated)**

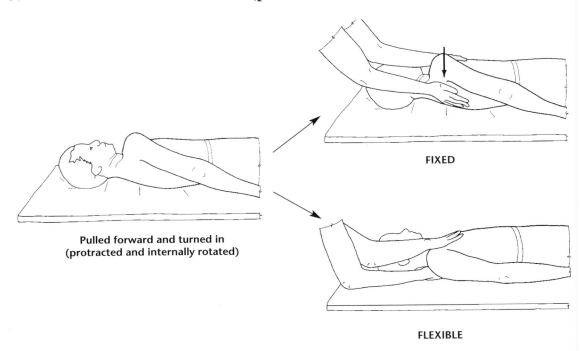

Pulled forward and turned in
(protracted and internally rotated)

FIXED

FLEXIBLE

c. **Pulled backward and turned out (retracted and externally rotated)**

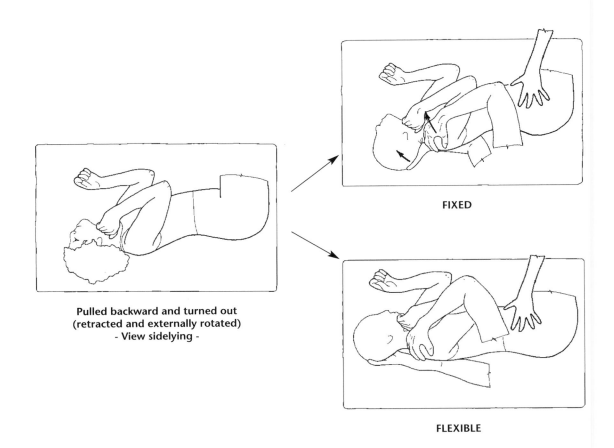

Pulled backward and turned out
(retracted and externally rotated)
- View sidelying -

FIXED

FLEXIBLE

8. Arm Flexibility

Assess if there are any joint or muscular limitations in the elbows. Be aware that the supine position may exaggerate the tension and/or movement patterns in the arms. Again, flex up the person to reduce spasticity. Opening the palm, thumb and extending the wrist can also help to reduce spasticity. Assess the practical flexibility if the arms are:

- Stiffly bent (flexed)
- Stiffly straight (extended)

a. Stiffly bent (flexed)

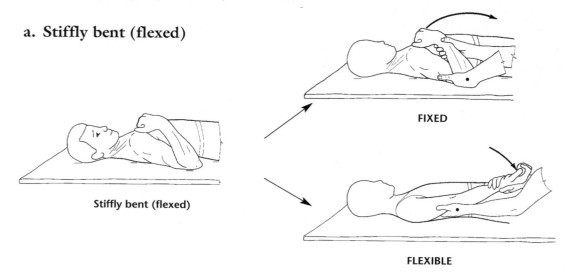

Stiffly bent (flexed)

FIXED

FLEXIBLE

b. Stiffly straight (extended)

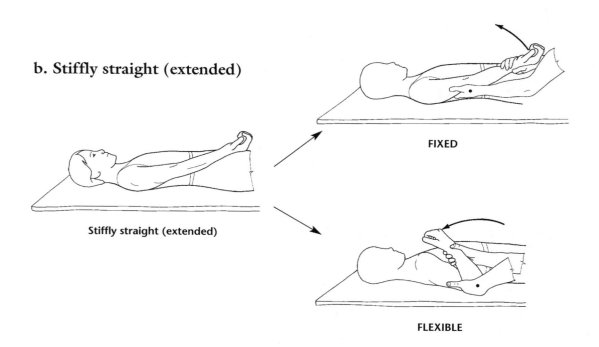

Stiffly straight (extended)

FIXED

FLEXIBLE

Joint and Muscular Flexibility Assessed Lying on Back

Aaron's pelvis, which rolls backward (posterior tilt), is 50% flexible at the lower spine, and the right lateral pelvic tilt is flexible. His trunk, which curves forward and curves sideways with a right-sided convexity, is flexible. Both of his hips flex to 90°, and even though the right hip tends to move and turn in toward midline, it (and the left hip) are flexible to come to a neutral posture. The left knee, which tends to extend, is flexible so that it bends to 90°. The right knee, which flexes, can straighten to 90°. Even though his ankles and feet turn in, they are flexible to attain a neutral posture. His left shoulder, which shrugs upwards, is 50% flexible, and the right shoulder, which tends to pull and turn in, is flexible, as is his right arm.

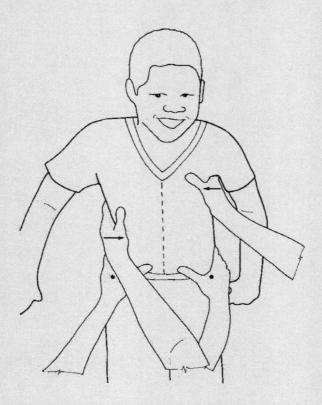

**His trunk, which curves to
the right, is flexible**

D Balance and Postural Control in Sitting

Before assessing the person's joint flexibility, posture and movement in sitting, get a general idea of the person's balance and trunk control when she sits on a firm surface with her feet on the floor. How much independent postural control does the person have?

1. Can the person sit alone and use her hands for activities? Can she shift her weight from side to side and front to back (good balance and trunk control)?

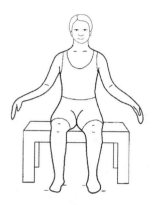

Good balance and trunk control

2. Can the person sit alone but needs to hold onto the surface (fair balance and trunk control)?

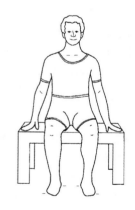

Fair balance and trunk control

3. Is the person unable to sit alone and requires assistance from another person (poor balance and trunk control)?

Poor balance and trunk control

E   Assessment in Sitting: Flexibility and Postural Support

A person's sitting posture(s) may be influenced by muscle tightness, weakness, movement patterns, and gravity. First, we assess the person's joint and muscular flexibility, in reference to *the* neutral sitting posture. We will also observe and feel the person's muscular activity and movement patterns. Then, with our hands, we will begin to assess where the individual's body needs support to achieve *the person's* neutral posture. The person will be assessed while sitting on a firm surface, like a mat table, with her feet flat on the ground. Note both the flexibility and the need for postural support on your assessment form.

Once again, we begin with the pelvis. Remember, the posture of the pelvis affects the posture of the whole body. If the pelvis is in the neutral posture, the rest of the body has a better chance of being balanced and active.

The posture(s) of the pelvis is affected by tissues:
- **Behind, in front and above the pelvis:** Tension, contractures, tightness in the spinal joints, muscles and tissues between the pelvis, sacrum and lumbar spine, and from the pelvis to the sternum and ribcage. (Assessed on pages 43, 44.)
- **Under and to the sides of the pelvis:** Tension, contractures, tightness in the spinal joints, muscles and tissues from the sides of the pelvis to the ribs and spine. (Assessed on page 44.)

In order for the pelvis to achieve the neutral posture:
- The hip joint, muscles and tissues around the hip joint need to be flexible so that the hip can bend (flex) to at least a 90°.
- Muscles and tissues in the lumbar spine and between the lumbar and sacral spine need to be flexible to achieve a neutral posture.
- Muscles and tissues in front of the pelvis attached to the sternum and ribcage need to be flexible.

To focus on the pelvis/lumbar spine, we need to allow for (accommodate) any limitations in hip motion. Before you continue, check your notes in Section C3. For instance, a person might be sitting with a laterally tilted pelvis because the hip is fixed in external rotation. Thus, we need to accommodate the hip external rotation so we can assess the true pelvic flexibility. Another common example is a hip that does not flex to 90°. If this is the case, place a wedge under the pelvis and thighs to create an open hip flexion angle. The wedge angle correlates to the amount of

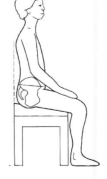

Wedge creating open hip flexion angle

limitation in hip flexion. If in the seated posture, the seat-to-back support angle is less than the person's hip flexion angle, you cannot truly be testing the pelvic/lumbar spine flexibility.

> **Note:** In the following sections, we first refer to the typical posture that the person tends to assume (if the person has a typical posture).

1. The Pelvis/Low Back

Assess the flexibility and control of the pelvis and low back.

  a. Is the person able to actively move her pelvis into the neutral posture and maintain that posture? (**neutral pelvis**)

  b. Can she move through different pelvic postures in a controlled manner? (**active pelvic control**)

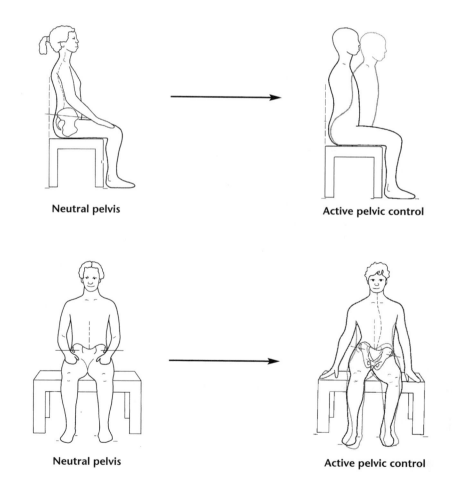

Neutral pelvis   Active pelvic control

Neutral pelvis   Active pelvic control

If the person's pelvis tends to assume one of the following postures, and she cannot move it to neutral by herself, assess the flexibility passively. With your hands on the ASIS and PSIS (or iliac crest if you can't reach the PSIS) move the person's pelvis at the lumbar spine. If you can move the pelvis into a neutral posture, it is *flexible*. If you can not move it out of its typical posture, it is *fixed*. Sometimes the pelvis is *partially flexible*. If so, note the percentage of flexibility, or practical flexibility. If the pelvis is *fixed*, we cannot expect the seating system to "correct" the pelvis to the neutral posture.

Is the pelvis:

   c. **Rolled backward (posterior pelvic tilt)**

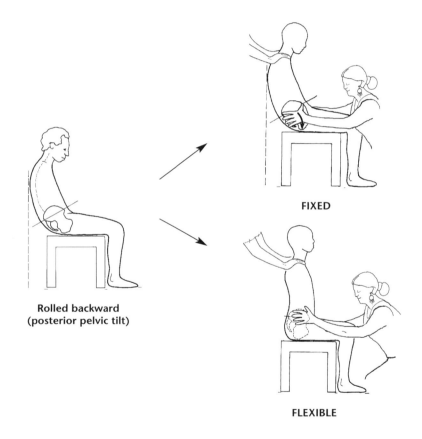

Rolled backward
(posterior pelvic tilt)

FIXED

FLEXIBLE

When the person's pelvis is "corrected" or reduced to its optimal posture, look at and feel the contour of the low back (lumbar spine). Some people's lower backs will be arched (lordosis), others' will be flat, and other lower backs will round and curve forward (kyphosis).

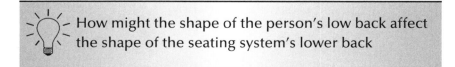

How might the shape of the person's low back affect the shape of the seating system's lower back

d. Stiffening and sliding forward (extensor thrust)

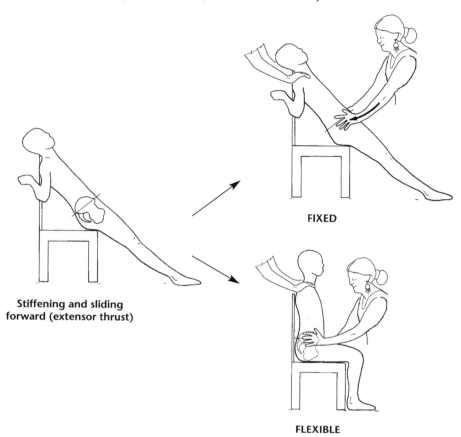

Stiffening and sliding forward (extensor thrust)

FIXED

FLEXIBLE

e. Rolled forward (anterior pelvic tilt)

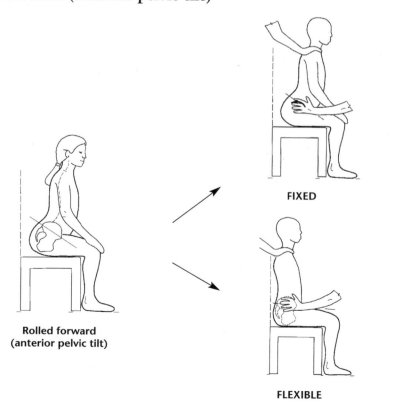

Rolled forward (anterior pelvic tilt)

FIXED

FLEXIBLE

f. Tilted to the side (lateral pelvic tilt)

Because the spine and pelvis are connected, the person's spine may accommodate in different ways to keep the head centered over the pelvis. The person's spine may form the shape of a "C" or "S". Additional curves may also be present. Remember to accommodate lack of hip flexibility.

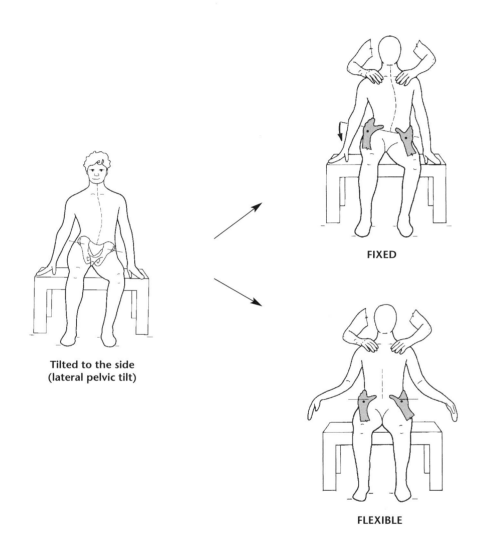

**Tilted to the side
(lateral pelvic tilt)**

FIXED

FLEXIBLE

g. Turned (rotated)

As with a lateral pelvic tilt, a pelvic rotation is often associated with a rotation in the spine. Note the practical flexibility.

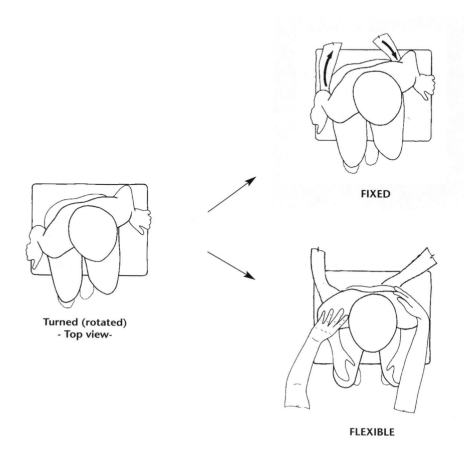

FIXED

Turned (rotated)
- Top view-

FLEXIBLE

How your hands are providing pelvic support:

After assessing the pelvic/low back flexibility, note specifically how your hands are providing pelvic support to help the person achieve *her* neutral posture. Questions to keep in mind:

- **Where** are your hands supporting, "correcting," or stabilizing the pelvis?
- In **what direction** are you applying the support with your hands?
- **How much force** are you using to "correct" the person's pelvic posture?
- What is the **minimal amount of support** necessary to stabilize and/or control the pelvis?

 How might this information affect the shape of the lower back support; the size, shape, and location of lateral (side), and anterior (front), pelvic supports?

2. The Trunk

Next, assess the flexibility and control of the person's trunk (mid-back or thoracic region, and chest).

a. Is the person able to move her trunk into the neutral posture and maintain that posture? (**neutral trunk**)

b. Is she able to move her trunk through different postures and control that movement? (**active trunk control**)

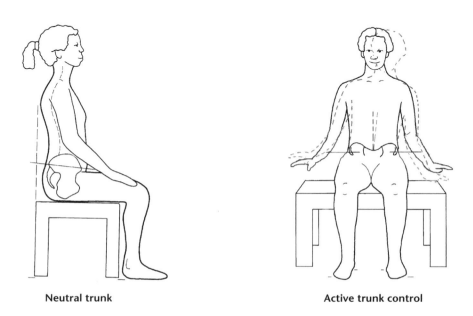

Neutral trunk   Active trunk control

If the person cannot move her trunk into the neutral posture, assess the trunk's flexibility. Make sure that your helper is holding the person's pelvis, hips, legs, and ankles in her neutral posture or its limit of flexibility. With the pelvis stable, what is the posture of her trunk? Can you "correct" the person's posture so that the spine is in a neutral posture (*flexible*), or is it stuck (*fixed*)? Precisely where are the trunk and mid-back flexible and fixed? How practically flexible are the spine and trunk?

In the following sections, we first refer to the typical posture that the person tends to assume (if the person has a typical posture). Note the percentage of flexibility, when the trunk is:

c. Curved forward (kyphosis)

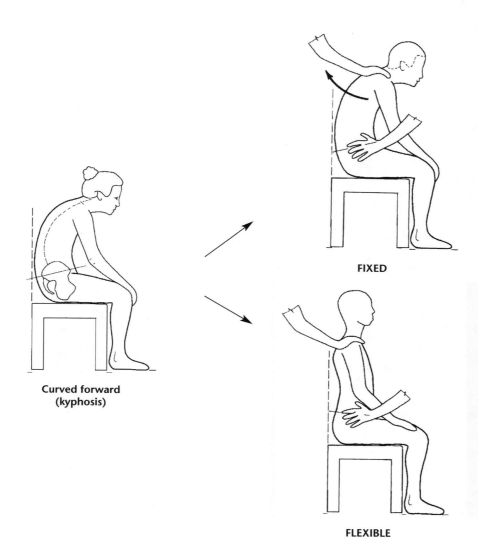

**Curved forward
(kyphosis)**

FIXED

FLEXIBLE

d. Curved to the side (scoliosis)

The spine can curve and twist in different ways in order to keep the head upright. The person's spine may form the shape of a "C" or "S." Additional curves may also be present. It is helpful to define the curve by the side of the convexity. For instance, the person below has a lower thoracic *convexity* to the left.

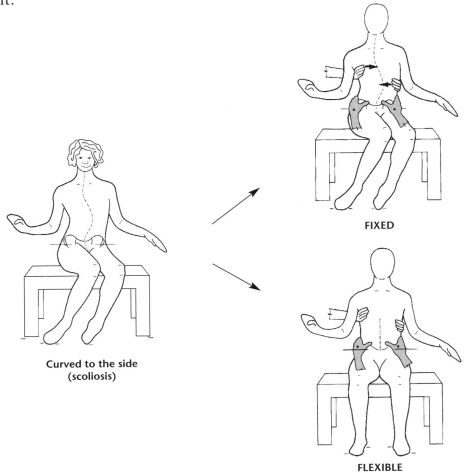

Curved to the side (scoliosis)

FIXED

FLEXIBLE

Note whether the ribs stick out on one side (rib hump).

Rib hump

e. Rotated backward on one side (rotated)

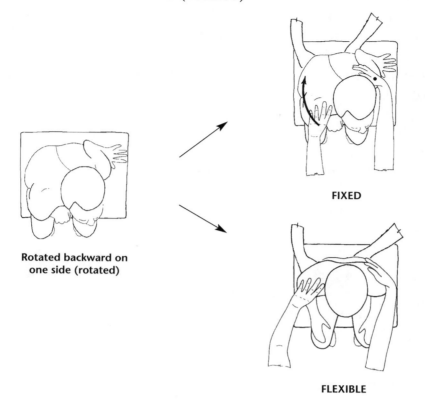

Rotated backward on
one side (rotated)

FIXED

FLEXIBLE

f. Arched backward (extended)

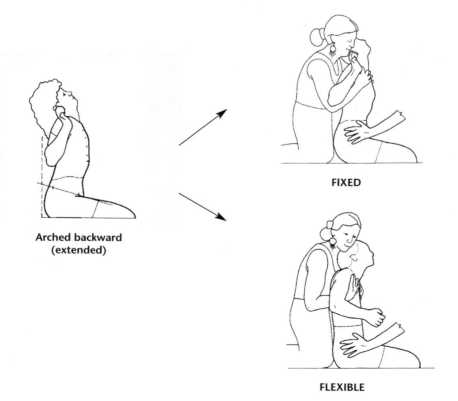

Arched backward
(extended)

FIXED

FLEXIBLE

How are your hands providing trunk support?

While assessing trunk flexibility, note specifically how your hands are providing support to the trunk, to help the individual achieve *the person's* neutral posture. Questions to keep in mind:

- In **what posture** of the **spine over the pelvis** does the head feel most balanced?
- **Where** are you hands supporting, "correcting," or stabilizing the trunk?
- **How much force** are you using to "correct" the person's trunk posture?
- **In what direction** are your hands applying the support?
- What is the **least amount of support** necessary to stabilize and/or control the trunk?
- How much **surface contact** is necessary to provide support?

 How might this information affect the shape, of the back support; the size, shape and location of lateral (side), and anterior (front) trunk supports?

3. The Hips and Legs

While assessing the posture(s) and movement of the person's hips and legs, observe how the legs are stabilizing to support the person's posture.

a. Is the person able to move her hips and legs into the neutral posture (slightly apart in 5-8° of abduction)? Can she use her legs and feet as a stable base of support? (**neutral hips**)

b. Can she move her hips in and out, up and down in a controlled manner? (**active hip control**)

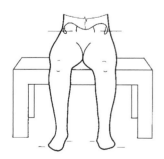

Neutral hips

Active hip control

If the person cannot move her hips and legs to the neutral posture, assess the amount of flexibility available. As in Section C 3a-e, assessing the joint flexibility in the supine position, stabilize the pelvis and move the leg at the hip joint. If the hips and legs can be corrected to the neutral posture, without changing the posture of the pelvis, the hip is *flexible*. If not, it is *fixed*. Note the percentage of flexibility and practical flexibility.

> **Note:** We first refer to the typical posture the person tends to assume (if the person has a typical posture).

Assess the flexibility if the hips and legs tend to assume one or a combination of the following postures:

c. Hips/legs moved towards midline (adducted)

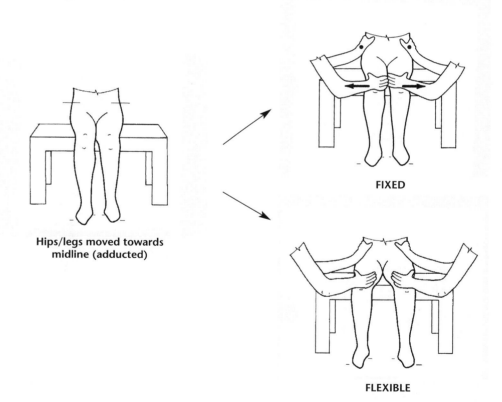

Hips/legs moved towards midline (adducted)

FIXED

FLEXIBLE

d. Hips turned in (internally rotated)

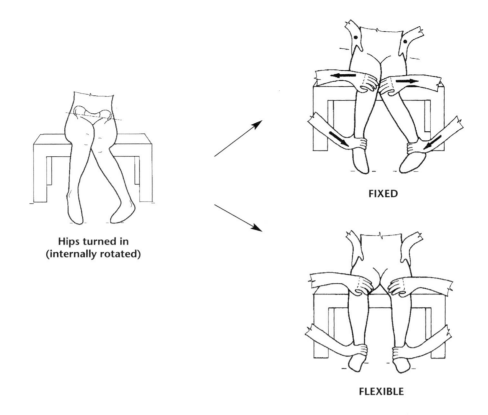

Hips turned in
(internally rotated)

FIXED

FLEXIBLE

e. Hips/legs spread open (abducted)

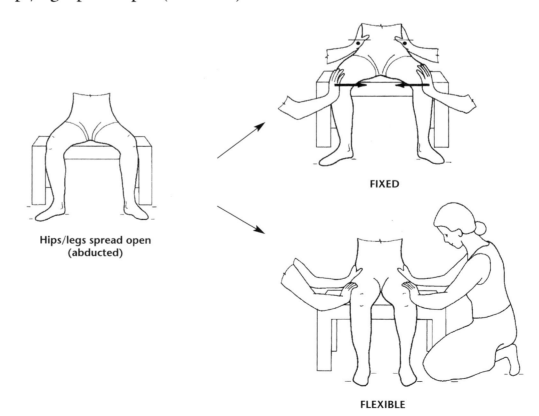

Hips/legs spread open
(abducted)

FIXED

FLEXIBLE

f. Hips turned out (externally rotated)

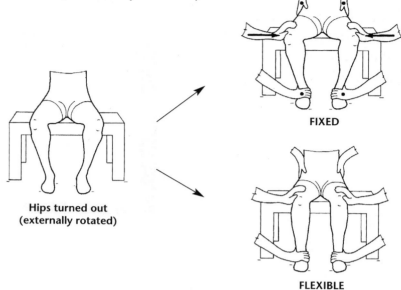

Hips turned out
(externally rotated)

FIXED

FLEXIBLE

g. Both legs turned to the same side (windswept)

If the hips and legs are fixed, it is difficult to measure the amount of rotation. You can place a large sheet of paper under the person's buttocks and thighs and trace the outline of her buttocks and thighs. Use this as a guide when deciding on seating components.

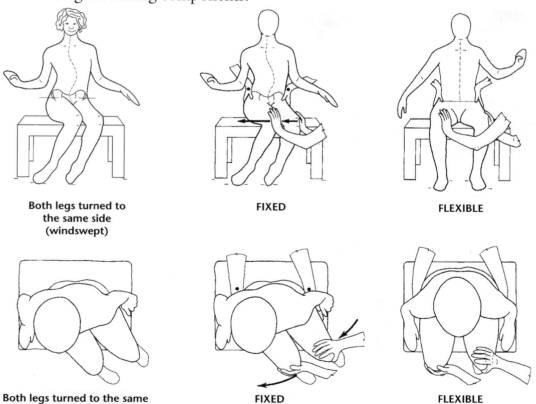

Both legs turned to
the same side
(windswept)

FIXED

FLEXIBLE

Both legs turned to the same
side (windswept) with left
hip external rotation, right
hip internal rotation
- Top view -

FIXED

FLEXIBLE

h. Legs moving constantly

Can you provide support with your hands to:
- Prevent the leg(s) from moving?
- Calm the leg(s)?
- Create a place where the leg(s) can rest and have a chance to stop moving?

Legs moving constantly

How are your hands providing hip and leg support?

While assessing the flexibility, note specifically how your hands are providing support to the hips and legs to achieve their neutral posture. Questions to keep in mind:
- **Where** are your hands providing stability for the hips and legs?
- In **what direction** are your hands applying the support?
- **How much force** are you using to provide stability and prevent excessive movement?
- What is the **minimal amount** of postural support needed?

 Can you imagine how this information might help you specify shapes and sizes of supports, wedges, and straps for the hips and legs?

4. The Knees

a. Can the person bend her knees to 90° so that the bottoms of her feet contact the floor/foot supports? (**neutral knees**)

b. Can the person control bending and straightening of her knees? (**active knee control**)

Neutral knees   Active knee control

If her knees cannot assume the neutral posture, assess her knee flexibility. The helper needs to stabilize the pelvis and prevent it from moving (usually into a posterior pelvic tilt). Assess the knee flexibility if the person's knees tend to be:

c. Bent (flexed): Typical posture

> **Movement to assess:** Straightening (extending) the knee(s). With one hand on the thigh above the knee and the other hand behind the lower leg, begin to straighten the leg(s) at the knee(s). When the helper feels the pelvis start to roll backward (posterior tilt), *stop* straightening the knee(s). Measure the angle. This is an especially important area to assess the practical flexibility.

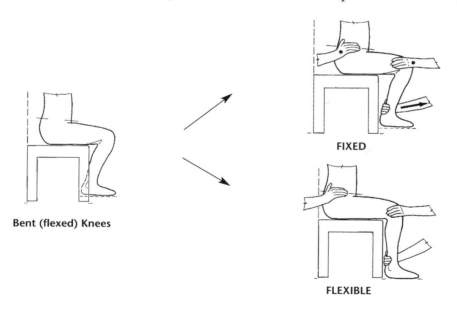

FIXED

Bent (flexed) Knees

FLEXIBLE

Place the angle measure with the axis at the center of the knee joint. If the knees straighten to 90°, they are considered flexible.

d. **Straight (extended):** Typical posture

Movement to assess: Bending (flexing) the knees. The muscles in the front of the leg can also be tight. The person's pelvis should be stabilized as in **c**. With one hand on the thigh above the knee and the other hand in front of the lower leg above the ankle, begin to flex the knee(s). If the knees flex to at least 90°, they are considered flexible. Note practical flexibility.

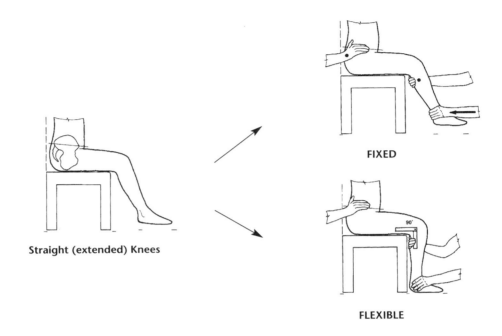

Straight (extended) Knees

FIXED

FLEXIBLE

How are your hands providing lower leg support?
- **Where** are you stabilizing the knees and legs?
- **How much** force do you need to apply?
- **In what direction** are your hands applying the support?

Also assess other knee flexion angle(s) that may allow the person to better use her legs and feet as a stable base of support over which movement can occur.
- Starting from *the* neutral posture, allow the knees to flex at different angles greater than 90° (foot more under the seat) maintaining foot contact with the floor or other support surface. Assess the effect on her posture and movement.

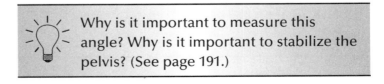

Why is it important to measure this angle? Why is it important to stabilize the pelvis? (See page 191.)

5. The Ankles and Feet

a. Can the person actively bend her ankles to 90° so that her feet rest on the floor or support surface? (**neutral ankles**)

b. Can she actively control her ankle/foot movements (bending ankle up, down, in, and out)? (**active ankle control**)

Neutral ankles   Active ankle control

If the person is unable to move her ankles and feet to a neutral posture, check your notes in Section C5 (page 57) about the degree of flexibility in the ankles and feet. Given the limitations in flexibility, note how your hands are providing support for the ankles and feet.

- **Where** are your hands supporting, "correcting," or controlling the ankles and feet?
- **How much stability** are your hands providing? Are they totally limiting any ankle/foot movement or allowing some movement? Which movements?
- **In what direction** are your hands applying the support?
- What is the **minimal amount of support** needed?

How might this information determine the foot support-to-leg angle in the seating system? Can you imagine how you might specify shapes and sizes of supports, wedges, and straps for the ankles and feet?

6. The Head and Neck

With the pelvis and spine supported in *the person's* neutral posture, describe her head/neck posture and movement.

    a. Is the person able to hold her head up? (**neutral head**) How long can that posture be maintained? (The person must have interesting things to look at in her environment.)

    b. Can the person turn her head to both sides to look at people and things in her environment? (**active head control**)

If the person does not have active head control, think of how her body and head can be supported in her neutral posture. Often head control is difficult to adequately assess until the person is sitting in a simulated (trial) seating system, because the posture of the body will greatly impact head balance and control. Assuming the person's pelvis, trunk and lower extremities are adequately supported, assess her head posture and movement:

- In **what posture** of the **spine over the pelvis** does the head seem most balanced?
- If you **alter the person's body in relationship to gravity** (tilt the seating system), does the person's head control improve or worsen?
- **Where** are your hands providing support for her head? Does the person feel comfortable with the support of your hands or does she push against it?
- Can you alter the head posture by providing **more support to the shoulders, arms, and upper back?**
- What happens if you **fully support the arms**, taking their weight away from the head and shoulder girdles?
- What is the **least amount of support** required?
- Describe the *contact surface* that you are providing with your hands, that is, the shape, amount of contact, and location.

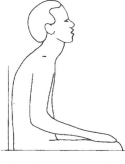

Head/neck extended

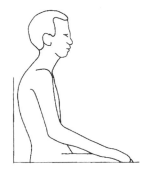

The person's neutral posture

 From this information, can you begin to imagine the location, shape, and size of a head/neck support?

7. The Shoulder Girdles

With the pelvis and spine stable, assess the posture(s) and movement of the shoulder girdles.

    a. Is the person able to actively bring her shoulders and arms into a neutral posture? (**neutral shoulder girdles**)

    b. Can she actively control her arm movements? (**active arm control**)

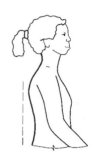

Neutral shoulder girdles

Active arm control

If the person is unable to bring her shoulders to a neutral posture, are any or a combination of the following postures assumed? Are the shoulder girdles:

    c. Shrugged upwards (elevated)

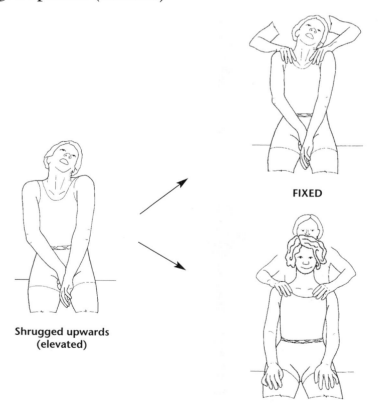

Shrugged upwards
(elevated)

FIXED

FLEXIBLE

d. Pulled forward and turned in (protracted and internally rotated)

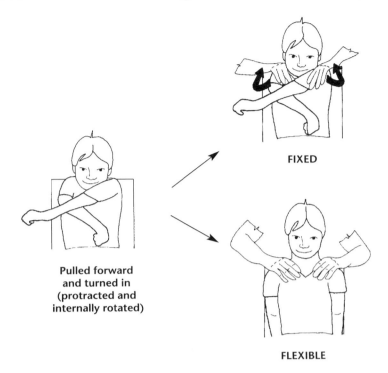

Pulled forward
and turned in
(protracted and
internally rotated)

FIXED

FLEXIBLE

e. Pulled backward and turned out (retracted and externally rotated)

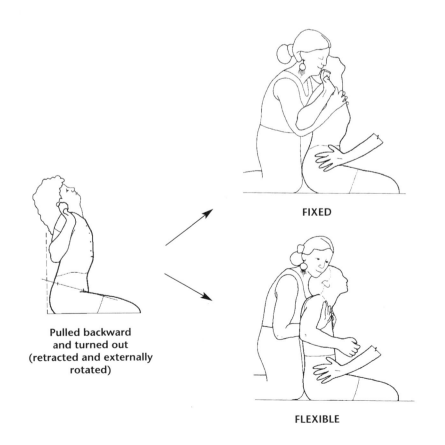

Pulled backward
and turned out
(retracted and externally
rotated)

FIXED

FLEXIBLE

How are your hands providing support for the shoulder girdles?

While assessing flexibility, note how your hands are providing support and/or control for the shoulder girdles.

- **Where** are your hands applying the support to "correct," or control the person's shoulder girdles?
- **How much stability** do the supports need to provide? Totally limit any shoulder movement? Allow some movement?
- **In what direction** are your hands applying the support?
- What is the **surface contact area** necessary to provide support?

8. The Arms

In Section C8 (page 61), you discovered whether there are any joint or muscular limitations of the elbow(s). If the person has active control of her arms, it will be important to assess functional activities while the person is sitting well supported in a simulated seating system. Assessment of functional skills will be addressed later (see page 111). The following section is geared toward the person who does not have active control of her arms. Ask yourself the following questions:

- **Where** are your hands providing support to the arms to affect abnormal movement patterns or provide postural stability?
- **How much force** are you using to "correct" the arm posture?
- **In what direction** are your hands applying the support?
- **How much surface contact area** is necessary to provide support?
- What is the **shape of the surface contact area**?

 How might this information affect your seating component selection for arm supports? Consider widths, flexibilities, and angles of pull of straps; location of supports and wedges; and specific needs for laptrays.

Assessment in Sitting: Balance, Flexibility and Postural Support

Aaron's balance and postural control in sitting are fair. He can sit on a bench independently; however, he is afraid of falling, especially if no one is nearby. Even though his pelvis rolls backwards (posterior tilt), it is 50% flexible such that it can almost be corrected to *the* neutral posture. With hand support behind his sacrum and pelvis below the PSIS, pressing forward with moderate force, his pelvis is more upright and neutral. Even though his pelvis tilts to the side, it is flexible. His pelvis can be held in neutral with support close to the right side of his pelvis. Also, minimal support over the top of his thighs gives Aaron a feeling of security so that he can tilt his pelvis forward and backward without fear of falling.

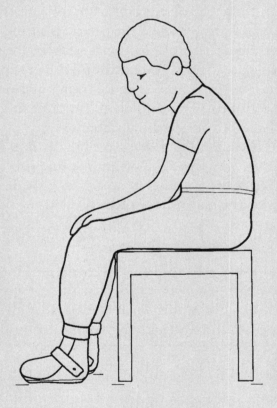

Aaron sitting independently on a bench

Aaron's trunk curves forward starting at about the 12th thoracic spinal level; however, it is 50% flexible. If his pelvis is supported, Aaron can move his trunk forward, backward, and lean side to side. If his back is supported from behind up to and including the lower ribs, so that his lower ribcage is "cupped," he feels secure. In this neutral trunk posture his head is slightly forward of his hip joints. When he brings his trunk and head farther back than that, he feels uncomfortable and afraid.

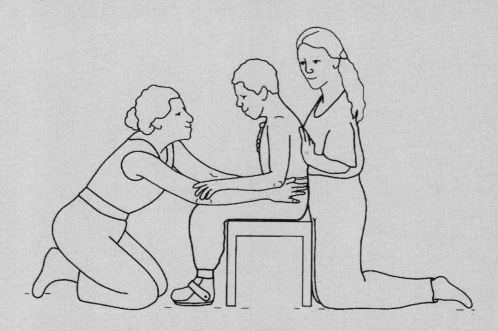

Aaron's neutral posture: head forward of hip joints

Aaron has active control of his left hip and leg. He is able to bend (flex) his left hip and leg, and move it towards and away from midline. Even though his right hip and leg move and turn in towards midline, they are flexible to come to neutral. Minimal support pressing against the inner aspect of his right knee prevents the right hip from turning and moving in excessively. This support also helps to prevent the left side of his pelvis from rotating backward.

Aaron likes to bend his right knee farther under his seat especially when reaching forward or getting ready to stand. The right knee is flexible, such that it can extend to 90° without rolling the pelvis backward (posterior tilt). His left knee tends to extend especially when he is excited; however, it can be flexed to 90°. Moderate support pressing down just below his left ankle prevents this excessive knee extension. The posturing of his ankles and feet are well controlled by customized rigid ankle/foot orthoses.

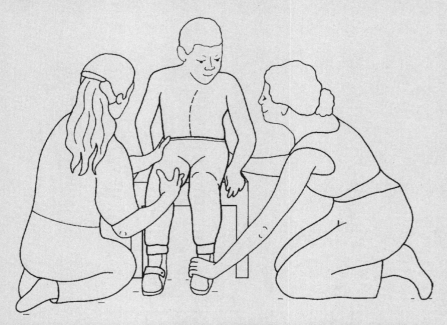

Supporting pelvis, sacrum, and trunk from behind, right side of pelvis, inner right knee, and left ankle

Aaron has active control of his head and neck. When his pelvis and trunk are supported, his head and neck no longer bend forward and turn to the left.

Aaron has active control of his left shoulder girdle and arm. His shoulder tends to shrug due to shortening of muscles and tissues between his neck and shoulder girdle. His right shoulder tends to pull forward and turn in and his right elbow tends to stiffen into extension. Supporting his forearm underneath such that his elbow is under his shoulder joint minimizes the turning in of his right shoulder, elbow extension, and leaning of his trunk to the right.

Aaron becomes fearful if the seating system is tilted backwards. If it is upright or slightly tilted forward, he is able to sit up comfortably.

F The Effect of Gravity in Sitting

In section E6 (page 82), we looked at gravity's effect on the person's head and neck posture in the upright position. In this section we will address the effect of gravity on the person's sitting posture when the entire seating system is tilted at different angles.

If possible, assess the effect of gravity when the person is in a simulated seating system. The person's body should be well supported; otherwise, the true effect of gravity will not be assessed. Assuming that the person's pelvis, trunk and legs are supported as well as possible, *slowly* tilt the seating system backwards at different angles. How does the person respond? Does she:

- Relax?
- Pull forward?
- Arch her back?
- Hold her head upright easier?

Note how much tilt seems optimal.

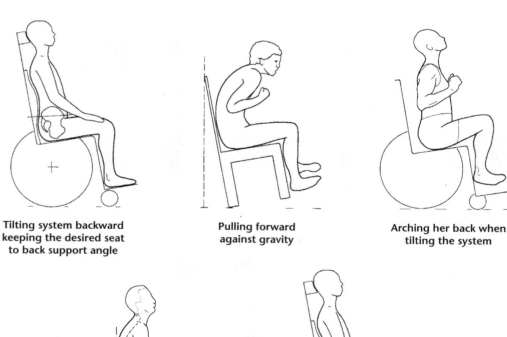

Tilting system backward keeping the desired seat to back support angle

Pulling forward against gravity

Arching her back when tilting the system

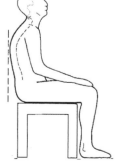

Poor head control in the upright posture

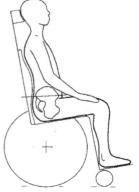

Improved head control when the seat is tilted back

G Pressure

Pressure under vulnerable boney prominences must be assessed in people who lack sensation (such as those with spinal cord injuries or *spina bifida*), the elderly, and people who lack the ability to weight shift and move to relieve pressure.

1. Risk Areas at the Seat Surface

Vulnerable bony prominences at the seat cushion include *ischial tuberosities*, *coccyx* (tailbone), *pubis*, *sacrum*, and *greater trochanters* (of the femurs).[6-8] Also, any bone that sticks out under the skin, like a rib in severe scoliosis, or a vertebrae in severe kyphosis, inferior angle of the scapula, PSIS, head of the *fibula*, ankle bones and so on, may be at risk for tissue breakdown. Areas at risk for high levels of pressure at the seat cushion include:

- *Sacrum/coccyx* (tailbone): Very little protection; however, generally not in contact with the cushion unless the pelvis is in an extreme posterior tilt.
- *Ischial tuberosities* (sitting bones): Normally the highest risk of pressure sores.
- *Greater trochancters* (bones on the outside of the hips): Less risk than ischial tuberosities, but also a concern.
- **Upper part of the thighs**: The best for taking the pressure load.

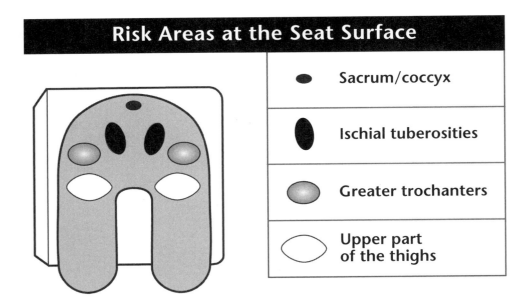

Risk Areas at the Seat Surface

●	Sacrum/coccyx
●	Ischial tuberosities
●	Greater trochanters
○	Upper part of the thighs

2. Measuring for Pressure

As an adjunct to a thorough assessment, pressure mapping and measuring systems can be a very useful tool for assessing areas of high pressure. We recommend always putting your hands under the buttocks to feel the pressure. Jamie Noon uses the "wiggle test."[9]

a. Wiggle test

Put your fingers under the above bony prominences and assess whether:

    (1) You can wiggle your fingers.

    (2) Your fingers are pinched but you can easily pull your fingers out.

    (3) Fingers are pinched and it is difficult to pull your fingers out.

Meaning of the wiggle test

    If (1) Don't do anything special to relieve the pressure.

    If (2) The pressure is okay, as long as there are no concerning factors, such as activity level, skin integrity, cleanliness of skin, continence, and you are confident about the person's pressure relief practices.

    If (3) Do something, that is, modify pressure relief cushion and educate regarding prevention of pressure sores.

b. Pressure mapping

Pressure mapping is one tool that can provide feedback to the person with the disability and the therapist. It is particularly useful for persons whose sensation is absent. A pad is placed between the person and any supporting surface. Pressure distribution is mapped and visually displayed on a computer. It can assist with checking static pressure as well as assessing the effectiveness of pressure relief methods. Pressure mapping should be used in conjunction with the wiggle test as part of a complete assessment[10]. Pressure mapping is frequently used to help design or choose the seat cushion.[11-13] It is also used to provide feedback to the wheelchair user about pressure-relieving methods including tilting of the seating/mobility system.[14,15] However, pressure alone is not the only cause of pressure sores. Other factors include tissue integrity, nutritional status, heat, continence, shear, health, age, scar tissue from previous pressure sores, activity level, smoking, and commitment to a pressure-relief routine.[16-18] Protocols for measuring pressure mapping have been developed.[19,20]

c. Low-cost pressure-measuring tool

During the 1991 International Seating Symposium, Michael Heinrich, Nigel Shapcott, Ralf Hotchkiss, David Werner, and Mari Picos (from Proyecto Prójimo in Mexico) developed a low-cost pressure-measuring tool using small balloons and columns of water[21].

Five small balloons (2 x 5 cm) are filled with colored water (can use food coloring). Each balloon is tightly tied to the end of a thin plastic tube (IV tubing, 2 mm inner diameter) 3 meters long. The tubes are mounted on a long strip of cloth, hung so that the bottom of the cloth is at the height of the seat cushion. Three horizontal ribbons are sewn across the cloth: green at 45 cm from the cloth bottom, yellow at 90 cm, and red at 135 cm. The ribbons mark three pressure zones: green = safe, yellow = caution, and red = danger. The balloons are taped onto the seat cushion in areas of potential pressure (ischial tuberosities, sacrum/coccyx, greater trochanters).

The pressure-measuring tool can be used to educate people at risk for skin breakdown as to dangerous pressure areas. Also, when the colored water rises in the tubes, a person can see which weight-shifting techniques will relieve pressure in specific areas. Lastly, it can help in the fabrication or choice of pressure-relief cushions and/or back supports.

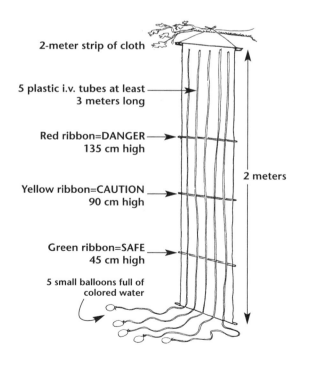

Figures from Werner[21]

After usage in Mexico, innovations to the design include:

- Injecting the water into the tubes using a large syringe made it easier to get water into the tubes. Adding T-connectors a few centimeters from the balloon helped even more.

- When the water level in the tube drops, bubbles form. Adding a little detergent and tapping the tube helped reduce bubbles.

- It may be difficult to set up all five balloons and position them accurately. So, some wheelchair riders preferred three balloons, and sometimes using only one balloon was sufficient to troubleshoot problem pressure areas.

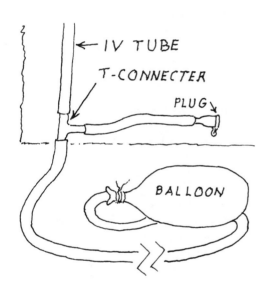

Figure from Werner[21]

References

1. Bergen A, Presperin J, Tallman T. *Positioning for Function: Wheelchairs and Other Assistive Technologies.* Valhalla, NY: Valhalla Rehabilitation Publications, Ltd.; 1990.

2. Trefler E, Hobson D, Taylor SJ, Monahan L, Shaw CG. *Seating and Mobility for Persons with Physical Disabilities.* Tucson, AZ: Therapy Skill Builders; 1993.

3. Presperin J. Seating Systems: The therapist and the rehabilitation engineering team. *Phys Occup Ther Pediatr.*, Spring 1990.

4. Ward D. *Prescriptive Seating for Wheeled Mobility.* Ft. Lauderdale, FL: HealthWealth International; 1994.

5. Minkel, J. Seating/positioning evaluation instructions. *Proceedings from the 19th International Seating Symposium* 2003:71-4.

6. Barton A, Barton M. *The Management of Pressure Sores.* London: Faber and Faber; 1981.

7. Peterson NC, Bittman S. The epidemiology of pressure sores. *Scand J Plastic Reconstr Surg.* 1971;(5):62-6.

8. Zacharow D. *Posture: Sitting, Standing, Chair Design and Exercise.* Springfield, IL: Charles Thomas; 1988.

9. Noon, Jamie. Personal communication, Fall 2008.

10. Brienza D, Pratt S, Sprigle S. Measurement of interface pressure–research versus clinical applications. *Proceedings from the 21st International Seating Symposium.* 2005:65-6.

11. Ferguson-Pell M, Wilkie IC, Reswick JB, Barbenel JC. Pressure sore prevention for the wheelchair-bound spinal injury patient. *Paraplegia.* 1980;18:42-51.

12. Ferguson-Pell M, Sprigle S, Davis K, Hagisawa S. Detecting incipient pressure sore onset. *Proceedings from the 13th International Seating Symposium.* 1997:357-66.

13. Drummond D, et al. A study of pressure distributions measured during balanced and unbalanced sitting. *J Bone Joint Surg.* 1982;64-A(7):1034-9.

14. Lipka D. An overview of pressure mapping systems. *Amer Occup Ther Assoc Tech Special Interest Section Quarterly.* 1977;7(4):1-4.

15. Shapcott N, Levy B. *Team Rehab Report.* 1999 January;10(1):16-21.

16. Schmeler M, Boninger M, Cooper R, Viteck M. Using peer-reviewed literature and other evidence to justify wheelchair seating and mobility interventions. *Proceedings from the 18th International Seating Symposium.* 2002.

17. Hobson D. Contributions of posture and deformity to the body-seat interface variables of a person with spinal cord injuries. *Proceedings from the 5th International Seating Symposium.* 1989:153-71.

18. Ferguson-Pell M, Wilkie IC, Reswick JB, Barbenel JC. Pressure sore prevention for the wheelchair-bound spinal injury patient. *Paraplegia.* 1980;18:42-51.

19. Swaine J, Janzen L, Oga C, Martens C, Swinton L, Jacobson B, Culver K, Preusser A, Swaine F, Sprigle S. Clinical protocol for the administration and interpretation of interface pressure mapping for sitting. *Proceedings from the 21st International Seating Symposium.* 2005:81-3.

20. Swaine J, Stacey M. Development of the Calgary interface pressure mapping protocol for sitting. *Proceedings from the 22nd International Seating Symposium.* 2006:59-62.

21. Werner D. *Nothing About Us Without Us.* Palo Alto, CA: Healthwrights: 1998.

Chapter 3
Simulation & Measurements

A Hand Simulation

Hand simulation means using your hands and often different parts of your own body to provide postural support for the person. Feel, sense, and observe how she responds to specifically placed support in different areas of her body. Hand simulation is actually done in conjunction with assessing joint flexibility and balance in sitting. In Chapter 2, many questions were posed to start you thinking about *how* your hands are supporting the person.

The individual continues to sit on a firm, level surface with her feet well supported. First, we position the person to accommodate or allow for fixed joint and muscular limitations (contractures and deformities). For example, place a block of firm foam under one side of the pelvis to accommodate a fixed pelvic obliquity. After accommodating the fixed contractures, use your hands to assess where she requires postural support. It is helpful to have at least one other person to assist.

Observe and feel how stability and movement in one part of the body affects other parts. How does she respond to your hands? Our intent is to help the person find and achieve her balanced **neutral posture**, a supported posture from which she can initiate movement to function. Simulating with your hands demands all of your senses. I often feel like an octopus, using my trunk, hands, pelvis, legs, and feet to provide just the right amount of support in just the right places.

> A challenge: Without using a single seating component, can you help the person find her neutral posture, and with your hands and body determine where she needs postural support? Quick, take a photo, or have someone draw a picture. Then describe how you are supporting each part of the person's body. **?**

Always keep in mind the person's original objectives when providing postural support. The person's need for comfort, movement, and/or stability for function will guide where and how much postural support the person requires. Ask yourself the following questions:

1. Specifically **where** are your hands supporting the person's body (i.e. posterior pelvis, where in the posterior and lateral spine, legs, arms, etc.)?

2. **What** are your hands doing? Are they "correcting" or "reducing" the person's posture? Are they providing stability? Are they preventing abnormal movement patterns?

3. **How much force** are you applying with your hands to support, stabilize, or correct each part of the body? Remember, do not correct beyond what is practical and comfortable. Watch for signs of resistance to correction, including facial expressions, increased spasticity, and discomfort.

> **Helpful Hint**
>
> A person will feel comfortable and relaxed when minimal effort is required to sit up. If the person relaxes in your hands, then you may have achieved the balance point.

4. In what **direction** are your hands applying the support?

5. How much **surface contact** is necessary to provide postural support? One finger? A full hand? This will give you an idea of the shape and contour of contact surfaces.

6. What is the **least amount of support** needed?

7. Describe the posture of the pelvis and trunk when the head is most **balanced** over the pelvis. Where are your hands supporting the person?

8. In what posture(s) is the person active and ready for **functional movement**? If the person does not have good active movement and control, assess this during **simulation with materials** because the person may first require a lot of postural support.

> **Helpful Hint**
>
> A photograph taken of the person in her neutral posture is a very helpful tool, as it is often difficult to adequately observe and describe all the details of her posture.

Aaron's Postural Objectives

Pelvis: Aaron's pelvis requires a stable support surface that allows space for his ischial tuberosities. Also, moderate support pressing forward behind his sacrum and pelvis below the PSIS, keeps his pelvis in a neutral and upright posture. Support close to the right side of his pelvis prevents his pelvis from tilting to the side. Minimal support over the top of his thighs further stabilizes his base of support.

Trunk: His back needs to be supported from his sacrum up to and including the lower ribs so that his lower ribcage is "cupped". With this support, he feels secure. His trunk needs to be supported in his neutral, kyphotic posture which means that his head is forward of his hip joints.

Hips and legs: If the hips are flexed to 90°, his pelvis can achieve a more upright neutral posture. Minimal support pressing against the inner aspect of the right knee prevents the right hip from turning and moving in excessively.

Knees, ankles, and feet: The right knee needs to be able to bend farther under the seat cushion especially when he is moving his trunk forward to function. Moderate support pressing down just below his left ankle prevents excessive left knee extension. His ankles and feet are supported by the orthoses.

Head and neck: The posture of his head and neck is affected by the posture and support of the rest of the body.

Shoulder girdles and arms: The right shoulder girdle should be positioned by supporting the forearm from underneath. This support prevents both turning in of the right shoulder girdle, elbow flexion, and leaning of the trunk to the right.

B Translating Information from Your Hands into Words

It is important to describe in words specifically where, how much, and what type of support the person requires from your hands. This will clarify the person's postural objetives. This specific information will guide the process of simulation with materials and the design of the seating system. The more precise we are about the person's postural needs, the clearer we will be about the characteristics of the seating system. This step is important, because sometimes we choose a component without really understanding *why* the person needs it. Following are examples of clarifying the person's postural objectives. Remember, every person will be different.

1. Alicia with Cerebral Palsy (her Pelvis)

- **Back of the pelvis:** "I stabilize the back of her pelvis at the PSIS. My hands are 'correcting' her pelvis into the neutral posture. The force is minimal, more of a reminder, and the direction of force is level with the floor (back to front). I use three fingers held sideways to support the top of her pelvis."

- **Sides of her pelvis:** "My hands help to guide or center her pelvis, so that it does not tilt too much to either side. The force is minimal, more of a reminder. My hands extend from the top of the seat cushion to halfway up the pelvis, supporting the sides of the hips but not the thighs."

- **Front of the pelvis:** "I exert a moderate amount of force over her thighs at a 60° angle to the seat cushion."

2. Alfonso with a Spinal Cord Injury and Quadriplegia (his Trunk)

- **Back of his trunk:** "His neutral posture is with his pelvis slightly rolled backward, his lumbar spine flat, and his thoracic spine curved slightly forward (kyphosis). My hands provide stability and contact, but no force to the back part of his lower ribcage."

- **Sides of his trunk:** "I stabilize both sides of his trunk to prevent him from leaning excessively. He wants to have some side-to-side movement, so I lower my hands to 4" (10.2 cm) under the armpits and 1" (2.5 cm) to each side of the trunk. I use the full width of my hand. My hands are angled from top to bottom to match the shape of his ribcage."

C Pre-Simulation Objectives of the Seating System

Before we prepare a trial seating system, clarify the postural objectives of the seating system. What are the characteristics of each part of the seating system that will achieve the person's postural objectives? This is a natural continuation from describing the person's postural objectives. Consider the original objectives—her need for comfort, movement, or stability for function—when determining the objectives of the seating system. Instead of describing how your active and responsive hands are supporting the person, consider how the seating system will support the person. Two examples follow.

1. Alicia with Cerebral Palsy: Support for her pelvis

- **The back support** should stabilize the back of her pelvis at the PSIS, such that the force is minimal, and the direction of force is level with the floor (back to front).

- **The seat cushion** should have supports on the sides of her pelvis that guide, or center, her pelvis, but do not totally limit sideways movement. The contact surface should extend three fingers up from the top of the cushion, supporting the sides of the hips but not the thighs. A support over the top of her thighs should provide moderate force and be set at a 60° angle to the seat cushion.

2. Alfonso with a Spinal Cord Injury and Quadriplegia: Support for his trunk:

- **The back support** should contact and contour to his spine, lower ribcage, and back to support him in his neutral posture (flat lumbar spine and slightly curved forward [kyphotic] thoracic spine). It should extend to the spine of his scapulae, but allow space so that the scapulae can move in all directions.

- **The lateral (side) trunk supports** should prevent excessive leaning to either side. They should be located 4" (10.2 cm) under the armpits and 1" (2.5 cm) to each side of the trunk. They should be the full width of my hand, and be angled from the top to bottom to match the shape of his ribcage.

Pre-Simulation Objectives of the Seating System

Lower back support: Provide support behind his sacrum and pelvis (below the PSIS) with moderate force pressing forward. The lower back support should contour to the shape of the sacrum and pelvis.

Upper back support: Support his back from the sacrum up to and including the lower ribs, so that his lower ribcage is "cupped." The upper back support should contour to the shape of his back to accommodate his kyphosis so that his head is forward of his hips joints. The left shoulder girdle needs to be free to function (especially for wheeling the wheelchair).

Seat cushion: Provide a stable base of support for his pelvis and thighs, to prevent his pelvis from rolling backwards. This cushion should allow space for his ischial tuberosities.

Seat-to-back support angle: Correspond to his hip flexion angle (90°).

Lower back support-to-upper back support angle: Support him in his neutral trunk posture by accommodating his lower thoracic kyphosis, but allowing his trunk to extend.

Leg-to-seat surface angle: The right knee needs to be able to flex further than 90° under his seat for function. The left knee needs to be supported in 90° of flexion to prevent excessive extension.

Foot support-to-leg angle: Needs to be 90° to accommodate the angle of the orthoses.

Tilt of the seating system: Needs to be upright or tilted slightly forward so that he is able to sit up comfortably.

Anterior (front) pelvic support: Stabilize his pelvis and thighs with minimal support over the top of his thighs.

Lateral (side) pelvic support: Prevent his pelvis from tilting to the side with close support to the right side of his pelvis.

Medial (middle) upper leg support: Prevent the right hip from turning and moving in excessively with minimal support pressing against the inner aspect of the right knee.

Ankle/foot supports: Prevent excessive left knee extension with moderate support pressing down just below his left ankle.

Arm supports: Prevent turning in of the right shoulder girdle, elbow flexion, and leaning of the trunk to the right with support underneath the forearm.

D Measurements

Accurate anatomic (body) measurements should be taken of the person, not what you think the seating system may turn out to be. This is true except for **1e.**, **seat surface to top of evaluator's hands,** as this measurement will be more specific for lateral trunk supports. Measurements can be taken during hand simulation, if there are enough people to both support the person and measure. If not, measurements can be done in sidelying, and then rechecked after simulating with materials is complete. Note that some measurements wil not be necessary depending on the required level of support. For instance, a child with cerebral palsy and spastic quadriplegia will require more support than a person with L1 paraplegia.

The person should sit on a firm flat surface. The person should be well supported to achieve the posture desired in the seating system. Note that sometimes separate measurements are required of the right and left side of the body. Measure as straight as possible. If measuring in sidelying, make sure that the person is positioned in the posture desired in the seating system.

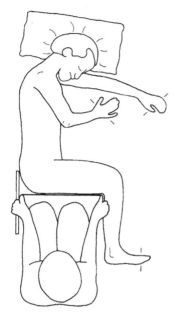

**Measuring seat depth
in sidelying**

Hints about Measurements

1. **Seat surface (contact point of the buttocks) to:**

   a. **PSIS**: Refer to page 10 for locating this bony landmark. If you cannot find the PSIS, measure from the seat surface to 1" (2.5 cm) below the iliac crest.

   b. **Elbows**: Measure for arm supports and laptray height. The shoulders and arms should be relaxed at the sides of the body with the elbows bent (flexed) to 90°.

   c. **Bottom of ribs**: Measure if the person will be using a lower back support. Feel for the last floating ribs (11 and 12). Measure from the seat surface to rib 11.

   d. *Inferior angle of the scapula*: Measure this for shorter back supports, or to make reliefs for the scapula. The inferior angle is the bottom point of the triangular-shaped scapula.

   e. **Top of evaluator's hands**: More accurate for trunk support location.

   f. *Spine of the scapula*: Measure for full-height back supports. The spine of the scapula is the horizontal ridge at the top of the shoulder blade (scapula).

   g. *Occipital shelf*: When palpating the occiput (lowest bone in the back of head), the occipital shelf is the area that protrudes. A head support may contact the head in this area.

   h. **Top of head**: Measure with the head in an upright, neutral posture.

2. **Farthest point in the back of body to:** Place a straight edge, like the triangle tool (described on page 103) or metal tape measure vertically at the furthest point in the back of the body (usually at the apex of the thoracic curve). The following horizontal distances can easily be measured:

   a. **Front of ribs (trunk depth):** Measure the distance from the straight-edge contact with back of the body to the front of the ribs. This will determine trunk support depth and cut out in the laptray.

   b. **PSIS (pelvis to trunk offset):** Measure the distance between the straight-edge contact of the thoracic curve to the PSIS. This measurement will determine the depth of a support behind the pelvis, and/or the shape of the upper back support in relationship to the lower back support.

   c. **Back of head (trunk to head offset):** Measure the distance from straight-edge contact with the thoracic curve to the back of the head. This will give you a starting point of the forward/backward location of the head support.

3. **Leg length:** Hold a rigid flat surface such as a hardcover book against the back of the buttocks. Measure from the book to the back of the knees. If a hamstring tendon is prominent, measure to the edge of the hamstring tendon.

4. **I.T. location to back of knee:** Measure the distance from the front of the I.T. (ischial tuberosity) to the back of the knee. This measurement will be important for an anti-thrust seat cushion, and any pressure-relieving cushions.

5. **Height of thigh:** Measure from seat surface to the top of the the thighs. This is important for the height of pelvic and upper leg supports.

6. **Back of knee to heel** (or weight-bearing area).

7. **Foot length:** Measure with the person wearing her usual footwear.

8. **Trunk width:** Your hands should simulate the support the person requires. Measure between your hands (or the flat supports). The supports should be at least 1" below the armpit so as not to press on important nerves in the armpit.

9. **Shoulder width:** Measure the width between the outer edges of the shoulders.

10. **Hip width:** Place a rigid flat surface such as a hardcover book or clipboard along each hip. Make sure the books are held at 90° to the seat surface. Measure the width between the books at the widest point. This is easier to do with two people. For obese people, this measurement is more accurate in sitting.

11. **Outer knee width:** Measure the width on the outside of the knees with the legs relaxed, supported, and knees apart (depending on the flexibility) in the person's neutral posture.

12. **Inner knee width:** Measure the distance between the knees when the legs are relaxed, separated (depending on the flexibility), and supported in the person's neutral posture.

Note: Measurements 11, 12, and 13 should be taken with the legs in the same position.

13. **Ankle width**
    a. **Inside width**: Measure the distance between the inside of the ankles when the legs are in their neutral posture.
    b. **Outside width**: Measure the distance between the outside of the feet when the foot is in the person's neutral posture, remembering that the foot is in line with the *femur*. We must allow enough room for feet, large shoes, foot supports.

14. **Ankle circumference**: With a flexible measuring tape, measure the distance encircling the top of the foot for footstrap considerations.

15. **Head width**: Measure the side-to-side width of the head at its widest part.

16. **Head circumference**: With a flexible measuring tape, measure the distance encircling the head from behind, from temple to temple (the area next to the outside of the eyes).

Tech Tip: Triangle Tool

Jamie Noon measures the body using a *triangle tool*.[1] Make a triangular base from 1/8" (7 mm) thick wood, plastic, or foamcore; height 38" (96 cm); width 14" (35.5 cm). Firm foam or rubber is attached to the long side that will be against the person. A measuring tape is attached to the long side facing you so that you can read it. Put the triangle tool against the most posterior or rear aspect of the person. The triangle tool is quite useful for measuring the pelvis to trunk offset, and trunk to head offset, because it allows for the natural rounding forward (kyphosis) of the thoracic spine.

Triangle tool

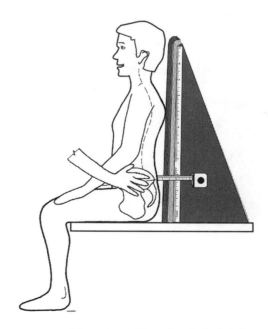

Measuring with a triangle tool

Measurements

	Left	Right

1. Seat surface (the contact point of the buttocks) to:
   a. PSIS
   b. Elbows
   c. Bottom of ribs
   d. Inferior angle of scapula
   e. Top of evaluator's hands
   f. Spine of scapula
   g. Occipital shelf
   h. Top of head

2. Back of body to:
   a. Front of ribs (trunk depth)
   b. PSIS (pelvis to trunk offset)
   c. Back of head (trunk to head offset)

3. Leg length
   (where hips touch flat surface to back of knees)

4. IT to back of knee

5. Height of thigh

6. Back of knee to heel (or weight-bearing area)

7. Foot length

8. Trunk width

9. Shoulder width

10. Hip width (greatest width)

11. Outer knee width (relaxed, with knees apart)

12. Inner knee width

13. Ankle width
    a. Inner width
    b. Outer width

14. Ankle circumference

15. Head width

16. Head circumference

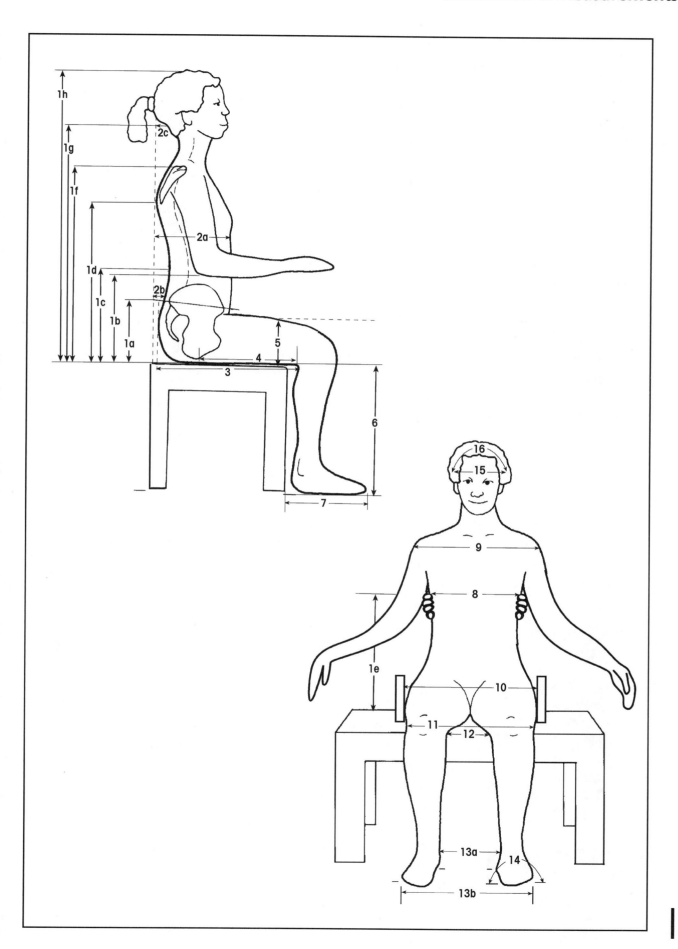

E | Simulation with Materials

When **simulating with our hands**, our intention is to help the person find her balanced neutral posture. When **simulating with materials** we want to create a trial seating system to support the person's neutral posture. We will then assess if this seating system will both support and assist the person to function optimally. In summary, we will be translating the information from our hand simulation into words, and then into static or dynamic postural supports. Simulation is an important part of the seating assessment process, because the person and her "team" can evaluate the comfort and fit of the trial seating system before the fabrication of the final seating system. Once a simulated seating system is created, we can assess her function and make

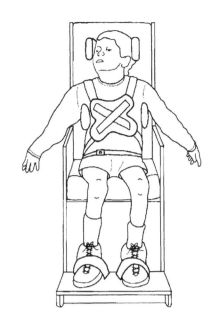

changes in the simulated seating system to enhance her function. Other benefits from simulation include educating the person as to the how the seat can support her, documenting and photographing for third-party reimbursement, and taking measurements.[2]

Different materials such as firm dense foam (like styrofoam), corrugated cardboard, wood, or other materials can be cut, shaped, and placed next to or under the person. Attach these materials with glue, velcro, or duct tape. An existing wheelchair or other type of chair gives you a base or a foundation from which to add various supports.

Tech Tip

"Pita Pocket"

Jamie Noon likes to use a "pita pocket" for customizing back supports.[1] He takes a thick firm foam for the back support and slices it like pita bread. He then puts the postural supports into the pita pocket. He can easily remove them to change size or shape. When the pita pocket is complete, he can then glue the slices together or make a custom-shaped back support.

"Pita pocket"

Helpful Hint

During simulation with materials, we also continue to simulate with our hands. It's a creative, integrative, problem-solving process.

Optimally, a seating evaluation chair or "simulator" can be used. A simulator may allow changes in:

- Seat depth and width
- Seat cushion type
- Back support height and type
- Seat-to-back support angle
- Seat angle
- Lower leg support length
- Leg-to-seat surface angle
- Foot support-to-leg angle
- Postural supports
- Seating system tilt

Optimally, the seat cushion should be wide enough to allow for "windswept" posture of the legs. Also, it should allow for a clear view from the sides to see spinal and pelvic alignment.[2]

Simulators can have flat, planar[3] components or molding bags. The molding bags are filled with particles, such as polystyrene beads, chunks of rubber, or beans. The bag is connected to a vacuum pump via a tube so that as the air is drawn out, the particles press together. The bags should be made of stretchable material, so that shapes can easily be created. In the beginning of the molding process, the vacuum pressure is set lower so that the beads can be moved around. As the final form takes shape, the vacuum pressure is increased.[4]

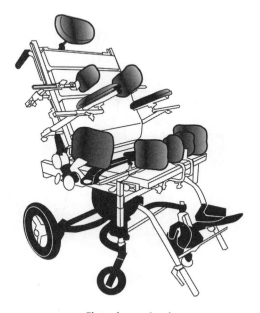

Flat, planar simulator

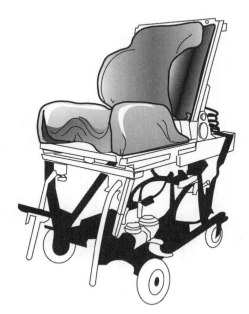

Simulator with molding bag

Note: It is easiest to take measurements after the simulated seating system is complete.

Jamie Noon and myself, along with the Project Prójimo team in Ajoya, Mexico designed and built a seating simulator. The seat-to-back support angle and seat angle changed separately by a telescoping tube and hinges. To achieve a posterior tilt (tilt-in-space) of the entire simulator, a wedge was put under the front casters. A very rigid foam was carved into pelvic, sacral, trunk, and hip supports. Velcro was attached on the back of the supports. Strips of velcro were attached to the back support and seat so that the supports could easily be moved. Foot supports were able to move up and down.[5]

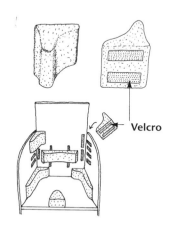

Velcro

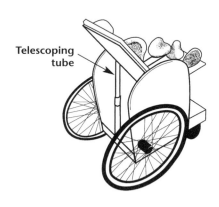

Telescoping tube

Monica Rock shared this design used in a project in Belize. Hip, pelvic, and trunk supports adjusted into the back support and seat via bolts in holes. The seat-to-back support angle was adjustable.[5]

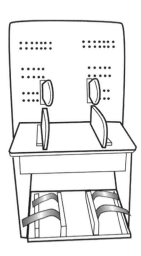

Adjustable pelvic and trunk supports

Adjustable seat-to-back support angle

Don't limit yourself to what you think should work. Be creative. Above all, observe, listen, feel, and stay open to new possibilities.

Chapters 5-13 include suggestions and ideas for components and postural supports for various types of postures. Remember, this section is intended to be thought provoking and give you some basic ideas. During simulation with materials, you may start by using some of the shapes suggested in this section, and then progress from there. Have a lot of blocks, wedges, and scraps of foam on hand to cut and shape. Have straps of different widths available so that you can try a variety of placements. Most importantly, always keep in mind the person's objectives and how the person's posture(s) needs to be supported to allow function and movement. Think how the specific parts of the seating system should be designed to achieve the objectives. Always ask, "Why am I choosing this support?" You should be able to explain why you use each component or support surface. Try different shapes, surfaces, and locations.

Simulation with Materials

A seating system is "mocked up" inside Aaron's wheelchair. A piece of wood is cut to fit on top of the seat rails, to act as a base for the seat cushion. A 1" (2.5 cm) piece of firm, dense foam is cut the same width of the wood and is positioned in front of his ischial tuberosities (pre-ischial shelf). A block of firm foam is placed between the right arm support and his pelvis. A piece of wood is cut that fits in front of the back support tubes to act as a structural base for the back support. The height of the back support is the distance between the seat surface to 1" (2.5 cm) below the bottom of his shoulder blade. A piece of firm, dense foam (lower back support) is cut and formed to the shape of his pelvis and sacrum but is slightly angled toward the top of the pelvis. A second piece of firm, dense foam (upper back support) is cut and contoured to the shape of his back. A positioning belt is taped onto the seat rails at a 90° angle to the seat cushion. A block of foam, positioned between the knees, is attached onto the seat cushion. A strap is taped to the left foot support so that it pulls around the left ankle at a 45° angle.

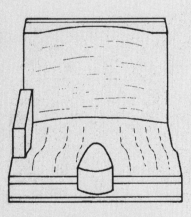

Simulated seating system

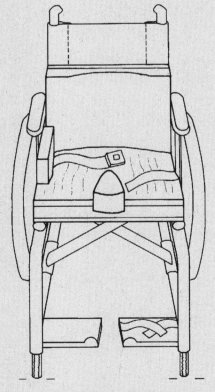

Simulated seating system in current wheelchair

E Functional Abilities in the Simulated Seating System

In Chapter 2B, the functional activities that the person performs in or from her current seating system/wheelchair, and how she performs these activities were identified. Now, reassess the functional activities that the person does in the simulated seating system. Ask:

- Can the person still do the activity?
- Observe *how* she does the activity. How does she stabilize her body and move to perform the function?
- Does the simulated seating system provide the needed postural stability, support, and freedom of movement for function?

If possible, assess all the important functional activities that the person does in or from her seating system. Some of these activities might be difficult from the simulated seating system, so figure out the movements required and assess whether these are able to be performed.

- Wheelchair propulsion
- Dressing
- Bathing
- Toileting
- Eating
- Communicating
- Tabletop activities

Do you remember the following people from the beginning of the assessment section, page 17?

Sammy

His therapist wants Sammy to be able to visually select choices from his communication board on his laptray. After he is well supported in the simulated seating system, we reassess his ability to visually select choices. We find that he still requires head support to be able to meet this objective. We then further modify our simulated seating system to include a head/neck support.

Maggie

Maggie's mother wants her to be able to reach and hit three circular switches placed on her laptray. After Maggie is well supported in her trial seating system, we reassess her arm function. The original specific objective described not only the **type** of arm function, but also **where** and **how** her arm should function. We find that she requires more trunk and shoulder support in order for her to perform this activity. We then modify the simulated seating system accordingly.

Functional Abilities in the Simulated Seating System

With Aaron sitting in this simulated seating system, we reassess important functional activities. When Aaron is wheeling the wheelchair, he shifts the lower part of his trunk to the right to stabilize against the arm support and leans his upper trunk to the left to reach the left wheel. The wheelchair must be narrow enough so that he does not have to lean too far to the left in order to reach the wheel. Further, he needs space for his shoulder blades to move freely in order to wheel.

Aaron likes to rock his trunk forward and backward and side to side to move and dance. The pelvic positioning belt provides sufficient stability but does not restrict this movement. He needs space to the sides of his trunk to allow that movement. In order to put on his shirt, he needs to bend his trunk forward and rotate it to the right. When he uses his left hand to function either to eat, draw, or use the Braille writer, his legs stay in neutral, but his right arm tends to flex more. If his right forearm is supported by a tabletop surface close to his chest so that his elbow is flexed, his left hand has more control to function.

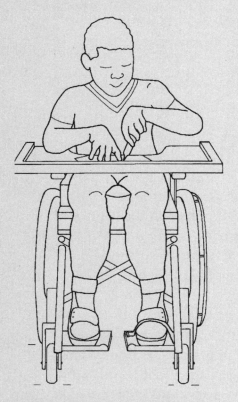

Improved posture and function in simulated seating system

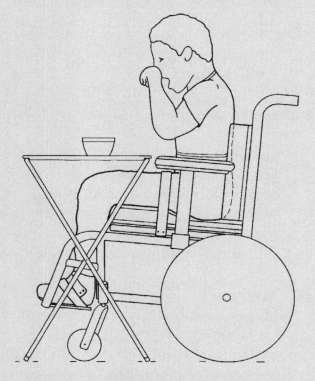

Greater postural stability and improved function in simulated seating system

References

1. Noon J. Personal communication. Fall 2008.

2. Bergen A. Information gathering through simulation. *Proceedings from the 21st International Seating Symposium*. 2005:71-4.

3. Waugh, K. Using a planar seating simulator as part of a comprehensive wheelchair seating assessment. *Proceedings from the 19th International Seating Symposium*. 2003:75-8.

4. Jones K, Bazata C. Simulation and molding: Understanding the differences and honing the skills. *Proceedings from the 22nd International Seating Symposium*. 2006:201-4.

5. Werner D. *Nothing About Us Without Us*. Palo Alto, CA: Healthwrights; 1998.

Chapter 4
Clarifying Objectives

Matching the Person's and Equipment's Objectives

Now we can begin to establish more specific and realistic objectives about how the seating/mobility system should serve the person. We summarize the person's specific postural and functional objectives, and then match them with the objectives of the seating/mobility system. The objectives may change depending on postural and functional information obtained in the simulation. Also, this section will include seating system requirements in relationship to the mobility base. For example, let us look at how the objectives are clarified for Alfonso, who has a spinal cord injury and quadriplegia.

1. Alfonso's Postural and Functional Objectives

a. Sit comfortably and balanced while pushing his wheelchair.

- **Pelvis**: Needs to be allowed to roll backward in a slight posterior tilt for extra stability.

- **Trunk**: Needs to be allowed to curve forward (kyphosis) for stability.

- **Shoulder girdles**: Needs to have space for his scapulae to move when propelling his wheelchair.

b. Have his back supported in a more upright posture when working at his computer.

- **Pelvis**: Needs to be supported from behind so that his pelvis is in a more upright, neutral posture (less posteriorly tilted). There should not be excessive pressure against the sacrum, because the spinous processes of his sacrum are prominent.

- **Trunk**: Requires moderate support and contact against the back of his lower ribcage, and lumbar and thoracic spine.

c. Have his trunk supported to the sides so that he does not have to rely on his arms for support. Be able to move his trunk side to side within a 2-3" range. Requires support angled from top to bottom to match the shape of his ribcage.

d. Be able to transfer independently using a sliding board onto his bed, toilet seat, and bath bench.

e. Brevent pressure sores under his ischial tuberosities and sacrum.

2. Objectives of the Seating/Mobility System

a. Posturally support Alfonso's pelvis and trunk in his neutral posture during wheelchair propulsion.

- The back support should contact and contour to his pelvis, spine, lower ribcage, and back to support him in his neutral posture (slight posterior pelvic tilt, flat lumbar spine, and slightly curved forward (kyphotic) thoracic spine). It should extend to the spine of his scapulae, but allow space so that the scapulae can move in all directions.

- The seating system should be positioned within the wheelchair so that he efficiently pushes the wheelchair. His elbows need to flex (bend) to 90° for efficient pushing and be behind his shoulders. The axle will be in line with, and directly under, his shoulder joint.

b. Provide more support behind his pelvis and back when he is working at the computer. Alfonso should be able to adjust the support for different activities. The support needs to press against the top of his pelvis and lower back when supported in a more upright posture, but be relieved in the area of the spinous processes of the sacrum.

c. Provide support for the sides of his trunk which allow 2-3" (5.1-7.6 cm) of sideways movement. The lateral (side) trunk supports should be located 4" (10.2 cm) under his armpits and 1" (2.5 cm) to each side of his trunk. They should be a full hand-width (3" [7.6 cm]) and be angled from the top to bottom to match the shape of his ribcage. They should flip away or be removable for transfers.

d. The seat surface height needs to be the same as the height of the bed, toilet, and bath bench. Arm supports need to remove. Lower leg supports need to swing away for transfers.

e. The seat cushion needs to be designed to prevent excessive pressure under the ischial tuberosities and sacrum. It should provide a stable support surface for the pelvis and the thighs.

Additional Objectives of Seating/Mobility System

After Aaron's function has been assessed in the simulated seating system, we realize there are other factors to consider (in addition to the pre-simulation objectives). Aaron needs a one-arm drive mechanism allowing him to wheel using only his left hand. Aaron's seat height must be low enough so that he can easily stand up from the wheelchair. Also, the seating system and wheelchair must be narrow enough so that he does not have to lean too far to the left in order to reach the wheel. If the tabletop surface is close to his chest so that it supports his right elbow and forearm, he has more control of his left hand.

Many of the components need to be accessible for Aaron to manipulate, such as the positioning belt, the medial upper leg support, swing-away leg supports, and ankle straps. His orthopedic surgeon is concerned about future right hip subluxation if his hip is permitted to move and turn in. A medial upper leg support should discourage this movement. Aaron's therapist is also concerned about his kyphosis getting worse. Even though his trunk is still kyphotic in the simulated seating system, his head is better balanced over his base of support and will not, hopefully, contribute to the progression of his kyphosis.

In order to maximize his wheeling efficiency with his left arm, the seating system needs to be positioned within the wheelchair so that Aaron's shoulder is centered over the wheel axle. The arm supports need to be adjustable in height for different activities and Aaron's growth. If the arm supports are shorter, he can get close to desks and tables more easily. The optimum push handle height is 36" (91.44 cm) so that his mother and father can comfortably push the wheelchair. The cushion covering needs to be easy to clean, since he tends to drop a lot of food in his lap. Aaron will need two seating systems: one for his new wheelchair, and one for his old wheelchair. For use at school and home, the seating system does not need to be removable from the wheelchair, as the seating system and wheelchair can be transported as one unit. However, the seating system that will fit into the old wheelchair needs to be removable so that the wheelchair can fold to be transported in his parent's van.

Part II

DESIGNING THE SEATING SYSTEM

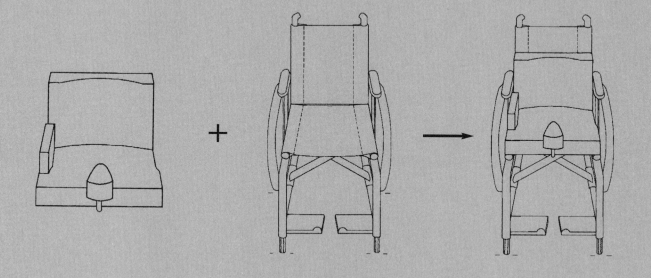

Chapter 5
General Guidelines for Seating

If a person is sitting in a typical wheelchair or does not have a seating system, how do we begin to provide seating? A typical wheelchair has a sling, or loose hammock material for the seat and back support. Over time the sling gets looser and sags, often conforming to the person's body and encouraging poor posture. In contrast, the foundation of a seating system is made of firm material and is designed to provide more postural support. In this book, firm does not mean hard or totally rigid. It refers to a surface with some rigidity to its structure so that it does not "give" a lot, or stretch excessively over time. The degree of firmness can vary. Examples of a firm surface are wood, plastic, layers of corrugated cardboard, or dense semi-rigid foam. The firm surface is usually covered with a softer, more compliant material that "gives" and conforms to the person's body. In the most basic form, the base of a seating system⊕ consists of a firm back support⊕ and a firm seat cushion⊕. A *postural support device*⊕ (seating system) is "a structure, attached to a wheelchair, which has a surface that contacts the occupants' body and is used to either modify or accommodate the occupant's sitting posture."[1]

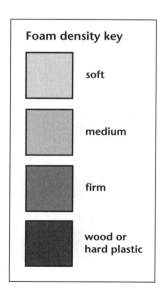

Foam density key

soft

medium

firm

wood or
hard plastic

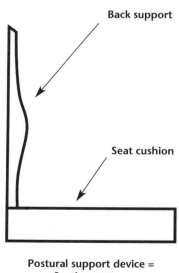

Back support

Seat cushion

Postural support device =
Seating system

Note: When ISO seating/mobility terminology is first used, a ⊕ is seen to the right side of the term.

A The Back Support

1. Purposes of Back Supports

Simulating with your hands should give you an idea of how the back support should perform or function for the person. If you translate support from your hands into words, you can describe the objectives of the back support necessary for each individual. Generally the back support should:

- Support the pelvis, sacrum, lumbar spine, and trunk in the person's comfortable **neutral posture**.
- Allow for the shape of the back of the body (the sacrum, ribcage, lumbar and thoracic spine), and provide space for the buttocks.
- Distribute the forces to prevent excessive pressure against sensitive bony areas (iliac crest, PSIS, ribs, spinous processes of the sacral, lumbar, and thoracic vertebrae).
- Provide the person with **postural options** from which to function.
- Not restrict movement needed for function.

2. Style

If the pelvis and trunk are flexible, the back support should be **firm**.[2-5] A sling back⊕ can encourage rolling backward of the pelvis (posterior pelvic tilt) and curving forward of the trunk (kyphosis). If a sling back is used, it should be tightened often to prevent sagging.

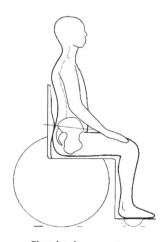

Firm back support

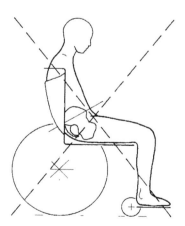

Sling back

3. Back Support Height⊕

The height of the back support depends on the person's trunk stability, control, and functional requirements.[2-5]

a. If the person has **poor trunk control and balance**, the back support height can extend to the **spine of the scapula**. This is the horizontal ridge at the top of the shoulder blade. The shoulder begins to round forward at this point, so the person's back will not contact the back support above this point. If a head support⊕ is needed and *not* a separate component, the back support should extend to the top of the person's head.

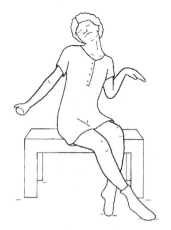

Poor trunk control and balance

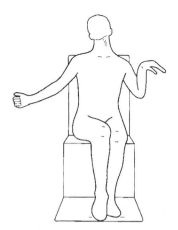

Back support height to the
spine of the scapula

b. If the person has **fair trunk control and balance**, the back support height can extend to **1/2 to 1" (1.3 to 2.5 cm) below the bottom tip of the shoulder blades (inferior angle of the scapulae).** This will allow the scapulae to move freely, which is necessary when using the arms.

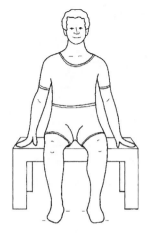

Fair trunk control

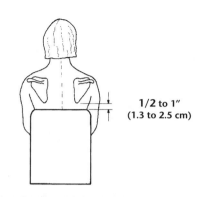

1/2 to 1"
(1.3 to 2.5 cm)

Back support height
1/2 to 1 inch (1.3 to 2.5 cm)
below the inferior angle
of the scapulae

c. If the **back support height is as high as the spine of the scapulae and the person needs to use her arms**, the area of the back support behind the scapulae may be **cut-out or relieved** to allow the scapulae to move freely. Also, the back support shape may be **contoured** to give the scapulae total freedom of movement.

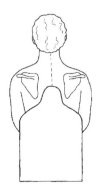

Contoured back support for scapular relief

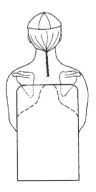

Scapular cut-outs or reliefs

d. If the person has **good trunk control and balance**, the above back support height might be appropriate (see b); however, if the person is an active wheelchair rider, **a back support extending to the lower, floating ribs, (ribs 11 and 12)**, may be sufficient.

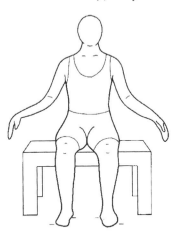

Good trunk control

Back support extending to the lower floating ribs

e. A person's **trunk control may improve progressively**, such as a child with hypotonia who is developing trunk stability. In this case, the person may need a **high back support at first, but as she gains more trunk control, the height can be decreased.**

B The Seat Cushion

1. Purposes of Seat Cushions

The objectives of the seat cushion will be specific for each individual, depending on the person's needs. Generally, a seat cushion should:

- Provide a stable support surface for the pelvis and the thighs.
- Provide pressure relief under the bony prominences (can include areas of the pelvis [ischial tuberosities, pubis], sacrum, and greater trochanters of the femurs). The ischial tuberosities are bony points that stick down from the bottom of the pelvis. They are approximately 1" (2.5 cm) in diameter. Pressure at these bony points can cause discomfort and sometimes tissue breakdown, especially in thin people. Seat cushions should allow space for the ischial tuberosities to sink into, so that pressure is more evenly distributed between the ischial tuberosities and the under surface of the thighs. Allowing space for the ischial tuberosities will prevent excessive rocking of the pelvis over these bony points.
- Accommodate for lack of hip joint flexion (see page 142) and/or leg length difference (see page 126).

In terms of posture and movement, the seat cushion may need to function uniquely for different people. Hand simulation will guide you as to how the seat cushion should act or function for the person.

For some people, the seat cushion should:

- Provide postural options, allowing movement and weight shifting.

For other people, the seat cushion may need to:

- Limit movement and postural options to help control exaggerated muscular activity.

2. Style

The seat cushion should have a firm supportive base[2-5] instead of a loose sling seat. The firm surface is usually covered with a softer, more compliant material that distributes pressure under the person's pelvis and thighs. A sling seat can cause the pelvis to roll backwards (posterior pelvic tilt) and the legs to turn in. If a sling seat is used, it needs to be tightened often so that it does not sag.

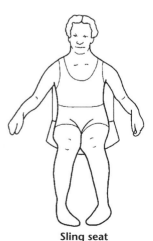

Sling seat

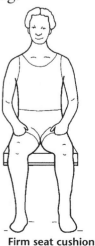

Firm seat cushion

3. Seat Depth⊕

The seat should support the full length of the thighs. Usually it should be the distance from the back of the buttocks to 1/2" (1.3 cm) behind the knees.[2-5]

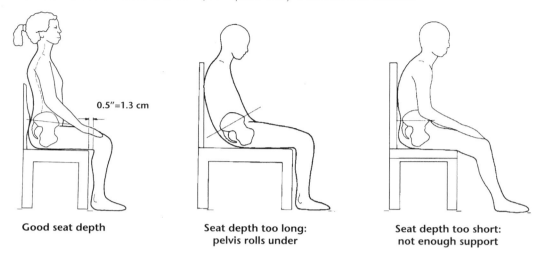

Good seat depth	**Seat depth too long: pelvis rolls under**	**Seat depth too short: not enough support**

Different leg lengths. If one leg is 1" (2.5 cm) or longer than the other leg, the seat will need to be longer under the longer leg to support it. If the seat is too long for the shorter leg, the pelvis will be pulled forward or rotated on that side.

Seat depth longer under the longer leg

126

C | Design Options

How might the seating system be joined with a mobility base (wheelchair, stroller)? Many possibilities exist. Four options follow.

1. Integrated Postural Support Device⊕

A wheelchair can be adapted. For example, wood covered with foam and fabric (postural support device) can be bolted or clamped into the wheelchair frame, so that it is not removable. This design does not allow the wheelchair to fold.

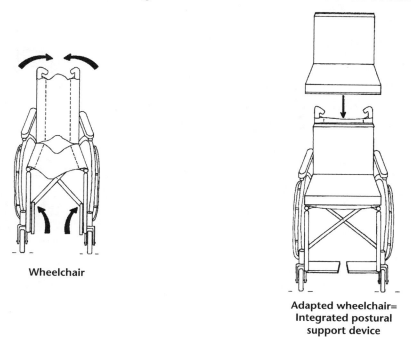

Wheelchair

**Adapted wheelchair=
Integrated postural
support device**

2. Postural Support Device Unit⊕

A seating system with its postural components can be made that fits into, but is removable from, the wheelchair frame. This can be made out of wood, plastic, or any available materials.

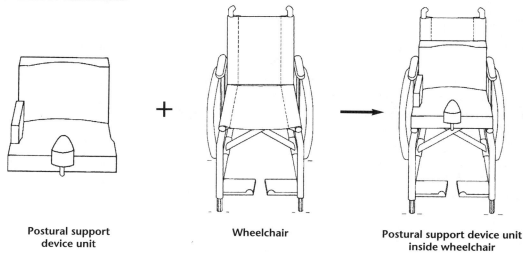

**Postural support
device unit**

Wheelchair

**Postural support device unit
inside wheelchair**

3. Postural Support Device Components⊕

Commercially available postural components can be matched to the person's needs and fit into the seating system and/or wheelchair.

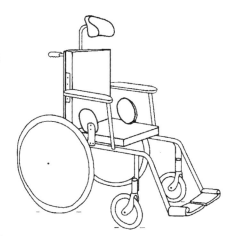

4. Seating System: Static vs. Wheeled Base

A seating system can be made with or without wheels. It can function on its own without a wheelchair frame. Often made out of wood or cane, this seating system may have large wheels if used outdoors and smaller wheels if only used indoors. This device does not fold for transport.

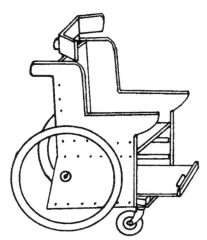

Figure from Werner[6]

References

1. 2008 ISO Standards from RESNA (Inderdisciplinary Association for the Advancement of Rehabilitation and Assistive Technologies). RESNA Technical Standards Board.

2. Bergen A, Presperin J, Tallman T. *Positioning for Function: Wheelchairs and Other Assistive Technologies.* Valhalla, NY: Valhalla Rehabilitation Publications, Ltd.; 1990.

3. Trefler E, Hobson D, Taylor SJ, Monahan L, Shaw CG. *Seating and Mobility for Persons with Physical Disabilities.* Tucson, AZ: Therapy Skill Builders; 1993.

4. Ward D. *Prescriptive Seating for Wheeled Mobility.* Ft. Lauderdale, FL: HealthWealth International; 1994.

5. Presperin J. Interfacing techniques for posture control. *Proceedings from the 6th International Seating Symposium.* 1990:39-45.

6. Werner D. *Disabled Village Children.* Palo Alto, CA: Hesperian Foundation; 1987.

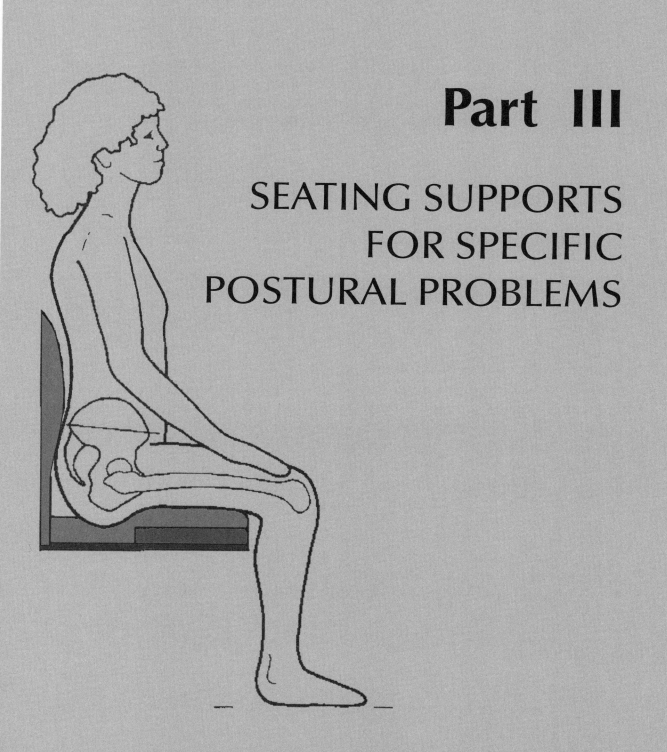

Part III

SEATING SUPPORTS
FOR SPECIFIC
POSTURAL PROBLEMS

This part suggests a systematic approach for providing specialized seating. Seating support options are presented for postures of various body parts. In this way, it correlates with Part I, Assessment. This chapter also includes pressure relief cushions and wheelchair considerations. Seating supports are presented for the: pelvis, trunk, hips and legs, ankles and feet, head and neck, shoulder girdles and arms. But please remember, **the person must be approached as a whole being**. As with assessing, you will look at the whole person, and then focus on supporting and stabilizing specific body parts. As you provide seating supports, you need to constantly reassess. It is like a dance, a dance between providing support to one part of the body and observing and feeling the responses in other areas of the body. During this dance, you will step back and come in close, sometimes looking at the whole person, and at other times focusing on specific parts of the body.

Each person's postural options, functional and health needs are unique. Approach each person with a fresh open mind — a beginner's mind, full of questions instead of answers. You do not need to have the answers right away; don't worry, they will come. Give yourself time and space to be with the questions. Open your eyes, ears, hands, mind, and intuitive sense to all possibilities. You will need them all to help you provide the best seating system for the person. **Fit the seating system to the person and not the person to the seating system.** Simulation with your hands will help guide you as to what the postural supports need to do for the person.

Seating is an art. It is a process, and as such, there are no formulas. If you try to fit the person to a seating system that is not quite right, it is like buying shoes that do not fit well. The shoes end up always irritating your feet, then your ankles start aching, and pretty soon your knees, hips, and back hurt so much that it painful just to walk around the block. Take the time you need to be in this creative seating process.

----

* For additional information regarding seating supports, see Bergen, Presperin and Tallman (1990)[1], Trefler et al (1993)[2], Presperin (1990)[3], Ward (1994)[4].

Chapter 6
The Pelvis

We almost always begin at the pelvis. Remember, in sitting, the pelvis is the base of support, the foundation. If the pelvis is stuck in a certain posture, the rest of the body may also be stuck. If the pelvis is able to achieve the neutral posture, the rest of the body has a better chance of achieving the neutral posture. Thus, if the pelvis is flexible at the lower back, we start by supporting the pelvis in the person's upright and neutral posture. From your assessment, is the pelvis:

- Rolled backward (posterior pelvic tilt), or sliding forward?
- Rolled forward (anterior pelvic tilt)?
- Tilted to the side (oblique)?
- Turned to the side (rotated)?

A | Pelvis Rolled Backward or Sliding Forward (Posterior Pelvic Tilt)

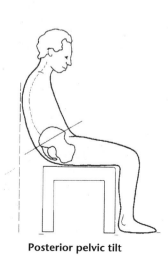

Posterior pelvic tilt

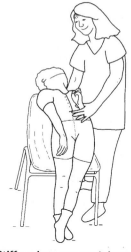

Stiffens legs out straight and slides forward

If the **pelvis is rolled backwards (posterior tilt)**, or if the person **stiffens her legs out straight and slides forward in the seat**, design of the following components will be considered:

1. Back support
2. Seat cushion
3. Seat to back support angle
4. Anterior (front) pelvic supports
5. Tilt

Consider all five aspects together. Using just one or two of these options may not be sufficient to support the pelvis.

1. Back Support

The back support will be separated into two segments, the upper back support and the lower back support, because each has its unique purpose. The *lower back support* extends from the seat cushion to the top of the pelvis/sacrum. Information from simulating with your hands will guide you as to the postural support required:

- **Where** are your hands supporting, "correcting," or stabilizing the pelvis?
- **How much force** are you using to "correct" the person's pelvic posture?
- **In what direction of force** are you applying the support with your hands?

The lower back support should:

- Support the pelvis, sacrum and lumbar spine in the person's comfortable **neutral posture**.
- Allow for the shape of the back of the person's body (the sacrum and pelvis), and provide space for the buttocks.
- Distribute the pressure to prevent excessive pressure against sensitive bony areas — iliac crest, PSIS, spinous processes of the sacrum, and lumbar vertebrae.

FLEXIBLE

The following are ideas for the lower back support if the person's pelvis is flexible (at the lumbar spine), and her **hip flexion angle is 90° or more** (more closed than a right angle). Remember, to provide more postural support than that which the sling back provides, start with a lower back support which is firm.

Possible Lower Back Support Options

a. **Posterior sacral and/or pelvic support⊕.** Add **a support behind the top of the pelvis and sacrum** to maintain the pelvis in its upright and neutral posture.[5-7] If the sacral/pelvic support is wider on the sides matching the shape of the pelvis, it can "cup" the pelvis, thus providing more support.

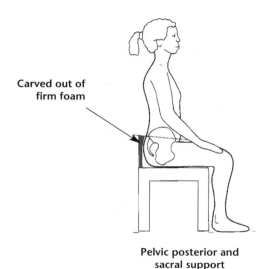

Carved out of firm foam

Pelvic posterior and
sacral support

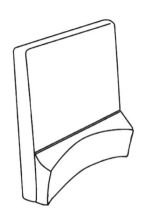

Sacral/pelvic support
cupping pelvis
- Front view -

b. **Change the shape or angle of the lower back support** so that its top point contacts just below the top of the pelvis (iliac crest), and the lower back support is parallel to the sacrum.[8-10]

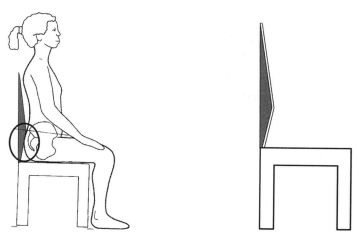

Change the shape of the lower back support

c. **Firm support behind the sling back**. If the person continues to use a sling back, add a firm support behind the sling back to support the person's pelvis and sacrum. The firm support can be made from a firm contoured foam, rubber or padded plastic. One or two straps (with a buckle, if possible) behind the firm support allow for tightening and loosening.[11,12]

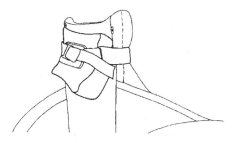

Firm support behind the sling back

Design Challenge

Adjustability

Our first postural objective is to support the person's pelvis in her neutral posture. Can the lower back support also allow or support different postures for functional movement? This may mean providing support to roll the pelvis more forward than the person's neutral posture (for activities in front of her, i.e., at a tabletop). Or perhaps, the person wants to roll her pelvis backwards at times, such as for greater postural security when pushing her wheelchair downhill. An adjustable lower back support may be:

- Removable
- Changeable in shape or size (inflatable air cushion, adjustable straps)

What others can you think of?

FIXED

If the pelvis is rolled backward (posterior pelvic tilt) and fixed at the low back (lumbar spine):

a. **Do not use a posterior support in the lower back which is shaped for an upright, neutral pelvis.** It may push the pelvis forward out of the seat. Instead, support the pelvis by shaping the lower back support to the pelvis and sacrum. You will probably need to tilt the seating system backwards and/or open the seat-to-back support angle.

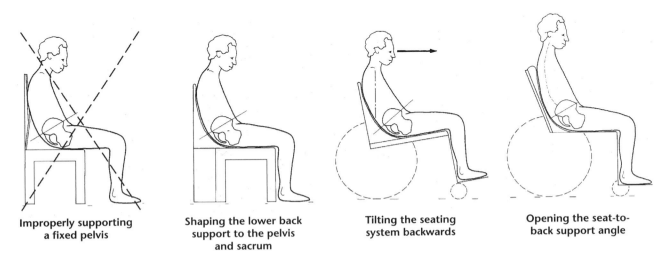

Improperly supporting
a fixed pelvis

Shaping the lower back
support to the pelvis
and sacrum

Tilting the seating
system backwards

Opening the seat-to-
back support angle

b. Sometimes if the person has been sitting in this posture for a long time, her back, head and neck become fixed and balanced in this posture. You may not want to change the current back support. However, if the person is using a wheelchair with a sling back, consider **reinforcing the sling back with straps** or replace the sling back with a tension-adjustable back support to prevent it from stretching further.[13]

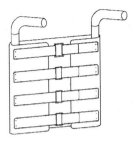

Reinforcing sling back
with straps

> **Note: If a person has such limitation in hip and spinal motion, she should seek medical and/or therapeutic help. Manual therapy and alternative positioning (such as supported standing, prone positioning) is recommended (see page 266.)**

2. Seat Cushion

The lower back support is the primary support for the back of the pelvis and sacrum. How can the seat cushion help to prevent the pelvis from excessively rolling backwards (posterior tilting)? A seat cushion should:

- Provide a stable support surface for the pelvis and the thighs.
- Provide pressure relief under the bony prominences.
- Accommodate for lack of hip joint flexion (see page 142) and/or leg length difference.

For some people it should:

- Provide postural options, allowing movement and weight shifting.

For other people, the seat cushion may need to:

- Limit movement and postural options because of exaggerated muscular activity.

Possible Seat Cushion Options

a. **Contoured cushion.** The seat cushion can be gently contoured to accommodate the ischial tuberosities. This cushion provides minimal pelvic control and the foam is equally firm throughout. It allows a person to move and weight shift, if she has that ability. This cushion will not be as effective if the person's pelvis pushes with force into a posterior tilt, or if the legs stiffen out straight and she slides forward in the seat.[1,4]

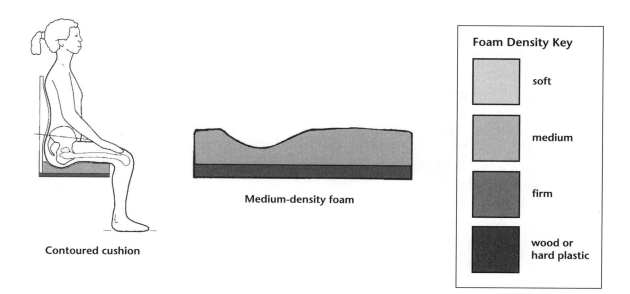

Medium-density foam

Contoured cushion

Foam Density Key	
	soft
	medium
	firm
	wood or hard plastic

Note: Throughout this book, various shapes of back supports are used, along with a range of seat-to-back angles. Why? So, you do not attach yourself to any one idea.

b. **Varied densities of foam** allow the pelvis to sink down into the softer foam. The firmer density foam in the front and bottom of the seat further prevent the pelvis from rolling backward (posterior tilt). This cushion will tend to control the pelvis more than the gently contoured cushion.[14]

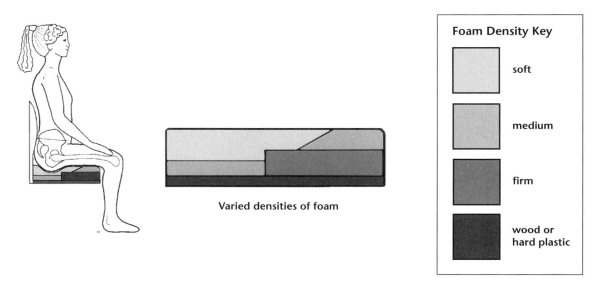

Varied densities of foam

Foam Density Key

soft

medium

firm

wood or hard plastic

c. **Anti-thrust seat**⊕ has a block of firm foam (pre-ischial shelf), which is positioned approximately 1" (2.5 cm) in front of the ischial tuberosities and is covered with softer foam padding.[15-18] The anti-thrust seat, when used with a well-designed back support, should provide more pelvic control than **a and b** above. If the pelvis begins to roll backward (posteriorly tilt), and the person passively slides or thrusts forward, the ischial tuberosities will contact the block and discourages further posterior tilting. The block must be made out of firm foam (e.g., 1.8-2.2 pound-density, rigid polyethylene foam). Soft foam will compress. Also, do not taper or wedge the rear edge of the block. This will allow the ITs to move.[19]

Usually the block is one-half to two-thirds of the seat depth, but it is better to feel the ischial tuberosities to make sure of the block's location. The height of the block ranges from 3/4" to 2" (2-5 cm), depending on the person's size and weight. It should always be covered with at least 1" (2.5 cm) of soft foam. Be very cautious using the anti-thrust seat if a person has a bony butt, pain, a tendency for pressure sores or very tight hamstrings.

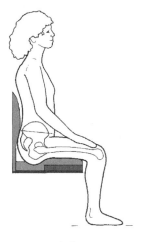

Anti-thrust seat

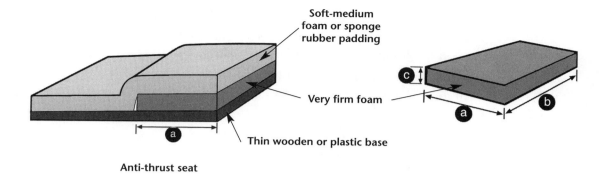

Anti-thrust seat

Soft-medium foam or sponge rubber padding

Very firm foam

Thin wooden or plastic base

a **The depth of the firm foam is critical,** as it depends on the measurement of the ischial tuberosity location (see below).

b **The width of the firm foam** is the same as the seat width.

c **The height of the firm foam** will depend on the height of the ischial tuberosities of the person. If the pre-ischial shelf is made too high, the pelvis (and overall posture) will lose stability.

Measuring for the very firm pre-ischial shelf (anti-thrust shelf block)[19]:

1. Check that the pelvis is upright.

2. Measure from the front of the ischial tuberosity to the back of the knee.

3. Subtract for the softer foam and relax room.

4. Subtract for space behind the knee.

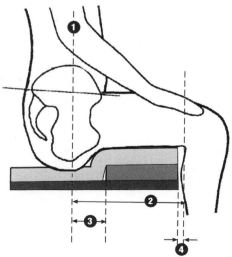

Measuring for pre-ischial shelf

Further options and modifications of the anti-thrust seat:

- **Front sloped down**. The front of the anti-thrust seat can be sloped down if the *hip flexion angle* is greater, or more open, than 90°.
- **Front wedged**. The front of the anti-thrust seat can be wedged if a person stiffens and straightens her legs with a lot of force.
- **Uneven**. The pre-ischial shelf may need to be uneven (front to back) to accommodate a pelvis which is fixed in rotation (rotating backward on one side and forward on the other side).
- **Split**. The pre-ischial shelf can be split if one hip does not bend up (flex) as much as the other hip (different *hip flexion angles*).

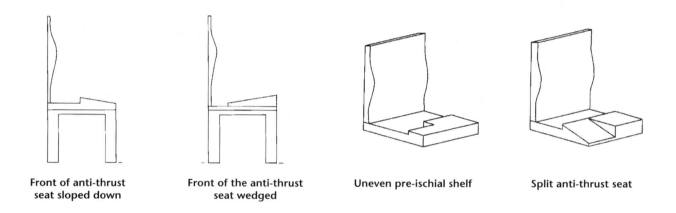

Front of anti-thrust
seat sloped down

Front of the anti-thrust
seat wedged

Uneven pre-ischial shelf

Split anti-thrust seat

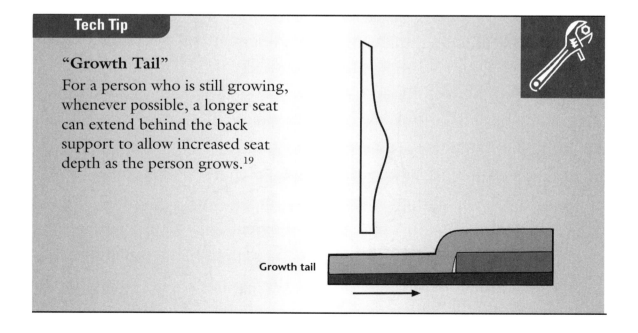

Tech Tip

"Growth Tail"

For a person who is still growing, whenever possible, a longer seat can extend behind the back support to allow increased seat depth as the person grows.[19]

Growth tail

3. Seat-to-Back Support Angle⊕

After identifying the characteristics of the back support and seat cushion, determine the angle between the seat cushion and the back support.

The appropriate seat-to-back support angle should:

- Allow the pelvis to be in the person's neutral posture.
- Allow for limited hip joint and spinal flexibility.
- Allow the head to be balanced and upright over the pelvis.

For some people:

- Promote trunk activity and stability (as in children with hypotonia).

For other people:

- Limit the degree of spasticity and abnormal movements.

How do we determine this seat-to-back support angle?

Start by: Matching the seat-to-back support angle to the person's *hip flexion angle*.

Next: Try different angles to assess their effect on the following factors:

- Head balance
- Trunk control
- Spasticity and abnormal movement

FLEXIBLE

If the pelvis is flexible (at the lumbar spine) and the *hip flexion angle* comes to 90° or more:

a. Seat-to-back support angle can be within a range of **90° to 110°**.

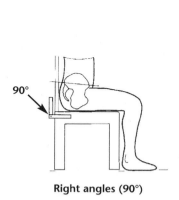

Right angles (90°)

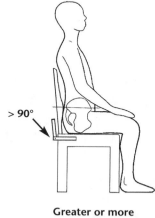

Greater or more open than 90°

Remember, there are no absolutes, no one right way for every person. Some people will require 95°, some 105°, and so on. You must try different angles, if possible.

The seat-to-back support angle will depend on the shape of the back support. In this book, the lower and upper back supports (see page 132) are separated, as the pelvis/sacrum and the upper back have different requirements in terms of postural support.[13] However, the support shape and angle (or offset between these two aspects) will affect each other. If a posterior pelvic/sacral support is provided for a flexible pelvis and spine, the upper back will need some space for the natural back contours, scapulae, and posterior curve of the thoracic spine. Most importantly, the head must feel balanced and aligned over the pelvis — the person's neutral posture. However, if the entire back support is flat and the seat-to-back support angle is 90°, the person will feel like she is falling forward. In this case, it is helpful to open the seat-to-back support angle to 95°.[20-22]

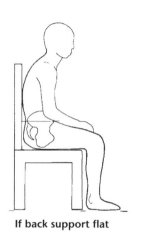

If back support flat

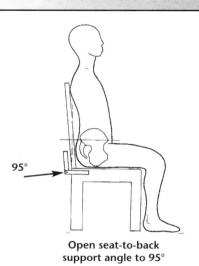

95°

Open seat-to-back
support angle to 95°

b. **Slightly opening the seat-to-back support angle by sloping the seat cushion down towards the front** encourages an upright and neutral trunk. This option can be beneficial for people with weak or floppy trunks.[23-25] In this posture, the child will have to work hard to sit up and will need active trunk musculature. It may be better to use this option for short periods of time or in specific situations such as with tabletop activities or to improve trunk control. Make sure that the person has time to rest in other postures, so the postural muscles required to sit upright are not overworked. An anti-thrust seat may help stabilize her pelvis and prevent it from sliding down and posteriorly tilting. Anterior knee blocks can also be used (see page 146).[20,26]

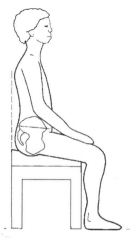

Open seat-to-back support
angle: seat cushion sloped
down towards the front

d. **Saddle seats** can also be used by hypotonic children. The child stabilizes her thighs, knees, and legs against the saddle seat, thus increasing her base of support.[27]

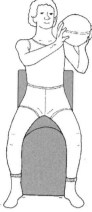

Saddle seat

e. **Dynamic seat-to-back support angle.** Some people need to move into an extended posture as this is their option of movement and expression. A dynamic seat allows the seat-to-back support angle and the seat-to-lower leg support angle to open and extend when the person extends, but then comes back to neutral.[28-31]

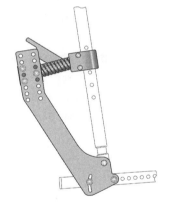

Dynamic seat-to-back support angle

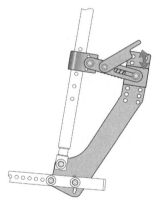

- Inside view -

Design by Dave Cooper, M.Sc. Kines., Rehab. Tech., Sunny Hill Hospital for Children

---

Design Challenge

Adjustability

Our first postural objective is to support the person's pelvis in her neutral posture. Now, can the person adjust the seat-to-back support angle to support different postures required for various functions and/or health needs? The seat-to-back support angle may need to increase (greater than 90°) for functional requirements such as wheeling downhill. The angle may need to change for health needs such as the inability to be upright for long periods of time due to lightheadedness or respiratory problems.

FIXED

If the pelvis is fixed (at the lumbar spine) or the person's *hip flexion angle* is less than, or more open than 90°, the seat-to-back support angle should:

a. **Correspond to the person's** *hip flexion angle.*[14]

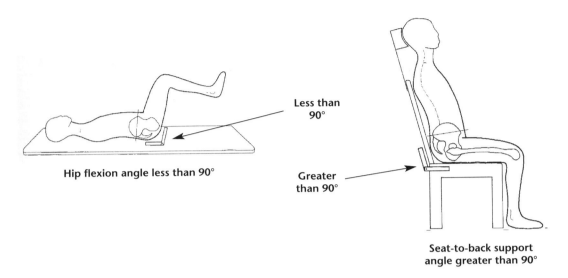

Hip flexion angle less than 90°

Less than 90°

Greater than 90°

Seat-to-back support angle greater than 90°

b. In some cases, even though the person's hip flexion angle is significantly less than 90°, the **seat-to-back support angle** will need to be **less** (more closed) than the person's hip flexion angle. This may happen if the person has a lot of spasticity. Or perhaps the person has been sitting in this posture for a long time, and her hips, back, head, and neck are fixed and balanced in this posture. In either case, the seat-to-back support angle will be the angle needed to optimize the person's head and trunk control, comfort, and function; and to minimize spasticity and abnormal movements.[32]

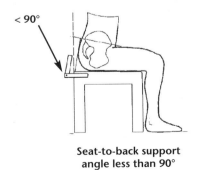

< 90°

Seat-to-back support angle less than 90°

4. Anterior (Front) Pelvic Supports⊕

In addition to a well-designed seat cushion and back support, the pelvis must almost always be supported from the front. If the pelvis is not supported from the front, the pelvis might still slide forward or thrust out of the seat. How do you know which anterior pelvic support is appropriate for the person with the disability? Simulating with your hands and materials will guide you.

Where and in what direction are your hands providing support in the front of the pelvis?

- **How much force** do you use to provide stability and prevent excessive movement?
- When simulating with materials, hold or tape straps at **different locations and angles of pull**. If you think a rigid bar or knee block may be the answer, create one and try it first!

Anterior pelvic supports should:
- Provide stability, but not prevent functional movement.
- Be safe and easily removable in case of emergency.
- Not irritate prominent bony areas, abdominal contents, or soft tissue.
- Conform to the person's body structure.

Possible Anterior Pelvic Support Options
a. **Positioning belts.**
    45-60° belt. A positioning belt is set at a diagonal (45-60°) to the seat cushion so that it pulls down and back passing under the ASIS (bony prominences in the front of the pelvis).[1,2,33] It usually attaches 1" (2.5 cm) to 2" (5 cm) in front of the junction of the back support and seat cushion and close to the sides of the pelvis to "hug" or secure the pelvis. If the person is using lateral hip supports on the outside of the hips, run the positioning belt under and inside the hip supports. Note that if the positioning belt is attached to the wheelchair frame at a 45° angle, it may not necessarily be 45° to the seat cushion. Also it may not be close enough to the sides of the pelvis to provide adequate stability.

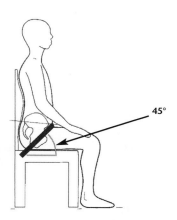

Positioning belt at 45° to seat cushion

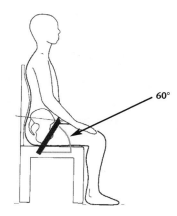

Positioning belt at 60° to seat cushion

90° belt. This belt is set 90° to the seat cushion. This type of positioning belt crosses the thighs and pulls straight down. It allows the person to move her pelvis forward over her thighs into an anterior tilt. It is appropriate for a person who has some active control of her pelvic movements.

Four-point positioning belt. This belt provides a pull both down and back to secure the pelvis. It has four points of attachment to the wheelchair. If the 90° positioning belt shifts due to movement, the four-point belt may be used to limit excessive movement. The major tightening force comes from the 90° angle strap; however, the rear strap helps to stabilize the 90° angle strap.[19]

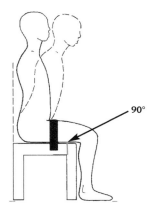

Positioning belt at 90° to seat cushion

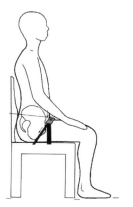

Four-point positioning belt

Belt Widths

For all positioning belts, the belt width depends on the size of the person. Depending upon the pressure exerted from the person on the belt, these sizes and amount of padding may vary.[19] Typically, use a padded:

- 1" (2.5 cm) wide belt for a seat depth under 12" (30.5 cm).
- 1 ½" (4 cm) wide belt for a seat depth between 12-16" (30.5-40.5 cm).
- 2" (5 cm) wide belt for a seat depth greater than 16" (40.5 cm).

Buckle Size

The buckle size corresponds to the belt width. Determine the best buckle for the person's function. For instance, if the person is independent, she needs a buckle that she can easily open and close herself.[19]

Pads vs. Padding

Padding is used so that the belt does not dig into the person's skin.

- Force-localizing pads are used to help direct pressure specifically, for example, a pad over the ASIS to limit pelvic rotation.
- Two thicker, firmer pads can be used under the belt just below each ASIS to provide pressure needed on the pelvic bone, but limit pressure on the intestines and bladder.

Pull Styles

- **Dual-Pull.** The buckle is in the middle with a tightening strap on each side of the buckle. These straps can be tightened after the buckle is fastened, providing even pressure on each side of the pelvis. This belt is especially helpful for a person with a lot of spasticity, uncontrolled movement or extensor thrust.

- **Single Pull.** The buckle is in the middle with a tightening strap to one side. This style belt is typically used for a person with hypotonia or muscle weakness. With a force-localizing pad over the ASIS, it can also be used to limit pelvic rotation (see page 153).

b. **Rigid sub-ASIS bar.** A padded rigid bar can be used if the person's legs stiffen and she slides out of the seat, or stands on her foot supports with positioning belts.[34,35] The bar should be placed under the ASIS and press down and back. It should always be padded, and the person should be checked for any signs of discomfort, rubbing, or skin breakdown. Because the rigid bar needs to fit under the ASIS, the diameter of the metal rod needs to be as narrow as possible. The bar can be contoured or straight. The contoured bar allows for the natural contour of the abdomen. It should remove easily for transfers.

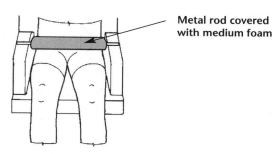

Metal rod covered with medium foam

Padded rigid sub-ASIS bar

c. **Dynamic pelvic support.** A dynamic, semi-rigid, but moveable device can support the sacrum and sides of the pelvis while controlling unwanted movement. For instance, it can control posterior tilting of the pelvis, while allowing anterior tilting. It can control tilting of the pelvis to the side and pelvic rotation. The semi-rigid support hugs the pelvis, and has a pivoting mechanism attached to the seat which allows and controls anterior and posterior pelvic tilt.[36]

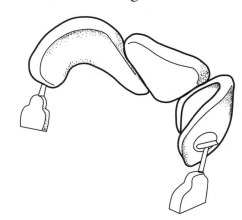

Dynamic pelvic support

d. **Thigh straps.** These straps attach under the thighs and come up between the legs, pulling diagonally (45° angle) over the thighs. Be very careful with regard to the strap location to prevent irritation of the person's genitalia.[3]

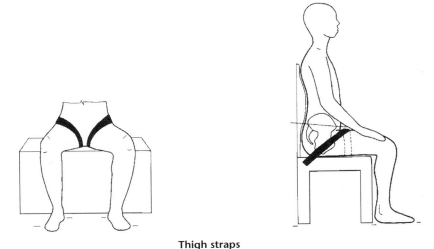

Thigh straps

e. **Anterior knee supports (blocks).** These blocks should apply pressure to the kneecaps and lower legs. Knee blocks can be used if the person has pain, skin redness and/or sores from positioning belts or rigid bars. Do not use knee blocks with hip and/or knee problems, without a physician's approval. Be sure to provide extra padding over any bony prominences in the back of the pelvis and sacrum because the force and lack of movement will increase the pressure over these boney areas. If used for a child who is growing, monitor these blocks closely for fit. These blocks should have a removable cover so that the foam can be modified as needed.[1,3,5,37,38]

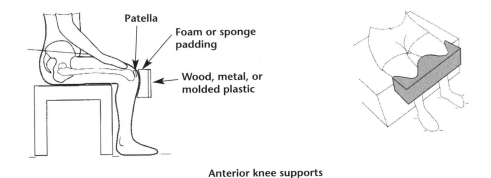

Patella

Foam or sponge padding

Wood, metal, or molded plastic

Anterior knee supports

5. Tilt⊕

After the seat cushion, back support, seat-to-back support angle, and anterior pelvic support are chosen, look at the angle of the entire seating system. The whole seating system may need to be tilted backwards permanently or have the ability to be tilted back at different angles during the day, for head control, feeding, rest, and so on. If the seat-to-back support angle is greater than 90°, the seating system may need to be tilted back, so the person does not slide out of the seating system.

Tilted backwards with seat-to-back support angle greater than 90°

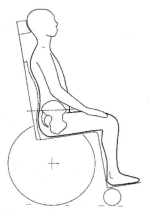

Tilted backwards with 90° seat-to-back support angle

B Pelvis Rolled Forward (Anterior Pelvic Tilt)

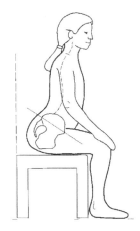

Anterior pelvic tilt

FLEXIBLE

If the pelvis is flexible at the low back (lumbar spine), do we want to "reduce" or "correct" it towards the neutral posture? Is this rolled forward (anteriorly tilted) posture causing problems for the person? For example:

- Is the person in pain?
- Does she lose her balance and fall forward so that she needs to lean on her arms for support?
- Is the person's function impaired?
- If this posture is not corrected, will it lead to a fixed deformity?

If you decide to "reduce" the posture, let the person's head balance and function guide you to determine how much to "reduce" the posture.

Possible Options

1. Use a **firm back support.**[1]

   The back support (upper and lower parts) should:

   - Support the pelvis, sacrum, and lumbar spine in the person's comfortable **neutral posture.**
   - Allow for the shape of the back of her body - the sacrum, ribcage, lumbar and thoracic spine, and provide space for the buttocks.
   - Follow the natural curves of the back.

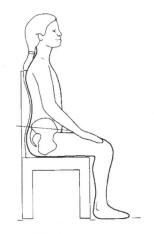

Firm back support

2. **Wedging the seat cushion under the pelvis** may help the pelvis attain a neutral posture. The wedge is located directly under the ischial tuberosities (butt bones) and acts like a "ramp," encouraging the pelvis to tilt towards a neutral posture.[26]

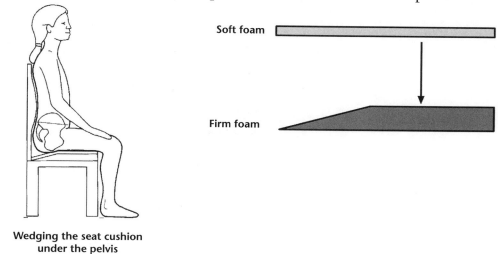

Soft foam

Firm foam

Wedging the seat cushion
under the pelvis

3. **Two positioning belts** can be used to "correct" the pelvis, one at a diagonal (45° angle), and one crossing the ASIS (bony prominences in the top/front of the pelvis) and attaching to the back support. These positioning belts need to be used together to be safe and effective.[1]

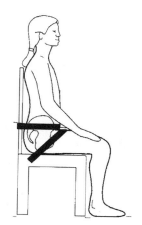

Two positioning belts

4. **Anterior abdominal support** or binder that can provide support, but elastic enough that it allows movement. Prior to tightening the support, the anterior pelvic tilt should be corrected.[39] When measuring for the binder, tilt the person back in the wheelchair to reduce the effect of gravity. It is recommended that the binder cover the bottom few ribs.

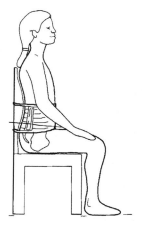

Anterior abdominal
support

FIXED

1. If the anterior tilt is fixed, the person **may or may not want the curve to be supported**.

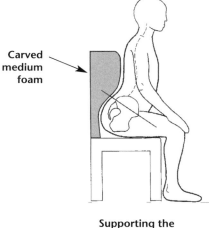

Carved medium foam

Supporting the fixed curve

2. **Rigid anterior (front) trunk support⊕.** If the person leans on her arms, she may benefit from a support in front of her trunk, to free her arms for function. Ideas for front trunk supports include a chest strap with or without elastic, a vest, or a rigid shaped support extending from the laptray.

Rigid anterior trunk support

3. **Tilt**. Along with the other options, tilting the seating system backwards may be useful for periods of rest; however, the seating system should be able to come to the upright position.

Tilting the seating system backwards

C Pelvis Tilted to the Side (Lateral Pelvic Tilt)

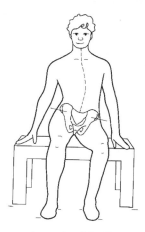

Lateral pelvic tilt

FLEXIBLE

If the pelvis is flexible at the low back (lumbar spine), postural supports on the sides of the pelvis (lateral pelvic supports) may prevent the pelvis from tilting to the side. Let your hands help guide you as to the location and amount of support necessary.

- **How close are your hands** to the sides of the pelvis and thighs?
- **What is the least amount of postural support** needed? A full hand contacting the whole side of the hip or only a fingertip?

Possible Pelvic Support Options[1,37]

1. **Lateral pelvic supports (blocks)**: If the person requires a lot of support and stability, use blocks on both sides of the pelvis to stabilize the pelvis. The size and shape of the sides of the pelvis and hips will determine the height and shape of the blocks. The closer the blocks are to the sides of the hips, the more stability they will provide.

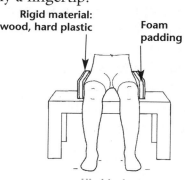

Rigid material: wood, hard plastic

Foam padding

Lateral pelvic supports

2. **Gentle contours** from the seat cushion can be used if the person requires only a small amount of support to prevent tilting to the side.

Gentle contours

Note: Some people need postural support that allows for movement and weight shifting. Other people need a lot of support limiting excessive movement and muscular activity.

3. **Inferior pelvic support**. A small platform under the low side of the pelvis may be used for **short periods during the day**, as an "encouragement" for the pelvis to come to a neutral posture. A lateral pelvic block should be used on the outside of the other hip to prevent this hip from shifting to the side.[39]

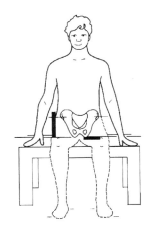

Small platform of firm foam under the low side of the pelvis

FIXED

1. **Position head first**. If the lateral pelvic tilt is fixed, the intent of our support is **not** to "correct" the pelvis to neutral, but instead to position the head in a neutral and balanced position first, and then accommodate, or allow for, the fixed pelvic position. The person's spine will react in one of several ways in order to keep the head upright, because the spine and pelvis are connected. The person's spine may form the shape of a "C" or a "S." Additional curves may also be present.

2. **Bringing the seat up to meet the pelvis** might be necessary. Since most of the person's body weight goes through one ischial tuberosity, the seat cushion will need to relieve pressure in that area. This can be done by using different densities of foam, or other pressure relieving materials. A good idea is to use level buildups of specific heights under each ischial tuberosity and greater trochanter for a stable base with good pressure distribution. Do not use wedges under the pelvis, as they will create instability.

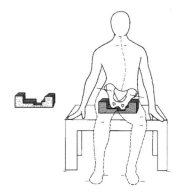

Bring the seat up to meet the pelvis

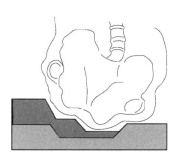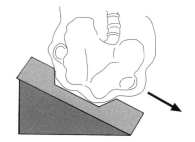

Level buildups, not wedges

D Pelvis Turned (Rotated)

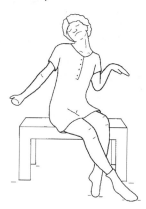

Pelvic rotation

FLEXIBLE

If the pelvic rotation is flexible so that it can be corrected to neutral at the low back (lumbar spine), the components should prevent or limit the pelvic rotation.[1,37] Refer to how your hands are controlling pelvic rotation to determine the component characteristics.

- **Where** are your hands located to control the pelvic rotation?
- **In what direction** are you applying the support to prevent the pelvic rotation?
- Even though the pelvic rotation is flexible, does the person still push strongly into rotation, and if so, **how much pressure** do you use with your hands to control the rotation?

Possible Options

1. **Angled positioning belt**. Attach the positioning belt at an angle to pull the forward side of the pelvis backwards. The target point of the pull should be just under the ASIS. The belt can have extra padding to focus the support where it crosses the ASIS.

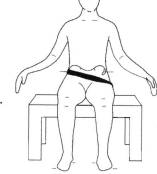

Attach the positioning belt at an angle

Sub-ASIS bar

2. **Sub-ASIS bar**. A padded rigid bar is often used when a positioning belt cannot keep the pelvis from rotating forward. This should always be padded and the person should be continuously checked for any signs of rubbing or skin breakdown.[34]

3. **Pelvic and leg supports for windswept posture**. A pelvic rotation is often associated with the tendency of the legs to "windsweep" or turn to one side. The leg on the same side of the pelvis that is rotated forward also moves forward, and turns out to the side (abducts and externally rotates). The opposite leg moves and turns in (adducts and internally rotates). A flexible pelvic rotation may be controlled by **blocking one leg from turning out to the side and moving forward, and the other leg from turning in**. The pelvic shift can be reduced with blocks on the sides of the hips (lateral pelvic supports).[1,37]

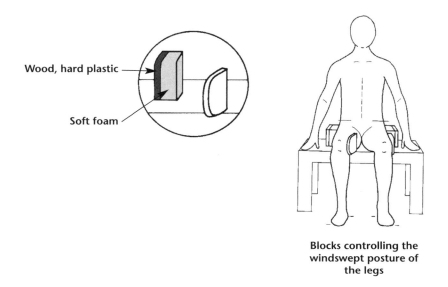

Wood, hard plastic

Soft foam

Blocks controlling the
windswept posture of
the legs

4. Create **channels for the legs**, so that the pelvis is supported in a neutral posture and the legs do not turn out to the side.

Carve channels out of
firm foam, or mold the
seat cushion to the
shape of the person

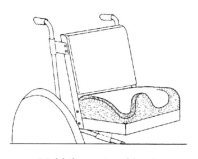

Mold the seat cushion to
the shape of the person

FIXED

1. **Position the head first**: If the pelvic rotation is fixed, the intent of our postural support, as with the fixed lateral pelvic tilt, is not to get the pelvis in neutral, but to get the head into a neutral and balanced position. When the pelvic rotation is fixed, the head posture is more important than the pelvic posture. First, position the head so that the eyes face forward, and the person feels that her head is balanced. Allow the pelvis to rotate. Accommodate and conform the seat cushion and back support to the position of the rotated pelvis and trunk. This can be accomplished by carving or molding the seat cushion.

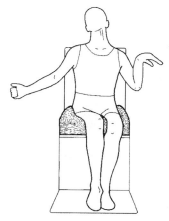

Fixed pelvic rotation

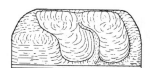

Accommodate the seat cushion and back support to the fixed position of the rotated pelvis and trunk

Note: Whether the pelvis is fixed or flexible, the pelvis will also need to be supported from the front as discussed on pages 143-6.

Benefits of Molding

1. Increases surface contact.[4]

2. Provides more sensory input, so that the person can feel more secure in the seat and possibly reduce spasticity.

3. Increases points of stability within the seat, thus enhancing postural support.[4]

4. Inhibits excessive movement in the seat.

Disadvantages of Molding

1. Limits movement and weight shifting.

2. Limits potential for change needed for growth or change in joint motion.

3. Molded systems are hotter because of close contact with surface areas.

References

1. Bergen A, Presperin J, Tallman T. *Positioning for Function: Wheelchairs and Other Assistive Technologies.* Valhalla, NY: Valhalla Rehabilitation Publications, Ltd.; 1990.

2. Trefler E, Hobson D, Taylor SJ, Monahan L, Shaw CG. *Seating and Mobility for Persons with Physical Disabilities.* Tucson, AZ: Therapy Skill Builders; 1993.

3. Presperin J. Interfacing techniques for posture control. *Proceedings from the 6th International Seating Symposium.* 1990:39-45.

4. Ward D. *Prescriptive Seating for Wheeled Mobility.* Ft. Lauderdale, FL: HealthWealth International; 1994.

5. Monahan L, Shaw G, Taylor S. Pelvic positioning: Another option. *Proceedings from the 5th International Seating Symposium.* 1989:80-5.

6. Zacharow D. Problems with postural support. *Physical Therapy Forum.* 1990; IX(35):1-5.

7. Mulcahy CM, Poutney TE. The sacral pad—description of its clinical uses in seating. *Physiotherapy.* 1986 Sept;72(9):473-4.

8. Margolis S. Lumbar support issues. *Proceedings from the 8th International Seating Symposium.* 1992:19-22.

9. Margolis S. The biangular back revisited: Use, misuse and clinical potentials. *Proceedings from the 18th International Seating Symposium.* 2002.

10. Wengert ME, Margolis K, Kolar K. A design for the back of seated positioning orthoses that controls pelvic positioning and increases head control. *Proceedings from the 10th Annual RESNA Conference.* 1987:216-18.

11. Zollars J, Axelson P. The back support shaping system: an alternative for persons using wheelchairs with sling seat upholstery. *Proceedings of the 16th Annual RESNA Conference.* 1993:274-6.

12. May L, Butt S, Kolbinson K, Minor L. Back support options: Functional outcomes in SCI. *Proceedings from the 17th International Seating Symposium.* 2001:175-6.

13. Engstrom B. *Ergonomics Wheelchairs and Positioning.* Hasselby, Sweden: Bromma Tryck AB; 1993.

14. Wright D, Siekman A, McKone B, Hockridge T, Margolis S. Notes from Stanford Rehabilitation Engineering Center Seating Seminar. February 1990.

15. Siekman A, Flanagan K. The anti-thrust seat: A wheelchair insert for individuals with abnormal reflex patterns of other specialized problems. *Proceedings from the 6th Annual RESNA Conference.* 1983:203-5.

16. Siekman A. Seating hardware: New age solutions to age old problems: The antithrust seat. *Proceedings from the 5th International Seating Symposium.* 1989.

17. McKone B. Return to functional seated positioning and mobility. *Presentation at 11th Annual Heal Trauma Conference: Coma to Community.* Santa Clara Valley Medical Center, CA, 1988.

18. Siekman A. The anti-thrust seat: Proper implementation and use. *Proceedings from the 22nd International Seating Symposium.* 2006:193-4.

19. Noon J. Personal communication. Fall 2008.

20. Bergen A. Personal communication. Fall 2008.

21. Waugh K. Personal communication. Fall 2008.

22. Waugh K. Measuring the right angle. *Rehab Manag.* 2005 Jan-Feb;18(1):40:43-7.

23. Post K, Murphy TE. The use of forward sloping seats by individuals with disabilities. *Proceedings from the 5th International Seating Symposium.* 1989:54-60.

24. Myhr U, von Wendt L. Improvement of functional sitting position for children with cerebral palsy. *Dev Med Child Neurol.* 1991;33:246-56.

25. Dilger N, Ling W. The influence of inclined wedge sitting on infantile postural kyphosis. *Proceedings from the 3rd International Seating Symposium.* 1987:52-7.

26. Wright D, Siekman A, McKone B, Hockridge T, Margolis S. Notes from Stanford Rehabilitation Engineering Center Seating Seminar. February 1990.

27. Reid DT. The effects of the saddle seat on seated postural control and upper-extremity movement in children with cerebral palsy. *Dev Med Child Neurol.* 1996 Sep;38(9):805-15.

28. Cooper D, Dilabio M, Broughton G, Brown D. Dynamic seating components for the reduction of spastic activity and enhancement of function. *Proceedings from the 17th International Seating Symposium.* 2001:51-6.

29. Hahn M, Simkins S. Effects of dynamic wheelchair seating in children with cerebral palsy. *Proceedings from the 24th International Seating Symposium.* 2008:153-7.

30. Magnuson S, Dilabio M. Dynamic seating components: The best evidence and clinical experience. *Proceedings from the 19th International Seating Symposium.* 2003:109-11.

31. Connor PS. A bit of freedom for full-body extensor thrust: A non-static positioning approach. *Proceedings from the 13th International Seating Symposium.* 1997:185-7.

32. Nwaobi O, Hobson D, Trefler E. Hip angle and upper extremity movement time in children with cerebral palsy. *Proceedings from the 8th Annual RESNA Conference.* 1987:39-41.

33. Bergen A. A seat belt is a seat belt is a ....*Assist Technol.* 1989;1(1):77-9.

34. Margolis S. Jones R, Brown B. The Subasis bar: An effective approach to pelvic stabilization in seated positioning. *Proceedings from the 8th Annual RESNA Conference.* 1985:45-7.

35. Cooper D, Treadwell S, Roxborough L. The meru rigid pelvic stabilizer for postural control. *Proceedings from the 10th Annual RESNA Conference.* 1987:573-5.

36. Noon J, Chesney D, Axelson P. Development of a dynamic pelvic stabilization support. *Proceedings from the 19th Annual RESNA Conference.* 1998:209-11.

37. Cooper D. Biomechanics of selected posture control measures. *Proceedings from the 7th International Seating Symposium.* 1991:37-41.

38. McDonald R. Development of a method of measuring force through a kneeblock for children with cerebral palsy. *Proceedings from the 17th International Seating Symposium.* 2001:47-8.

39. Zacharow D. *Posture: Sitting, Standing, Chair Design and Exercise.* Springfield, IL: Charles Thomas; 1988.

Chapter 7
The Trunk

After supporting the pelvis and sacrum, and accommodating the hips and legs, we will address support for the trunk (lumbar/thoracic spine, back, and chest). Recognize that often the hips and legs must be supported first, before the trunk.

Suggestions will be given for a trunk that is:
- Curved forward (kyphosis)
- Curved to the side (scoliosis)
- Rotated forward on one side (rotated)
- Arched backward (extended)

Note: A person can have a combination of these four postural tendencies or fixed deformities.

Purposes of the Upper Back Support

As stated previously, the **lower back support** is considered independently from the **upper back support**. The **upper back support** is the part of the back support above the pelvis/sacrum, supporting the thoracic/lumbar spine, back and ribcage. The upper back support should:

- Support the trunk in **the person's** neutral posture, so that her head is well balanced over her pelvis.
- Not restrict movement needed for function, such as bending backwards (extending) in the mid-back; turning around; leaning to one side; "hooking" an elbow around the backrest tubes; or freely moving her arms and shoulder girdles.
- Respect the natural curves of the trunk and ribcage and accommodate any bony prominences (ribs, spinous processes of the vertebrae, scapulae, etc.).

Keep in mind the general guidelines. Begin with a firm, supportive back support. For suggested back heights, see page 123.

A Trunk Curved Forward (Kyphosis)

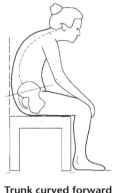

**Trunk curved forward
(kyphosis)**

If the **trunk is curved forward (kyphosis)**, we will look at the

- The upper back support and the relationship between the upper and lower back support.
- Anterior (front) trunk supports.

1. Upper Back Support and the Relationship Between Upper and Lower Back Support

Again, refer to your hands to understand how the person's trunk needs to be supported to achieve her neutral posture.[1]

- In what posture of the spine over the pelvis does her head feel most balanced?
- Where are your hands supporting, "correcting," or stabilizing the trunk?
- How much support is necessary to prevent the trunk from curving forward?
- Where specifically is the spine flexible enough to extend backwards? Can these area(s) be used as pivot points to balance the head over the pelvis?

FLEXIBLE

Possible Options

a. **Firm and contoured upper back support**. The upper back support can be firm supporting the contours of the person's spine, so that the person's **head and trunk are comfortably balanced** over her pelvis. Refer to the pelvis to trunk offset in your measurements to determine the horizontal distance between the PSIS and the apex of the thoracic curve.[2]

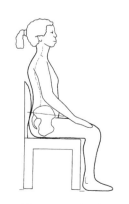

**Firm upper back
support**

b. **Angle upper back support**. The upper back support can **angle backwards beyond** the person's neutral balance point. This option allows her to bend back (extend) in the mid-back. [1, 3-5] Make sure you are not over-correcting the pelvis and trunk.

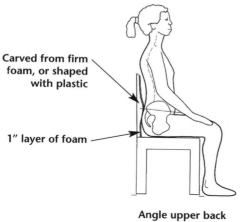

Carved from firm foam, or shaped with plastic

1" layer of foam

Angle upper back
support backwards

c. **Semi-rigid support**. If the person continues to use the wheelchair's sling back, a semi-rigid but flexible support behind the sling back can support both the person's pelvis/spine and lower ribcage. Note that the angle between the lower and upper back support should correspond to the flexible area(s) in the person's spine. This angle allows the upper back to bend backward (extend).[6]

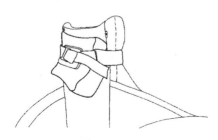

Semi-rigid support behind the sling back

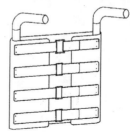

Straps behind the sling back

d. **Tilt**. Tilting the seating system and/or wheelchair backwards may keep the head and trunk from flopping forward.

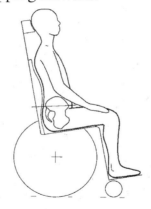

Tilt the seating system
and/or wheelchair backwards

e. **Increasing seat-to-back support angle.** Sometimes **slightly opening the seat-to-back support angle by sloping the seat cushion down towards the front,** as suggested with a flexible posterior pelvic tilt (page 140) encourages an upright and neutral trunk. Remember, use this therapeutically and functionally for short periods of time so the person does not fatigue. If used for longer periods of time, anterior knee blocks can be used. See page 146.

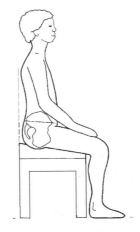

**Seat cushion sloped down
towards the front**

f. **Contour.** The upper back support can be **gently contoured,** particularly if the person does not want to use trunk supports. This differs from a sling back in a wheelchair. The sag of the sling tends to increase over time, encouraging rounding of the upper back. The contoured back support is made out of firm material so that its curvature will not increase over time.

**Gently contoured
upper back support**

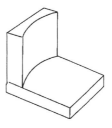

**Firm foam, or
shaped plastic**

g. **Lateral (side) trunk contours** specifically placed on both sides of the trunk, may give the person just enough guidance and the sense of stability to sit more upright and neutral. Make sure that these contours do not hinder the trunk movement needed to function.

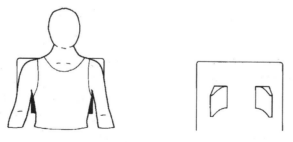

Lateral (side) trunk contours

h. **Lateral (side) trunk supports⊕.** These can provide more guidance and stability than the lateral contours. These supports should be thin, adjustable, and high enough to provide support but not dig in under the armpits. The trunk supports should curve and contour to the shape of the ribcage. These supports can extend from the back support towards the front of the chest to provide more stability, or can be shorter if less control is needed. Lateral trunk supports should be thin should not interfere with arm movement. Covering them with medium-firm foam will assure that they do not bottom out. If the person needs lateral trunk supports only for certain activities, the supports should be easily removable or move out of the way when not needed.[7]

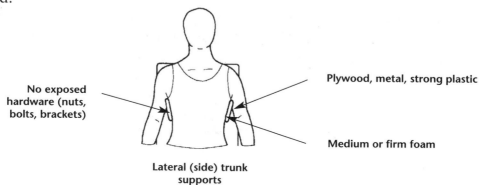

No exposed hardware (nuts, bolts, brackets)

Plywood, metal, strong plastic

Medium or firm foam

Lateral (side) trunk supports

Design Challenge

Adjustability

Our first postural objective is to support the person's trunk in her neutral posture. Can the upper to lower back support angle also be adjustable to allow for or support different postures needed for other functional movements? Can it allow the person to lean backwards (extend), but also support the trunk when she is sitting more upright?

FIXED

If the **trunk is curved forward (kyphosis)**, and is fixed, the intent of the back support is to support the back such that her head is upright and balanced. The guiding question for a fixed kyphotic trunk is:

- In **what posture** of the **spine over the pelvis** does the head feel most balanced?

Possible Options

a. Instead of a flat back support, make the back support **rounded** to accommodate the person's trunk posture.[2,8]

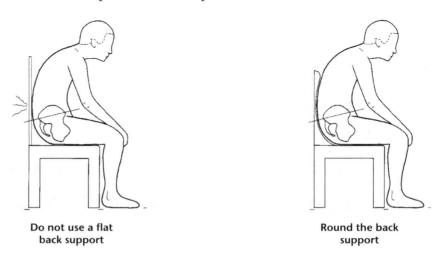

| Do not use a flat back support | Round the back support |

b. **The seat-to-back support angle** may need to be **greater than 90°**, and the upper to lower back support angle will need to conform to the curve of the person's kyphosis so that her head is upright and balanced.

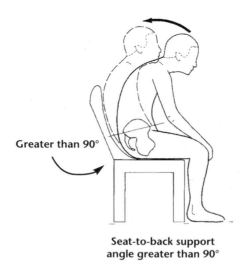

Greater than 90°

Seat-to-back support angle greater than 90°

c. After the fixed kyphosis is supported, the entire seating system can be **tilted backwards slowly**, until the person's head is upright and balanced.

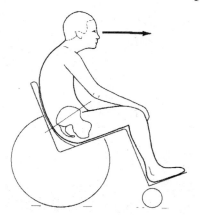

Tilt the seating system backwards

d. The back support may need to be **relieved or cut out** in specific areas where the bones stick out (often the spine, ribs, scapulae).

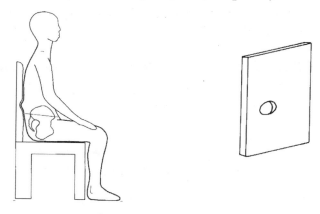

Back support relieved or cut out

e. If the person has been sitting in this posture for a long time, and her back, head, and neck are fixed and balanced in this posture, you may not need to change the current back support. However, if the person is using a wheelchair with a sling back, you may need to **reinforce the sling back** with straps to prevent it from stretching out more.[1,9]

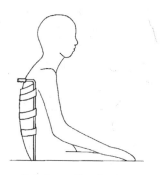

**Reinforce sling back
with straps**

2. Anterior (Front) Trunk Supports

The person may need the front of her trunk supported to sit upright. Before supporting the trunk from the front, try different shapes and angles of back supports and tilts of the seating system to balance the person's head over her pelvis. If anterior trunk supports are used, the person should also have time out of them. If a person is always strapped into a seating system, she may have fewer chances of developing her trunk control. Anterior trunk supports can be used for people whose spines are either flexible or fixed.

Anterior (front) trunk supports should:
- Provide stability, but not prevent functional movement.
- Be safe, neither limiting respiration nor causing choking, and be easily removable in case of emergency.
- Not irritate prominent bony areas.
- Conform to the person's body structure.
- Be padded so the straps do not dig into soft tissue.

Let your hands guide you as to what the trunk supports/straps should do. Try different types of trunk supports/straps attached at different angles to evaluate what works best.[10]
- **Where** are your hands providing the stability for, or the force to "correct" the trunk and shoulder girdle?
- **How much stability** do the supports need to provide? Total limitation of any forward trunk movement? Allowance of some movement?
- **What direction of pull** of the strap provides stability? Reduces unwanted movement patterns?

CAUTION!

If the pelvis is not properly stabilized by an anterior (front) pelvic support, the use of an anterior trunk support can be hazardous and even fatal. If the pelvis is not properly stabilized, the person can slide or slump down in the seat, and the anterior chest support could press against the anterior neck region. This could lead to choking, strangulation, or death.

Possible Anterior Trunk Support Options

a. **Trunk strap around the chest** may prevent the trunk from falling forward. This strap allows forward reaching with the arms and forward movement of the scapulae. This design will not work well if a person tends to hang over the top of the strap.

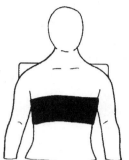

Trunk strap around the chest

b. **Trunk strap with elastic** allows more trunk movement and expands with breathing.[11]

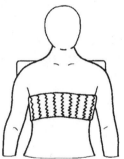

Trunk strap with elastic

c. **Puller strap** is used if a person leans into a side (lateral) trunk support. It is connected to the *inside* of the trunk support that the person is leaning against and pulls across the chest to the *outside* of the other trunk support. This strap can cross the chest at a diagonal if one shoulder tends to rotate forward. [11]

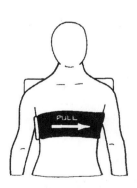

Puller strap

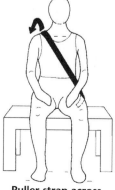

Puller strap across the chest

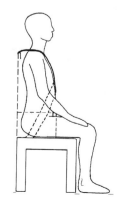

Back support attachment sites of puller strap

167

d. In **H-straps**, the upper strap attaches to the back support at, or slightly below, the shoulders. At this attachment site, the straps will hug the shoulders and pull the shoulders back if they tend to round forward. Buckles on the straps make it easier to get the H-strap on and off and allow adjustability.[2,11]

H-straps

Back support attachment sites of H-straps

e. A **chest panel** is X-shaped and made from plastic or semi-rigid material. It presses against the breastbone (sternum). Position it below the top of the breastbone to prevent choking and discomfort.[2,11]

Chest panel

✋ CAUTION! & Tech Tip

What determines safety risk of an anterior trunk support? Answer: The ability of the lower strap to catch at the axilla before the upper strap catches at the throat. So be very cautious when using the chest panel. Any strap, vest, or chest panel should be positioned so that the bottom strap will be closer to the axilla than the top strap is to the throat.

f. A **vest** can be made out of sturdy but flexible material. It contacts more of the person's body than the straps. People who need extra sensory contact and stability may prefer the vest.[12]

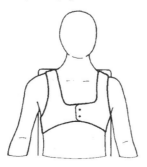

Vest

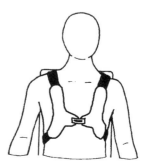

Vest with buckle

g. **Shoulder straps can attach to the trunk supports** to gently pull the shoulders back. These are especially good for women, as the straps do not cross the breasts.

Shoulder straps attached to trunk supports

h. **Chest strap with H-strap.** With this design, looped webbing is sewn on the left and right side of the chest strap. The chest strap has a buckle in the middle. The shoulder strap can go through any loop on the chest strap, depending on the person's need.[13]

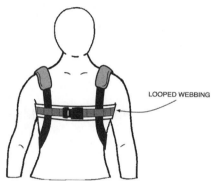

LOOPED WEBBING

Chest strap with H-strap

i. **Dynamic trunk strap.** Webbing is sewn in the loop style as above onto elastic straps. This allows for some movement of the trunk, but the looped webbing also provides some control to the movement. This can be used with trunk or chest straps.[13]

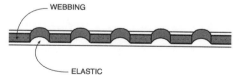

WEBBING

ELASTIC

Dynamic trunk strap

Tech Tip

Shoulder strap guides attaching onto the back support can make sure the straps do not fall off the shoulders or cut into the neck.

B Trunk Curved to the Side (Scoliosis)

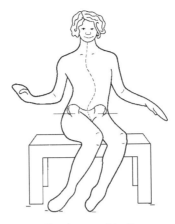

Trunk curved to the side (scoliosis)

If the curve is flexible, postural supports on the sides of the trunk should guide or prevent the trunk from curving or leaning to the side. Remember we have already supported the pelvis, which usually means lateral pelvic supports on each side of the pelvis.

FLEXIBLE

Again, let your hands help you decide where and how much support the person requires.

- In **what posture of the spine over the pelvis** does the head feel most balanced?
- **Where and in what direction** are your hands supporting or "correcting" the trunk to prevent curving to the side?
- **How much stability** do the supports need to provide? Total limitation of any sideways movement? Allowance of some movement?
- What is the **least amount of surface contact** necessary to support and/or control the trunk? A full hand, one to two fingertips?

Possible Options

1. **Lateral (side) trunk supports** at equal heights may provide sufficient guidance and trunk stability. The height of the trunk supports will depend on the amount of postural control and stability required. The supports can be positioned close to the sides of the ribcage to limit movement or placed farther away from the ribcage to allow some side-to-side movement. Also, these supports can extend from the back support towards the front of the chest for more support, or can be shorter if less support is needed. If lateral trunk supports are required only for certain activities, the supports should be easy to remove or move out of the way when not needed.[7]

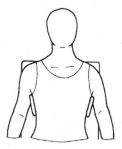

Lateral (side) trunk supports

2. **Three points of control**. If the person's trunk is curving to the side and needs more control to prevent this posture, the lateral trunk supports should be offset to provide three points of pressure. Place one support just below the point where the spine curves out (convex side **ⓐ**). On the other side of the spine (concave side **ⓑ** and **ⓒ**), one support should be placed above, and one below, the curve. The location of the supports depends upon the size and shape of the trunk curve(s). The supports should be thin, contoured to the body shape and adjustable. The highest support should be high enough to provide support but not cut under the armpits. Often the lowest support is placed to the side of the pelvis. There should be one to two ribs in between the left and right trunk supports for these to be effective.[8,14,15]

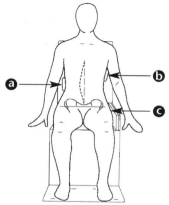

Three points of control

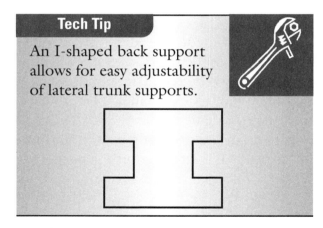

Tech Tip

An I-shaped back support allows for easy adjustability of lateral trunk supports.

3. Anterior (front) trunk supports as outlined on pages 167-9 may be useful in stabilizing the trunk.

FIXED

1. **Conform the back support to accommodate the deformity.** Support the curve, but do not try to correct it. Areas may need to be relieved in the back support for bony prominences (spine, ribs). As with the fixed lateral pelvic tilt and rotation, the intent of our support is **not** to position the trunk in neutral, but to first **position the head in a neutral and balanced position.** We then accommodate the fixed trunk and pelvic position. The scoliosis may be in the shape of a "C" or an "S," or an "S" with an additional curve. Conform the back support to the fixed trunk position.[8] The back support can be custom molded to the person, or it can be carved out of semi-rigid material such as firm foam. Please refer to page 155 regarding benefits and disadvantages of molding.

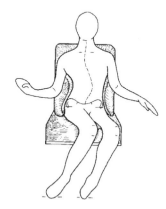

Accommodate the back support to the fixed position of the trunk

Custom or sculpted back support

2. Anterior (front) trunk supports as outlined in pages 167-9 may be useful in stabilizing the trunk.

C Trunk Rotated Forward (Rotated)

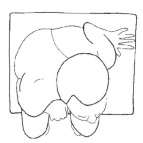

Upper trunk rotated
- Top view -

If the **upper trunk is rotated forward on one side (rotated)** and the rotation is flexible, the intent of the support is to correct or prevent excessive rotation. Your hands will help you understand the necessary shape of the trunk supports/straps and how they should contact the body.

FLEXIBLE

- **Where** are your hands located to control the forward rotation of the upper trunk and shoulder girdle?
- **To what degree** do the supports need to stabilize and control the rotation? Limit all forward rotation of the trunk? Allow some rotation?
- **What is the optimal direction of pull** of the strap?
- Note the **shapes and surfaces** of the areas in the upper trunk requiring support. Respect bony prominences.

Possible Options

1. A **puller strap** can cross the chest at a diagonal if one shoulder tends to rotate forward. A "force-localizing pad" at the shoulder can be used to focus the support.

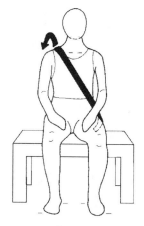

Puller strap

2. **Lateral (side) trunk support that curves around the front** of the trunk and ribcage may prevent excessive rotation. This support will need to be removable or be able to pivot out of the way when the person transfers.

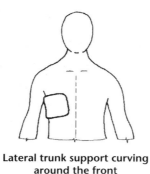

Lateral trunk support curving
around the front

- Top view -

3. A **vest** made out of sturdy but flexible material may be able to provide enough evenly distributed pressure to prevent excessive rotation.

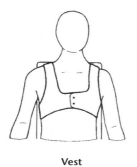

Vest

Vest with buckle

4. **Tilting the seating system backwards** may prevent the trunk from rotating forward excessively.

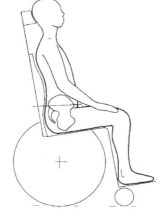

Tilt the seating
system backwards

FIXED

If the upper trunk is rotated forward on one side (rotated) and the rotation is fixed, the head position should guide the posture of the rest of the body. Refer to page 172 for guidelines.

B   Trunk Arched Backward (Extended)

If the **upper trunk is arched backward (extended)**, the posture is often associated with shoulder girdles that pull backward and turn out (retract and externally rotate).

**Upper trunk arched
backward (extended)**

FLEXIBLE

If the upper trunk is flexible, the intent of the back support will be to reduce the excessive extension of the upper back and the posturing of the shoulder girdles. Think of how your hands are reducing the extension:

- **Where** are your hands placed to control the upper back arching?
- Note the **shapes and surfaces** of the upper back and shoulders requiring support. Respect the bony prominences.

Possible Options

1. Begin with a **firm back support** which matches the contours of the person's back when the person's upper trunk is in her neutral posture.

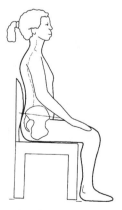

Firm back support

2. **Wedges** can assist the shoulder blades to move forward.[2]

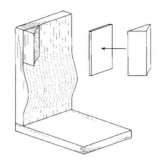

Wedges behind shoulder blades

3. **Gently contour** the back support.

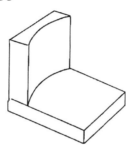

**Gently contour the
back support**

4. **Tilt the seating system backwards**. The excessive upper back extension may or may not improve with the entire seating system tilted backwards.

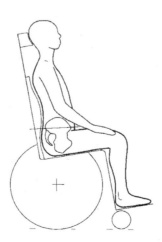

**Tilt seating system
backwards**

5. **Anterior (front) trunk supports** as outlined on pages 167-9 may be useful in stabilizing the trunk.

FIXED

If the upper trunk is fixed, the intent of the back support will be to support and accommodate the trunk for comfort and function.

1. **Support the curve**, but do not try to correct it. Some people may want the curve supported with shaped material, while others may not.

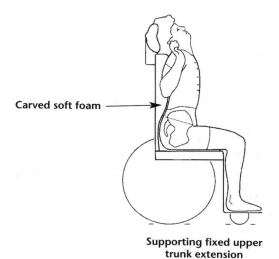

Carved soft foam

Supporting fixed upper trunk extension

2. **Supporting the trunk from the front** as outlined in pages 167-9 may be useful in stabilizing the trunk.

References

1. Zollars JA, McKone B. Above and beyond the pelvis: Taking a closer look at the head and trunk. *Proceedings from the 9th International Seating Symposium.* 1993:87-93.

2. Bergen A, Presperin J, Tallman T. *Positioning for Function: Wheelchairs and Other Assistive Technologies.* Valhalla, NY: Valhalla Rehabilitation Publications, Ltd.; 1990.

3. Margolis S. Lumbar support issues. *Proceedings from the 8th International Seating Symposium.* 1992:19-22.

4. Margolis S. The biangular back revisited: Use, misuse and clinical potentials. *Proceedings from the 18th International Seating Symposium.* 2002.

5. Wengert ME, Margolis K, Kolar K. A design for the back of seated positioning orthoses that controls pelvic positioning and increases head control. *Proceedings from the 10th Annual RESNA Conference.* 1987:216-18.

6. Zollars JA, Axelson P. The back support shaping system: An alternative for persons using wheelchairs with sling seat upholstery. *Proceedings of the 16th Annual RESNA Conference.* 1993:274-6.

7. Presperin J. Deformity control. In *Spinal Cord Injury: A Guide to Functional Outcomes in Occupational Therapy.* Rockville: Aspen Publications; 1986.

8. Wright D, Siekman A, McKone B, Hockridge T, Margolis S. Notes from Stanford Rehabilitation Engineering Center Seating Seminar. February 1990.

9. Engstrom B. *Ergonomics Wheelchairs and Positioning.* Hasselby, Sweden: Bromma Tryck AB; 1993.

10. Trefler E, Angelo J. Comparison of anterior trunk supports for children with cerebral palsy. *Assist Technol.* 1997;9(1):15-21.

11. Presperin J. Interfacing techniques for posture control. *Proceedings from the 6th International Seating Symposium.* 1990:39-45.

12. Carlson JM, Lonstein J, Beck KO, Wilke DC. Seating for children and young adults with cerebral palsy. *Clin Prosthet Orthot.* 1987;11(3):176-98.

13. Noon J. Personal communication. Fall 2008.

14. Mao HF, Huang SL, Lu, HM, Wang YH, Wang TM. Effects of lateral trunk support on scoliotic spinal alignment in person with spinal cord injury: A radiographic study. *Arch Phys Med Rehabil.* 2006 Jun;87(6):764-71..

15. Trefler E, Hobson D, Taylor SJ, Monahan L, Shaw CG. *Seating and Mobility for Persons with Physical Disabilities.* Tucson, AZ: Therapy Skill Builders; 1993.

Chapter 8
The Hips and Legs

Along with the pelvis, the legs should provide a stable base of support from which the body can move for function. If the legs are tight, contracted, or move uncontrollably, they can affect the posture of the pelvis and the rest of the body. We need to support the hips and legs in conjunction with the pelvis and trunk. In this section, we will address the following typical postures and movements:

- Hips/legs moved towards midline (adducted) and turned in (internally rotated)
- Hips/legs spread open (abducted) and turned out (externally rotated)
- Both legs turned to the same side (windswept)
- Hips bent up excessively (flexed)
- Legs moving constantly

Use your hands to determine how the components need to act to provide stability and support.
- **Where and in what direction** are your hands providing support for the hips and legs?
- **How much support** are you using to provide stability and prevent excessive hip and leg movement?
- **What is the minimal amount of postural support** needed to provide stability to the hips and legs?
- **What are the qualities of the contact area**, including the shape, size, amount of tissue and bony prominences where the postural supports will contact the person's body?

Pelvis and upper leg supports should:
- Support the person's hips and legs in their neutral posture within the limits of flexibility.
- Allow for the shape of the thighs.
- Be removable or flip-down if necessary for transfers.

A   Hips Moved Towards Midline (Adducted) and Turned In (Internally Rotated)

**Hips and legs adducted
and internally rotated**

FLEXIBLE

If the hips/legs are flexible enough to come to neutral, the intent of the medial (middle) upper leg support⊕ is to limit or prevent the legs from always moving towards midline.

Possible Medial Upper Leg Support Options

1. **Mild contoured bump** can be used in between the legs. This bump can be used if a person's legs only need a reminder, or a little support to keep them apart.

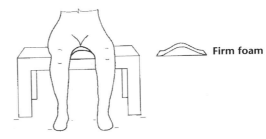

Firm foam

Mild contoured bump

2. **Wedged-shaped block**. If more support or force is needed to keep her legs apart, use a wedged-shaped block in between her knees. This block can extend from the front of the knees to one third up the length of the thigh.[1] The depth and width of the block depends on the person's tightness and spasticity. With a lot of tightness or spasticity, the legs may pull more towards each other.[2,3] Making the block larger spreads the pressure over a greater surface area. The block should follow the shape of her thigh. This usually means making it wider at the knees and narrower towards the pelvis. The block should be able to remove or flip-down for transfers and toileting.[1] A post attached on the underside of the block can slip into a hole in the seat cushion to make the block removable. If removable, it should be tethered to the seating system so that it does not get lost.

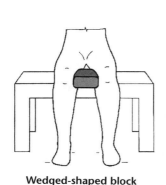

Wedged-shaped block

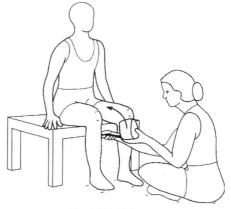

Block that flips down

FIXED

If one or both of the **hips/legs are moved towards midline (adducted) and turned in (internally rotated)** and fixed, the intent of the middle (medial) thigh support is to provide support to prevent tightness, contractures and to protect the skin of the knees from being irritated.

1. **Support the hips and lower legs** within their flexibility.

   STEP 1: Position the hips. Place a small padded block between the knees, but do not force the hips and legs out to the sides. Make sure that the hip is not dislocated or subluxed. Get this checked by a doctor. It is important not to force a dislocated or subluxed hip out to the side, because it will cause pain.

Small padded block between the knees

   STEP 2: Support the lower legs. Use the information obtained from the flexibility assessment about the difference between the hips/legs moved towards midline (adducted) or turned in (internally rotated). We need to respect the rotation limitations in the hip joints.

   If in this position (adducted), the hips cannot **turn out** (externally rotate) so that the lower legs and feet line up vertically with the knees, **support the lower legs and feet in this position**. DO NOT force the feet towards midline, you may cause pain and damage in the hips and knees, and cause the pelvis to move out of place.

Support the pelvis and hips with lateral pelvic supports before using a medial upper leg support.

B Hips Spread Open (Abducted) and Turned Out (Externally Rotated)

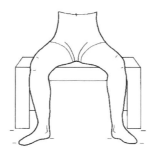

**Hips/legs abducted and
externally rotated**

FLEXIBLE

If one or both of the hips/legs are spread open (abducted) and turned out (externally rotated) but flexible enough to come to neutral (5-8° of abduction), the intent of the lateral (side) pelvic and upper leg supports⊕ is to encourage the hips to come to a more neutral posture.

Possible Options for Lateral Pelvic and Upper Leg Supports[1,4]

1. **Contoured supports or blocks on the outside of the pelvis and legs.** The amount of stability that the person requires (assessed with your hands) will guide you as to the height and length of the supports. The shape of the person's legs will further guide you as to the shape of the supports.

   a. Some people need **blocks or contours only at their pelvis.** If the person needs more postural control and stability, make the supports higher.

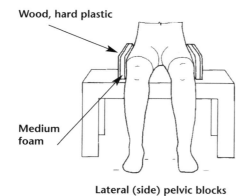

Wood, hard plastic

Medium foam

Lateral (side) pelvic blocks

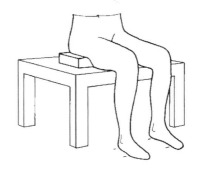

Lateral (side) pelvic contours

b. Some people need **supports that extend past the knees**.

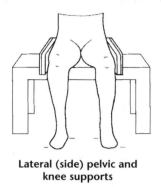

Lateral (side) pelvic and
knee supports

FIXED

If the hips and legs are fixed, the intent is to provide support to minimize tightness and contractures.

1. **Support the legs out to the side** (the abducted position), to prevent further turning and spreading out.

> **STEP 1: Position the hips.** Support the hips and legs at the comfortable limit of moving inward (adduction).
>
> **STEP 2: Support the lower legs.** Use the information obtained from the flexibility assessment about the difference between the hips/legs **spread open** (abducted) or **turned out** (externally rotated). Respect the **rotation limitations** in the hips.
>
> If in this position the hips cannot **turn in** (internally rotate) so that the lower legs and feet line up vertically with the knees, support the lower legs and feet in this position ("frog-legged position"). DO NOT force the feet to line up with the knees, as you may cause pain and damage in the hips and knees, and cause the pelvis to move out of place. A footplate that is wedged may be needed to fully support the feet.

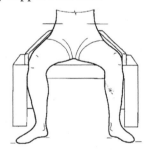

Support the legs in
the fixed position

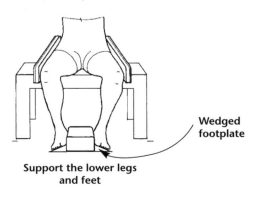

Wedged
footplate

Support the lower legs
and feet

C   **Both Hips Turned to Same Side (Windswept)**

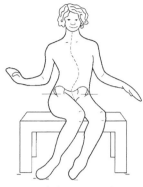

**Both legs turned to
the same side (windswept)**

FLEXIBLE

If both legs are flexible, the intent of the postural support is to support the upper legs in a comfortable neutral posture of the hips.

1. **Pelvic and upper leg supports for windswept posture.** Block the knees from turning out to the side, and the pelvis from shifting and rotating. The amount of stability that the person requires will guide you as to the height and length of the supports. The shape of the person's legs will guide you as to the contours of the support surfaces. [1,5]

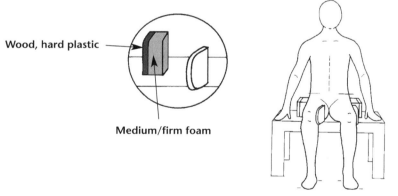

Wood, hard plastic

Medium/firm foam

**Pelvic and upper leg supports
to control windswept posture
of the legs**

FIXED

1. **Allow the legs to go to the side**, so that the pelvis will be upright and in a
   neutral position. Conform the seat cushion to support the legs. As in the case of
   a fixed lateral pelvic tilt, rotation, and/or fixed scoliosis, the intent of our seating
   system is to support the person's posture so that her head is upright and
   balanced over her base of support. The seat cushion can be carved out of semi-
   rigid foam or molded to the person's pelvic and leg posture.[4-8]

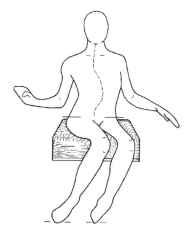

Conform the seat cushion to
support the legs

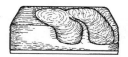

Mold or carve out of
semi-rigid foam

D Hips/Legs Bent Up Excessively (Flexed)

Hips/legs flexed excessively

FLEXIBLE

1. **Superior upper leg support**⊕: Use straps over the thighs or a padded block under a laptray to prevent excessive flexing up of the legs.[1]

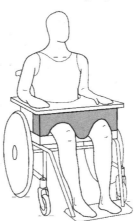

**Padded block under
a laptray**

E Legs Moving Constantly

The person's legs may be looking for stability if they tend to move excessively, uncontrollably, or constantly. With your hands, try different hand placements, not only to limit or to prevent movement, but also to create contact surfaces for the person to rest her legs. Often, if a person's legs are moving a lot, they may quiet and move less if in close contact with contoured surfaces. Assess how she responds to different shapes, contact surfaces, and textures.

Possible Options

1. **Troughs** contoured to the person's legs may give them a place to rest.[9]

Leg troughs

2. **Wide anterior lower leg straps** may limit excessive movement and/or provide close contact with seating surfaces so that the person feels more secure and stable.[1]

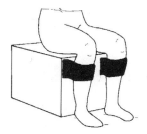

Wide anterior lower
leg straps

References

1. Bergen A, Presperin J, Tallman T. *Positioning for Function: Wheelchairs and Other Assistive Technologies.* Valhalla, NY: Valhalla Rehabilitation Publications, Ltd.; 1990.

2. Myhr U, von Wendt L. Improvement of functional sitting position for children with cerebral palsy. *Dev Med Child Neurol.* 1991;33:246-56.

3. Trefler E, Hobson D, Taylor SJ, Monahan L, Shaw CG. *Seating and Mobility for Persons with Physical Disabilities.* Tucson, AZ: Therapy Skill Builders; 1993.

4. Presperin J. Interfacing techniques for posture control. *Proceedings from the 6th International Seating Symposium.* 1990:39-45.

5. Cooper D. Biomechanics of selected posture control measures. *Proceedings from the 7th International Seating Symposium.* 1991:37-41.

6. Presperin J. Seating and mobility evaluation during rehabilitation. *Rehab Manag.* 1989 April-May.

7. Wright D, Siekman A, McKone B, Hockridge T, Margolis S. Notes from Stanford Rehabilitation Engineering Center Seating Seminar. Feb. 1990.

8. Monahan L, Shaw G, Taylor S. Pelvic positioning: Another option. *Proceedings from the 5th International Seating Symposium.* 1989:80-5.

9. Ward D. *Prescriptive Seating for Wheeled Mobility.* Ft. Lauderdale, FL: HealthWealth International; 1994.

Chapter 9
The Knees

In this section, we will address the **leg-to-seat surface angle**⊕ and the following typical postures and movements:

- Knees bent (flexed)
- Knees straight (extended)

How is the **leg-to-seat surface angle** determined? It should:
- Allow for the person's knee joint limitations and flexibility.
- Provide postural options for functional movement.

For some people, it may need to:
- Limit movement because of exaggerated muscular activity.

A | Knees Bent (Flexed)

Flexed knees

FLEXIBLE

If the knees are flexed, but flexible, so that the legs can be straightened to at least 90° without causing the pelvis to roll backward (posterior tilt), consider the following.

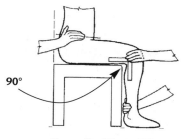

Knees flexible to 90°

Possible Options[1,2]

1. The **leg-to-seat surface angle can be set at 90°** to the seat cushion. This may require modifying the lower leg and foot supports of the wheelchair, as standard wheelchair leg-to-seat surface angles are set greater than 90°. Also the position and size of the caster wheels may need to be adjusted.

   If the **leg-to-seat surface angle** is greater than 90°, people tend to sit with a pelvis that is rolled under (posterior pelvic tilt). The muscles in the back of the knees (hamstrings) attach to the pelvis and below the knee joint. Therefore, moving (straightening) the knee will directly affect the posture of the pelvis.

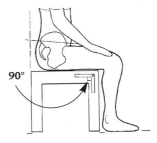

Leg-to-seat surface angle 90°

2. The **leg-to-seat surface angle can be less than 90°** if the person needs to bend (flex) her knees so that her feet are under her during functional activities.[3,4] Also, this angle can be used if a person has significant flexor spasticity so that she pulls into flexion when putting her into the seating system.[5] It is helpful in this case to undercut the front edge of the seat cushion.[6]

   Undercutting also accommodates calf bulk and prevents pressure on the top part of the calf and AFOs.[6] Bergen points out that it never hurts to cut back the front edge of the seat cushion, but it can hurt not to undercut it.[6]

Leg-to-seat surface angle less than 90°

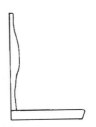

Cut back the front edge of the seat cushion

3. A **posterior foot support**⊕ may prevent the knee from bending (flexing) excessively. **A block or strap** can be positioned behind the heel or lower leg.

Block behind the heels

> **Note:** Sometimes people need to adjust the leg-to-seat surface angle. An example may be a person who needs the lower leg elevated to alleviate swelling due to a below-the-knee cast, a below-the-knee amputation, or circulatory problems. In these cases, the lower leg support should support and shape to her lower leg.[2]

FIXED

If the knee flexion angle is fixed, the hamstrings are tight, and the angle is less than 90°.

1. **Cut back the front edge of the seat cushion** so the legs and feet can go under the seat cushion without the pelvis rolling backwards (posterior tilting).

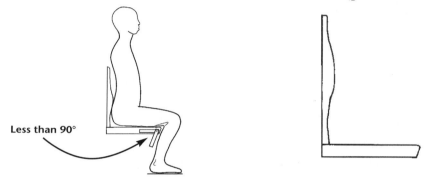

Less than 90°

Cut back the front edge of the seat cushion

 If a person with a knee flexion angle less than 90° is forced to sit at a 90° seat-to-lower leg support angle, what do you think will happen?

The pelvis will roll backward (posterior pelvic tilt) because of the pulling of the *hamstrings* (muscles on the backs of the thighs).

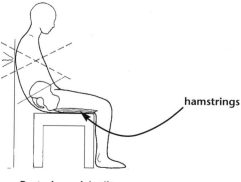

hamstrings

Posterior pelvic tilt

B   Knees Straight (Extended)

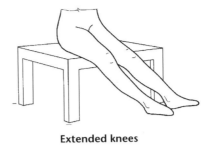

Extended knees

FLEXIBLE

From simulating with your hands, note:

- **Where** and in what direction are you applying the support to flex and stabilize the knees and legs?
- **How** much force do you need to apply?

Use this information when deciding on the postural supports to control excessive knee extension. Again think of your intent of controlling excessive knee extension. Do you want to totally limit knee extension, allow some extension, or allow all knee movement (flexion and extension)?

Possible Options for Anterior Lower Leg Supports⊕[1]

1. **Wide strap.**

Wide strap

2. **Anterior knee blocks.** These blocks should apply pressure to the kneecaps and lower legs. Do not use these if the person has a history of hip and/or knee problems.[7]

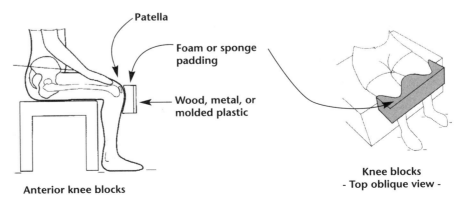

Patella

Foam or sponge padding

Wood, metal, or molded plastic

Anterior knee blocks

Knee blocks
- Top oblique view -

3. **Circumferential ankle supports = ankle straps.**

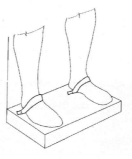

Ankle straps

FIXED

1. **Posterior lower leg support**⊕. Support the knees in extension; do not force them to 90°. Note that elevating lower leg supports usually come with flat calf panels that may not allow for correct leg-to-seat surface angle or comfortable support of the calf. A curved calf panel will be closer to the shape of the calves.

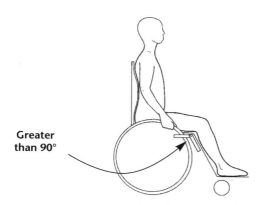

Greater
than 90°

Posterior lower leg support

References

1. Bergen A, Presperin J, Tallman T. *Positioning for Function: Wheelchairs and Other Assistive Technologies.* Valhalla, NY: Valhalla Rehabilitation Publications, Ltd.; 1990.

2. Ward D. *Prescriptive Seating for Wheeled Mobility.* Ft. Lauderdale, FL: HealthWealth International; 1994.

3. Kangas K. Clinical assessment and training strategies for the mastery of independent powered mobility. *Proceedings from the 9th International Seating Symposium.* 1993:121-6.

4. Engstrom B. *Ergonomics Wheelchairs and Positioning.* Hasselby, Sweden: Bromma Tryck AB; 1993.

5. Waugh K. Measuring the right angle. *Rehab Manag.* 2005 Jan-Feb;18(1):40:43-7.

6. Bergen A. Personal communication. Fall 2008.

7. McDonald R. Development of a method of measuring force through a kneeblock for children with cerebral palsy. *Proceedings from the 17th International Seating Symposium.* 2001:47-8.

Chapter 10
The Ankles and Feet

Postural supports for the ankles and feet will be considered along with supports for the pelvis, trunk, hips, and legs. What is the intention of postural supports for the lower legs, ankles, and feet?

- To provide a stable support surface for the feet over which the body can move.

For some people they should:
- Allow movement of the ankles, feet, and lower legs.

For other people, they may need to:
- Limit movement because of exaggerated muscular activity.

A   Foot Support-to-Leg Angle⊕

The foot support-to-leg angle should be set so that the feet are fully supported on the foot supports/footplates.[1-4]

Feet fully supported on the foot supports/footplates

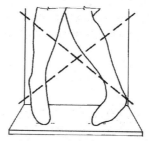

Inadequate foot support

FLEXIBLE

If the ankles are flexible and come to the neutral posture, consider one of the following.

Possible Options

1. **Foot support-to-leg angle** can be 90°.

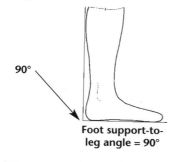

90°

Foot support-to-leg angle = 90°

2. **Foot support-to-leg angle may be less than 90°.** If the person moves her feet under and behind her knees for functional activities, the foot support-to-leg angle should allow this range of movement.

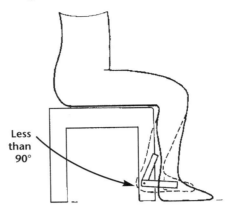

Less than 90°

Foot support-to-leg angle less than 90°

FIXED

If the ankles/feet are fixed (in plantar flexion, dorsiflexion, inversion, eversion, or a combination of the above), change the foot support-to-leg angle to support the position of the ankle/feet.

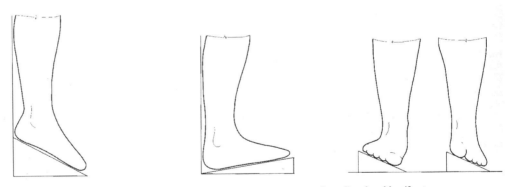

Angle of foot support-to-leg angle changed to accommodate fixed ankles/feet

B Ankle/Foot Supports

By the nature of the numerous joints in the ankle and foot, many combinations of movements and postures can occur. Again, your best guide for determining what the ankle/foot supports should be doing for the person are your hands.

- **Where** are your hands supporting or "correcting" the ankles and feet?
- **How much stability** do the supports need to provide? Total limitation of any ankle/foot movement? Allowance of some movement? Which movements?
- What **direction of force** are you using to control movement?
- What is the **least amount of support** needed?
- Do the lower leg and/or foot supports need to remove, flip up, or swing away for transfers?

Note: If the person wears ankle-foot orthoses (AFOs), this may affect the choice of ankle/foot supports, length of lower leg support, and foot support-to-leg angle.

Possible Circumferential Ankle/Foot Support⊕ Options[1,2]

1. **Ankle straps** can be used to prevent unwanted movement because of exaggerated muscular activity. The straps should be attached at a diagonal (45°) to control movement. For more control, ankle straps should attach close to the side of the foot. Straps can be attached with buckles or velcro. Sew velcro on one strap and thread that strap through a ring on the end of the second strap.

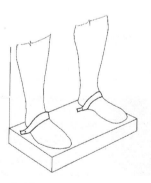

**Ankle straps set at 45°
to the foot supports**

2. **Toe straps** in the front of the foot can be used to control movement, especially unwanted turning in (inversion) or turning out (eversion) of the feet. Toe straps should be used with ankle straps. Toe straps alone will not control the ankle movement.

**Toe straps used with
ankle straps**

3. **Wide dynamic straps** can be made out of strong elastic material. This type of strap prevents excessive movement, but allows some movement and gives the foot/ankle a lot of sensory input.

Wide dynamic straps

4. **Vertically reinforced ankle straps** or wide circumferential support around the ankles, reinforced by vertical straps, can provide secure positioning of the ankle and foot. Remember, some people need broad contact like a wide strap to feel safe in their seating system.

**Vertically reinforced
ankle straps**

Possible Medial and Lateral Ankle/Foot Support⊕ Options [1,2]

1. **Blocks or shoeholders** can be used to control and limit turning in (inversion), toeing in (adduction), turning out (eversion), or toeing out (abduction) of the ankles/feet. The height and length of the blocks depends on the amount of control and stability needed.

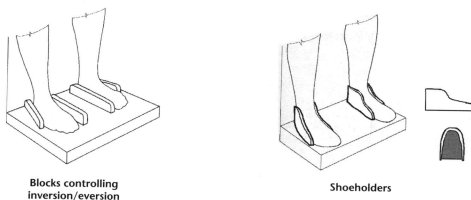

**Blocks controlling
inversion/eversion**

Shoeholders

2. **A foot box** can be used if the person's feet need to be protected from injury, as in the case of a person whose skin or bones are fragile.

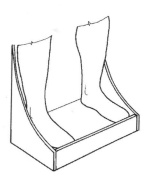

Foot box

Design Challenge

Dynamic Foot Support

Sometimes a foot support surface that moves with the person's movement may be desirable. For example, someone who has a lot of extensor spasticity may need to extend her legs, but also needs encouragement to flex them. A spring-loaded foot support that moves down with her leg movements, then comes back up to help her flex her legs may be beneficial.[5]

References

1. Bergen A, Presperin J, Tallman T. *Positioning for Function: Wheelchairs and Other Assistive Technologies.* Valhalla, NY: Valhalla Rehabilitation Publications, Ltd.; 1990.

2. Presperin J. Interfacing techniques for posture control. *Proceedings from the 6th International Seating Symposium.* 1990:39-45.

3. Ward D. *Prescriptive Seating for Wheeled Mobility.* Ft. Lauderdale, FL: HealthWealth International; 1994.

4. Waugh K. Measuring the right angle. *Rehab Manag.* 2005 Jan-Feb;18(1):40:43-7.

5. Whitmeyer J. Dynamix in seating: Don't sit still for too long. *Proceedings from the 7th International Seating Symposium.* 1991:301-4.

Chapter 11
The Head and Neck

The posture and stability of the person's body will greatly impact her head balance and control. Thus, the person's head should be supported only after her pelvis, trunk, lower extremities, and sometimes shoulders and arms, are adequately supported. Because the head and neck can move in so many different directions, it is difficult to isolate one movement, one postural problem. Most movements are a combination of movements. Keep this in mind as we address the following postures and movements, when the head:

- Falls or pushes back (extends).
- Falls to one side (laterally flexes), turns and pushes to one side (rotates), or pushes back and turns (extends with rotation).
- Falls or pulls forward (flexes).
- Moves excessively in all planes but has difficulty staying in neutral.
- Is large.

What are the characteristics of a head/neck support? What are we trying to achieve? The head/neck support should:

- Support the person's head/neck in her neutral posture.
- Shape and contour to the person's head/neck.
- Allow the person to move her head/neck within her range of control.

For some people, the support should be:

- Adjustable or removable.

To help the person find her neutral head/neck posture, and determine the necessary support, ask the following questions:

- In **what posture** of the **spine over the pelvis** does the head feel most balanced?
- Does **altering the person's head in relationship to gravity** (tilting the seating system) improve or worsen the person's head control?
- **Where** are your hands providing support for the head? Does the person feel comfortable with the support of your hands or does she push against it?
- Can you alter the head posture by providing **more support to the shoulders and upper back**?
- What is the **least amount of support** necessary when the person is sitting at rest?

- Describe the **contact surface** you are providing with your hands (the amount of contact, location and direction of support).

For support during functional movement:
- Does the person need **more or different head support** when performing a functional activity?
- Can the person independently **remove or adjust** the head support?

A Head Falls or Pushes Back (Extends)

If the person's head still tends to **fall or push backwards** even after tilting the entire seating system at different angles and finding the optimal balance of her head in relation to her pelvis and gravity, begin by giving support behind her head.

**Head falls backwards
(extends)**

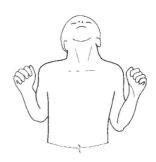

**Head pushes backwards
(extends)**

Possible Posterior Head Support⊕ Options[1,2]

1. **Gentle curved support.** The size of the curved support will depend on the amount of support needed. The shape will depend on the shape of the person's head. The location of the support will depend on where the person needs and likes support. For instance, a person may want support behind the upper part of her head, or the lower part of her head. Perhaps support is needed both at the upper and lower parts of her head.

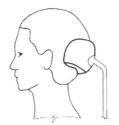

Small gentle curved support

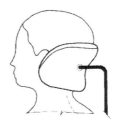

Large gentle curved support

2. A **neck roll** fits under the ridge at the lower part of the skull. This may provide just enough support for the person to tilt her chin down to see directly in front of her. The length of the neck roll depends on her comfort and amount of lateral control needed. If the neck roll is longer and curved, it can give the person a place to rest her head even when turning it from side to side. A neck roll is made out of strong rigid material such as metal rod, and covered with foam. Sometimes a neck roll is uncomfortable, irritates the neck, or stimulates arching of the neck and spine. Try it before making a final decision.

Short neck roll

Longer and curved
neck roll

B Head Falls (Laterally Flexes) or Rotates to One Side

If the person's head **falls or pushes to one side (laterally flexes)**, turns and **pushes to one side (rotates)**, or **pushes back and turns (extends with rotation)**, first provide **support behind the head** (outlined in A), and then provide support on the **sides of the head/neck** as needed. These combination movements will probably need creative combinations of head/neck supports. Allow the information you get from your hands to design the appropriate head/neck support.

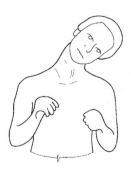

Head falls to one side
(laterally flexes)

Head turns and pushes
to one side (rotates)

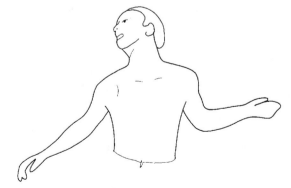

Head pushes back and turns
(extends with rotation)

Possible Lateral and Posterior Head Support⊕ Options[1,2]

1. **Gentle curved support** may be used if the person only needs a little support.

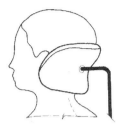

Gentle curved support

2. **Lateral (side) head blocks** will limit more movement. Locate the blocks above the ears. The closeness of the blocks to the head will depend on the amount of movement you want to allow or prevent.

Lateral (side) head blocks

3. A **neck ring** may also prevent bending or excessive turning of the head to one side. One problem with a neck ring is that the person may bring her head forward and under the front edge of the neck ring, getting her head stuck. To prevent this problem, the ends of the support can be flared out.

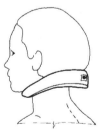

Neck ring

Long neck ring

4. **Lateral (side) head and the jaw support**. If more control is needed, try a support which blocks the side of the head and the jaw. A relief should be made for the ears. Be very careful with this support. The pressure of the support against the jaw may injure the jaw joint (temporomandibular joint).

**Lateral (side) head
and the jaw support**

C   Head Falls or Pulls Forward (Flexes)

If the person's **head still falls or pulls forward (flexes)** after supporting behind and beside the head, and tilting the seating system backwards, reassess the posture of the person's pelvis and back. Is there any way you can change the postural supports so that the person's head is not forward of her pelvis? Try again to get her head balanced over her base of support. If no other options work, try controlling the person's head from the front.

Head falls forward

Possible Anterior Head Support⊕ Options [1,2]

1. A **headband** around the forehead with a chin strap can be used with a neck support. The headband can be adjusted with a buckle in the back strap.

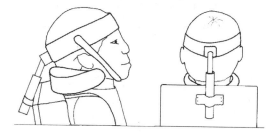

Headband

CAUTION!   Choking Risk

2. A **helmet/cap** can provide more control for the head. Elastic straps at the back of the helmet will allow some controlled movement.

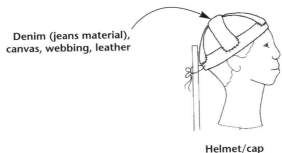

Denim (jeans material), canvas, webbing, leather

Helmet/cap

3. A **chin support or soft collar** can be used to limit the forward movement of the head. Make sure that this does not make the person cough or gag. The chin support should not attach to the seating system, but be placed directly on the person.[3]

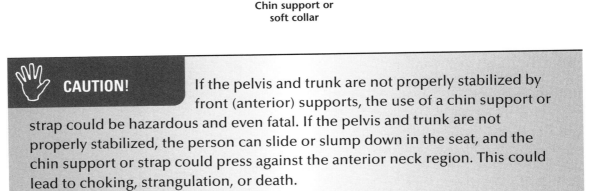

Carved soft foam

Chin support or soft collar

✋ CAUTION! If the pelvis and trunk are not properly stabilized by front (anterior) supports, the use of a chin support or strap could be hazardous and even fatal. If the pelvis and trunk are not properly stabilized, the person can slide or slump down in the seat, and the chin support or strap could press against the anterior neck region. This could lead to choking, strangulation, or death.

4. A **dynamic headband** attached to the front of the person's head can allow head rotation. The headband can be threaded through a guide or pulley system at the back of the head support so that it is free to slide. This headband will need to be used in conjunction with a headrest supporting the back and/or sides of the head/neck.[4]

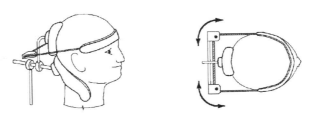

Dynamic headband*

*Used with permission of Whitmeyer Biomechanics.

D | Head Moves Excessively in All Planes

If the person's **head moves excessively in all planes** but has difficulty staying in neutral, the person will probably require a combination of supports.

Possible Options [1,2]

1. **Two curved supports** behind her head may help to provide a place of centering and security for the person to rest her head.

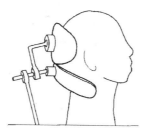

Two curved supports*

2. A **neck ring which supports both the lower part of skull and contacts both sides of her neck** may help to limit the excessive side-to-side and forward-to-backward head movements.

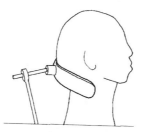

Neck ring*

*Used with permission of Whitmeyer Biomechanics.

E   Head Is Large

If the person's **head is large**: (hydrocephaly, infants)

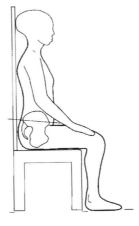

Large head

Recess the head support or **modify the back support** and seat depth to allow space for the head. Refer to the pelvis to trunk offset and trunk to head offset measurements.

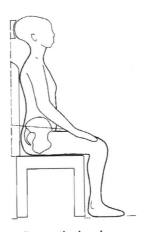

Recess the head support

Adjustable and Changeable Head Support: Azim's story

Submitted by Jamie Noon[5]

When Azim was 1 year old, he started using a special seat. His head control was very weak. In a 25° backwards tilt of his seating system, his head still dropped down and he was unable to lift it back up. He attempted to slide his head to the left and right, but did not have the strength to move it over the side of the posterior head support to come to an upright position.

The first thought was to restrict Azim's head movement with lateral head supports. However, with observation, the team began to understand that Azim was exploring his environment with the part of his body he controlled—his head. During hand simulation, the team noticed that hands placed at the sides of the head support allowed a ramp for Azim to slide his head from the dropped position to the upright position. Two padded plastic "wings" were attached to the head support. After 2 weeks of use, Azim's head control increased and the "wings" were cut shorter. After another 2 weeks, the "wings" were cut shorter still. Within 2 months, Azim could independently and saftely place his head where he wanted it. His teacher noted an acceleration in interaction and learning corresponding to his supported, independent movement.

Azim in seating system

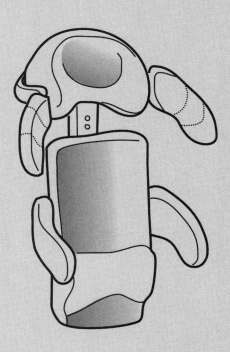

Changeable head support

References

1. Bergen A, Presperin J, Tallman T. *Positioning for Function: Wheelchairs and Other Assistive Technologies.* Valhalla, NY: Valhalla Rehabilitation Publications, Ltd.; 1990.

2. Cooper D. Head control: We're not there yet. *Proceedings from the 10th International Seating Symposium.* 1994:69-72.

3. Trefler E, Hobson D, Taylor SJ, Monahan L, Shaw CG. *Seating and Mobility for Persons with Physical Disabilities.* Tucson, AZ: Therapy Skill Builders; 1993.

4. Whitmeyer J. Dynamic head supports. Biomechanix, Inc. 1992.

5. Noon J. Personal communication. Fall 2008.

Chapter 12
The Shoulder Girdles

Once the pelvis, hips, legs, and trunk are stabilized, we can focus on supporting the shoulder girdle (shoulders and scapulae, or shoulder blades). The upper back, head, and neck are intimately connected with, and will significantly affect, the shoulder girdle. In this section we will address the shoulder girdles if one or both are:

- Shrugged upwards (elevated).
- Pulled forward and turned in (protracted and internally rotated).
- Pulled backward and turned out (retracted and externally rotated).

The intent of shoulder girdle supports is usually to assist the person's shoulders/scapulae into a more neutral posture (within limits of flexibility). Refer to how your hands are providing postural support to this region.

- **Where and in what direction** are your hands supporting or "correcting" the posture of the person's shoulder girdle?
- **How much stability** do the supports need to provide? Totally limit any shoulder movement? Allow some movement?
- Does **adding more pelvic and trunk support** help the person feel more stable and secure and affect the posture of the shoulder girdles?
- Note the **shapes and surfaces** of the shoulder girdle and upper back requiring support. Respect bony prominences.

A Shoulders Shrugged Upwards (Elevated)

**Shoulders shrugged
upwards (elevated)**

Possible Options[1-3]

1. **Pressure downward through straps** attached to the back support below the shoulder level may provide the necessary stability to the shoulders.

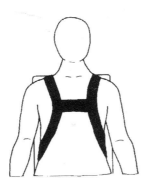

H-straps

**Back support attachment
sites of H-straps**

2. **Laptray.** By providing forearm support, a laptray, may allow the shoulders to relax.

**Laptray providing
forearm support**

B ## Shoulders Pulled Forward and Turned In (Protracted and Internally Rotated)

Shoulders pulled
forward and turned in
(protracted and
internally rotated)

Possible Options

1. **Anterior (front) trunk supports** such as H-straps or shoulder straps can encourage the shoulder girdles to move back and turn out (retract and externally rotate) to a neutral posture.

Shoulder straps

2. **Laptray with forearm support** may prevent some of this unwanted movement.

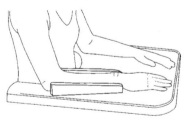

Laptray with forearm support

3. **Tilt the system** at different angles to assess whether the posture changes. Sometimes this posture is a response to gravity.

C Shoulders Pulled Backward and Turned Out (Retracted and Externally Rotated)

If the shoulder girdles are pulled backward and turned out (retracted and externally rotated), remember that this posture is associated with the upper trunk arching backward. Providing support and stability for the pelvis and trunk can influence this posture.

**Shoulder girdles pulled
backward and turned out
(retracted and externally rotated)**

Possible Options

1. **Wedges behind the shoulder blades** may encourage the shoulder blades to move forward.

Wedges behind the shoulder blades

2. **Gently round** the upper back support.

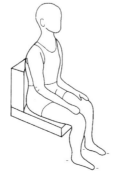

**Gently rounded upper
back support**

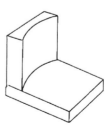

**Rounded upper
back support**

3. **Blocks can be positioned behind the elbows** and attached either to the back support or to the laptray. By moving the elbows forward, the posturing of the shoulder girdles can be indirectly affected.

Blocks behind the elbows

4. **Anterior trunk supports**: If you find that pressure over the mid-chest area helps to decrease this posture, try using anterior trunk supports, as outlined on pages 167-9.

5. **Tilt the system** at different angles to assess whether different positions in gravity affect the posture. The shoulder girdle posture may or may not improve with the entire seating system tilted backwards.

References

1. Bergen A, Presperin J, Tallman T. *Positioning for Function: Wheelchairs and Other Assistive Technologies.* Valhalla, NY: Valhalla Rehabilitation Publications, Ltd.; 1990.

2. Presperin J. Interfacing techniques for posture control. *Proceedings from the 6th International Seating Symposium.* 1990:39-45.

3. Ward D. *Prescriptive Seating for Wheeled Mobility.* Ft. Lauderdale, FL: HealthWealth International; 1994.

Chapter 13
The Arms

In reality, it is impossible to separate the arms from the shoulder girdles. Address these areas together, now focusing on the arms. We will look at the following arm postures[1-3]:

- One arm stiffened straight (extended), the other bent (flexed).
- One arm strong, the other weak or stiff.
- Both arms stiffly bent (flexed).
- Both arms stiffly straight (extended).
- Arms moving uncontrollably.
- Stabilize one arm to improve function of the other arm.
- Self-abusive behaviors.

What is the intent of arm supports?

- Support the person's arms and shoulder girdles in her neutral posture during rest and for optimal function.
- Provide a surface on which the arms and hands can function.

For some people the intent is to:

- Prevent or limit unwanted movement.

Ask yourself the following questions:

- **Where and in what direction** are your hands providing support to the arms to affect abnormal movement patterns or provide postural stability?
- What is the **amount and shape of the contact area** of the shoulders and arms necessary to provide support?
- Do the arm supports need to **remove or flip away** for transfers and different activities?
- Does **adding more pelvic and trunk support** help the person feel more stable and secure and affect the arm posture?

A   One Arm Stiffened Straight (Extended), the Other Bent (Flexed)

One arm extended,
the other flexed

1. **Posterior upper arm supports**⊕. Blocks behind the elbows attached either onto the back support or to the laptray can help bring both arms in front of the body and towards midline.

Posterior upper arm supports

B   One Arm Strong, the Other Weak

If one arm is strong and the other weak or stiff, the latter may be supported on **a laptray, a half laptray or with an arm trough** attached to an arm support. If the weak or stiff arm is supported, it may act as a postural support so that the other arm can function optimally. If the seating system tilts backwards, the trough should also support the back of the elbow so that the arm does not slide backwards.

One arm strong,
the other weak or stiff

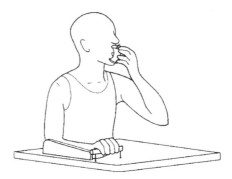

Supporting the weak or stiff arm

C Both Arms Stiffly Bent (Flexed)

Arms bent (flexed)

Possible Options

1. **Supporting the shoulder girdle** may allow the arms to relax and move into a more neutral posture.

2. **Providing support for the forearms with a laptray** may also help to decrease this flexed posture. The angle of the laptray may need to be adjusted to accommodate the flexed posture of the elbows.

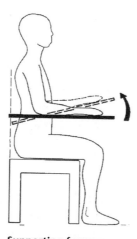

**Supporting forearms
with a laptray**

D   Both Arms Stiffly Straight (Extended)

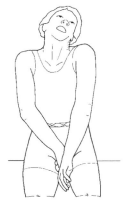

**Arms straight
(extended)**

FLEXIBLE

1. If the elbows are flexible, **support the arms on a laptray**. A **trough** (forearm channel) may help to position the forearms and decrease some of the excessive muscle activity.

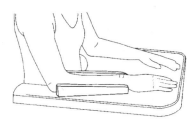

Forearm trough

FIXED

1. If the elbows are **fixed or function better in extension**, they will need to be supported by **adjusting the angle or height of the laptray**. If the person has hand function, she may want the laptray or tabletop surface to be lower to accommodate her position.

**Adjusting the angle or
height of the laptray**

E Arms Moving Uncontrollably

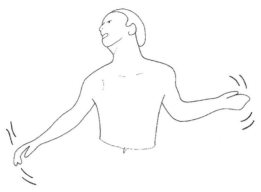

Arms moving uncontrollably

If the person's arms exhibit excessive or uncontrolled movement, they may be looking for stability. Hand simulation will help you determine where and how support is needed. Most probably the person will need more central postural support for the trunk and pelvis.

1. If a person is moving her arms around a lot, she may respond to **close contact with different types of surfaces**. Assess her responses to different shapes, contact surfaces, and textures.

2. **Troughs** contoured to the person's arm(s) may provide a place for her arms to find stability and rest.

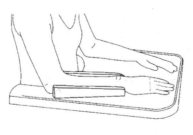

Arm troughs

F Stabilize One Arm to Improve Function of Other Arm

Possible Options

1. The person may hold onto a **grasping bar** mounted to a laptray or tabletop. An advantage to this is that the person can decide when to use the support.

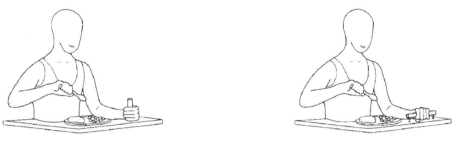

Vertical grasping bar   Horizontal grasping bar

2. Some people may want **straps to limit excessive movement**.

Denim (jeans material), canvas, webbing, leather. Best if secured with a buckle or velcro that threads through a D-ring.

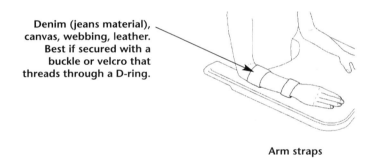

Arm straps

G Self-Abusive Behaviors

If the person has tremendous movement or self-abusive behaviors, the arms can be **stabilized under a laptray**. The edges of the laptray must be padded with no exposed hardware that can injure the hands. Blocks on the armrest should prevent the tray from pressing against the person.[4]

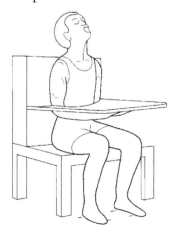

Stabilize arms under a laptray

References

1. Bergen A, Presperin J, Tallman T. *Positioning for Function: Wheelchairs and Other Assistive Technologies.* Valhalla, NY: Valhalla Rehabilitation Publications, Ltd.; 1990.

2. Presperin J. Interfacing techniques for posture control. *Proceedings from the 6th International Seating Symposium.* 1990:39-45.

3. Ward D. *Prescriptive Seating for Wheeled Mobility.* Ft. Lauderdale, FL: HealthWealth International; 1994.

4. Trefler E, Hobson D, Taylor SJ, Monahan L, Shaw CG. *Seating and Mobility for Persons with Physical Disabilities.* Tucson, AZ: Therapy Skill Builders; 1993.

Chapter 14
Pressure-Relief Cushions

Individuals who lack sensation (such as those with spinal cord injuries or *spina bifida*), the elderly and people who lack the ability to move, must use cushions that assist in limiting tissue breakdown.

A Extrinsic and Intrinsic Factors

Extrinsic and intrinsic factors that put people with disabilities at higher risk for pressure sores are summarized below.

Extrinsic factors (factors outside the person)[1,2]:
- **Pressure**: Tissue cell death begins to occur within minutes of high, sustained pressure.[3-5]
- **Heat**: Tissue damage increases as temperature increases.[6-9]
- **Moisture**: Sweat and moisture weaken the tissue and reduce air flow.
- **Shear**: As the person moves, the tissue between the bone and the skin will slide, rub, and *shear*, restricting blood flow and causing tissue damage.[3,10-12]
- **Friction/trauma**: Scrapes and bruises can initiate and/or keep an open pressure sore from healing.

Intrinsic factors (factors within the person)[1,2,12]:
- **Age**: Older skin is less elastic.
- **Sensation**: If sensation is partial or absent, the excessive pressure will not signal the person to shift weight.
- **General health**: Some conditions put a person at higher risk, such as diabetes.
- **Scar tissue from previous pressure sores**: These areas are always at higher risk for pressure sores.
- **Posture**: If a person sits with a posterior pelvic tilt, and rounded spine, pressure increases under the ischial tuberosities and sacrum.[13-15] If a person sits with a lateral pelvic tilt, there will be more pressure under the lower ischial tuberosity and greater trochancter.
- **Activity level and movement**: To keep healthy, the body needs to move. This will enhance blood and fluid flow as well as organ health.[16]
- **Commitment to following a pressure-relief routine.**[17]
- **Smoking** increases the risk of pressure sore development and slows healing of pressure sores.[18]

B Pressure

Sitting on canvas, nylon, vinyl, or wood can cause pressure sores, because there is excessive pressure under the bony prominences (ischial tuberosities, coccyx, pubis, sacrum, and greater trochanters of the femurs).

Risk Levels at the Seat Surface

Areas at risk for high levels of pressure at the seat surface include:

- *Ischial tuberosities* (sitting bones): Normally the highest risk for pressure sores.
- *Coccyx* (tailbone): Very little protection; however, generally it is not in contact with the cushion unless there is an extreme posterior pelvic tilt. Sometimes pressure sores develop under the coccyx because of poor transfers or bathroom equipment.
- *Sacrum*: Sacral pressure sores are often due to bed positioning. As with the coccyx, generally the sacrum is not in contact with the cushion, unless the person sits in an extreme posterior tilt.
- *Greater trochanters* (hip bones): Less risk than ischial tuberosities, but also a concern, especially with improperly fitted contoured cushions designed to alleviate more central pressures.
- **Upper part of the thighs**: The best for taking the pressure load; however, tissue breakdown can happen with excessive pressures and/or shearing, especially with more firmly contoured cushions.

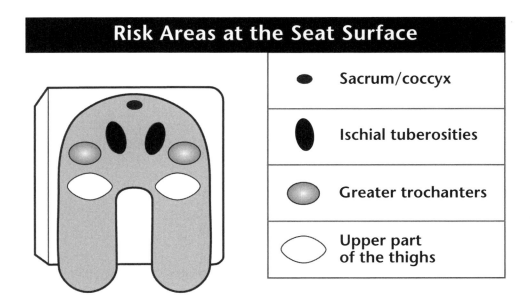

Risk Areas at the Seat Surface

●	Sacrum/coccyx
⬛	Ischial tuberosities
⬭	Greater trochanters
⬯	Upper part of the thighs

C Tips for Keeping Tissue Healthy

Pressure mapping systems and the "wiggle test" (both described on page 91) can be very useful for assessing areas of high pressure.

In addition to using a cushion, the person must:

- Move, that is, shift her weight off her butt bones. This can be done by pushing up on the arm supports, leaning forward, to the side, reclining the back support, tipping the wheelchair backward against a bed (or other surface), or lying down. People who have difficulty moving must have assistance from other people to change positions, or utilize a wheelchair that can tilt and/or a back support that can recline to relieve pressure.[12,14]
- Check the skin at risk for excessive pressure daily.
- Keep the skin clean and dry.
- Eat healthy foods.
- Not smoke or use nicotine products.

D Qualities of Cushions

Cushions should[1,19]:

- **Distribute pressures** to relieve pressure under vulnerable bony prominences.
- Provide a **stable support** surface for the pelvis and thighs.[20, 21]
- **Function effectively in different climates** (not retain a lot of heat, or freeze and harden in the cold).
- **Dissipate heat and moisture** so that excessive heat and humidity does not build up.[8,9]
- **Be lightweight**, especially if a person is transferring independently.
- **Be durable**.

The categories of cushions include fluids, gels, and foams. Each type of cushion has advantages and disadvantages. Each person, with knowledgeable help, should decide which cushion works best for her, depending on her body, where she lives, and what she does. No single cushion is best for everyone.[22-25] It is important that a cushion does not "bottom out." To "bottom out" means that the butt bones push through the cushion, thus pressing onto the wheelchair upholstery or seat surface.

E Cushion Covers

Covers over the cushions should be loose, stretchy, and able to absorb sweat and urine.[1] If the cover is not stretchable, it can change the effect of a cushion. For example, an inelastic cover will create a "hammock effect,"[26] tethering like a hammock so that the cushion cannot "give" to distribute pressure. Sweatshirt-type fabric works well as a cover. Cushion covers should be easily removable for washing. Plastic waterproof covers are easy to keep clean, but can cause serious problems for some people, as they are thick, inelastic, and nonabsorbent. The surface of waterproof covers can keep wetness next to the skin for a long time and may contribute to tissue breakdown.

F Types of Cushions

1. Fluid

Air and water cushions. These cushions shape to the buttocks and provide good pressure distribution by dispersion of the fluid, thereby equalizing or balancing the pressures. Both cushions can leak, so may require maintenance. Optimally, fluid cushions are segmented, meaning comprised of separate compartments that will provide more postural stability. Water cushions tend to be heavy.[10,27]

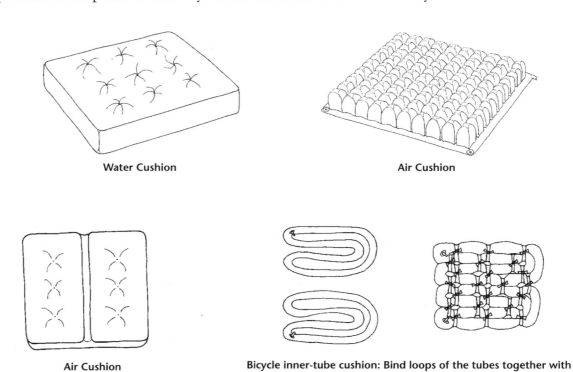

Water Cushion

Air Cushion

Air Cushion

Bicycle inner-tube cushion: Bind loops of the tubes together with thin straps of inner tubes. (Idea from a wheelchair builder at Tahanan Walang Hagdanang Quezon City, Philippines.)

Figure from Hotchkiss.[28]

228

2. Gel

Gel cushions flow somewhat like fluid cushions but with less dispersion, and provide more stability. Gels provide good pressure distribution.[29] Some gels are heavy and may get soft in hot weather.[10]

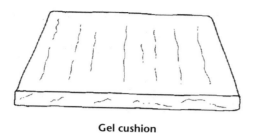

Gel cushion

3. Foams

Foam cushions can provide more stability, depending on the compressibility of the foam. If different densities of foam or contoured foam are used, good pressure relief can be obtained. Foams do not draw heat well from the body and can break down in 6 months time or less.

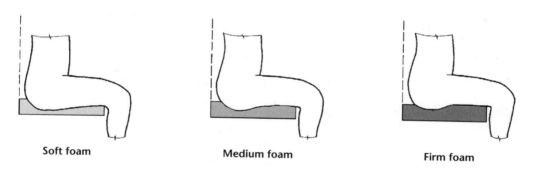

Soft foam   **Medium foam**   **Firm foam**

4. Molded

A cushion can be custom molded to the shape of the person's buttocks. Then, the cushion is individually shaped to relieve areas that are at risk for high pressure. Each time the person sits in the cushion, she must sit the same way. If not, there could be pressure and/or shearing at vulnerable bony areas.

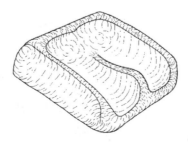

Molded cushion

5. Contoured Cushion

This cushion loads the pressure in safer areas, and relieves pressure at the vulnerable areas.[21,30] The cushion base is carved from firm foam, and then covered with a compressible, spongier top surface foam. This design has been used in many countries as a low-cost option for a supportive, pressure-relieving cushion. Some materials that have been used for the firm foam include koir (compressed coconut fiber), and compressed chipped foam.

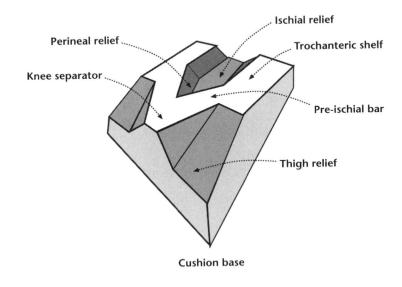

Cushion base

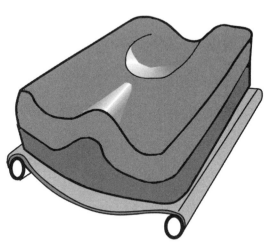

Finished contoured cushion

Note: Even though the intention of the molded and contoured cushions is to take pressure off of vulnerable areas (e.g., ischial tuberosities, sacrum, coccyx, greater trochanters), and load the upper thighs, if not done properly, tissue breakdown can happen under the thighs.

A contoured base for the foam can be made out of many layers of thick corrugated cardboard glued together. Wet the top layers of cardboard and have the person sit on it so that the bony prominences indent the cushion. These areas can be carved out to relieve excess pressure. Dry the cushion and coat it with waterproof varnish. Cover the cushion with 6" (15.2 cm) of high-density foam.

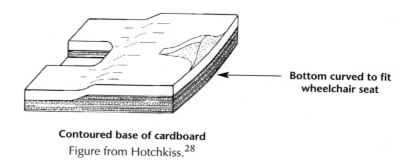

Bottom curved to fit
wheelchair seat

Contoured base of cardboard
Figure from Hotchkiss.[28]

6. Composite

A composite cushion consists of a combination of various cushion materials. The cushion can consist of a firm contoured base to provide pelvic stability, covered with fluid, viscous fluid gel, or foam. A composite cushion can be made from a combination of foams of different firmness and densities. This cushion provides both pressure distribution as well as postural stability.

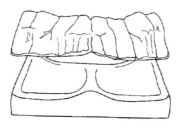

Composite cushion

References

1. Ferguson-Pell M. Seat cushion selection. *J Rehabil Res Dev (Clinical Supp 2)*. 1990:49-73.

2. Noon J. Personal communication. Fall 2008.

3. Zacharow D. *Posture: Sitting, Standing, Chair Design and Exercise*. Springfield, IL: Charles Thomas: 1988.

4. Bar CA. Predicting ischaemia from an analysis of dynamic pressure records. *Proceedings from the 5th International Seating Symposium*. 1989:145-52.

5. Ferguson-Pell M, Wilkie IC, Reswick JB, Barbenel JC. Pressure sore prevention for the wheelchair-bound spinal injury patient. *Paraplegia*. 1980;18:42-51.

6. Kosiak M, Fisher SV, Szymke TE, Apte S. Wheelchair cushion on skin temperature. *Arch Phys Med Rehabil*. 1978; 59:68-72.

7. Ferguson-Pell M, Minkel J. Tissue trauma: Understanding it and preventing it. (Notes from course). *15th Annual RESNA Conference*. 1992.

8. Siekman A. Testing the heat and water vapor transmission characteristics of wheelchair cushions. *Proceedings from the 24th International Seating Symposium*. 2008:59-62.

9. Kokate JY, et al. Temperature-modulated pressure ulcers: A porcine model. *Arch Phys Med Rehabil*. 1995;76:666-73.

10. O'Neill H. Tissue trauma: Postural stability, pelvic position and pressure sore prevention. *Proceedings from the 4th International Seating Symposium*. 1988:71-5.

11. Hobson D, Comparative effects of seated postural change on seat surface shear. *Proceedings from the 12th Annual RESNA Conference*. 1989:83-4.

12. Hobson D. Contributions of posture and deformity to the body-seat interface variables of a person with spinal cord injuries. *Proceedings from the 5th International Seating Symposium*. 1989:153-71.

13. Drummond DS, Narechania RG, Greed AL, Lange TA. The relationship of unbalanced sitting and decubitus ulceration to spine deformity in paraplegic patients. *Proceedings of the 17th Annual Meeting of the Scoliosis Research Society*. Milwaukee, WI: Scoliosis Research Society; 1982:94.

14. Hobson DA, Tooms RE. Seated lumbar/pelvic alignment: a comparison between spinal cord injured and non-injured groups. *Spine*. 1992;17:293-8.

15. Sprigle S, Schuch JZ. Using seat contour measurements during seating evaluations of individuals with SCI. *Assist Technol*. 1993;5(1):24-35.

16. Barral JP, Mercier P. *Visceral Manipulation*. Seattle, WA: Eastland Press; 1988.

17. Henderson JL, Price SH, Brandstater ME, Mandac BR. Efficacy of three measures to relieve pressure in seated persons with spinal cord injury. *Arch Phys Med Rehabil*. 1994;75:535-9.

18. Lamid S, El Ghatit AZ. Smoking, spasticity and pressure sores in spinal cord injured patients. *Am J Phys Med*. 1983 Dec;62(6):300-6.

19. Pratt S. Selecting the appropriate seat cushion: Is it really that much of a challenge? *Proceedings from the 24th International Seating Symposium*. 2008:242-3.

20. Aissaoui R, Boucher C, Bourbonnais D, Lacoste M, Danseareau J. Effect of seat cushion on dynamic stability in sitting during a reaching task in wheelchair users with paraplegia. *Arch Phys Med Rehabil*. 2001 Feb;82(2):274-81.

21. Sprigle S, Wooten M, Sawacha Z, Thielman G. Relationships among cushion type, backrest height, seated posture, and reach of wheelchair users with spinal cord injury. *J Spinal Cord Med*. 2003 Fall;(3):236-43.

22. Garber SL, Krouskop TA, Carter RE. System for clinically evaluating wheelchair pressure relief cushions. *Am J Occup Ther*. 1978;32(9):565-70.

23. Garber SL, Krouskop TA. Wheelchair cushions for spinal-cord injured individuals. *Am J Occup Ther*. 1985;39(11):722-5.

24. Garber SI, Dyerly LR. Wheelchair cushions for persons with spinal cord injury: An update. *Am J Occup Ther*. 1991;45(6):550-4.

25. Gilsdorf P, Patterson R, Fisher S, Appel N. Sitting forces and wheelchair mechanics. *J Rehabil Res Dev*. 1990;27(3):239-46.

26. Iizaka S, Nakagami G, Urasaki M, Sanada H. Influence of the "hammock effect" in wheelchair cushion cover on mechanical loading over the ischial tuberosity in an artificial buttocks model. *J Tissue Viability*. 2009 May; 18(2): 47-54.

27. Guimaraes E, Mann WC. Evaluation of pressure and durability of a low-cost wheelchair cushion designed for developing countries. *Int J Rehabil Res.* 2003 Jun;26(2):141-3.

28. Hotchkiss R. *Independence through Mobility: A Guide to the Manufacture of the ATI-Hotchkiss Wheelchair.* Washington, DC: Appropriate Technology International; 1985.

29. Takechi H, Tokuhiro A. Evaluation of wheelchair cushions by means of pressure distribution mapping. *Acta Med Okayama.* 1998 Oct;52(5):245-54.

30. Perkash I, O'Neill H, Politi-Meeks D, Beets CL. Development and evaluation of a universal contoured cushion. *Paraplegia.* 1984 Dec;22(6):358-65.

Chapter 15
Wheelchair Considerations

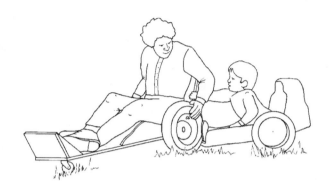

These are things to think about when making the seating system, putting it in a wheelchair, or getting a wheelchair.

A Seat Surface Height at Front Edge⊕

The seat surface height at the front edge is the height of the top edge of the seat cushion to the floor. This measurement depends on many factors. Be sure to add the height of the cushion when deciding on the seat height of the wheelchair. The foot supports should be approximately 2" (5 cm) from the floor to clear obstacles.[1] If the person has short legs, she may require much higher foot supports. The foot supports will need to be adjusted when changing the seat height. The seat height should be:

1. **Low enough** so that:

   - The person's knees can get under tables, counters, and sinks.
   - Transfers are as safe and easy as possible.
   - If the person propels her own wheelchair, pushing will be as easy and efficient as possible.
   - The seating/mobility system is stable. If the person and seating system are too high, she may feel unstable.
   - The person, while seated in the wheelchair, fits inside a vehicle (e.g., a bus or van with a lift).
   - If the person pushes her wheelchair with her feet, the bottoms of her feet should touch the floor.

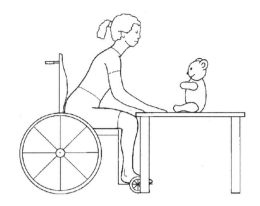

Seat surface height: too high

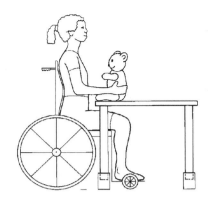

Seat surface height: appropriate

Seat surface height: too high

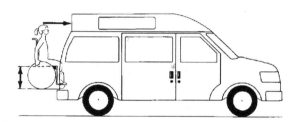

Seat surface height: appropriate height

2. **High enough** so that the person:

- Is sitting at the appropriate level for various activities.
- Is able to see and communicate with people.
- Can be transferred by the caregiver. If the person needs to be lifted and carried, it will be less of a strain on the caregiver's back if the seat is higher.

Sitting at the appropriate height for various activities

3. **For optimal pushing**, consider:

- Lowering the rear seat height from the front seat height (adding "dump") so that the person is more stable during pushing and braking.
- Setting the rear seat height such that the person's elbow is flexed to approximately 90-100°[2,3] (some say 100-120°)[4-6] when gripping the top of the handrim. Recognize that lowering the rear seat height is more stable, but if too low, the shoulder joint can turn in, predisposing it to injury.[6]
- Using larger rear wheels for taller users (e.g., 26" = 66 cm) and smaller wheels (20-24" = 51-61 cm) for shorter users to avoid extreme "dump" angles.

**Lowering rear seat height ("dump")
so that elbow is flexed at 90°-100°**

B Width of the Wheelchair/Mobility System

1. The wheelchair/mobility system must be **narrow enough to get through doors** and around furniture.

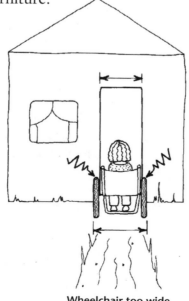

Wheelchair too wide

2. If the person propels her own wheelchair, the wheelchair should be **narrow enough so that pushing is as easy as possible**. For optimal pushing, the handrims should be as close to the body as possible. Many wheelchairs are too wide.

**Wheelchair too wide
for efficient pushing**

3. The wheelchair should be wide enough to provide good **side to side** stability. Sometimes this is accomplished by *wheel camber:* the top of the wheel is slanted toward the seating system or mobility frame. An increased camber brings the pushrims closer to the body and protects the hands when going close to walls and through doorframes.[1] However, increasing camber will increase the overall width of the wheelchair, which will reduce accessibility.[1] For general use, camber should be minimized (0-3°).[3] Sports chairs may use greater than 3° for better stability and responsiveness.

Wheel camber

4. The **back support** should be wide enough to provide trunk support, but **not too wide or tall to interfere with propelling the wheelchair**. The person's elbows should be behind her shoulders when pushing the wheelchair.

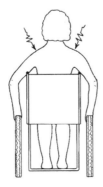

Back support too wide

Tech Tip

If the person requires trunk supports, use an I-back or narrow the back support at the top. Adjust the rear axle to allow better access to the rear wheel.

C The Position of the Seating System Within the Mobility System

Rear axle position. Some wheelchairs allow for adjustability vertically (up and down) and horizontally (forward and backward). Raising the axle lowers the seat and lowering the axle raises the seat. Moving the axle forward brings the seat back in relation to the wheels. Moving the axle backwards brings the seat forward.

1. **Pushing efficiency**. If the person pushes her own wheelchair, the maneuvering wheel⊕ (rear wheel) axle should be positioned so that most (80-90%) of the person's weight is over the maneuvering wheels.[2] This usually means the wheel axle is in line with, or slightly in front of the shoulder for most effective pushing. However, this may make the chair tip easily, and cause the person to fall backwards. With practice, a person can learn to balance the wheelchair with the axle forward of the back support tubes, but if the person needs more stability, move the maneuvering wheel back.[7] In each case, we are looking for a balance between stability and effective pushing.

Training wheelchair riders to be comfortable in a tippy wheelchair can have significant advantages in everyday propulsion. A tippier wheelchair rolls easier since most of the weight is over the larger maneuvering wheels. A tippier wheelchair is much easier to push on a side slope because the maneuvering wheels resist the tendency for the wheelchair to be pulled down the slope.[8] A tippier wheelchair is also less affected by obstacles such as sidewalk cracks, since less weight is on the caster wheels⊕.

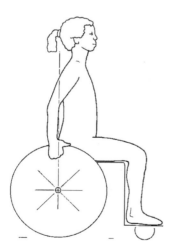

The person's weight in
front of the rear axle

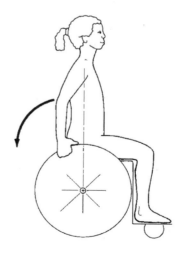

The person's weight
over the rear axle

2. **Stability of seating system inside the wheelchair/mobility system**. If the seating system is set inside the wheelchair in front of the back support tubes, make sure it does not unbalance the wheelchair so that the wheelchair tends to tip forward.

3. **Caster wheels**. The person's feet either need to be far enough in front of, above, or behind the front casters so that the casters can freely rotate without hitting the feet. The position of the foot supports will depend on the person's size and individual leg-to-seat surface support angle requirements (see pages 190-3, 241).

D Arm Supports⊕

Some people use arm supports (armrests) or laptrays to support their arms. Depending on how the person transfers, the arm supports may need to flip up or be removable. Arm supports should be as close to the person as possible so the person can retrieve or reposition herself. Whenever possible, arm support height should be adjustable.[9]

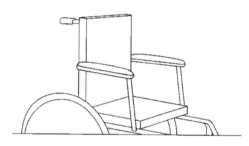

Fixed arm supports

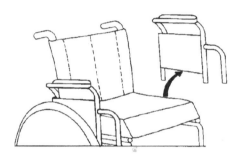

Removable arm supports

E Lower Leg Supports⊕ and Foot Supports

1. **Transfers**. Lower leg supports and foot supports may need to remove, swing away, or flip up to get out of the way during transfers.

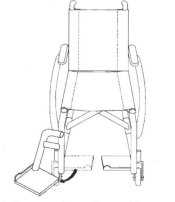

Swing-away lower leg and foot supports

Flip-up foot supports

2. **Foot boxes** or **bumpers** on the sides of the foot supports can be used if the person's feet need to be protected from injury, as in the case of a person whose skin or bones are fragile. Be sure the frame is wide enough to accommodate the foot boxes when the feet and legs are properly aligned.

Foot boxes

3. **Leg-to-seat surface angle** should be as close to vertical (90°) as possible to minimize the overall length of the wheelchair. This allows the person to turn around in the least possible space. However, if the person has limited knee flexion or other issues (assessed previously), the leg-to-seat surface angle may need to be greater than 90°.

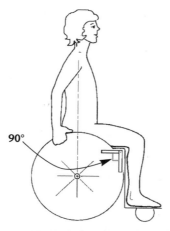

**Vertical (90°) leg-to-seat
surface angle**

F Cushion Covering

Covers over the cushions should:
- Be stretchy so as to not limit the compressive quality of the foam.
- Be easily cleanable.
- Allow air flow to prevent excessive heat build-up.
- Allow accessibility to the cushion so that changes can be made to the cushion if necessary.

G System Tilt

Tilting the entire seating system has been used for specific postural problems in the previous sections. Recognize that there may be a specific tilt angle for the person's optimal function. For instance, a person may need to be more upright to eat, use her hands and communicate. Also, the person may need another angle, such as tilted back, to rest. In this case, the seating/mobility system must have an adjustable tilt method.

1. Rear (Posterior) Tilt

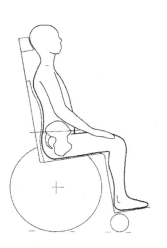

With a posterior tilt (tilt-in-space), the seat-to-back support angle does not change. Tilting the postural support device unit or seating/mobility system rearward (posteriorly) to reduce the effect of gravity can be helpful to:

- Decrease fatigue and conserve energy for people who have muscular weakness or limited endurance in the upright position.
- Decrease pressure under the bony areas of the buttocks.[13-16]
- Enhance comfort, especially if the person has decreased ability to move and shift weight.
- Improve posture.[17-18]
- Possibly slow the progression of spinal deformities.
- Control swelling of the lower extremities.
- Improve breathing[17], circulation, and digestion.
- Enhance function.[18-19]

The options of posterior tilt include:
- A fixed tilt of the mobility system (wheelchair).
- A fixed posterior tilt of the postural support device unit inside the mobility base.
- Adjustable tilt controlled either manually or by power.

2. Recline⊕

Recline means reclining the back support in order to increase the seat-to-back support angle. This is different than tilting the seating system backwards as a unit. Recline can be used for the same reasons as posterior tilt. However, if the person has increased tone and movements that are difficult to control, such as in persons with cerebral palsy, it is usually best to tilt the system rather than recline. Changing the seat-to-back support angle will change the support at the pelvis, the key area of postural support. In many situations, recline is helpful. For instance, in a boy with Duchenne's muscular dystrophy, recline will allow the boy to rest, use the urinal easily, and also to stretch his hip flexor muscles.

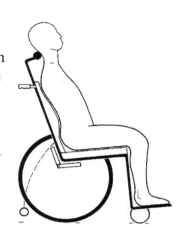

3. Adjustable Lateral (Sideways) Tilt

Tilting the seating system laterally (to the side) has been used with persons with profound neurological and orthopedic conditions such as fixed pelvic obliquity and scoliosis. Some deformities cause overlapping of bones, such as the pelvis and lower ribs, which can cause skin breakdown.[20] With these bony deformities, respiration, circulation, eating, and digestion[21, 22] can be affected. So, lateral tilt has been used to[20,23]:

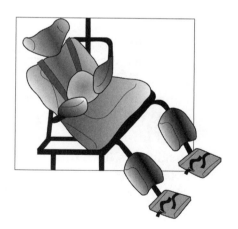

- Reduce the effect of gravity, to decrease overlapping of bones.
- Reduce skin breakdown in areas of high pressure and bone overlap.
- Improve comfort.
- Relieve pressure under the bony areas.[24]
- Assist with the movement of food through the digestive tract.[22]
- Increase sitting tolerance.
- Improve head balance
- Manage saliva.

Persons with the following diagnoses have utilized the lateral tilt: spastic quadriplegia due to cerebral palsy or other diseases to the brain, Duchenne's muscular dystrophy, *metatrophic dwarfism* and *torticollis, spinal muscle atrophy, spina bifida,* and *multiple sclerosis.*[20-26] Sometimes an oblique angle of tilt is necessary, but should be designed and used with caution.[12,26]

4. Forward (Anterior) Tilt

Tilting the postural support device unit forward (anteriorly) for short periods of time is used for functional activities or to improve trunk control. As with opening the seat-to-back support angle by sloping the seat cushion down towards the front (see page 140), this option can be beneficial for children with weak or floppy trunks.[18,33] In this posture, the child will have to work hard to sit up and will need active trunk musculature. Make sure that the child has time to rest in other postures, so the postural muscles required to sit upright are not overworked. An anti-thrust seat may help stabilize her pelvis and prevent it from sliding down and posteriorly tilting.

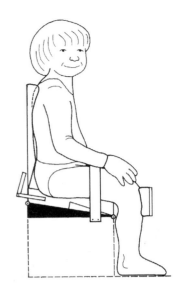

H Transporting the Seating/Mobility System

1. **Foldability.** The environments in which the person uses the seating/mobility system, and the necessity of transporting the seating/mobility system will help you decide if it needs to fold. The seating system may need to be taken out of the mobility base for transport, or the seating/mobility system may be transported as one unit.

2. **Safety during transport.** When traveling in a motor vehicle, it is generally safest for the person to transfer to a vehicle seat and use the vehicle seat belt system. If the person is to be transported in the wheelchair, the wheelchair must be facing forward and secured to the vehicle. The person should be secured to the vehicle with crash-tested seat belts. A wheelchair that has been designed and tested for use in motor vehicles is referred to as a WC19 wheelchair. These wheelchairs have four crash-tested securement points where wheelchair tiedown⊕ straps and hooks can be attached. If the person does not have a WC19, the tiedown straps should be attached to welded or strong, non-moveable junctions of the wheelchair frame. Do not attach tiedowns to adjustable or removable parts of the wheelchair. Wheelchair tiedowns should be crash-tested and strong enough so that the wheelchair frame is securely held to the vehicle floor. It is best if floor anchor points for rear tiedown straps are located directly behind the rear securement points on the wheelchair. The front tiedown straps should anchor to the vehicle floor at points that are spaced wider than the wheelchair. The wheelchair rider must be restrained by a pelvic belt⊕ and shoulder belt⊕, which are connected to the vehicle. All other components of the seating system are used for postural supports, not for vehicular safety. Seating system components will not restrain the wheelchair rider in a crash. For further information, please refer to *Ride Safe* from the University of Michigan Health System.[34]

References

1. Cooper R, Boninger M, Cooper R, Koontz, A, Eisler H. Considerations for the selection and fitting of manual wheelchairs for optimal mobility. *Proceedings from the 21st International Seating Symposium.* 2005:59-60.

2. Richter WM, Axelson PW. Opti-fit wheelchair fitting system final report. 2007. NIH SBIR Phase I Grant #1 R43 HDO47071-01.

3. Richter WM. Personal communication. Fall 2008.

4. Boninger ML, Baldwin M, Cooper RA, Koontz A, Chan L. Manual wheelchair pushrim biomechanics and axle position. *Arch Phys Med Rehabil.* 2000 May;81(5):608-13.

5. Van der Woude, LHV, Veeger RH, Rozendal, RH, Sargeant TJ. Seat height in handrim wheelchair propulsion. *J Rehabil Res Dev.* 1989:31-50.

6. Consortium for Spinal Cord Medicine. *Preservation of Upper Limb Function following Spinal Cord Injury: A Clinical Practice Guideline for Health-Care Professionals.* PVA; 2005.

7. Samuelsson KA, Tropp H, Nylander E, Gerdie B. The effect of rear-wheel propulsion on seating ergonomics and mobility efficiency in wheelchair users with spinal cord injuries: A pilot study. *J Rehabil Res Dev.* 2004 Jan-Feb;41(1):65-74.

8. Richter WM, Axelson PW. Low-impact wheelchair propulsion: Achievable and acceptable. *J Rehabil Res Dev.* 2005 May-Jun;42(3 Suppl 1):21-33.

9. Bergen A, Presperin J, Tallman T. *Positioning for Function: Wheelchairs and Other Assistive Technologies.* Valhalla, NY: Valhalla Rehabilitation Publications, Ltd.; 1990.

Ride Safe. Rehabilitation Engineering Research Center on Wheelchair Transportation Safety from the University of Michigan Health System, University of Michigan Transportation Research Institute. 2005. Available at: www.travelsafer.org.

10. Jones CK, Kanyer B. Review of tilt systems. *Proceedings from the 8th International Seating Symposium.* 1992:85-7.

11. Michael SM, Porter D, Pountney TE. Tilted seat position for non-ambulant individuals with neurological and neuromuscular impairment: A systematic review. *Clin Rehabil.* 2007 Dec 21(12):1063-74.

12. Ward D. *Prescriptive Seating for Wheeled Mobility.* Ft. Lauderdale, FL: HealthWealth International; 1994.

13. Hobson D, Comparative effects of posture on pressure and shear at the body-seat interface. *J Rehabil Res Dev.* 1992 Fall;29(4):21-31.

14. Pellow TR. A comparison of interface pressure readings to wheelchair cushions and positioning: A pilot study. *Can J Occup Ther* 1999;66:140-49.

15. Burns SP, Betz KL. Seating pressures with conventional dynamic wheelchair cushions in tetrapelgia. *Arch Phys Med Rehabil.* 1999;80:566-71.

16. Henderson JL, Price SH, Brandstater ME, Mandac BR. Efficacy of three measures to relieve pressure in seated persons with spinal cord injury. *Arch Phys Med Rehabil.* 1994;75:535-9.

17. Chan A, Heck CS. The effects of tilting the seating position of a wheelchair on respiration, posture, fatigue, voice volume and exertion outcomes in individuals with advanced multiple sclerosis. *J Rehabil Outcomes Meas.* 1999;3:1-14.

18. McClenaghan BA, Thombs L, Milner M. Effects of seat-surface inclination on postural stability and function of the upper extremities of children with cerebral palsy. *Dev Med Child Neuro.* 1992;34:40-8.

19. Nwaobi OM. Seating orientations and upper extremity function in children with cerebral palsy. *Phys Ther.* 1987;67:1209-12.

20. Tanguay S, Peterson B. When to think about lateral tilt and why. *Proceedings from the 24th International Seating Symposium.* 2008:117-9.

21. Hardwick K, Handley R. The use of automated seating and mobility systems for management of dysphagia in individuals with multiple disabilities. *Proceedings from the 9th International Seating Symposium.* 1993:271-3.

22. Hardwick K. Therapeutic seating and positioning for individuals with dysphagia. *Proceedings from the 22nd International Seating Symposium.* 2006:46.

23. Cooper D. A retrospective of three years of lateral tilt-in-space. *Proceedings from the 17th International Seating Symposium.* 2001:87-8.

24. Ma E, Banks M. Head-righting with lateral tilt and seating: Are there pressure management consequences? *Proceedings from the 22nd International Seating Symposium.* 2006:138-40.

25. Clements K, Geddes J, Bebb M, Reeves J. Lateral tilt-in-space: An innovative design for a unique problem. *Proceedings from the Australian Rehabilitation and Assistive Technology Association.* 2004:1-7.

26. Whitmeyer J. A dual axis positioning in space system to reduce the effect of gravity on spinal curves. *Proceedings from the 9th Annual RESNA Conference.* 1989:167-8.

27. Dilger N, Ling W. The influence of inclined wedge sitting on infantile postural kyphosis. *Proceedings from the 3rd International Seating Symposium.* 1987:52-7.

28. Myhr U, von Wendt L. Improvement of functional sitting position for children with cerebral palsy. *Dev Med Child Neurol.* 1991;33:246-56.

29. Myhr U, von Wendt L, Norrlin S, Radell U. Five-year follow-up of functional sitting position in children with cerebral palsy. *Dev Med Child Neurol.* 1995;37(7):587-96.

30. Post K, Murphy TE. The use of forward sloping seats by individuals with disabilities. *Proceedings from the 5th International Seating Symposium.* 1989:54-60.

31. Meidaner JA, The effects of sitting positions on trunk extension for children with motor impairment. *Pediatr Phys Ther.* 1990;2:11-14.

32. Janssen-Potten YJ, Seelen HA, Dukker J, Hulson T, Drost MR. The effect of seat tilting on pelvic position, balance control, and compensatory postural muscle use in paraplegic subjects. *Arch Phys Med Rehabil.* 2000;81:401-8.

33. Reid DT, Sochaaniwskyi A. Effects of anterior-tipped seating on respiratory function of normal children and children with cerebral palsy. *Int J Rehabil Res.* 1991; 14(3):203-12.

34. Ride Safe. Rehabilitation Engineering Research Center on Wheelchair Transportation Safety from the University of Michigan Health System, University of Michigan Transportation Research Institute. 2005. Available at: www.travelsafer.org

Aaron's Seating and Mobility System

The team decided that Aaron requires a seating system inside a new wheelchair with a left one-arm drive mechanism. This wheelchair will be used at school and at home. A seating system for his current wheelchair will also be fabricated. This wheelchair will be used by the family when they leave the house because it is easier to fold and transport. The following details of the seating/mobility system are given for the one-arm drive wheelchair.

1. **Lower back support:** Contoured support behind pelvis and sacrum
2. **Upper back support:** Firm but contoured to the shape of Aaron's back. Extends to 1" (2.5 cm) under his shoulder blades.
3. **Seat cushion:** Anti-thrust seat.
4. **Seat-to-back support angle:** 90°.
5. **Lower back support-to-upper back support angle:** Angled backwards slightly.
6. **Leg-to-seat surface angle:** 90°, but allowing more flexion of knees.
7. **Foot support-to-leg angle:** 90°.
8. **Tilt of the seating system:** 0° in relationship to gravity.
9. **Anterior (front) pelvic support:** 1" (2.5 cm) wide positioning belt with a push-button set at 90° to the seat cushion.
10. **Lateral (side) pelvic support:** Hip block on right side of pelvis.
11. **Medial (middle) upper thigh support:** Wedged-shaped block on a flip-down bracket with a push button that Aaron can control.
12. **Ankle/foot supports:** Left ankle strap set at 45° to foot support.
13. **Arm support:** Laptray.

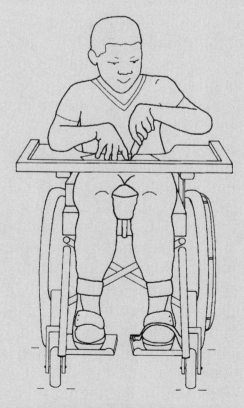

Final seating/mobility system

Seating System in Relationship to Mobility Base

14. **Seat height:** Low as possible for Aaron to stand from wheelchair.
15. **Width of seating/mobility system:** Narrow as possible, but wide enough to allow room for shoes over Aaron's AFO's.
16. **Position of seating system within mobility system:** Set far enough back in the wheelchair so that his shoulders are in line with the axle.
17. **Arm supports:** Desk-length, height-adjustable arm supports.
18. **Leg supports:** Swing-away for transfers.

19. **Foot supports:** Flip-up for transfers.
20. **Cushion covering:** Washable and well ventilated.
21. **Seating system removable from mobility system:** Does not need to remove from one-arm drive. A second seating system will be fabricated that needs to remove from original wheelchair.
22. **Wheelchair foldability:** Does not need to fold.
23. **Push-handle height:** 36" (91.4 cm).
24. **Left one-arm drive mechanism.**

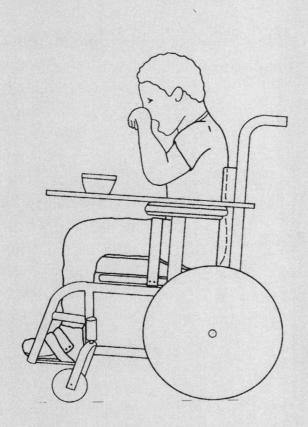

Improved function in final seating/mobility system

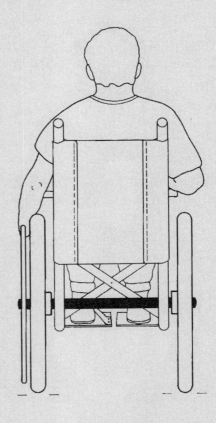

Left one-arm wheelchair

Part V

PUTTING IT ALL TOGETHER

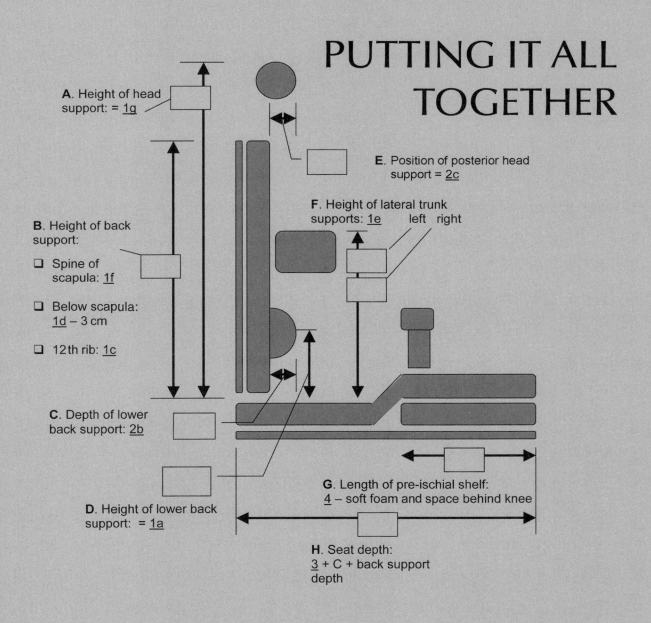

A. Height of head support: = <u>1g</u>

B. Height of back support:

- ❑ Spine of scapula: <u>1f</u>
- ❑ Below scapula: <u>1d</u> – 3 cm
- ❑ 12th rib: <u>1c</u>

C. Depth of lower back support: <u>2b</u>

D. Height of lower back support: = <u>1a</u>

E. Position of posterior head support = <u>2c</u>

F. Height of lateral trunk supports: <u>1e</u>   left   right

G. Length of pre-ischial shelf: <u>4</u> – soft foam and space behind knee

H. Seat depth: <u>3</u> + C + back support depth

Chapter 16
Summarizing

We need to organize and summarize our findings from the assessment and simulation in order to design the seating/mobility system. There are many ways to do this. The following outline is one way to organize the significant findings. It is also included in the Assessment Form in Appendix A. Summarize the following five elements:

- The person's postural and functional objectives.
- The objectives of the seating system.
- The objectives of the mobility system and other objectives.
- The characteristics and components of the seating system.
- The seating system in relationship to the mobility system.

Summarize:

A The Person's Postural and Functional Objectives

Remember, we obtained these specific objectives from translating information from hand simulation into words (page 96-9). These objectives were further clarified while assessing the person's function when simulating with materials (page 111).

B The Objectives of the Seating System

The objectives of the seating system should correspond directly to the person's postural and functional objectives. Simulating with materials helped to clarify the objectives of the seating system (pages 115-6).

C | The Objectives of the Mobility System and Other Objectives

This section includes issues covered in chapters 15 and 17:
- How the person relates to the mobility base, such as wheeling efficiency, transferring to and from the wheelchair, manipulating components such as brakes, seat belts, arm, lower leg, and foot supports.
- How the mobility base relates to the environment, such as issues of stability, seat surface height at the front edge, wheelchair width, and transportability.
- Other considerations include health concerns such as reducing the forces that contribute to contractures and deformities; considering the person's bowel and bladder control, tolerance to sitting, and growth or changes in the person's condition.

D | The Characteristics and Components of the Seating System

Summarize the charateristics of the Seating System components:

- Lower back support
- Upper back support
- Seat cushion
- Seat-to-lower back support angle
- Lower back support-to-upper back support angle
- Leg-to-seat surface angle
- Foot support-to-leg angle
- Tilt of the seating system
- Pelvic supports
  Anterior (front)
  Lateral (side)
- Trunk supports
  Anterior (front)
  Lateral (side)

- Upper leg support
  Medial (middle)
  Lateral (side)
  Superior (top)
- Lower leg supports
  Anterior (front)
  Posterior (back)
- Ankle/foot supports
- Head/neck supports
- Shoulder girdle supports
- Arm supports
- Laptray
- Wedges (scapulae, arms)
- Troughs (legs, arms)
- Straps
- Adjustability of components and angles

E   The Seating System in Relationship to the Mobility System

- Seat surface height at front edge
- Width of seating/mobility system
- Position of seating system within mobility system
- Rear axle position
- Cushion covering
- Seating system removable from mobility system
- Wheelchair foldability
- Push handle height
- System tilt or recline

F   Translating Body Measurements into Seating Components

Below are helpful hints when translating body measurements into seating component measurements:

- Allow for the thickness of foam padding you plan to use for the different parts of the seating system. This is especially important when determining the seat cushion depth, back support height, and leg support length.
- Add the thickness of the back support when determining the seat cushion depth. Of course this depends on if and how the back support is connected to the seat cushion.
- The relationship between the seat cushion and back support will determine the back support height.
- Add the seat cushion thickness at the front edge when determining the leg support length.
- Thickness of foam padding over trunk, pelvic, leg, and arm supports must be added into the measurement of these supports.

Seating systems that allow for adjustability are helpful so fine-tuning can be done at the fitting. Appendix C provides one example of seating component measurements. See Appendix C for specific translation of body measurements to component measurements.

G Fitting Tips

1. **Anti-thrust seat/pre-ischial shelf**
   An adjustable pre-ischial shelf is helpful. If possible, the seat cover should be made in such a way that the seat shape (pre-ischial shelf) can be easily accessed and modified during the fitting. The same is true for the lower back support.

2. **Pelvic control**
   a. **Direction of positioning belt**: The direction of the positioning belt will greatly affect the resulting pelvic support. The belt can be positioned at 90, 60, or 45° to the seatbase. Both sides of the belt can be positioned the same or assymetrically to achieve *the person's* neutral posture.
   b. A **"force-localizing pad"** can be placed under the positioning belt at a location where a specific force is required.
      - For example, to de-rotate a pelvic rotation with the left side back, place the left side of the positioning belt at 90° to the seatbase and the right side of the belt at 45° to the seatbase with a force-localizing pad just in front of or slightly below the right ASIS. This, along with other pelvic control techniques, will help to reduce the forward rotation of the right side of the pelvis.

3. **Seat depth: Type of back support**
   The seat depth of the seat system can depend greatly on the type of back support used. For example, when using an adjustable back upholstery to accommodate a thoracic kyphosis, the seat depth can be measured based on upper leg measurements. But, when using a rigid back support for the same case, the seat depth may need to allow for the both the kyphosis and the thickness of the solid back support. A back support with varied angles (e.g., bi-angular back support) can also help to accommodate the extra depth of a kyphosis.

4. **Consider all aspects of pelvic support**
   The pre-ischial shelf, lower back support, and anterior pelvic support work together to hold the pelvis to the rear of the seat cushion and as upright as is possible and practical. Only when this is achieved can the rest of the fitting be effective.

5. **Lateral (side) trunk supports**
   When using lateral trunk supports, it may be helpful to have the trunk supports (pads and hardware) ready for the fitting, but to find the specific location and angle during the fitting. Mark the location and mount the trunk supports in the same fitting session.

Note: See page 258 for "Tech Tips for Growth Adjustability".

Part VI

SPECIAL CONSIDERATIONS

Chapter 17
Seating/Mobility Guidelines for Specific Conditions

A General Considerations

The concepts in this book can be applied to anyone who requires a seating/mobility system. However, according to the person's diagnosis or condition, there may be a few added special considerations.

1. **Limited tolerance to upright sitting**. If the person has limited tolerance to sitting upright because of *hypotension*, pain, fatigue, or problems with breathing, circulation, pressure, or swallowing, the seating system may need to be tilted backwards, as needed, during the day. This consideration also applies to a person who uses a forward-sloped seat for functional activities, and needs to tilt back for times of rest.

2. **Seizures**. If the person has seizures, safety straps may be needed to prevent a fall out of the chair. If the person stiffens with force during a seizure, the components and hardware will need to be particularly durable and reinforced. If a person is prone to unpredictable, severe seizures leading to involuntary movement, power mobility may not be a safe option.

3. **Bowel/bladder control issues.** If the person lacks bowel and/or bladder control, the seat cover should be easy to wash. Waterproof material must be used with care. It is not elastic, can keep moisture next to the skin for a long time, and as a result may contribute to pressure sores. See pages 228 and 242 for further information on cushion covers.

4. **Surgery**. If the person is scheduled for surgery that may affect her seated posture, movement, and/or function, wait until after surgery to make or order the seating system.

5. **Anticipated body changes**:
   a. **Growth**. If the seating/mobility system is being made for a child or young adult, make it adjustable for the expected growth of the child.
   b. **Progressive conditions**. If the person's physical status is expected to either progressively improve or deteriorate, the seating/mobility system should have built-in adjustability for future changes. This means creating a system with parts that can be removed, adjusted, or modified at a later date. This category includes persons with traumatic injuries whose bodies may change due to weight gain, *atrophy*, spasticity, and so on. If a person has a progressive disease and is getting her first power wheelchair, it needs to be upgradeable.

c. **Weight changes**. If a person is expected to gain or lose weight, consider adjustability. For example, many people with traumatic injuries lose weight before the wheelchair is ordered, then regain the weight later.

Tech Tips

Growth Adjustability
- Growth tail will allow easy changes in seat depth.

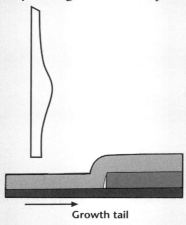

Growth tail

- Removable covers will allow easy access to adjust supports.
- "I" or "T" shaped back supports will allow lateral trunk supports to be closer to the body, and then move laterally when the child grows.

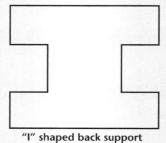

"I" shaped back support

- Adjustable lower back supports at the sacrum will allow the sacral support to grow with the child.
- Adjustable lower leg support assembly⊕ can extend in length when the child grows.
- Adjustable seat and wheelchair frames (both width and depth) will allow the wheelchair to grow with the child.

Note: If it has been 4 months of more since the assessment until fitting of the seating/mobility system, check to make sure that there are no changes. It might be helpful to re-measure if the child is growing.

Note: If a person has had a disability for a long time, it may be difficult for her to accept suggestions for changes in the seating/mobility system. In this case, it is best to make a few temporary changes and have her try it out prior to ordering any new equipment. See Richard's story.

6. **Orthosis/prosthesis.** If a person will be wearing an orthosis (brace) or prosthesis (artificial limb) while seated in the system, the seating system must accommodate the size and shape of the orthosis or prosthesis. Typically, less postural support will be required of the seating system when the person wears the orthosis or prosthesis. If the person sometimes wears the orthosis or prosthesis, and sometimes does not, the seating supports will have to accommodate both situations. For example, lateral trunk supports for a child with cerebral palsy wearing a spinal orthosis may need to prevent excessive side-to-side movement. When not wearing the orthosis, the trunk supports may need to provide more postural control.

B Cerebral Palsy

For persons with celebral palsy (CP), follow the assessment presented in this book, but always remember that while the book separates the parts of the body for the purposes of clarification, the body must be viewed as a whole. Look at the child's movement patterns. Movement is expression. Ask and observe what movements are available to the child. What movement can be encouraged to allow the child to function? What movement should be restricted to allow the child to function? Is the child looking for stability and more surface contact? How does supporting one part of the body affect the other parts of the body? For instance:

- A child who stiffens and extends her legs and thrusts out of the seating system, may be looking for stability. If you provide her with a lot of contact and stability to her pelvis, trunk, and legs, she may start to relax.

- A different child who stiffens and extends her legs may be employing these movements as a form of expression. So, some of this movement must be allowed. This child may require more support during some activities and more freedom of movement during other activities. Dynamic seating components may be appropriate for this child.

There is no cookbook recipe, as each child is different. That is why it is critical to get input from the entire team, fully assess the child, and simulate with your hands and materials. This process cannot be rushed.

With aging, changes may occur in regards to pain levels, bowel and bladder function, and bone density. Heart, breathing, and gastrointestinal problems are reported to increase as adults with CP age.[1-3] Because of a lifetime of muscle imbalance, skeletal and postural asymmetries, and overuse issues, pain tends to progress as persons with CP get older.[4-6] Also, *osteopenia* is common in older persons with CP.[6,7] Fractures are five times more common in older persons with CP than in younger persons with CP.[8] Also, people commonly have less energy and need more rest as they age.[9] So, when assessing an older person with CP, recognize that the seating/mobility system will need to change as the person's needs change. Additional seating supports may be needed. Options for tilt may provide some rest and relief from pain. Consider power mobility, if appropriate, to increase function and conserve energy.[9]

C Traumatic Brain Injury

In adults or children, *traumatic brain injuries* (TBI) occur from many sources, including accidents, falls, sports, abuse, and gunshot wounds. Each person with a TBI will present differently. The most important element to consider when seating a person with a TBI is that her needs will change as she progresses through the different phases of recovery.[10] In the early phase of TBI, the person is typically in a coma, has high tone, and is in a flexed or extended posture (or a combination of the two).[11] As the person's brain begins to recover, she will come in and out of consciousness. Changes in cognition, perception, tone, movement, and function can occur quickly or over time. The later stages of recovery are identified when the person reaches her first plateau in terms of motor, functional, and cognitive abilities.[12]

Differences between Persons with CP and TBI

Persons with TBI differ from children with cerebral palsy in the following ways[13]:

- Tone and movement patterns can be varied and may change over time.
- There may be contractures due to poor bed positioning or *heterotopic ossification* after the accident.
- Endurance is limited in the early phases of a TBI.
- A variety of cognitive deficits, such as distractibility, memory and judgment impairments, affect safe power mobility.
- The TBI often affects the person's emotions and can manifest as impulsiveness, aggressiveness, and irritability.
- Visual perceptual problems are common, and can affect mobility.

Because of these factors, when seating a person with a TBI, generally follow the seating advice for children with cerebral palsy listed above and in the rest of this book. However, note that the seating and mobility system for a person with a TBI must be able to change and adjust as the person improves over time. Wheelchairs that allow tilt and changeable angles, specifically adjustable seat-to-back support angle and leg-to-seat surface angles, are optimal. Seating systems should provide more support in the initial stages of recovery. Consider the person's alertness, orientation, in addition to cognitive and perceptual status, especially when deciding if power mobility is an option. A person with a TBI might physically be able to drive a power wheelchair, but might lack the visual perception, cognition, and judgment to do so safely.

Seating/Mobility Intervention in the Early Phases of Recovery

The following components allow for easy adjustability[14,15]:

- **Seat cushions** that are firm and supportive. Depending on the person's ability to move, the seat cushions may need to relieve pressure. Typically, molded systems are not used in the first year because the person is changing and requires a seat cushion that can also change.

- **Back supports** that are firm but can be easily modified. The pelvis and sacrum may require a lower back support. The upper back support should be firm, supportive, and easy to modify.

- **Seat-to-back support angle** should be adjustable for changes in hip flexion, as well as pelvic and trunk flexibility.

- **Trunk supports, leg supports, laptrays, and head supports** should be adjustable.

- **Adjustable tilt.** If the seating/mobility system has an adjustable tilt, it can be tilted backwards for rest, and also be upright for functional activities.

- **Foot propulsion.** Some people need access to the floor for foot propulsion. Floor access requires a lower seat height and/or a shorter seat depth than might be used otherwise.

In the late phase of the recovery process, the focus is less on the adjustability of the seating and mobility system and more on the longer-term functional goals.[12] Independent mobility, whether that is walking or propelling a wheelchair, is a high-priority goal. If the person does not have the motor function or energy to propel efficiently and effectively, and the person has the necessary perceptual and cognitive skills, then consider power mobility.[11]

A particular challenge in this population is projecting what the person may require in the future. When the person is discharged from rehabilitation, a wheelchair must be purchased, because it is virtually impossible to rent wheelchairs with tilt and extensive seating supports. In a person with a TBI, recovery can take many months. In later stages, the person may progress to sitting upright and using her arms and legs for propulsion. At some point, power may be an option as well. Deciding on a new wheelchair when the person has not yet fully recovered is difficult.[16] The team must use their knowledge and experience with TBI, along with the recovery course of the particular person with the TBI to predict and plan for the person's seating/mobility needs.

D Orthopedic Issues

In juvenile rheumatoid arthritis (JRA), the child develops swelling and pain in the joints, often leading to *contractures.* In arthrogryposis multiplex congenita (AMC), the baby is born with joint contractures, often accompanied by muscle weakness. Two types of contractures are commonly seen in AMC. In one type, the person has flexed and dislocated hips, extended knees, *equinovarus deformity* of the feet and ankles, internally rotated shoulders, and flexed elbows and wrists. In another type, the hips are abducted and externally rotated, the knees are flexed, there are equinovarus deformities of the feet and ankles, internally rotated shoulders, extended elbows, and flexed wrists.[17] Scoliosis is present in up to one-third of AMC cases.[18]

Baby with AMC:
first type of contractures

Baby with AMC:
second type of contractures

Seating/Mobility Priorities

Follow the guidelines in this book, but prioritize the following seating objectives[19]:

- **Enhance comfort**, especially if the person has difficulty moving or weight shifting.
- **Accommodate the joint contractures**; do not try to correct them, unless the contractures are beginning to change due to therapy, exercises, or surgery.
- **Enhance function** with seating/mobility choices and technical aids. Consider power mobility at an early age to diminish fatigue.[18]

Often persons with AMC or JRA walk, but require a mobility device for longer distances. Also, they may require modifications for a variety of seating surfaces at home, school, and work, such as, in the kitchen to prepare meals, and at the computer or desk.

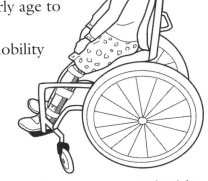

Seating system to accomodate joint
contractures for a girl with AMC

E Osteogenesis Imperfecta

Osteogenesis imperfecta (OI) or "brittle bone disease" is an inherited disorder of the connective tissue. It is characterized by fragile bones, frequent fractures, short height, limited joint mobility, and full sensation. The level of involvement varies dramatically from person to person.[20] Even though the person's bones are fragile and need to be protected, overprotecting a person with OI can be just as emotionally devastating as fractured bones.[21] The seating/mobility system should[18,19]:

- **Protect** the person from collisions and potential fractures (add bumpers, lightweight trays).

- **Be lightweight** for easy propulsion.

- **Provide shock absorption** (pneumatic tires and suspension systems).

- **Be adaptable and adjustable**. Components should be easily removable.

- **Enhance function**. A person with OI is typically of short stature, so to enhance access wheels and brakes, try various wheel sizes, axle locations, and extension handles on brakes.

- **Provide postural support and stability**. The seating system should provide postural support to enhance arm function. It should also provide extra stability to prevent unwanted movement within the seat that can lead to fractures.

- **Adapt to casts**. For leg fractures, the knees may be in extension. Elevating leg supports or a plywood insert under the seat cushion can be used temporarily. If the person fractures an arm, consider renting a power chair temporarily.[19]

- **The seating system can be built as a one-piece unit** that is removable from the wheelchair, allowing it to be used as a lifting/transfer device. This can reduce the risk of fractures that can occur when the child is lifted out of the seat.[22]

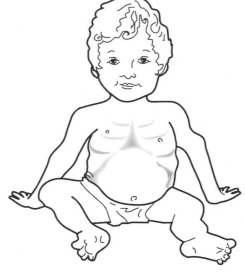

Child with OI

F   Muscular Dystrophy

Muscular dystrophy (MD) is a condition in which the muscles progressively become weaker. One common type, Duchenne's muscular dystrophy (DMD), occurs in boys and usually is detected by 5 years of age. The boy walks with a waddling gait and has difficulty climbing stairs because of weakness in the pelvic and abdominal musculature. Usually between 8 and 10 years of age, the boy falls more and becomes more fatigued.[23] At this point, a power wheelchair with a manual wheelchair backup becomes necessary. A power wheelchair is helpful to avoid excessive fatigue. One of the biggest difficulties in a boy with DMD is the development of spinal deformities, usually lordosis, scoliosis, or *kyphoscoliosis*[24-26] because of the weakening of the abdominal muscles. By the age of 15, usually the young man requires postural support to sit upright. As muscular weakness progresses, respiration is affected. This occurs by the early 20s, and sometimes earlier. Respiratory insufficiency is a sign of the pre-terminal stage of DMD. Seating supports depend on the boy's level of weakness and function.

Seating Goals

In the early stages of MD, the seating goals are[11]:

- **Independent mobility**. This may mean providing powered mobility sooner so that the boy can keep up with his peers.
- **Maximize function**. Postural support should enhance arm and hand function. Sometimes when the abdominal muscles are weak, the boy relies on his arms for support. Providing abdominal support can free his arms for function. Also, seating intervention should make transfers as easy as possible.
- **Delay spinal deformities and hip flexion contractures**. In conjunction with range of motion exercises, power tilt, recline, and seating supports can help keep the boy more in midline. Timing is critical for seating intervention. Once the spinal deformity begins, it can progress rapidly.[27] Some have found that the progression of scoliosis can be slowed by supporting the spine in extension to increase weight bearing through the facet joints.[28,29]
- **Enhance comfort**. Postural support can help improve comfort by preventing excessive pressure in one area, for instance, on one ischial tuberosity.[30]

As the disease progresses, the child may or may not undergo spinal surgery. In either case, as the disease progresses, the seating goals are[11]:

- **Maximize comfort** because shifting weight to relieve pressure is more difficult, a pressure relief cushion, tilt, and back support recline may be appropriate.
- **Encourage independent mobility**.
- **Maximize function.**
- **Accommodate spinal deformities, contractures, and/or a fused spine** by using postural supports.

- **Prevent secondary complications** such as tissue breakdown and respiratory problems.

If the boy undergoes spinal surgery, his ability to weight shift to relieve pressure is decreased. The weight-bearing pressures may actually be increased following surgery, because, in many cases, the weight is brought back over the pelvis when the spine is aligned. Therefore, seating must help with pressure relief, such as, tilting the seating system and modifying the pressure-relief cushion.[22]

Seating Intervention[11,24,27]

In the early stages of DMD, when the boy has **mild weakness**, less support is needed. During this period, the boy may only need a firm flat seat cushion, plus adding some pelvic, hip and thigh supports such as gentle contours on the seat cushion. Assess each boy individually. Remember, it is essential to maximize function and independent mobility.

For a child with **moderate weakness**, it becomes important to support the boy's weakened pelvis and trunk, so that the child can rest these areas in a good posture while using his hands, legs, and head to function. Use a seat cushion and back support with appropriate postural supports. Consider an elastic anterior abdominal support,[24] binder, or corset to support the weak abdominal muscles, so that he does not need to lean on his legs or laptray to function. An anterior abdominal support can also prevent too much anterior pelvic tilt and lumbar lordosis (see page 149). At this point, or even sooner, consider power tilt and recline. Often boys with DMD need to lean forward for better arm function. However, with the powerful effect of gravity and weakened abdominal muscles, the hip flexors get very tight, leading to more anterior tilt and lumbar lordosis. Power recline and tilt can allow the boy to rest, stretch the *hip flexor muscles*, and allow for easier urinal use.[22]

When a boy develops **significant weakness and involvement**, it is important to help him to stay in his chair as long as possible and use whatever function is available. Consider power mobility, recline, and tilt, as well as appropriate seating supports. If scoliosis develops, lateral pelvic and trunk supports, a molded seating system, or an orthosis may support the trunk. If the seating system is too rigid, it may interfere with the boy's activities of daily living. Overall, the team must find the balance between seating supports and important functional activities. In the later stages of muscular dystrophy, consider the need to relieve pressure with pressure-relief cushions, tilting, or reclining the seating system. At this point, a caregiver or mechanical lift will be needed for transfers. The seating system should accommodate for this situation. It should also accommodate for urinals. As the disease progresses, tilting the system is important for comfort, fatigue, and relief from the gravitational forces on the spine. One of the few blessings with DMD is that the musculature around the mouth is often spared, making it a dependable control site for many years.[22] Older, ventilator-dependent young men may use mini joysticks with very light resistance, operated with lip and tongue movement.[22] Mouthsticks and tongue switches may also be utilized. The power wheelchair may need to accommodate ventilators.

G Pain

Many people who require seating and mobility systems have pain or uncomfortable sensations. When determining seating for these people, it is helpful to know whether the pain comes from the *peripheral nervous system* or the *central nervous system*.[31] This may require some additional assessment by medical professionals. If the pain comes from the peripheral nervous system, changing the seating/mobility system may help relieve the pain by using specific supports, tilt, or pressure-relief cushions as presented in this book.[32] Certain types of pain might respond in whole or in part to other modalites that do not involve seating options. In such cases, consider the following options before addressing seating issues:

- Movement therapy such as *Feldenkrais, neurodevelopmental therapy*, and *Aston patterning.*
- Manual therapy (hands-on therapy) such as *craniosacral therapy, visceral manipulation, nerve manipulation, myofascial release, joint mobilization, strain/counterstrain*, and the *McKenzie approach.*
- Exercise.
- *Oriental* and *ayurvedic medicine.*
- Medicines, herbs, and *homeopathy.*

Remember, it is important that the person is fully assessed and the seating/mobility system modified so that it is as comfortable as possible.

H Multiple Sclerosis

Many persons with *multiple sclerosis* (MS) have either lost their ability to walk or are in fear of doing so. Within 15 years of onset, 50% of persons with multiple sclerosis (MS) will require assistance with walking.[33] On an emotional level, introducing seating/mobility to someone in the early stages of MS can be a tricky task. If the person's function has only decreased slightly, it may be difficult for her to face the fact that she may lose a lot of strength and function in the future, and be reliant on technology.[34] In such cases, it might help initially to rent equipment rather than buy it,[35] or to purchase an upgradeable wheelchair.[16]

The range of physical, emotional, urinary, and cognitive issues varies widely in persons with MS, as does progression of the disease. Because of these factors, each person with MS must be individually assessed. It is essential to get input from the team familiar with the person and answer the following questions[36,37]:

- Do the person's symptoms progress between attacks? Does the person have a progressive loss of function and no remissions?
- What are the changes in function in the last 1-2 years?
- Does the person fatigue? Fatigue is very common in persons with MS, especially in hot weather.
- If considering power mobility, does the person have the motor control, visual processing, and cognitive judgment required for the safe use of power mobility?

Seating/Mobility Interventions

Based on the assessment and the answers to these questions, the seating team must consider the following and be willing to try a variety of seating options[37]:

- **Change**. Because of the unpredictable course of MS, seating and mobility components must be able to change. Sometimes a person may require more postural support, and sometimes less support. Sometimes a person with MS requires a wheelchair, but might not during a remission. When a person needs wheeled mobility for the first time, it is more practical and psychologically gentler to acquire a loaner wheelchair rather than buy a wheelchair.[38] The problem with loaner wheelchairs is that they are difficult to customize.[16] Another option is to start out with a lightweight wheelchair with necessary postural supports, and upgrade it as the person's needs change. An advantage to purchasing an upgradeable wheelchair is that seating system upgrades can be purchased as the person changes without purchasing a whole new wheelchair.[16]
- **Fatigue**. Even though a person with MS might be able to walk or propel a wheelchair, these activities might take so much energy that pain sets in and affects the person's quality of life.[39,40] In this case, consider power mobility, such as a power wheelchair or scooter. Lightweight and ultralight wheelchairs are critical to reduce energy expenditure.

- **Spasticity and contractures**. Changes in tone, often resulting in contractures, are common. Consider postural supports that can be adapted over time. Contractures of hamstring and adductor muscles are common. Adjustable footplates that allow more knee flexion and hip adduction are helpful.
- **Skin integrity**. As a person's disease progresses, the risk of skin breakdown also increases due to reduction in sensation, difficulty in repositioning, and moisture from incontinence. Consider pressure-relief cushions with appropriate covers (see Chapter 14).
- **Pain**. Many people with MS experience pain. The type and source of pain must be analyzed to determine whether seating intervention can be of help (see section on pain).[41]
- **Sensory problems**. A variety of sensory impairments and strange sensations are common in persons with MS. Plastic-coated handrims help with proprioception. Gloves, and the use of mag wheels instead of spoked wheels, help prevent fingers getting caught in the spokes.
- **Vision**. Eighty percent of people with MS have visual difficulties. The person must have functional driving vision to drive a power wheelchair safely.[41]

When moving to a power mobility base, the base should be upgradeable to permit changes in controllers (e.g., from joystick to switches to head control to sip and puff control). Tilt and recline may be added for positional changes that help maintain range of motion, distribute pressure, and provide angle changes for the hips and knees.[16]

I Leg Amputations[16]

A major seating and mobility concern for people with leg amputations is weight distribution in the wheelchair and the rear axle position. With or without the prosthesis (the prosthesis is lighter than a leg), the wheelchair will be tippy, so the rear wheels need to be moved back. Typically, sensation is intact for people with amputations. However, if the limb loss was due to a physiological problem that compromised the blood supply or tissue integrity, such as *diabetes*, pressure distribution can be critical. Also, support for the amputated limb is necessary. This postural support should be comfortable, supportive, and provide adequate pressure distribution, while allowing for functional transfers. The support should be removal when the prosthesis is worn. If the amputation is extremely high, such as in a hemi-pelvectomy, molded seating can provide stability as well as surface area support.

J The Elderly

For many people, aging brings decreased movement, joint mobility, and endurance, in addition to changes in urinary function, vision, hearing, heart and circulatory status. Despite the physical decline, our elderly carry wisdom and have many things to teach the younger generations. Let us help them physically through seating and mobility intervention, so that they can be comfortable, functional, and free of pressure sores that could shorten their lives. Let's shift our attitudes about the elderly. Let's not see them as passive observers in sling seats and geri-chairs, but rather as active people contributing and participating in society.

Some elderly are part-time wheelchair users, while others are more full-time users. Many of the elderly who live in residential facilities are dependent on wheelchairs.[42] The elderly who are often in need of appropriate seating and mobility are those in heavy, non-adjustable, sling seat wheelchairs.

Major Concerns[11]

- **Mobility**. Wheelchairs that are fit properly can enhance the elderly person's independent mobility. If a wheelchair is too large, heavy, and hinders propulsion, the elderly person will be reliant on others to push her.[43]

- **Pressure and skin integrity**. Because of general weakness, thinning of the skin, lack of movement, incontinence, tissue aging and fragility, the elderly are particularly susceptible to pressure sores.[44,45]

- **Posture**. Typically, an older person with limited mobility will sit in a sling seat wheelchair without an appropriate seat cushion and back support. The person will slide forward in the wheelchair, her pelvis posteriorly or laterally tilting, and her spine kyphotic or scoliotic.[46]

Elderly woman with kyphosis
in standard wheelchair

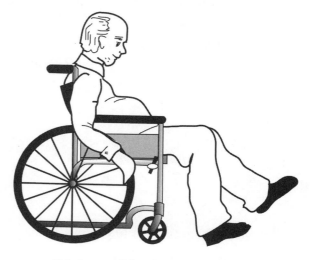

Elderly man sliding forward
in sling seat wheelchair

- **Comfort.** Many elderly have pain due to difficulty moving, poor posture, and joint changes. Seating should promote comfort, especially for full-time wheelchair users.[47]
- **Function.** For a part-time wheelchair user, it must be easy to transfer in and out of the wheelchair.[48] For a more full-time user, it is important to focus on appropiate seat height to access tables, beds, and toilets; propulsion ability; eating and swallowing; and so on.
- **Safety.** In the elderly, it is critical to prevent falls that could cause fractures. Loose brakes and foot supports that stick out are common culprits in falls.

Seating System

Follow the guidelines in this book, keeping the above concerns and goals in mind. Remember that postural supports should never hinder function.[48,49]

- **The seat cushion** should provide both pressure relief and postural support. A pressure-relief cushion should relieve pressure under bony prominences, depending on the person's posture and areas of greatest pressure[45,50,51] (see Chapter 14). A contoured cushion, gentle anti-thrust seat, or cushion with varied densities of foam can help the pelvis from sliding forward (see pages 135-8).
- **Anterior pelvic supports** should be used with caution. The person must be able to access and release the anterior pelvic support, whether that is a positioning belt or a rigid pelvic bar. Restraints, although intended to keep an elderly person from falling from wheelchair tips, are controversial in residential care facilities, as improper use has resulted in injury and even death.[52-55] However, when properly adjusted, positioning belts can help prevent injuries.[46,56-58]
- **The back support** should support the head and trunk to be in the person's neutral posture and accommodate any fixed aspects of the spine.
- **Lateral trunk supports** may need to swing away or remove for transfers, or for dressing in the wheelchair.[16]
- **The cushion cover** should absorb water and urine and be removable for ease in cleaning (see pages 228 and 242).

**Seating/mobility system for elderly
woman allowing greater comfort
and propulsion**

Wheelchair Considerations

In addition to guidelines previously stated in this book, areas to focus on regarding wheelchairs for the elderly are[11]:

- **Seat height**. Depends on the person's function. If the person is not using her feet to propel, a higher seat may ease transfers to standing. However, the seat height also needs to be low enough to get under tables. Tables and beds can be raised with blocks to accommodate a wheelchair. If the person propels the wheelchair with one or both feet, the seat should be low enough so the person's feet contact the floor for heel-to-toe propulsion (see Seating for Persons with Hemiplegia section below).

- **Arm supports**. The height of arm supports should allow the person's arms to rest comfortably, and at the same time allow the person to push up on the arm supports to stand.

- **Lower leg supports**. These must swing away to assist with transfers.

- **Lightweight wheelchairs**. The elderly, who tend to be more fragile and weak than others, are often given big, heavy, clunky wheelchairs. A properly fit, lightweight wheelchair makes it easier for elderly persons to propel independently.

- **Brakes**. Brakes should be reliable and within easy reach.

K Hemiplegia

Weakness, spasticity, or *flaccidity* on one side of the body can be the result of damage to the brain at any time from infancy to adulthood. *Hemiplegia* from a *stroke* is more common in adults.

Seating/Mobility Considerations

In addition to the guidelines in this book, consider these additional aspects:

- **Seat height.** If the person is propelling the wheelchair with one foot and one arm, the seat height needs to be low enough to allow the foot to come under the seat to propel heel to toe.[59]
- **Seat depth** may need to be a little shorter or cut back (see page 191) to allow the knee to flex under the seat cushion.
- **Seat cushion and back support.** If the person is propelling with one foot, a supportive seat cushion, lower back support (if it is flexible), and positioning belts, can encourage the pelvis to come into more of a neutral and anteriorly tilted posture, making propulsion easier. If a person tends to extend her trunk and hips when pushing with a foot, without proper support, she will tend to extend and slide forward out of the seat.
- **One-arm drive wheelchair.** A rod connecting one wheel to the other wheel is called a one-arm drive wheelchair. This type of chair allows a person with the functional use of one arm to propel both wheels by propelling one wheel. However, a one-arm drive wheelchair is much heavier than a traditional wheelchair, and a caregiver may not be able to transfer it to a car. Also, the weight requires good strength and endurance, which can be compromised in a person with hemiplegia. Maneuvering a one-arm drive requires good cognitive skills and motor planning, which may be impaired in people with hemiplegia.

**Elderly man with hemiplegia in
wheelchair fit to enhance propulsion
with right foot and hand**

L Spinal Cord Injury

For most persons with spinal cord injuries, a wheelchair is the only means of mobility in the home and community. As accessibility in the community improves, people with spinal cord injuries are leading increasingly active and productive lives. Consequently, their equipment needs to perform in a variety of situations. Most people with spinal cord injuries can benefit from more than one type of wheelchair to meet all of their needs. In reality, many people have only one wheelchair and seating system at a time, so it is important to carefully consider the choices and features, and also to prioritize equipment goals.

1. Seating Issues

The main seating issues for persons with spinal cord injuries are skin integrity, function, posture, and pain. It is very important to prevent these problems. Ongoing lifetime education about prevention is important, especially as more information about aging with a spinal cord injury becomes available.[60-63] Because pressure sores take a long time to heal, can be life threatening, and interfere with the person's ability to participate in normal activities, the primary seating goal needs to be distribution of pressure to decrease the risk of pressure sores.[64-66]

a. Skin Integrity

- **Lack of sensation.** A person with normal sensation will shift weight frequently to relieve pressure. A person with a spinal cord injury who has impaired or absent sensation does not have the reminder to weight shift, and so is at high risk for developing pressure sores. Even a person who has avoided problems with pressure sores for long periods of time can develop pressure sores as she ages. With aging the skin is less elastic, blood flow is decreased, healing time is longer, and there is more muscle atrophy.[67] The cushion and method of pressure relief that worked for years to distribute pressures may no longer be adequate. Tissues affected by shearing, moisture, trauma, friction, poor nutrition, and so on, are at even greater risk when a person has impaired sensation.

- **Skin inspection.** All areas at risk must be visually inspected on a regular basis. The person can do the inspection herself using a mirror, or a consistent caregiver can check for changes in the skin. During the seating assessment, inspect the skin for existing or potential problem areas. Scar tissue from healed pressure sores is always a risk factor for future skin breakdown.

- **Pressure distribution.** Optimal pressure distribution is a priority when choosing a seat cushion. The ischial tuberosities, coccyx, sacrum, and greater trochanters are under increased pressure because they become prominent with muscle atrophy.[68] Lateral pelvic tilt is common, and results in increased body weight and pressure on the lower ischial tuberosity and possibly the greater trochanter. Some cushions are better than others when it comes to accommodating prominent bony areas and correcting or accommodating the lateral pelvic tilt. Cushions need to have adequate depth and be made from materials that allow immersion of bony prominences. See Chapter 2 and 14 for information on pressure assessments and cushion design.

- **Pressure mapping.** Pressure mapping can provide valuable feedback to persons with spinal cord injuries and their therapists. It is particularly useful for persons who have absent sensation. In pressure mapping, a pad with electronic leads is placed between the person and the supporting surface. The leads are connected to the computer, which "reads" the person's pressure pattern and displays it on the computer. Pressure mapping can both check static pressures and verify the effectiveness or ineffectiveness of pressure relief methods. Pressure mapping should always be used in conjunction with manual palpation; the combination will help the therapist and the person with a spinal cord injury understand the person's pressure distribution (see page 91). Pressure mapping is frequently used to help select the appropriate seat cushion.

b. Posture, Pain, and Function

Postural asymmetries and deviations are caused by a variety of factors, including absent or weak muscle function, muscle imbalance, lack of adequate postural support, functional use patterns, gravity, spasticity, inability to change positions throughout the day, and contractures. Most full-time wheelchair users will develop postural issues over time. Pain that is related to postural patterns may be altered by seating intervention. Common postural deviations in the spinal cord injury population are:
- Pelvis rolled backward (posterior pelvic tilt) and thoracic curving forward (kyphosis) with resulting poor head position.[69,70]
- Pelvis rolled forward (anterior pelvic tilt) with accentuated lumbar lordosis.
- Pelvis tilted to the side (lateral pelvic tilt) with scoliosis.
- *Rotatory scoliosis* from functional asymmetries.

2. Seating Interventions

Follow the guidelines in this book on assessment, pressure-relief cushions, back support size and modifications, the seat-to-back support angle, lower leg support angle, and wheelchair considerations. The wheelchair is not only a mobility device, but also a postural support device from which to complete all functional activities. When assessing and designing the seating/mobility system, the person with a spinal cord injury must perform some key functional tasks. It is important that seating intervention enhances and does not hinder function.

a. **Back Support.** The back support should be an appropriate height, and wide enough to provide trunk support but not interfere with propelling the wheelchair. Often, the back support tubes of a wheelchair can be lowered to allow greater freedom for the shoulders and arms.

When considering pelvic, sacral, or low back support options, remember if the wheelchair folds, the back support needs to be removable or foldable. Ideally a pelvic/low back support should adjust, so that the person's pelvis and lower spine receive adequate support when she needs to be more upright, such as when working on a computer. If the person needs more stability, for example, when wheeling downhill, the person may need to be in a more posteriorly tilted pelvic posture. Thus, ideally, a back support can adjust for these and other functional needs, especially for a person with paraplegia.[71-73] Adjustability is helpful, but less relevant for a person with quadriplegia, as often she needs to round her trunk forward and posteriorly tilt her pelvis for stability during functional activities.

b. **Fixed Tilt/Angle of the Wheelchair.** Oftentimes people with spinal cord injuries will prefer to keep their wheelchairs fixed in a backwards tilt for stability. In addition, tilting the wheelchair backwards 20° can reduce pressure under the buttocks.[74,75] However, reclining the back support, while making no other adjustments, can increase the shear at the seat surface.[74] "Squeezing" the wheelchair, or lowering the rear portion of the seat while maintaining the back angle, has not been found to increase seat surface pressures.[76]

c. **Rear Axle Position and Upper Limb Pain.** Over time, many people with spinal cord injuries develop shoulder pain, *repetitive strain injuries,*[77,78] and *carpal tunnel syndrome.*[78-82] People with spinal cord injuries rely heavily on their arms for wheelchair propulsion[84] and transfers. Propulsion, especially when the shoulder is internally rotated and extended, has been linked to shoulder problems.[84-86] Paying attention to sitting posture and wheelchair setup, especially the rear axle position, may help to prevent future shoulder pain and carpal tunnel syndrome[86,87] (see pages 237 and 239). The shoulder will be healthier over time if it is aligned and is not turned in (internally rotated). This means that optimally the wheel axle should be directly under the shoulder and the elbow flexed to 90-100°[88] or 100-120°[89] when the hand is at the top of the pushrim. When the wheelchair is too wide, the shoulder will rotate internally, putting the shoulder at risk for problems.[86,87] Also, if the shoulder is internally rotated, the wrist will not be well aligned for efficient propulsion. Shorter strokes with high forces at the pushrim have been linked to increased compression at the nerves, especially the median nerve in the *carpal tunnel* of the wrist.[90,91] Education about propulsion, for example, pushing using longer, circular push strokes with less peak force, is helpful for wheeling efficiency and preventing injury.[92-94]

3. Additional Seating Considerations for Persons with Quadriplegia

A person with quadriplegia has less trunk stability than a person with paraplegia. In order to gain trunk stability to use her arms, she curves her trunk forward and posteriorly tilts her pelvis. Over time, sitting with a posteriorly tilted pelvis and a rounded forward spine (kyphosis) makes it harder to lift her arms, expand her chest for breathing, and look up to talk to people. This posture also increases neck problems and contributes to shoulder problems. A very kyphotic spine decreases trunk height and puts the arms at a disadvantage for propelling a manual wheelchair.

Person with quadriplegia with posteriorly tilted pelvis and kyphotic spine

a. **Postural Supports.** One way to prevent this posture is by using an appropriate back support.

b. **Power Wheelchair and Power Tilt.** Another consideration for persons with C6 level quadriplegia or higher is to use a power wheelchair with power tilt.[95] It may tilt partially or fully during the day to allow gravity to assist with spinal extension. If the person has been using a manual wheelchair for many years, she may not want to consider changing to power and power tilt. However, now that we know more about aging, the long-term effects of posture on neck, back, and shoulder pain, it is important to provide this information so that the person with a spinal cord injury can make an informed decision. Also, power tilt can be beneficial if the person experiences *autonomic dysreflexia (AD)*, in which an irritating stimulus causes a sudden increase in blood pressure. In this case, the person should sit upright and lower the legs to decrease blood pressure. After stabilizing the blood pressure, determine and treat the cause of the AD.

Changing seat cushion, sacral and upper back support, tilt and rear axle to improve postural alignment

c. **Back Support Considerations.** In addition to the back support options in this book, consider the thickness of the back support. A person with quadriplegia often needs to "hook" an elbow around a push handle in order to shift weight, use her arms, and turn around.[96] If the back support is too thick, hooking an elbow will be difficult.[97] For persons with higher-level spinal cord injuries, the back support needs to extend to the spine of the scapula and support the scapula. In this case, scapular reliefs should be cut into the back support to allow for full mobility of the shoulders and arms.[97] Lateral trunk supports, if used, should not interfere with transfers. They can swing away.

**Person with quadriplegia hooking
an elbow around the push handle
for stability**

M | Spina Bifida

Spina bifida is a congenital defect in which the posterior vertebral arches fail to fuse in midline to form the spinous process. There may or may not be a protrusion of the spinal cord and its membranes. Typically, these lesions are repaired close to birth. Approximately 80% of the lesions occur in the lumbar area,[98] but lesions can occur at any level of the spine. Approximately 25% of children with spina bifida also have *hydrocephalus*, which may or may not require a *shunt*. The child's physical manifestations depend on the level and extent of the spinal cord lesion, just as in spinal cord injuries. Besides lower limb contractures, spinal deformities are common. Congenital kyphosis occurs in 10-15% of infants.[99] By adolescence, approximately one third of the children have acquired paralytic kyphosis.[100] Kyphosis is found approximately at the level of the spinal defect.

Seating Considerations

Follow the guidelines for assessment and intervention presented earlier in this book and in the above section on spinal cord injuries. In addition, consider[11,101]:

- **Mobility**. Depending on the level of the lesion, some children walk, some require wheelchairs, and some do both. It is important to provide children with a variety of mobility devices. In a very young child, consider providing a mobility system that is at the floor level, so she can play with her peers.

- **Back support**. Besides providing the appropriate postural supports, provide a relief for the *gibbous*, the sharp, angular kyphosis at the spina bifida level. Surgery at this level involves tucking the exposed spinal cord and nerve roots back inside the membrane, and then covering the wound with muscle and skin flaps. This area often has decreased or absent sensation. The bones are often uneven and thinly padded by the skin, so it is especially susceptible to pressure sores.[102]

- **Head support**. If the child has hydrocephalus and the head is large, the child may require a head support.

As a person with spina bifida ages, she will experience aging issues similar to those of a person with a spinal cord injury. In addition, she may have issues with[103]:

- Shunt malfunctions that can produce chronic headaches, vomiting, and neurological problems.[104]
- Increased pain.
- Osteoporosis from lack of bone stimulation.
- Skin integrity, as changes in skin, fat, and muscle tissue may make some people more prone to skin breakdown. Leg wounds are one of the most common associated problems found in people with spina bifida.[102]
- Edema.
- Incontinence.
- Obesity.

As the person with spina bifida ages, consider her future and options to enhance function and mobility such as postural support and pressure-relief cushions.

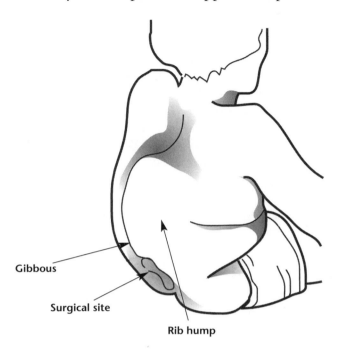

Gibbous

Surgical site

Rib hump

Child with spina bifida and gibbous deformity

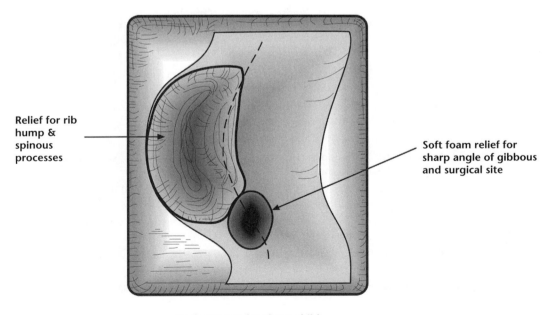

Relief for rib hump & spinous processes

Soft foam relief for sharp angle of gibbous and surgical site

Back support for above child

References

1. Strauss D, Ojdana K, Shavelle R, Rosenbloom L. Decline in function and life expectancy of older persons with cerebral palsy. *Neurorehabilitation.* 2004;19(1):69-78.

2. Murphey KP, Molnar GE, Lankasky K. Medical and functional status of adults with cerebral palsy. *Dev Med Child Neuro.* 1995; 37:1075-84.

3. Murphey K, Bliss M. Aging with cerebral palsy. In: Kemp B, Mosqueda L. *Aging with a Disability: What the Clinician Needs to Know.* Baltimore, MD: John Hopkins University Press; 2004.

4. Klingbeil H, Baer H, Wilson R. Aging with a disability. *Arch Phys Med Rehabil.* 2004;5 Suppl 3.

5. Ahmed M, Matsumura B, Cristian A. Age-related changes in muscles and joints. *Phys Med Rehabil Clin N Am.* 2005;16:19-39.

6. Zaffuto-Sforza C. Aging with cerebral palsy. *Phys Med Rehab Clin North Amer.* 2005;(16):235-49.

7. Rapp CE, Torres MM. The adult with cerebral palsy. *Arch Family Med.* 2009; (5):466-72.

8. Aging with a disability. Available at: http://www.jik.com/awdrtcawd.html. (Ranchos Los Amigos National Rehabilitation Center).

9. Presperin J. Aging with a developmental disability. *Proceedings from the 24th International Seating Symposium.* 2008:109-12.

10. Presperin J. Seating and mobility evaluation during rehabilitation. *Rehab Manag.* 1989 April-May.

11. Trefler E, Hobson D, Taylor SJ, Monahan L, Shaw CG. *Seating and Mobility for Persons with Physical Disabilities.* Tucson, AZ: Therapy Skill Builders; 1993.

12. Stewart AK. Seating and mobility for the child with traumatic brain injury. *Proceedings from the 9th International Seating Symposium.* 1993:103-9.

13. Monahan L, Trefler E. Seating persons with closed head injuries: Evaluation considerations. *Proceedings from the 5th International Seating Symposium.* 1989:90-85.

14. McKone B. Return to functional seated positioning and mobility. *Presentation at 11th Annual Heal Trauma Conference: Coma to Community.* Santa Clara Valley Medical Center, CA; 1988.

15. Presperin J. Positioning for the individual with a brain injury. *Proceedings from the 7th International Seating Symposium.* 1991:45-7.

16. Presperin-Pederson J. Personal communication. January 2009.

17. Donohoe M. Arthrogryposis multiplex congenita. In: Campbell S, VanderLinden D, Palisano R. *Physical Therapy for Children.* St. Louis, MO: Saunders/Elsevier; 2000:381-400.

18. Montpetit K, Mitchell V. Seating solutions for children with multiple congenital anomalies. *Proceedings from the 7th International Seating Symposium.* 1991:16-5.

19. Siekman A. Osteogenesis imperfecta and multiple congenital contractures (arthrogryposis): Seating and mobility issues. *Proceedings from the 4th International Seating Symposium.* 1988:9-15.

20. Bleakney D, Donohoe M. Osteogenesis imperfecta. In: Campbell S, VanderLinden, D, Palisano R. *Physical Therapy for Children.* St. Louis, MO: Saunders/Elsevier; 2000:381-400.

21. Axelson P, Zollars JA. Presentation on assistive technologies for the seating and mobility needs of persons with osteogenesis imperfecta. *Connect Tissue Res.* 1995;31(4):S45-7.

22. McKone B. Personal communication. December 2008.

23. Stuberg WA. Muscular dystrophy and spinal muscle atrophy. In: Campbell S, VanderLinden D, Palisano R. *Physical Therapy for Children.* St. Louis, MO: Saunders/Elsevier; 2000: 421-52.

24. Liu M, Mineo K, Hanayama K, Fujiwara T, Chino N. Practical problems and management of seating through the clinical stages of Duchenne's muscular dystrophy. *Arch Phys Med Rehabil.* 2003;84:818-24.

25. Carlson JM, Payette M. Seating and spine support for boys with Duchenne muscular dystrophy. *Proceedings from the 9th Annual RESNA Conference.* 1985:36-8.

26. Medhat M. Management of spinal deformity in muscular dystrophy. *Proceedings from the 3rd International Seating Symposium.* 1987:144-8.

27. Silverman M. Commercial options for positioning the client with muscular dystrophy. *Clin Prosthet Orthot.* 1986:10(4):159-79.

28. Gibson DA, Koreska J, Robertson D. The management of spinal deformity in Duchenne's muscular dystrophy. *Clin Orthop.* 1978;9:437-50.

29. Gibson DA, Wilkins KE. The management of spinal deformities in Duchenne's muscular dystrophy. *Clin Orthop.* 1975;108:41-51.

30. Lin F, Parthasarathy S, Taylor SJ, Pucci D, Hendrix R, Makhsous M. Effect of different sitting postures on lung capacity, expiratory flow, and lumbar lordosis. *Arch Phys Med Rehabil.* April 2006;87:504-9.

31. Presperin-Pedersen J, O'Connor A. Pain: Defining, categorizing, and determining its affect on seating. *Proceedings from the 21st International Seating Symposium.* 2005:101-2.

32. Presperin-Pedersen J., O'Connor A. Pain mechanisms and intervention regarding seating. *Proceedings from the 22nd International Seating Symposium.* 2006:118-120.

33. Noseworthy JH, Lucchineti C, Rodriguez M, Weinshenker BG. Multiple sclerosis. *N Engl J Med.* 2000;343(13):938-52.

34. Boninger ML, Cooper R, Minkel J. Review of medical, technology and psychosocial issues for persons with MS. *Proceedings from the 21st International Seating Symposium.* 2005:123-5.

35. Bhasin C. Multiple sclerosis: disease process and implications for seated/wheeled mobility. *Proceedings from the 9th International Seating Symposium.* 1993:69-74.

36. Minkel J. Multiple sclerosis: Understanding the beast within. *Proceedings from the 24th International Seating Symposium.* 2008:123-6.

37. Minkel J. Meeting the challenge: Trying to meet the needs of persons with MS. *Proceedings from the 24th International Seating Symposium.* 2008:186-9.

38. Bhasin C, Lewis D. Seating for multiple sclerosis: Strategies to accommodate disease progression. *Proceedings from the 9th International Seating Symposium.* 1993:97-100.

39. Ambrosio F, Boninger ML, Souza A, Fitzgerald SG, Koontz AM, Cooper RA. Wheelchair propulsion biomechanics in patients with multiple sclerosis. *Proceedings of the 24th Annual RESNA Conference*; 2002.

40. Fay BT, Boninger ML, Fitzgerald SG, Souza AL, Cooper RA, Koontz AM. Manual wheelchair pushrim dynamics in people with multiple sclerosis. *Arch Phys Med Rehabil.* 2004 Jun;85(6):935-42.

41. Savage F, Sweet-Michaels B. Multiple sclerosis-seating and mobility concerns for changing needs. *Proceedings from the 19th International Seating Symposium.* 2003: 79-81.

42. Shields M. Use of wheelchairs and other mobility support devices. *Health Rep.* 2004;15:37-41.

43. Engstrom B. *Seating for Independence: The Man and the Wheelchair–An Ergonomic Approach.* Waukesha, WI: ETAC USA; 1990.

44. Shaw G, Monahan L, Taylor S, Wyatt D. Peak sitting pressure for institutionalized elderly wheelchair users. *Proceedings from the 7th International Seating Symposium.* 1991:151-6.

45. Brienza D, Trefler E, Geyer MJ, Karg P, Kelsey S. A randomized control trial to evaluate pressure-reducing seat cushions for older person wheelchair users. *Adv Skin Wound Care Healing.* 2001;14(3):120-9.

46. Cooper D. Pelvic stabilitzation for the elderly. *Proceedings from the 3rd International Seating Symposium.* 1987:219-25.

47. Shaw G. Wheelchair seat comfort for the institutionalized elderly. *Assist Technol.* 1991;3(1):11-23.

48. Fernie G, Holder J, Lunan K. Chair design for the elderly. *Proceedings from the 3rd International Seating Symposium.* 1987:212-8.

49. Presperin-Pedersen J. Functional impact of seating modifications for older adults: An occupational therapist perspective. *Top Geriatr Rehabil.* 2000;16(2):73-85.

50. Conine TA, Hershler C, Daechsel CP, Pearson A. Pressure ulcer prophylaxis in older patients using polyurethane foam or Jay wheelchair cushions. *Int J Rehabil Res.* 1994 (5):92-105.

51. Shaw G. Seat cushion comparison for nursing home wheelchair users. *Assist Technol.* 1993;5(2):92-105.

52. Chaves ES, Cooper RA, Collins DM, Karmaker A, Cooper R. Review of the use of physical restraints and lap belts with wheelchair users. *Assist Technol.* 2007 Summer;19(2):94-107.

53. Calder CJ, Kirb RL. Fatal wheelchair-related accidents in the United States. *Am J Phys Med Rehabil.* 1990;69(4):184-90.

54. Weick MD. Physical restraints: An FDA update. *Am J Nursing.* 1992 (14):74-80.

55. Miles SH, Irvine P. Deaths caused by physical restraints. *Gerontologist.* 1992 (32):762-6.

56. Corfman TA, Cooper RA, Fitzgerald SG, Cooper R. Tips and falls during electric-powered driving: Effects of seat-belt use, leg rests, and driving speed. *Arch Phys Med Rehabil.* 2003;85(12):1797-802.

57. Kirby RL, Ackroyd-Stolarz, SA, Brown MG, Kirkland SA, Macleod DA. Wheelchair-related accidents caused by tips and falls among non institutionalized users of manually propelled wheelchairs in Nova Scotia. *Am J Phys Med Rehabil.* 1994;73:319-30.

58. Sosner J, Avital F, Begeman P, Sheu R, Kahan B. Forces, moments and accelerations acting on an unrestrained dummy during simulations of three wheelchair accidents. *Am J Phys Med Rehabil.* 1997;76(4): 304-10.

59. Engstrom B. *Ergonomics Wheelchairs and Positioning*. Hasselby, Sweden: Bromma Tryck AB; 1993.

60. Charifue S, Lammertse D. Spinal cord injury and aging. In Lin V, et al. *Spinal Cord Medicine: Principles and Practice*. New York: Demos Publications; 2003.

61. Krause JS, Coker JL. Aging after spinal cord injury: A 30-year longitudinal study. *J Spinal Cord Med*. 2006;29(4):371-6.

62. McGlinchey-Berroth R, Morrow L, Ahlquist M, Sarkarati M, Minaker KL. Late-life spinal cord injury and aging with long term injury: Characteristics of two emerging populations. *J Spinal Cord Med*. 1995 Oct;18(4):255.

63. Aging with a disability. Available at: http://www.jik.com/awdrtcawd.html. (Ranchos Los Amigos National Rehabilitation Center).

64. Richardson RR, Meyer PR. Prevalence and incidence of pressure sores in acute spinal injuries. *Paraplegia*. 1981;19:235-47.

65. Salzberg CA, Byrne DW, Cayten CG, et al. A new pressure ulcer risk assessment scale for individuals with spinal cord injury. *Am J Phys Med Rehabil*. 1996;75:96-104.

66. Young JA, Burns PE, Bowen AM, et al. *Spinal Cord Injury Statistics: Experience of the Regional Spinal Cord Injury Systems*. Phoenix, AZ: Good Samaritan Medical Center; 1982.

67. Yarkony G. Aging skin, pressure ulcerations, and SCI. In *Aging with Spinal Cord Injury*. New York: Demos Publications; 1992:39.

68. Gutierrez EM, Alm M, Hultling C, Saraste H. Measuring seating pressure, area, and asymmetry in persons with spinal cord injury. *Eur Spine*. 2004 Jul;13(4):374-9.

69. Hobson DA, Tooms RE. Seated lumbar/pelvic alignment: A comparison between spinal cord injured and non-injured groups. *Spine*. 1992;17:293-8.

70. Sprigle S, Schuch JZ. Using seat contour measurements during seating evaluations of individuals with SCI. *Assist Technol*. 1993;5(1):24-35.

71. Zollars J, Axelson P. The back support shaping system: An alternative for persons using wheelchairs with sling seat upholstery. *Proceedings of the 16th Annual RESNA Conference*; 1993:274-6.

72. Zollars J, Chesney D, Axelson P. The design of a back support shaping system: Clinical methodologies for measuring changes in sitting posture and function. *Proceedings from the 10th International Seating Symposium*. 1994:97-108.

73. May L, Butt S, Kolbinson K, Minor L. Back support options: Functional outcomes in SCI. *Proceedings from the 17th International Seating Symposium*. 2001:175-6.

74. Hobson D. Comparative effects of posture on pressure and shear at the body-seat interface. *J Rehabil Res Dev*. 1992 Fall;29(4):21-31.

75. Michael SM, Porter D, Pountney TE. Tilted seat position for non-ambulant individuals with neurological and neuromuscular impairment: A systematic review. *Clin Rehabil*. 2007 Dec; 21(12):1063-74.

76. Maurer CL, Sprigle S. Effect of seat inclination on seated pressures of individuals with spinal cord injury. *Phys Ther*. 2004 Mar;84(3):255-61.

77. Cole E, Bjornson A. Enhancing upper extremity repetitive strain injuries through wheelchair set-up. *Proceedings from the 19th International Seating Symposium*. 2003:113-7.

78. LaFrance A, Wilson D, Sawatzky B. Functional adaptation of bone and cartilage at the glenohumeral joint in manual wheelchair users. *Proceedings from the 22nd International Seating Symposium*. 2006:80-3.

79. Boninger ML, Dicianno BE, Cooper RA, Towers JD, Doontz AM, Souza AL. Shoulder magnetic resonance imaging abnormalities, wheelchair propulsion, and gender. *Arch Phys Med Rehabil*. 2003 Nov;84(11):1615-20.

80. Aim M, Saraste H, Norrbrink D. Shoulder pain in persons with thoracic spinal cord injury: Prevalence and characteristics. *J Rehabil Med*. 2008 Apr;40(4):277-83.

81. Nichols P, Norman P, Ennis J. Wheelchair users shoulder? *Scandinavian J Rehab Med*. 1979(11):29-32.

82. Pentland W. Upper limb function in persons with long-term spinal cord injury. *Proceedings from the 9th International Seating Symposium*. 1993:209-21.

83. Dubowsky SR, Sisto SA, Langrana NA. Comparison of kinematics, kinetics, and EMG throughout wheelchair propulsion in able-bodied and persons with paraplegia: An integrative approach. *J Biomech Eng*. 2009 Feb;131(2):021015.

84. Mercer JL, Boninger M, Koontz A, Ren D, Dyson-Hudson T, Cooper R. Shoulder joint kinetic and pathology in manual wheelchair users. *Clin Biomech* (Bristol, Avon). 2006 Oct;21(8):781-9.

85. Collinger JL, Boninger ML, Koontz AM, Price R, Sisto SA, Tolerico ML, Cooper RA. Shoulder biomechanics during the push phase of wheelchair propulsion: A multisite study of person with paraplegia. *Arch Phys Med Rehabil.* 2008 Apr;89(4):667-76.

86. Boninger ML, Baldwin M, Cooper RA, Koontz, A, Chan L. Manual wheelchair pushrim biomechanics and axle position. *Arch Phys Med Rehabil.* 2000 May;81(5):608-13.

87. Wei SH, Huang S, Jiang CJ, Chiu JC. Wrist kinematic characterization of wheelchair propulsion in various seating positions: Implications for wrist pain. *Clin Biomech* (Bristo, Avon). 2003 Jul;18(6):546-52.

88. Richter WM, Rodgriguez R, Woods KR, Axelson PW. Biomechanical consequences of a cross-slope on wheelchair propulsion. *Arch Phys Med Rehabil.* 2007 88(1):76-80.

89. Cooper R, Boninger M, Cooper R, Koontz A, Eisler H. Considerations for the selection and fitting of manual wheelchairs for optimal mobility. *Proceedings from the 21st International Seating Symposium.* 2005:59-60.

90. Boninger ML, Cooper RA, Baldwin MA, Shimada SD, Koontz A. Wheelchair pushrim kinetics: Body weight and median nerve function. *Arch Phys Med Rehabil.* 1999;80:910-5.

91. Boninger ML, Impink BG, Cooper RA, Koontz AM. Relation between median and ulnar nerve function and wrist kinematics during wheelchair propulsion. *Arch Phys Med Rehabil.* 2004 Jul;85(7):1141-5.

92. Boninger ML, Koontz AM, Sisto SA, Dyson-Hudson TA, Chang M, Price R, Cooper RA. Pushrim biomechanics and injury prevention in spinal cord injury: Recommendations based on CULP-SCI investigations. *J Rehabil Res Dev.* 2005 May-June;42(3 Suppl 1):9-19.

93. Richter WM, Axelson PW. Low-impact wheelchair propulsion: Achievable and acceptable. *J Rehabil Res Dev.* 2005 May-Jun;42(3 Suppl 1):21-33.

94. Robertson RN, Boninger ML, Cooper RA, Shimada SD. Pushrim forces and joint kinetics during wheelchair propulsion. *Arch Phys Med Rehabil.* 1996 Sep;77(9):856-64.

95. Sonenblum SE, Sprigle S, Harris F, Maurer C. Understanding wheelchair use patterns: Tilt-in-space. *Proceedings from the 24th International Seating Symposium.* 2008:179-80.

96. Padgitt J. Independence and dependence: Making seating and mobility choices for the person with C5-6 spinal cord injury. *Proceedings from the 22nd International Seating Symposium.* 2006:48-9.

97. Jones CK. The use of molded techniques for fitting C5-6 spinal cord injured five or more years post injury. *Proceedings from the 3rd International Seating Symposium.* 1987:189-92.

98. Volpe JJ, ed. *Neurology of the Newborn, 4th ed.* Philadelphia, PA: WB Saunders; 2001.

99. Mintz L, Sarwark J, Dias L, Schafer M. The natural history of congential kyphosis in myelomeningocoele. *Spine.* 1991;16(Suppl 5):348-50.

100. Brown JP. Orthopedic care of children with spina bifida: You've come a long way baby! *Ortho Nurs.* 2001;21:51-58.

101. O'Neill H. Clinical management of seating and mobility needs of children with myelodysplasia. *Proceedings from the 3rd International Seating Symposium.* 1987:197-201.

102. Okamoto GA, Lamers JV, Shurtleff DB. Skin breakdown in patients with myelomeningocele. *Arch Phys Med Rehabil.* 1983:64;20-3.

103. Presperin J. Aging with a developmental disability. *Proceedings from the 24th International Seating Symposium.* 2008:109-12.

104. Klingbeil H, Baer H, Wilson R. Aging with a disability. *Arch Phys Med Rehabil.* 2004 Jul;85 (7 Suppl 3):S68-73.

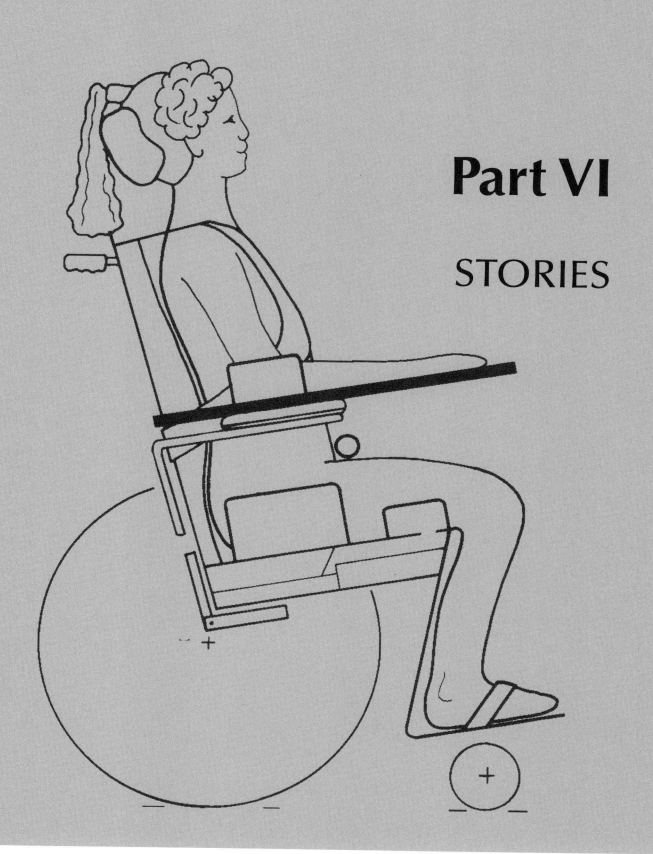

Part VI

STORIES

Chapter 18
Stories

The following stories of Martita, David, Kyo, Thomas, Nadia, and Richard demonstrate the seating assessment process, the establishment of goals, and how and why specific parts of seating systems are chosen. These are stories, not case studies, so many details are not included.

A Martita's Story

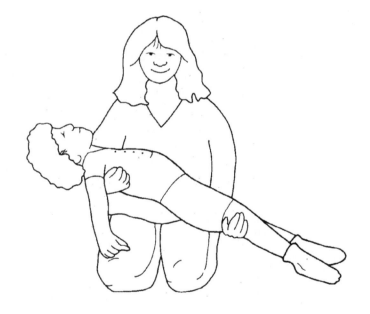

Martita is an 11-year-old girl with cerebral palsy. She lives with her family in a rural village. Martita has been carried since she was born because she cannot sit or move by herself. Recently her mother has been having back problems from carrying Martita. Her mother says Martita does not speak but understands what others are saying. Martita needs to be dressed, bathed, and fed by a family member. In order to feed Martita, her mother bends Martita's body and supports her head from behind so that it does not extend backwards. Members of the family rarely leave the village, but when they do, they travel by a neighbor's pickup truck or public bus. The family is poor and has no money for a seating system. Martita's mother brings her to the project because she wants a chair (seating system) with wheels so that:

- She can push Martita around the house and village.
- Martita can sit independently and comfortably.
- Martita can be fed while sitting in the seating system/wheelchair.
- Martita can play with toys and use her hands.

1. Physical Assessment

The team finds the following when they assess Martita's posture, movement, and function:

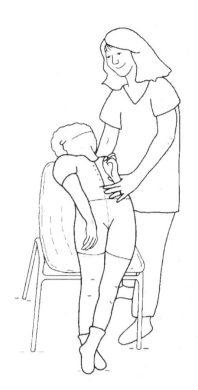

a. **Posture in a chair.** Martita is unable to sit alone. Her pelvis slides forward and her trunk arches backward, so that her head pushes against the top of the chair's backrest. Her hips and legs stiffen out straight, turn and move in towards midline. Her ankles and feet bend down and turn in. Her shoulder girdles pull backward and turn out, and both arms are stiff, either bent or straight.

b. **Joint and Muscular Flexibility Lying on her Back.** Her pelvis and spine are flexible such that they can attain the neutral posture. Both of Martita's hips are able to flex to 90°. Her hips/legs move and turn out to the side to neutral but are stiff when the worker moves them out to the side. Her knees and ankles are flexible to come to neutral as are her shoulder girdles and arms.

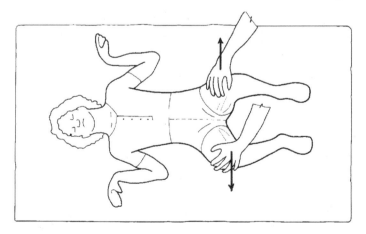

Martita's legs are stiff when moved out to the side

c. **Assessment in Sitting: Flexibility and Postural Support.** Although Martita's body tends to stiffen and her pelvis slides forward, her **pelvis** and **trunk** are flexible to come to their neutral posture. To maintain this posture, her pelvis needs to be supported from behind and the front. If Martita's **upper back and shoulder girdles** are rounded forward, such that her head is over her pelvis, she does not tend to arch and extend her trunk. Minimal pressure on the lower part of the *sternum* also decreases her arching and stiffness. Also in this posture, her head requires minimal support from behind to prevent if from falling

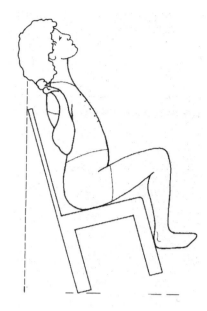

Pulling against gravity

backwards. Keeping her **hips, knees,** and **ankles** bent at 90° and her legs separated decreases her tendency to stiffen and slide forward out of the seat. When Martita is tilted back in a chair, she tends to arch her back, become fearful, and cry. Martita's body relaxes when the chair is upright.

d. **Objectives of Martita's Seating/Mobility System.** Martita's mother and the team decide the seating/mobility system must accomplish the following objectives:

- It needs to be a vehicle that will allow people to push Martita around the house and the unpaved roads of the village.
- It must support Martita's body so that she is sitting independently and comfortably as determined in the seating assessment.
- It must support Martita's body so that she can be fed by her mother and also allow Martita to use her hands to play with toys.

The team decides to make a **seating system with wheels**. They decide to use large wheels in the back and smaller casters in the front. The front casters cannot be too small because they will get caught in ruts when used outdoors. The seating/mobility system will be made out of wood because wood is inexpensive and available. The seating system will not remove from the mobility system, because Martita will be carried if she leaves the village. If the seating/mobility system needs to be transported, it will be transported in the neighbor's pickup truck. All parts of the chair will be well padded so that it is comfortable for Martita.

3. Seating System

Now let's look at the seating supports the team chooses for Martita.

(1) The **shape of the lower back support is changed** so that it angles in to control the top of her pelvis.

(2) An **anti-thrust seat** controls her pelvis from underneath, preventing it from sliding forward.

(3) A **seat-to-back support angle of 90°** is used because she has 90° of hip flexion, and 90° is found to be optimal to minimize her spasticity. If the seat-to-back support angle is greater than 90°, Martita tends to stiffen her body and slide out of the seat. If less than 90°, her head is not balanced over her pelvis.

(4) A **4-point positioning belt** provides support for the pelvis, pulling both down and back, as found by hand simulation.

(5) The **upper back support matches the natural curves** of her back. The upper part of the back support is gently contoured and rounds the shoulder girdles forward to reduce the excessive upper back arching.

(6) The **upper back support angles backward** from the lower back support so that her head is balanced over her pelvis.

(7) A **wedged-shaped block between her knees** prevents excessive turning in of her hips and legs.

(8) The **leg-to-seat surface angle and foot support-to-leg angle are 90°** to help reduce the excessive stiffening and straightening of her legs.

(9) **Ankle straps set at a 45° angle** help to prevent extension of her legs.

(10) **H-straps** provide minimal support across the front of the upper chest so that Martita does not fall forward.

(11) A **neck roll** underneath the ridge at the back of her skull prevents her head from falling backward.

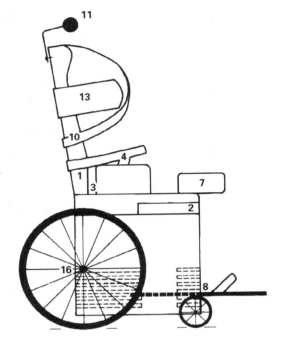

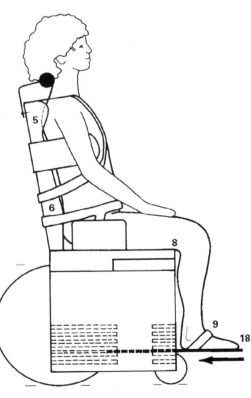

Martita's posture in a chair

After making these supports for Martita, such that her pelvis and legs are more stabile, the team members find that her trunk starts to curve to the right side. Her pelvis and the trunk have to be stabilized to prevent this curving, so the following supports are added.

(12) **Lateral pelvic supports (blocks)**, extending to the top of each side of the pelvis, prevent it from shifting to the side.

(13) **Lateral (side) trunk supports** positioned so that the right one is higher than the left one, prevent curving of her trunk to the right.

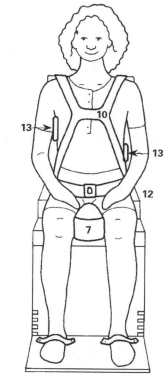

4. The Seating System in Relationship to the Mobility Base

(14) A **laptray** helps support her arms and gives her a surface on which to eat and play.

(15) The **width** of the seating/mobility system needs to be 26" (66 cm) or less so that it easily fits through the doorways.

(16) The **rear axle** needs to be far enough back for stability, but not too far back, so that the wheelchair can be tilted backwards to get over ruts.

(17) The **arm supports** need to be **adjustable in height** to allow for Martita's growth.

(18) The **footplate** can **slide in and out** like a drawer for transfers. The footplate also needs to be able to adjust in height for growth.

(19) The seat cushion will be **covered with easily cleanable material**.

5. The Final Check

After the seating system is made, the team always makes sure that they have reached the initial goals. Indeed, they find that Martita is comfortable, and enjoys sitting by herself in her new seating system. Her mother can feed her in the seating system, and Martita is even beginning to use her hands to play with toys. The team tells Martita and her mother to return in 6 months for a reevaluation and to make necessary changes in her seating/mobility system.

B | David's Story

David is a 32-year-old man who had a spinal cord injury 10 years ago at the thoracic 6 spinal level. He has associated paraplegia of his legs, abdominal, and back region and does not have sensation below the level of his spinal injury. David is an engineer who works long hours. He comes to the project because he has been experiencing pain in his upper back, neck, and shoulders. He lives with his wife and two children in a suburban home outside a major city. He drives his own compact car adapted with hand controls. Two years ago, he had a pressure sore in the middle of his buttocks, but has no pressure sores now. David pushes his own wheelchair that he built and repairs, and sits on a 2.5" (6.4 cm) piece of foam. David's health insurance will pay for a seating system because his doctor agrees that it is a necessary medical item.

He wants a seating system that:
- Can support his posture better so that he does not have so much pain in his neck, upper back, and shoulders, especially when he works at his desk.
- Will prevent future pressure sores.
- Will fit inside his wheelchair. He does not want to change his seat height or any part of his wheelchair frame.

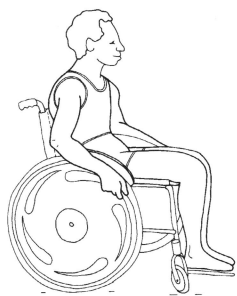

The team finds the following when they assess David's posture, movement, and function:

1. Physical Assessment

a. **Posture in his Wheelchair**
David's pelvis rolls backward (posteriorly tilts), his trunk curves forward (kyphosis), his hips and legs turn in and come together, his knees and ankles are bent to 90° degrees so that his feet rest on the foot supports.

His head control is good, but because his trunk curves forward, he excessively extends his neck in order to look in front of him. His shoulder girdles are rounded forward, but his arms are strong.

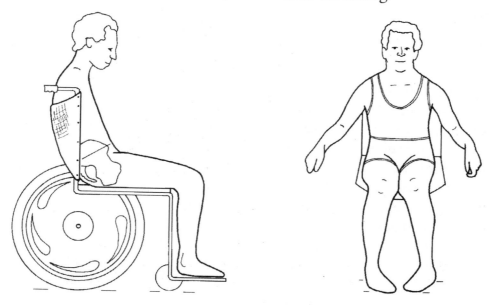

David's posture in his present wheelchair

b. Functional Abilities from Wheelchair

David transfers independently to and from his bed, toilet, bathtub seat, and car. The heights of the transferring surfaces range from 19 to 21" (48.3 to 53.3 cm). He transfers sideways into the car, and then takes out his seat cushion. He then folds his wheelchair and puts it behind the driver's seat. Desk, table, and counter heights at home and work range from 24 to 30" (61 to 76.2 cm). The axle of his rear wheels is in line with his shoulders.

c. Joint and Muscular Flexibility Lying on his Back

David's pelvis is fixed in a rolled back position (posterior pelvic tilt) at his low back, and his back curves forward (kyphosis) and is fixed. David's hips do not bend up (flex) to 90°, only to 70°. His hips move in and out well, and his knees and ankles are flexible.

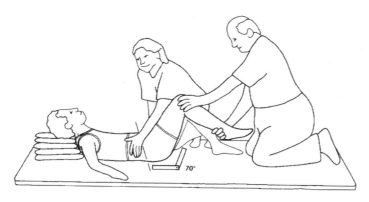

Hip flexion to 70°

d. **Assessment in Sitting: Flexibility and Postural Support:**
David needs to hold onto the mat table to sit independently (fair balance) especially if he tries to lean to one side or the other.

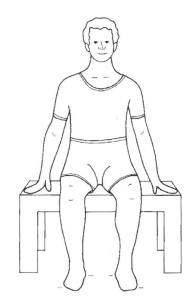

Fair balance

Because of the lack of hip flexion, he scoots to the front edge of the mat table, to allow the knees to be lower than the top of thighs. This accommodates the lack of hip flexion. David's pelvis tends to roll backward and is fixed. However, gentle support behind his pelvis (not sacrum) and low back (to the sides of his lumbar spine) prevents his pelvis from rolling back excessively. His trunk curves forward and is fixed. Supporting the lower part of his ribcage such that his head is balanced over his pelvis helps to reduce his neck and upper back pain. Even though his hips adduct and internally rotate (move and turn in), when moving and turning out, they are flexible to come to neutral. A minimal amount of support between his knees helps to keep the legs from coming together.

e. **Pressure.** Pressure was assessed both with the "wiggle test" and by using pressure mapping. The wiggle test found high pressures (3) under the ischial tuberosities, coccyx, moderate pressures (2) under the greater trochanters and lower pressures (1) under the thighs. Pressure mapping was consistent with the results from the "wiggle test".

2. Objectives of David's Seating System

David and the project team decide that a seating system for David must accomplish the following objectives:

- Help prevent pressure sores.
- Support David's body to accommodate the fixed nature of his joints. Specifically, his pelvis and low back need to be supported from behind such that his head is balanced over his pelvis.
- Not limit David's function (pushing the wheelchair, daily living, and working activities).
- Be comfortable!

3. Seating System

David helped the team make the following seating system for his wheelchair:

a. David's most important seating goal is preventing pressure sores, so a **contoured cushion** is made. The firm contoured base will provide stability for the pelvis. The base is made from firm foam that is cut out to relieve excessive pressure under the ischial tuberosities, sacrum and coccyx. The firm foam is covered with a layer of soft foam. The loose fitting, removable cushion cover is made from absorbable material.

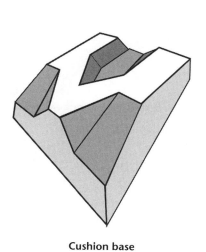

Cushion base

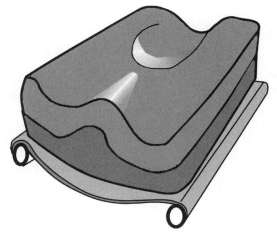

Finished contoured cushion

b. Because his hip flexion is 70° (20° less than 90°), the **seat-to-back support angle needs to be open to 110°.** The overstretched sling back essentially provides a seat-to-back support angle of 110°.

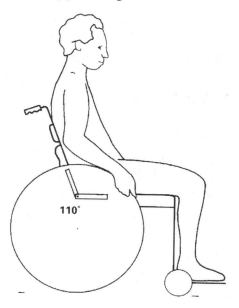

Seat to back support angle of 110°

c. Because his pelvis and trunk are fixed, the team does not try to position his pelvis upright and straighten his spine. David does not want a rigid back support, but the sling back does not provide enough support. Thus, **straps are used to reinforce the sling back**. In front of the straps, two firm supports are used to provide more specific postural support. **One support is shaped to the pelvis** and relieved in the area of the sacrum. The other **support is shaped to the lower ribcage to "cradle" or "cup" the lower ribcage**. His back is supported by these components and discouraged from rounding farther forward. David hopes that over time his pelvic and back flexibility will improve, and he can progressively tighten the straps to sit straighter. The top of the back support must be lower than the bottom of his shoulder blades so that it does not interfere with his arm and shoulder blade movement.

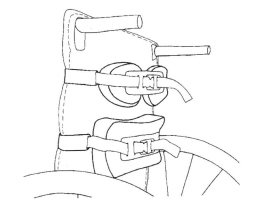

Firm supports in front of straps

d. To keep his legs slightly apart, David decides to add a mild **contoured bump** onto the top of the cushion between his knees. His knees and ankles can be supported at 90°.

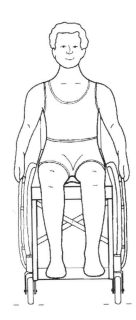

Mild contoured bump between his knees

4. **The Seating System in Relationship to the Mobility Base**

  a. **Seat height**. The seat cushion height must be the same as the height of his old seat cushion, 2.5" (6.4 cm), so that his ability to transfer, get under desks and tables does not change.

  b. **Removability**. The cushion must easily remove for transfers into the car. The cushion must also not slide around while in the wheelchair. Therefore, the bottom of the cushion will be covered with a rubberized material to provide some friction.

5. **The Final Check**

After the cushion is made, David and the team make sure that they have reached the initial goals. The team suggests that David carefully monitor the skin over his sacrum and buttocks to determine whether the seat cushion is truly helping to relieve pressure in these areas. The team tells him to come back to the project immediately if he has any pressure or seating problems. If not, they suggest he come back in 6 months for a recheck.

C Kyo's Story

Kyo is a 4-year-old boy with cerebral palsy and resulting hypotonia such that his body is weak and floppy. His mother has been carrying him since he was born because he cannot sit by himself. His mother takes Kyo from their village to a rehabilitation project in the nearby city. She tells the project team that he needs a chair with wheels so that:

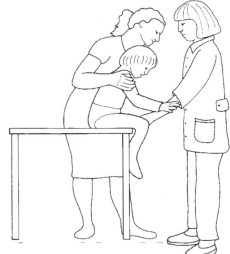

- She can push Kyo around the house and in the village, with the hope that Kyo will eventually push the wheelchair himself.
- She can feed Kyo while he is sitting in the chair.
- Kyo will sit up better as now he falls forward in any chair, making it difficult for him to breathe.
- Kyo can sit up in order to play with toys on a table top.

The family has collected enough money to pay for a seating system. The project will give Kyo a small wheelchair that was used by another child who outgrew it. Although Kyo is usually carried, the team finds out that he can stand with some assistance. Because he uses his arms to function, wheeling is a possibility, but he has not yet tried to wheel a wheelchair.

The team finds the following when they assess Kyo's posture, movement, and function:

1. Physical Assessment

a. **Posture in a Chair**

Kyo does not have a seating system, so his posture is assessed in a regular chair. Kyo's pelvis rolls backward (posterior pelvic tilt), his trunk curves forward and his hips and legs spread open and turn out to the sides. His head falls forward and to the right side, and his arms pull slightly forward and turn in.

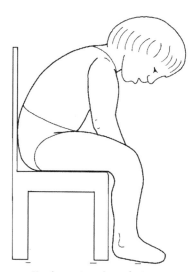

Kyo's posture in a chair

b. **Joint and Muscular Flexibility Lying on his Back**
His pelvis and spine are flexible such that they can attain neutral. Both of Kyo's hips are able to bend up to 90° and can be turned and moved towards the middle. His knee, ankle, shoulder girdle, and arm flexibility is good.

c. **Assessment in Sitting: Flexibility and Postural Support**
Kyo can sit by himself if he holds onto the edge of the bench with both hands (fair balance). Even though Kyo tends to roll his **pelvis** backward, his joints are flexible so that his pelvis and trunk can attain a neutral posture. To maintain this posture, his pelvis needs to be supported from behind just below the PSIS. With this guidance, he is able to move his pelvis and **trunk** forward and backward. His back needs to be supported from behind in his neutral posture. When he gets tired he tends to fall forward and needs support in the front of his trunk to remind him to sit up. Both of Kyo's **hips** are flexible. Support on the outside of his pelvis and knees prevents the hips from turning and moving out excessively and the pelvis from shifting to the side. Kyo likes to move his **legs**. If his **feet** are under his knees, he is able to push down through his feet helping him extend his trunk. When tilting the chair back, he tends to pull forward against gravity.

Pulling forward against gravity

d. **Wedging the Seat**
If Kyo's seat is wedged so that his thighs angle down, his back straightens. His mother found that this posture allows him to draw more easily. Moderate pressure against the front of his knees prevents him from slipping down.

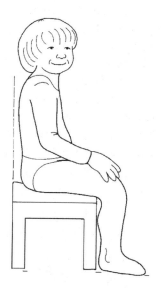

Wedging the seat

2. Objectives of Kyo's Seating System

The team decides that the device for Kyo must accomplish the following objectives:

- It can be pushed around the village and home, with the hope that eventually Kyo may be able to push the wheelchair independently.
- It must support Kyo's body especially to prevent his trunk from falling forward so that he can breathe better. Specifically, it should support his pelvis and back from behind in his neutral posture. His pelvis and knees need to be supported from shifting and moving to the sides. His legs must be free to move.
- It must support his body so that can use his hands, play with toys, and eat while he is sitting in the chair.
- It must be comfortable!

The team decides to make a seating system that fits into a small wheelchair. The family travels by public bus; thus, the seating system needs to remove from the wheelchair, and the wheelchair needs to fold. The seating system is made out of plywood, since plywood is inexpensive and available. The wheelchair has large wheels in the back and 6" front casters. All parts of the seating system are well padded so that Kyo is comfortable.

Now, let's look at what the team chooses for Kyo's seating supports.

3. Seating System

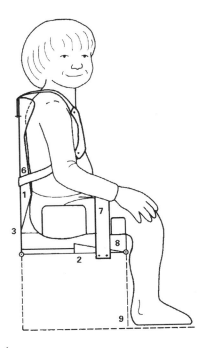

(1) Because his pelvis is flexible at his spine and moderate support behind the pelvis just below the PSIS guides him to his neutral posture, the **shape of the lower back support is changed** so that it angles in to control the top of his pelvis.

(2) An **anti-thrust seat** stabilizes his pelvis from underneath and helps to prevent his pelvis from rolling backward. **The front of the anti-thrust seat slopes down**, which helps Kyo sit up straighter.

(3) A **seat-to-back support angle of 85°** is used because his hips and pelvis are flexible; however, this angle is adjustable (see 13).

(4) The **upper back support** is relatively **flat and extends to the spine of his scapula** because he requires more back support at this time.

(5) The **foam behind his scapulae are cut out** or relieved so that his shoulder girdles and arms are free to move.

(6) The **upper back support angles backward** slightly from the lower back support to give Kyo space to extend his trunk.

(7) **A positioning belt set at 90°** to the seat cushion allows Kyo to move his pelvis forward over his legs. This movement makes it easier for him to play with toys on the table and to push the wheelchair.

(8) **The leg-to-seat surface angle is 90°**, but the long footplates allow him to move his feet under and behind the seatbase.

(9) The **foot support-to-leg angle is 90°**.

(10) The **long footplate** supports Kyo's feet as he flexes or extends his knees.

(11) Kyo likes to move his legs, so **ankle straps are not necessary**.

(12) He does not need a **head support** as his head control is good.

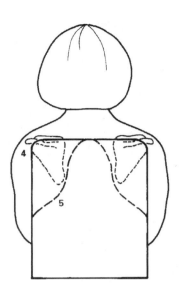

Because they found that Kyo sits up so well with the wedge under his pelvis, the team designs the seating system so that it can adjust for two postural options.

(13) Hinges at the **seat-to-back support angle and leg-to-seat surface angle allow adjustability** so that the seat cushion can slope down at times. A wedge is placed under the seat base to create this angle. When his thighs are lower than his hips, his back straightens, and it is easier for him to use his hands to draw.

(14) **Anterior knee supports (blocks)** are used for short periods of time (30 minutes), when the wedge is used. The knee blocks both prevent his pelvis from slipping down and give some sensory input for Kyo to extend his trunk.

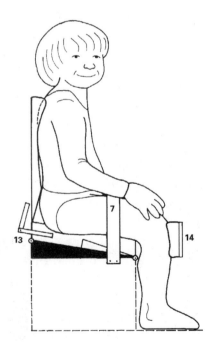

After making supports that provide more stability for his pelvis and legs, the team members find that Kyo's trunk starts to curve to either side when he tires.

The team adds the following to his seating system:

(15) **Gentle contours** at the outer aspect of his pelvis and knees prevent the hips from spreading open and turning out excessively and the pelvis from shifting to the side.

(16) **Small lateral (side) trunk supports** are positioned at the area of his lower ribs for some side support. The supports are positioned wider and lower than usual to allow Kyo to move his trunk.

(17) A **chest panel** helps Kyo sit upright only when he is tired. At other times he can sit without the chest panel.

(18) A **tray** provides a surface on which to eat and to use his hands to play.

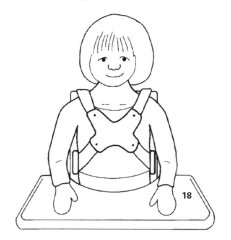

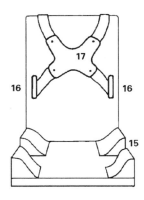

4. The Seating System in Relationship to the Wheelchair

(19) The **seat height** needs to be 12″ (30.5 cm) so that he can stand up from the wheelchair or crawl out of the seating system onto the floor. His seating system can be removed from the wheelchair and strapped in a chair allowing him to eat at the family's table.

(20) The **width** of his wheelchair is 15″ (38.1 cm) so that it easily fits through the doorways.

(21) Kyo will be wheeling the wheelchair in the future, so the **axle** is located under his shoulder joint.

(22) The **arm supports need to be adjustable** in height for growth and different functional activities.

(23) The **footplates** are attached to the footrests, so that they can flip-up for transfers.

(24) The seat cushions will be **covered with easily cleanable material**.

(25) **Push handle extensions** are added because the wheelchair is really low and is difficult for other people to push.

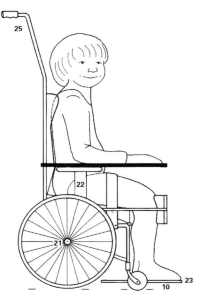

5. The Final Check

The team wants to make sure that they have achieved Kyo and his family's goals. Kyo's mother can push him in his wheelchair and he is already beginning to push the wheelchair himself. His posture has improved in the seating system such that his feeding and breathing are better. He is beginning to play with toys on a tabletop in front of him. The team asks his mother to bring Kyo back to the project in 6 months for a recheck.

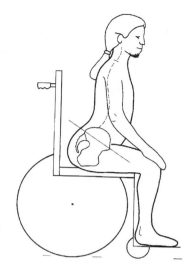

D Thomas's Story

Thomas is a 19-year-old man with spina bifida at the thoracic 12 spinal level. He has associated paraplegia of his legs, and the abdominal and back region. He lives in a small apartment in the city by himself and is in his second year at the university. He travels by public buses. Thomas pushes his own wheelchair and sits on a piece of 2" (5.1 cm) soft foam.

He comes to the project because he feels that the arching backward of his trunk is worsening, forcing his weight forward. Sometimes he has to hold himself up by pressing his hands on his thighs. Thomas's health insurance will pay for his seating system because it is medically necessary.

The team finds the following when they assess Thomas's posture, movement, and function:

1. Physical Assessment

a. **Posture in his Wheelchair**
Thomas's pelvis rolls forward (anteriorly tilts), his trunk arches backward (extends excessively), his hips and legs fall out to the sides and his knees and ankles are bent to 90°. He has good head control, and his arms are strong.

b. **Functional Abilities**
Thomas transfers independently to all surfaces. He is able to transfer independently to surfaces up to 4" (10.2 cm) higher than his seat height. When he pushes his wheelchair, he tends to sit in a more neutral posture. In this posture, his back is closer to the back support, and the axle position of the rear wheel is in line with his shoulder. While studying or sitting at a desk, he tends to lean forward onto the desk. Often he needs to support himself with his left arm to write with his right hand.

c. **Joint and Muscular Flexibility Lying on his Back**
Thomas's pelvis is slightly fixed in a rolled forward position (anterior pelvic tilt), but is 75% flexible as is his trunk. Thomas's hips bend up (flex) to 90°. His hips move in and out well, and his knees and ankles are flexible.

d. **Assessment in Sitting: Flexibility and Postural Support**
His balance is good enough that he can sit by himself on a mat table and move forward and backward; however, he needs to hold onto the mat table when shifting his weight to either the right or left. Both the rolling forward of his pelvis (anterior tilt) and arching backward of his trunk are 75%

flexible. If his pelvis is supported at the ASIS, the posture of his pelvis and trunk are in a more neutral posture. Thomas feels more stable in this posture, and he does not need to support himself with his hands to maintain his balance. His hips, which tend to spread open and turn out to the sides, are flexible. Support at the sides of the knees prevents turning out of the hips and legs and makes him feel more stable. Thomas's pressure was assessed using the wiggle test. The only areas of high pressure were the thighs.

2. Objectives of Thomas's Seating System

Thomas and the project team decide that a seating system for him must accomplish the following objectives. The seating system must:

- Support Thomas's body to improve the posture of his pelvis, trunk, and hips, specifically to prevent the excessive rolling forward of his pelvis and arching backward of his trunk.
- Not limit Thomas's function to push his wheelchair, use his hands, or transfer.
- Be comfortable!

3. Seating System

Thomas helped the team make the following seating system for his wheelchair:

(1) The **seat cushion** is made such that the back part is lower than the front part (**wedged**) to position his pelvis to be more upright and less rolled forward (anteriorly tilted).

(2) **Gentle contours** at the outer aspect of his knees prevent the hips from spreading open and turning out excessively.

(3) The cushion is covered with foam and a **loose, easily removable cover** sewn from sweatshirt material.

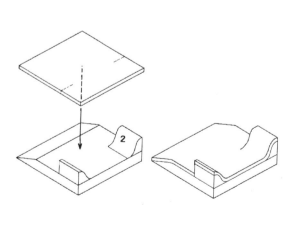 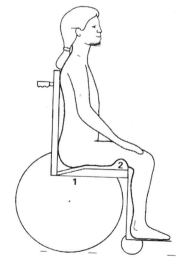

(4) Both the **leg-to-seat surface and foot support-to-leg angles** that he has been using are fine. Thomas does not want any straps for his pelvis, trunk, or ankles, because they are unnecessary.

(5) Thomas does not want a special back support because he rarely leans against it. He is concerned about making the wheelchair heavier to push.

4. Seating System in Relationship to Wheelchair

(6) The **seat height** is 3" high in the front and 2" high in the back, because the back of his cushion slopes down. The front of his seat cushion is 1" higher than his previous seat cushion. Thomas does not think this will be a problem as he is able to transfer onto surfaces of different heights.

(7) Because he is sitting in a more neutral posture, his weight will be shifted towards the back of the wheelchair. This more neutral posture allows **his shoulders to be in line with the rear axle** so that he is stable. This position makes it easier for Thomas to do wheelies, to get up and down curbs, and go down hills. (If he goes down hills without doing a wheelie, he falls forward and out of the wheelchair.)

(8) The **seat cushion needs to be lightweight** so that it does not add a lot of weight to his wheelchair. If it is lightweight, it is easier to remove and lift during transfers.

5. The Final Check

At this time, Thomas and the team hope that they have resolved Thomas's major postural problems. The team suggests that Thomas evaluate the cushion during his activities at home and school. Pressure was reassessed using the "wiggle test" with Thomas sitting on his new cushion. He still did not have high pressure under typical areas of concern (the ischial tuberosities, coccyx, greater trochanters). The team tells him to come back to the project immediately if he has any pressure or seating problems. If not, they suggest he come back in 6 months for a recheck.

E Nadia's Story

Nadia is a 12-year-old girl with cerebral palsy resulting in spastic-athetoid quadriplegia. She is unable to sit and move very much by herself. When she sits at home, she sits in a wheelchair without any seating supports except a strap around her waist. She is very uncomfortable in the wheelchair and tends to thrust out of it. She lives with her father, grandmother, and sister in a third-floor apartment without an elevator. The family does not have a car and relies on buses and taxis for transportation. The family has only been able to take Nadia on short trips to the doctor, park, or museum, because she gets very uncomfortable and slides out of her wheelchair. She has never gone to school prior to this year since there was no transportation. Her family arranges for the seating assessment because they want Nadia to go to school.

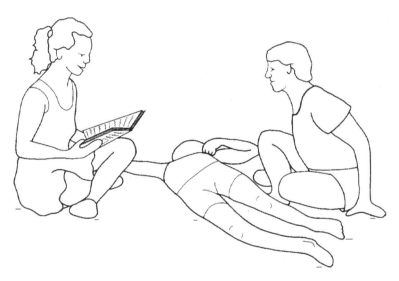

Her father wants a device:
- In which Nadia can be pushed around so that she can attend school.
- That can be transported on the schoolbus.
- That will support Nadia in a comfortable sitting position, and allow her to be fed more easily.

The team gathers the following additional information:

Nadia's breathing is shallow and uncoordinated. A family member needs to dress, bathe, and feed her. She communicates "yes" by smiling and by moving her limbs a lot. She communicates her dislikes by frowning, crying, or becoming agitated.

Her present wheelchair is 10 years old and the sling seat and back are very stretched out. The wheelchair frame is in good repair; however, the brakes and some bolts need to be tightened. There is no funding for a new wheelchair, but there is funding for a seating system from an special education project that realizes Nadia cannot go to school wihtout the seating system.

The team finds the following when they assess
Nadia's posture, movement and function:

1. Physical Assessment

a. **Posture in Present Wheelchair**
Nadia moves her whole body constantly.
Nadia's pelvis tends to rotate forward and
tilt down on the right side. Her upper
trunk curves (convex) to the left and her
head rotates to the right. Her hips and legs
both turn to the right (her knees angle to
the right). She moves her legs a lot, and her
knees bend and straighten. Her shoulder
girdles tend to pull back, turn out and
shrug (elevate). Her right arm pushes out
straight and her left arm bends.

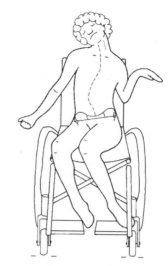

Nadia's posture in her
present wheelchair

b. **Joint and Muscular Flexibility Lying on Her Back**
Nadia's pelvis is fixed in the obliquity, but the rotation is flexible. Her trunk
is fixed with a curve (convex) to the left in the middle part of her spine
(thoracic) and a curve (convex) to the right in the lower part of her spine
(lumbar region).

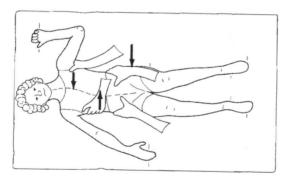

Fixed scoliosis

Both of Nadia's hips are able to bend up to 90°. Her left hip cannot move
out to the side or turn out to neutral; it is *fixed*. She experiences pain, and
the workers at the project think that her hip might be **dislocated**. The right
hip cannot move in to the middle and turn in to neutral; it is *fixed*. Both
knees are bent and do not straighten to 90°, but lack 10°. Ankle and foot
flexibility is good. Her arms and shoulder girdles are flexible.

c. **Assessment in Sitting: Flexibility and Postural Support:**
Even though Nadia's **pelvis** is flexible in rotation, she continues to push and rotate the right side of her pelvis forward. A lot of pressure against the upper right side of her pelvis (ASIS) is needed to prevent this rotation. The tilting down of her pelvis (obliquity) on the right side is fixed. When the workers put her pelvis in an upright and level position, her balance is disturbed and her head tilts to the left. However, when a block is placed under the left side of her pelvis, her head is aligned and balance restored. Supporting the pelvis very close to each side prevents the pelvis from shifting and tilting more to the side. Her **trunk** and spine are fixed in a S-type of scoliosis. For Nadia, this means the curves balance each other so that her head is upright.

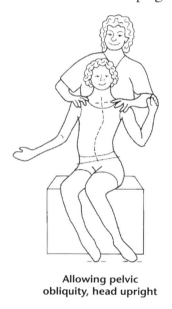

Allowing pelvic obliquity, head upright

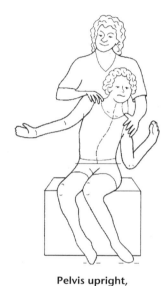

Pelvis upright, head not upright

Moving the **left hip** out to the side and turning it out causes pain in the hip and rotation of the pelvis. It is *fixed*. Moving and turning the **right hip** in towards midline causes rotation of the pelvis. It is *fixed*. Straightening her **knees** to 90° causes the pelvis to roll backward (posteriorly tilt). They lack 15° from 90° of flexion. The **ankles** and **feet** are flexible. Support behind the upper part of the **arms** and **elbows** and gentle pressure down through her shoulders support the **shoulder girdles** and arms in her neutral posture. Supporting the arms significantly changes the posture of **the head and neck** such that her head does not rotate so strongly to the right side. Tilting her and the chair backward improves her head control and balance.

The father and the project team decide to make a seating system that fits inside her present wheelchair. The special bus will transport Nadia in her seating system and wheelchair. Her wheelchair will be securely attached to the bus with the appropriate tie-downs, seat belt, and shoulder belt. During the week, the wheelchair will be used at school and for transport. On the weekends, the family will use the wheelchair at home. Nadia will be carried in the seating system from the special bus to their apartment, where it can be strapped into a regular chair. If transported in a taxi or car, the wheelchair can fold. The seating system is made out of a strong plastic, because the plastic is lighter weight than wood. All parts of the chair are well padded for comfort.

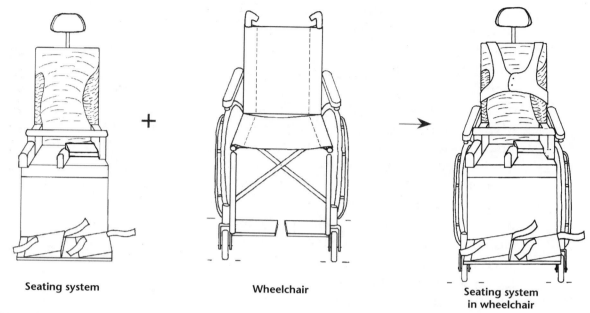

| Seating system | Wheelchair | Seating system in wheelchair |

Now let's look at what the team decides to choose for Nadia's seating supports.

2. Seating System

(1) **A seat cushion with varied densities of foam** provides a stable base of support for her pelvis allowing her ischial tuberosities (butt bones) to sink down into the soft foam.

(2) **A seat-to-back support angle of 95°** is found to be comfortable for her 90° of hip flexion and to balance her trunk and head over her pelvis.

(3) **The back support is conformed** to Nadia's fixed curved trunk, including the sides of her trunk, without trying to correct it. The back support is made by carving firm foam to closely match the contours of her trunk and back.

(4) Because the pelvic tilt to the side (obliquity) is fixed:

a. **A small platform under the left side** of her pelvis accommodates the obliquity.

b. **Lateral pelvic supports (blocks)** prevent her pelvis from shifting to either side. The blocks extend high enough to contact the sides of the pelvis, to "hug" the pelvis so that it does not move too much to the side.

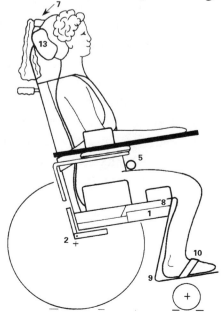

(5) The project team decides to use a padded **rigid bar** to control her pelvic rotation/thrust. No belts or straps are strong enough to control her pelvic rotation/thrust.

(6) **A medial knee support** is carefully positioned at the inside of the left knee to stop the left hip turning in while not forcing it past its flexibility. A lateral knee support is positioned at the outside of the right knee to stop the right leg turning out while not forcing it past its flexibility.

(7) The chair is **tilted backwards** slightly as this improves her head control and general level of spasticity.

(8) **The front edge of the seat cushion is cut back** to allow her feet to go under the seat cushion, because of the limitation in her knee straightening (extension). Thus, the leg-to-seat surface angle is 75°.

(9) The **foot support-to-leg angle is less than 90°**, because she has the available flexibility in her ankles.

(10) **Ankle straps** set at a 45° angle to the foot supports prevent some of her excessive leg movement.

(11) **The foot supports need to be slightly angled** to accommodate the posture of her hips and lower legs.

(12) **A vest** helps to stabilize her shoulder girdles so they do not shrug. The vest makes her chest feel more secure.

(13) **A head support which both contours** to and supports the back and sides of her head will discourage excessive extension and rotation to the right.

(14) **A removable laptray** provides a surface for her to eat and use her hands to play.
a. **Blocks** are bolted onto the back part of the tray to help her upper arms and elbows come to midline.

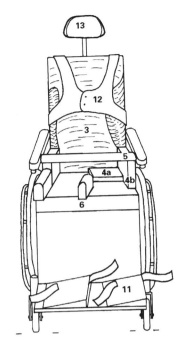

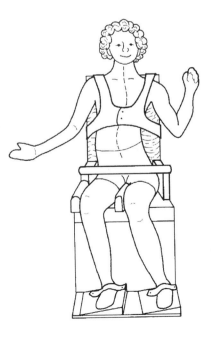

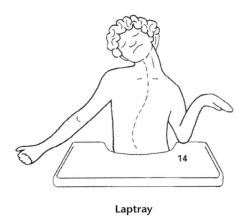

Laptray

**Laptray with blocks help
to position the arms**

3. Seating System in Relationship to Mobility Base

(15) The **seat height** needs to be between 22-24" (55.9-61 cm) so that she can sit at the family's table.

(16) The **width** of the seating system will allow it to fit inside the wheelchair.

(17) Nadia will not be wheeling the wheelchair, so her shoulders need to be **in front of the axle** for stability.

(18) The **arm supports** of the wheelchair will be used.

(19) The **leg and foot supports** will be part of the seating system allowing her legs and feet to always be supported even when she is not using the wheelchair as a base.

(20) The **seat cushion** will be covered with **easily cleanable material**.

4. The Final Check

After making the seating system, the team makes sure that they have achieved the initial goals. Nadia is comfortable in her new seating system, but since this is her first experience in a seating system, she does not want to sit in it for very long. She needs time to get used to it. Her father can feed her in the seating system, and Nadia is even beginning to use her hands to play with toys. The team tells Nadia and her father to return in 6 months to reevaluate her progress and make necessary changes in her seating/mobility system.

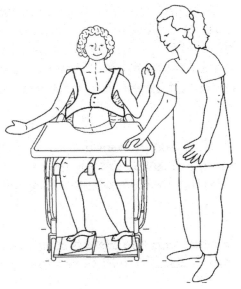

F Richard's Story

Richard is a 48-year-old man who had a traumatic brain injury 17 years ago. Prior to his injury, he worked as an engineer. He is no longer able to work. Richard lives alone and semi-independently. He has assistance 20 hours/week for foot care, transportation, shopping, household tasks, and socialization. He uses a power chair with a left joystick. He has significant tone throughout the right side of his body. After his injury, he developed **_heterotopic ossification_** in his shoulders, elbows, and hips. This significantly limits his joint mobility and he has a lot of pain with movement. Also post-injury, his right femur fractured many times. His left femur fractured one time. The right femur is now 2" (5.1 cm) shorter than the left femur. Over the last 5 years, Richard developed serious circulatory problems in his right foot, which developed into multiple **_decubitus ulcers_**, edema, and "purple foot syndrome." Besides the right foot, he has not had any other problems with skin breakdown.

He wants a seating system that:
- Will improve comfort, particularly of his pelvis, hips and back.
- Support the right leg to improve the circulation to his foot.
- Maintain his present level of independence.

The team finds the following when they assess Richard's posture, movement and function:

1. Physical Assessment

a. **Posture in his Wheelchair**
Richard's pelvis is posteriorly tilted (rolled backward) and oblique (tilted) down on the left. His spine is scoliotic, with the convexity of the curve to the left in lumbar spine. The left femur is forward of the right femur. The right hip is adducted and internally rotated. His right knee is flexed to about 45°, his left knee to 75°. His right leg tends to extend with his spasticity so that his foot comes up off the foot support. His head control is good, but he excessively extends his neck and tilts it to the left. His left arm is functional; however, his shoulder flexion is limited to 90°. His right arm is held tightly with a pattern of shoulder adduction, internal rotation, elbow flexion of 90°, forearm pronation,

Richard's posture in his present wheelchair

and fingers that are tightly fisted. His left elbow rests on the arm support, so that he can use his hand to operate the joystick.

Richard standing up using the grab rail

b. **Functional Abilities from Wheelchair**
Richard transfers using a stand-pivot transfer from his wheelchair to bed, toilet, and shower with the help of specialized placement of grab bars. For other transfers, he requires the assistance of a person to stand and pivot. It is important that seating intervention does not change the height of his seat cushion as this is critical for his independence. The heights of the transferring surfaces range from 19-21" (48.3-53.3 cm). Desk, table, and counter heights at home and work are 27-30" (68.6-76.2 cm). Height of kitchen countertops are 27" (68.6 cm), where Richard prepares his meals. The refrigerator shelves are 30-32" (76.2-81.3 cm). Richard accesses the kitchen and bathroom counters from his left side, as forward leaning is possible. Richard uses his left arm for activities of daily living. His reach is very limited due to joint limitations in his shoulder and elbow.

c. **Joint and Muscular Flexibility Lying on his Back**
Richard's pelvis is fixed in a posterior pelvic tilt and left pelvic obliquity. His lumbar scoliosis is fixed. Richard's right hip flexes to 70°, and his left hip flexes to 90°. Both hips come to neutral abduction and rotations. His right knee only flexes to 80°, and his left knee flexes to 90°. His right ankle lacks 10° of dorsiflexion, and left ankle is able to come to neutral. His left shoulder flexes to 90°, and his right shoulder flexes to 60°. He has 30-60° of right elbow flexion.

d. **Assessment in Sitting: Flexibility and Postural Support**
Richard is able to sit on the mat table with left arm support and he can lean forward and to the left. He loses his balance to the right. When Richard sits on a flat surface with his feet well supported, his **pelvis** is posteriorly tilted and oblique down to the left and is fixed. However, support under the right side of his pelvis, behind his pelvis, and on the outside of his right thigh helps Richard relax and feel more comfortable. Also supporting his fixed pelvic obliquity aligns his head over his trunk and pelvis. His **trunk** curves convex to the left in the lumbar spine. Supporting the back and sides of his trunk and ribcage with curved contact of the hands helps the muscles of his back relax. Allowing the right **hip** to flex only to 70° by putting a wedge under the front part of the seat also reduces pain in his low back.

Mild support on the inside of the right knee reduces the tendency for the right hip to pull in. Allowing the knees to be somewhat extended at their range of mobility is comfortable for Richard.

2. Objectives of Richard's Seating System

Richard and the project team decide that a seating system must accomplish the following objectives:

a. Enhance not hinder his independent function. For Richard this specifically meant:
  - Enhancing transfers to and from the wheelchair.
  - Repositioning himself in the wheelchair.
  - Reaching forward with his left arm in the kitchen.
  - Accessing kitchen countertops, refrigerator, sinks, and computer.

b. Decrease pain under right ischial tuberosity, right hip joint, both knees, and low back. Because of the nature of Richard's fixed joints, the joint limitations must be accomodated.

c. Improve circulation for right leg. This means not compressing the femoral artery in the right groin.

3. Seating System

Richard helped the team modify the following seating system for his wheelchair:

(1) **Seat cushion:** One of Richard's seating goals is reducing pain. The seating team decided to modify Richard's **composite cushion**.

  (a) A **right pelvic shelf** was added to the firm contoured base to accommodate his fixed pelvic obliquity.

  (b) A **lateral pelvic contour** was added to the right side of the contoured base to prevent his pelvis from drifting to the right.

  (c) The **medial thigh support** was built up on the right side to prevent the right hip from adducting too much.

  (d) The contoured base was covered with **flowable gel**. The entire cushion was **covered with loose absorbable material,** which is easily removable to clean.

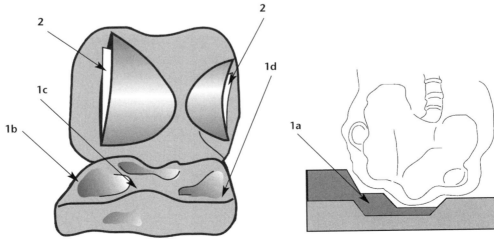

Composite cushion   Right pelvic shelf

(2) **"Pita pocket" lateral trunk contours.** Because his pelvis and trunk are fixed, the team did not try to position his pelvis upright and straighten his spine. In order to support Richard's neutral posture, lateral trunk contours were created. As Richard is quite sensitive to changes in postural support, the **pita pocket** was utilized. Two pieces of foam were sliced, than contoured. Different sizes of foam were put inside the pita pocket. The two pita pockets were velcroed onto Richard's current back support. These two pockets were modified over time until just the right support was provided. At this point they were covered with a loose cover that could be removed for cleaning or future modifications.

(3) Because his right hip flexes only to 70° (20° less than 90°), the **seat-to-back support angle needed to be open to 110°.**

(4) To accommodate his limited right knee flexion, and tendency to extend his right knee, the **leg-to-seat surface angle was set at 70°.** This was accomplished through leg supports with an adjustable leg-to-seat surface angle.

(5) An **arm trough** was added to support Richard's right arm in internal rotation and adduction.

(6) **Foot boxes** were provided to prevent Richard's feet from being injured.

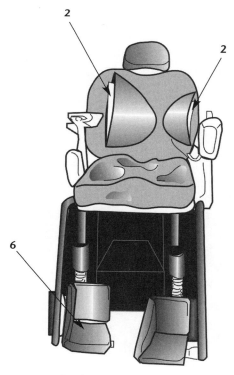

Seating system in wheelchair

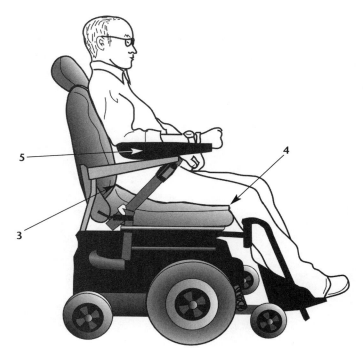

Seating/mobility system

4. The Seating System in Relationship to the Mobility Base

The **seat cushion height** needed to be the same as the height of his old seat cushion, so that his ability to transfer, get under desks, counter tops, and tables did not change..

5. Progression of Changes in the Seating/Mobility System

Because Richard has been disabled for 17 years, had a lot of pain, spasticity, joint limitations and a narrow window of comfort, it was critical to make a few changes at a time, then try them out prior to the final seating system. This required a lot of time, patience and understanding from the seating designer/provider, but this process was very important.

6. The Final Check

After the modifications to his seating system and wheelchair were finished, Richard and the team made sure that they had reached the initial goals. Richard and the team knew that Richard would need some slight modifications over time. The team scheduled follow-up visits at 2-week intervals until Richard was satisfied with the changes to his seating/mobility system.

7. Update on Richard

After 17 years of not walking, Richard has begun to walk with a 4-pronged cane. He began acupuncture treatments which decreased his pain. The seating system assisted with this progress, as he was not in constant pain anymore, so his body began to relax more.

Glossary

Achilles tendon lengthenings: The Achilles tendon is the heelcord that connects the back of the heel with the muscles behind the calf, the gastrocnemius and soleus. In an Achilles tendon lengthening, the gastrocnemius muscle is surgically lengthened.

Adductor releases: The adductor muscles, which are located in the inside of the thigh, close to the groin, are surgically cut.

Ankle-foot orthosis (AFO): A brace, often made out of plastic which controls unwanted movement of the lower leg, ankle, and foot.

Arthrogryposis multiplex congenita (AMC): A rare non-progressive congenital disorder characterized by multiple joint contractures, and sometimes muscle weakness and fibrosis (thickening of tissue).

ASIS: The anterior superior iliac spine of the pelvis. This is the bony prominence that sticks out in the top front part of the pelvis. See drawing in **pelvis** entry.

Aspiration: Food or liquids go "down the wrong pipe" or go through the trachea and into the lungs instead of being swallowed (through the esophagus to the stomach).

Aston patterning: A system of movement education, body work, fitness, and products developed by Judith Aston, movement specialist.

Atrophy: Partial or complete wasting away of a part of the body.

Augmentative communication device: This device assists a person who is unable to communicate verbally. It can be a simple board with pictures on it or it can be an electronic computerized system. The person can access it directly using different body parts (fingers, sticks, head sticks, eye gaze) or indirectly by using switches activated by body parts.

Autonomic dysreflexia (AD): An over-activity of the sympathetic nervous system, occurring in persons with spinal cord injuries above the T5 spinal cord level. AD occurs when an irritating stimulus is introduced to the body below the level of the spinal cord injury, such as an overfull bladder. The impulses cannot reach the brain because of the spinal cord injury. Instead, a reflex is activated, which causes a rise in blood pressure. The person may have a pounding headache, sweating above the level of the spinal cord injury, red face, nausea, and slow pulse, among other symptoms. Causes can be bladder and bowel problems, skin wounds, irritants to the body, and so on. Blood pressure must first be stabilized, and then the cause of the irritant (i.e., bladder or bowel problem) must be taken care of.

Ayurvedic medicine: Holistic medicine originating in India, which includes food, lifestyle adjustments, treatments, and herbal therapies.

Base of support: Our foundation supporting the weight of our body. In sitting, the pelvis, thighs, and feet are our base of support providing us with a stable foundation from which we shift our weight to move.

Bony prominence: Specific area of a larger bone that sticks out. Examples are the ASIS and PSIS of the pelvis, and the greater trochanter of the femur.

Bursae: A fluid-filled sac located where tendons or muscles pass over bony prominences near joints. Bursae assist with ease of joint movement.

Carpal tunnel: This tunnel is a narrow passageway of ligaments and carpal bones at the base of the hand. The median nerve passes through this tunnel.

Carpal tunnel syndrome: The tendons swell and put pressure on the median nerve. The person experiences numbness, tingling, pain, and sometimes weakness in the hand.

Central nervous system (CNS): The CNS includes the brain and the spinal cord. The CNS coordinates the function of the body.

Cerebral palsy: A disorder of movement caused by damage to an immature brain around or during birth. Some people have spasticity, some are floppy and weak, some have uncontrolled and uncoordinated movements, and some have combinations of the above.

Cerebrospinal fluid (CSF): A clear fluid that is produced and reabsorbed in the ventricles of the brain. CSF nourishes and flows around the brain and spinal cord.

Cervical spine: The bones (vertebrae) of the neck. There are seven cervical vertebrae. The cervical spine joins the head above to the thoracic spine below.

Coccyx: The tailbone, located at the bottom tip of the sacrum. See **pelvis**.

Components: Individual postural supports of a seating system. Components have specific purposes depending on their shape, size, and placement. Examples include head/neck supports, pelvic and trunk supports, chest straps, and pelvic positioning belts.

Contact surface: A description of the shape, size, and characteristics of your hand or a component that is contacting or supporting the person's body.

Contractures: When muscles become tight, sometimes the muscles and tissues around the joint become permanently shortened. The joint will then lose some of its flexibility.

Convexity: This term is often used when describing a curve in scoliosis. Referencing a circle, the outer part of the curve is convex, whereas the inside part of the curve is concave.

Craniosacral therapy: A gentle hands-on therapy which aims to balance the cerebrospinal fluid flow through the brain and spinal cord by releasing restrictions in the skull, spine and membranes surrounding the brain, spinal cord and nerve roots.

Decubitus ulcer: See **pressure sores.**

Deformities: After contractures occur for a long time, the bones themselves can deform or change. Deformities can be seen in the femurs if the muscles are constantly pulling the hips in, or in the spine with fixed scoliosis. Deformities are often seen in the ankles, feet, and spine, along with other areas.

Derotation osteotomy: A surgical procedure where the bone (osteo) is cut (tome). A typical derotation osteotomy is done for the femur (thigh bone) in children with cerebral palsy, if their femurs turn in due to spasticity. A cut is made in the femur so that the femur is angled more into the socket. This is done to prevent dislocation.

Diagnosis: The name of the disease or injury. Examples of diagnoses are spinal cord injury, cerebral palsy, spina bifida, muscular dystrophy, and so on.

Diabetes: A metabolic disease that causes abnormally high blood sugar levels. Diabetes can lead to kidney, nerve, and eye problems. Damage to the blood circulation leads to poor healing of wounds.

Dislocation: A dislocation occurs when a bone comes out of its socket. Typical dislocations occur in the hip, ankle, shoulder, and hand. Dislocations can be caused by spastic and tight muscles. Muscles that pull and turn the hips in (adductors, internal rotators, flexors) may eventually cause hip dislocation if tight or spastic.

Environmental control unit: An electronically controlled device used to turn on/off and regulate electronic appliances in the environment. Examples include a remote control to turn on/off a light, radio, television, or thermostat.

Equinovarus deformity: A deformity in which the ankle is plantarflexed (bent down) and inverted (turned in) and the foot is curved inward.

Feldenkrais method: Movement education and hands-on therapy to help people learn how to move and function through exploration. This method was originated by Moshe Feldenkrais.

Femur: The thigh bone.

Fibula: The outer bone of the lower leg. The head of the fibula is at the top of this bone.

Fixed: In this manual, "fixed" is the same as contracture, as when the joint and muscle are not flexible.

Flaccidity: See **floppy.**

Flexible: In this manual, "flexible" is the opposite of "fixed", so that even though the joints may tend to be in a certain posture, there is full or partial joint flexibility.

Floppy: An arm or leg that feels limp, soft, or heavy. A person might slump forward, and feel loose and weak. This can result from brain, spinal cord, or muscular and connective tissue damage as well as from various genetic syndromes or nutritional and metabolic disorders.

Gastroesphogageal reflux: Acidic contents rise up from the stomach irritating the lining of the esophagus. Reflux causes a burning and uncomfortable feeling, and can cause damage to the lining of the esophagus.

Gastrostomy tube: A tube is surgically inserted through the adominal wall directly into the stomach. Food is then inserted directly through this tube. A gastrostomy tube is used if a person is unable to take in or swallow food.

Gibbous: A sharp, angular kyphosis of the spine. This is often seen at at the level of the spina bifida. Surgery at this level involves tucking the exposed spinal cord and nerve roots back inside the membrane, and then covering the wound with muscle and skin flaps. The bones are often uneven and thinly padded by the skin, so a gibbous is especially susceptible to pressure sores.

Greater trochanters: Bony prominences at the upper and outer aspects of the femurs.

Hamstrings: Muscles behind the thighs that go from the ischial tuberosity to the tibia and fibula (lower leg bones).

Hand simulation: Providing support with our hands and body, without seating components to assess how the person responds to support in different areas, and to different shapes and relationships to gravity. Hand simulation informs us about the qualites of the necessary postural supports.

Hemiplegia: Weakness, spasticity, or flaccidity on one side of the body that occurs from damage to the brain, at any time between infancy and adulthood.

Heterotopic ossification: Development of bone in abnormal areas, usually in soft tissue such as muscles and joints.

Hip flexor muscles: Muscles in the front of the hip that cause either the thigh to flex (bend up) or the lower back to arch.

Hip flexion angle: The angle in which the hip joint can bend (flex) before causing the pelvis to roll backwards (posterior tilt). When the hip flexion angle is assessed, the pelvis must be held stable.

Homeopathy: A system of holistic medicine that uses greatly diluted forms of a substance that would ordinarily make a person ill, to stimulate the immune system in order to improve health.

Hydrocephalus: An increased amount of cerebrospinal fluid in the ventricles (reservoirs) in the brain. This can be caused by an overproduction of fluid, or a blockage in the drainage system in the brain. Hydrocephalus causes pressure on the brain, and potentially brain damage.

Hypersensitive: An increased sensitivity to touch. Some people with brain damage may be hypersensitive in that they cannot tolerate specific textures of materials. Sometimes "hypersensitive people" do not want certain parts of their bodies contacted, such as hands, feet, head, or upper part of the shoulders.

Hypotension: Decreased blood pressure.

Hypotonia: Less than normal tone or tension, similar to an arm or leg feeling limp or heavy. When trying to sit up, the person may slump forward. Hypotonia can result from brain, spinal cord, or muscular and connective tissue damage as well as from various genetic syndromes or nutritional and metabolic disorders.

Iliac crest: The bony ridge at the top of the pelvis. See drawing in **pelvis** entry.

Ischial tuberosities: The bony prominences under the pelvis. These are the bones that we sit on. See drawing in **pelvis** entry.

Joint mobilization: Hands-on treatment in which bones are mobilized or moved when a joint is stuck.

Juvenile rheumatoid arthritis (JRA): Arthritis in one or more joints before the age of 16, which lasts at least 6 weeks. Some symptoms include joint pain, limited joint motion, and swollen joints.

Kyphosis: The spine and trunk curve forward. This naturally occurs to a certain degree in the thoracic and sacral spines.

Kyphoscoliosis: A combination of both kyphosis and scoliosis, so that the spine is both curved forward and to the side.

Lordosis: The spine and trunk extend or arch backward. This naturally occurs to a degree in the cervical and lumbar spines.

Lower back support: Extending from the seat cushion to the top of the pelvis/sacrum, it supports the pelvis, sacrum, and lumbar spine.

Lumbar spine: The bones (vertebrae) of the lower back. There are five lumbar vertebrae. The lumbar spine joins the thoracic spine above and the sacral spine below.

Mat table: A low padded table often used for therapy and seating evaluations. Because the mat table is low, the person can transfer from a wheelchair onto it fairly easily. The person can lie down on the mat table for joint and muscular flexibility assessment. Also the person can be assessed in a sitting posture, so that the knees can bend (flex) under the mat table if necessary.

McKenzie method: Also known as Mechanical Diagnosis and Therapy, it is a system of education and active patient involvement for neck, back, arm, and leg problems.

Metatrophic dwarfism: Rare form of dwarfism involving short limbs and a long trunk.

Midline: An imaginary line through the middle of the body from head to toe, midway between the left and right sides.

Mobility system: The base that allows the person to move from place to place. This is different from the seating system, because the seating system is the part that provides postural support. Examples of mobility systems are wheelchairs, power wheelchairs, strollers, wagons, monoskis, horses, boats, and so on.

Motor planning: How the brain organizes and initiates movements.

Multiple sclerosis (MS): Believed to be an autoimmune disease, which means that the body's immune or defense system attacks its own nervous tissue. Symptoms are varied, but may include weakness, numbness, balance problems, fatigue, bladder and bowel problems, blurred speech, dizziness, and blurred vision. MS is a progressive disease, and is characterized by remissions (feeling better) and exacerbations (feeling worse).

Muscular dystrophy (MD): A condition in which the muscles progressively get weaker. One common type, Duchenne's muscular dystrophy (DMD), occurs in boys and usually is detected by 5 years of age.

Myofascial release: Gentle elongation of the muscles and associated fascia (connective tissue).

Myositis ossifications: Development of bone in deep muscle tissue.

Nasogastric tube: A tube that passes from the nose through the esophagus to the stomach. This tube is used when a person has significant problems feeding either temporarily (i.e., after surgery) or permanently.

Nerve manipulation: Gentle manipulation of the nerves to decrease pain and improve mobility.

Neurodevelopmental therapy (NDT): A movement therapy used to work with anyone with neurological problems, particularly children with cerebral palsy and adults with strokes. The approach, created by the Bobaths, is based on infants' normal development.

Neutral posture: In this book, we refer to *the* neutral posture and *the person's* neutral posture. *The* neutral posture is the posture chosen in this book as a common reference point.

The neutral posture

- Pelvis upright and level (neutral) or slightly rolled forward (anterior pelvic tilt)
- Trunk upright with the back following its natural curves
- Hips and legs separated (each leg 5-8° from midline)
- Knees and ankles bent (usually at 90°), so that the feet rest flat on the floor/foot support
- Head upright, in midline, and balanced over the body, allowing the person to look at things in front of her
- Shoulders relaxed, arms free to move and function

The person's neutral posture

The posture in which the person is balanced and stable, but is active and ready to function. In her neutral posture, the person is more restful, so her muscles do not have to work a lot to maintain this posture. However, she is not collapsed and inactive, but instead is ready for action. This posture is her home base or place to come back to between extremes of postural changes.

Nissan fundal plication: A surgical procedure used to treat gastroesophageal reflux and hiatal hernia. The upper part of the stomach is wrapped around the bottom of the esophagus to reinforce the sphincter or valve at the bottom of the esophagus.

Occipital shelf: The occiput is the lowest bone in the back of head. When palpating the occiput, the occipital shelf is the horizontal area that protrudes.

Oriental medicine: Holistic therapy utilizing acupuncture, herbs, and other modalities to restore balance in the body.

Orthoses: Braces or assistive devices that help hold parts of the body in useful positions. Orthoses are typically made for ankles, feet, and legs; forearms and hands; or spine and trunk, and so on. Often they are made out of plastic, or metal bars and leather.

Osteogenesis imperfecta (OI): Also called "brittle bone disease." An inherited disorder of the connective tissue, characterized by fragile bones, frequent fractures, short height, limited joint mobility, and full sensation.

Osteopenia: A condition where the bone mineral density is lower than normal. A person with osteopenia may or may not develop osteoporosis.

Osteoporosis: Softening of the bones. Osteoporosis can be caused by hormonal imbalance and can occur in women after menopause. It also has been seen after bony injury and rickets, and can be associated with long-term use of steroids.

Paralysis: The absence of voluntary movement.

Peripheral nervous system (PNS): The PNS consists of motor and sensory nerves. Sensory nerves carry information from the skin and organs to the CNS. Motor nerves carry information from the CNS to muscles, glands, and organs.

Pelvis: The hip bone. The posture of the pelvis is very important in seating. In sitting, the pelvis is in the neutral posture when the bony prominences in the front of the pelvis (ASIS) are slightly lower than the bony prominences in the back of the pelvis (PSIS), when the lower spine is slightly arched.

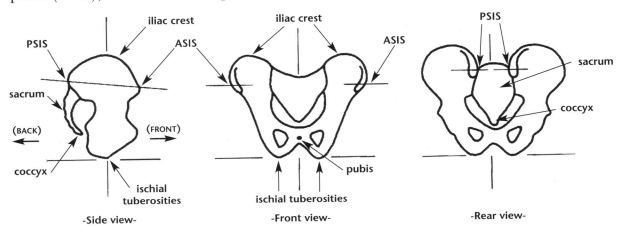

Position: Position is a static, inactive term referring to nonliving things, such as seating components.

Postural control: The ability to hold oneself upright against gravity and move the body through different postures.

Postural options: Choices of various sitting postures needed in order to function.

Postural support: A contact surface providing the body with stability and control necessary to function and move. Your hands, body, or seating components can be postural supports.

Postural support device (PSD): A structure (seating system) attached to a mobility base that helps to support the person's posture.

Postural support device unit: PSD that is not removeable from the mobility device.

Postural support device components: Components that can be added to a wheelchair or PSD to improve support.

Posture: Posture is how the body parts are aligned at any one moment. It is active and dynamic, meaning that the body is ready to move. Normally our posture is constantly shifting and changing so that we can move to function.

Practical flexibility: The degree of comfortable flexibility for the person's joints.

Pressure: The force that a person's body exerts on the seating surface. Pressure is especially relevant to a person who lacks the sensation to feel this pressure, because she or he will be at risk for pressure sores.

Pressure sores: Pressure sores can occur when a person is unable to feel pressure under her buttocks or other bony areas of the body. Consequently, the person does not, or cannot, shift weight off that area. This excessive pressure decreases blood supply to the tissues and the tissues begin to ulcerate and die. Depending on the severity of the pressure sore, layers of the skin, muscle, fascia, and even bone can be affected. Pressure sores can also be caused by sliding of the tissues against the bone, moisture, and poor nutrition. Pressure sores are a leading cause of death and hospitalizations of persons with spinal cord injuries.

Proprioception: The body's awareness of position, location, movement, and orientation of body parts.

PSIS: The posterior superior iliac spine of the pelvis. This is the bony prominence that sticks out in the upper back part of the pelvis. See **pelvis** entry.

Pubis: The center of the front lower part of the pelvis, where the two sides of the pelvis come together. The bony prominences (pubic tubercles) can be found by sliding your hands up to the top of the inner thighs. See **pelvis** entry.

Reduce: Refers to partially or totally correcting, changing, or improving part of a person's body so that that body part is in better alignment (closer to the neutral posture).

Repetitive strain injuries: Pain and tightness in areas of the body because of repetitive motions, such as keyboarding (typing) a lot, playing tennis or other sports, or pushing a wheelchair.

Respirator: A device that supplies oxygen or a mixture of oxygen and carbon dioxide for breathing.

Resting posture: The posture that a person tends to assume when at rest or when not attempting to perform a functional task.

Right angle: 90°.

Rotatory scoliosis: Scoliosis with a rotational component, meaning that in addition to the spine being curved to the side, it is also twisted so that one side of the spine is in front of the opposite side.

Sacrum: The wedge-shaped bone located between both sides of the back of the pelvis. The sacrum's bottom end is connected to the tailbone (coccyx). Its upper end is connected to the bones of the low back (lumbar vertebrae). The sacrum is actually five vertebrae (bones of the spine) fused together. See **pelvis** entry.

Scapula: Shoulder blade.
> **Spine of the scapula:** Horizontal ridge at the top of the scapula.
> **Inferior angle of the scapula:** Bottom point of the triangular-shaped scapula that often sticks out.

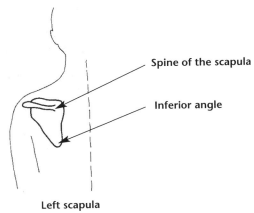

Spine of the scapula

Inferior angle

Left scapula

Scoliosis: The spine curves to the side. Sometimes it curves as a single, large C-shaped curve, and sometimes it has two curves so that it forms a S-shaped curve. In this book, scoliosis is labeled left or right by the side of the convexity.

Seat-to-back support angle: The angle between the seat cushion and the lower part of the back support.

Seating system: Seating components that are put together with the purpose of supporting the person's posture. A seating system can be a simple seat cushion, or a combination of a back support, seat cushion, and other postural supports (e.g., head/neck supports, pelvic and trunk supports, chest straps, pelvic positioning belts).

Seating/mobility system: The seating system and the mobility system combined.

Seizures: A person who has a seizure becomes unconscious for a very short period of time. A person who has a "petit mal" or mild seizure can appear to blank out for a few moments. If a person has a "grand mal" or bigger seizure, her whole body can move uncontrollably. A seating system for a person with grand mal seizures should protect her from falling forward out of her seating system when she has seizures.

Sensation: The ability to physically feel light touch, firm pressure, and heat and cold. A person with a complete spinal cord injury usually has impaired ability to feel these sensations at and below the level of the spinal injury.

Shear: The horizontal force caused by a sideways (lateral) sliding movement between tissues and bones. Shear can increase the risk of pressure sores in areas of bony prominences. Increased shearing can occur when the person slips and slides down out of her seating system.

Shoulder girdle: The shoulder joint, clavicle, shoulder blade (scapula), and the muscles and tissues in that area.

Shunt: A hole or passage that moves fluid from one part of the body to another. In persons with hydrocephalus, a shunt is a tube with a valve that drains excessive cerebrospinal fluid from the brain to either the abdominal cavity (most common), the pleural cavity (surrounding the lungs), or into the heart (rare).

Sidelying: Position of lying on the side. Sidelying in the concept of the seating assessment presented in this book is with the hips bent (flexed) to 90° or to the limit of hip flexibility.

Simulation: The process of representing, mocking-up, or imitating. In this book, simulation can be done with hands or with materials. Hand simulation is providing support with our hands and body, without seating components to assess how the person responds to support in different areas, and to different shapes and relationships to gravity. Simulation with materials is making a trial representation of the seating system to assess and change it prior to deciding on the final design.

Simulator: A seating evaluation chair that may have the capabilities of changing seat depth and width, seat-cushion type, back-support height and type, seat-to-back support angle, lower-leg support length, leg-to-seat surface angle, foot-support-to-leg angle, postural supports, and system tilt.

Spasticity: Spasticity is tightness in the muscles caused by damage to either the brain or spinal cord. Muscles on one side of the joint tend to be tighter than muscles on the other side of the joint.

Special seating: Providing a seating system for a person with a disability to achieve the person's individual goals, such as to improve posture, function, relieve excessive pressure and shear, enhance comfort, and improve bodily functions.

Spina bifida: Also called meningocele or myelomeningocoele. It is a vertebral (backbone) defect in which the vertebrae do not close over the spinal cord. This defect occurs in utero, before the baby is born. An unprotected bag of nerves bulges through the skin, so the baby essentially has a spinal cord injury. The physical effects of spina bifida depend on the levels of the spinal cord at which the defect is located. (See **spinal cord injury** entry.)

Spinal cord injury: A spinal cord injury usually occurs with a traumatic accident, such as a car accident or a fall. The physical effects of a spinal cord injury depend on where the back is broken and spinal cord is damaged. If the spinal cord is injured in the neck, a person may lose a lot of function in the hands, and usually all function in the trunk and legs. If the spinal cord is damaged lower in the back, a person will lose function in the legs. If the injury is incomplete, not all function will be lost below the level of the injury. Other effects of a spinal cord injury are lack of sensation, problems with bowel and bladder control, temperature regulating mechanisms, and sexual function.

Spinal muscle atrophy: A term applied to a number of genetic disorders that affect the nervous system so that the person has muscular weakness and atrophy.

Spinous process: The bony prominences on each vertebrae that stick out towards the back of the body.

Sternum: The breastbone, situated between the left and right ribcage in the front of the body.

Strain/counterstrain: A gentle hands-on therapy used to treat muscle and joint pain and problems. The spasmed muscles and joints are positioned towards positions of tissue ease or comfort in order to gently release the spasms.

Stroke: A blood vessel carrying blood to the brain is either blocked or breaks open. When blood flow stops for longer than a few seconds, the brain cannot get enough blood and oxygen. Brain damage can result.

Subluxation: A subluxation occurs when a bone comes partially out of its socket. Typical subluxations can be caused by spastic and tight muscles and can occur in the hip, ankle, shoulder, hand, and so on. A hip subluxation may eventually lead to a hip dislocation if not treated.

Supine: The position of lying on the back, face up, looking at the ceiling.

Tactile sensitivity: See **hypersensitive**. A sensory issue in which touch is perceived as uncomfortable and sometimes even dangerous. A person who is tactilely sensitive may avoid touching, can become fearful or bothered by shirt tags, a hug, dirty hands, and bare feet on grass or sand.

Thoracic spine: The bones (vertebrae) of the mid-back. There are 12 thoracic vertebrae. The thoracic spine joins the cervical spine above and the lumbar spine below and the ribs to the side.

Tissue: Muscle, skin, and fascia.

Torticollis: A condition in which the head is tilted toward one side and rotated to the opposite side. It can be congenital or acquired, and has different causes.

Traumatic brain injury (TBI): Adults or children may incur a brain injury from accidents, falls, sports, abuse, gunshot wounds, and so on. Because of the complex nature of the brain, each person with a TBI will present differently.

Ventilator: A machine that helps to move breathable air into the person's lungs.

Vertebrae: Individual bones of the spine.

Vestibular system: This sensory system provides information about the body's movement and orientation in space. In essence, it is the main system that controls balance and equilibrium.

Visceral manipulation: Gentle mobilization of the organs and their associated structures to improve both movement and function of the organs and associated muscles, joints, and fascia.

Visual perception: The ability to recognize and identify what you see.

Wheel camber: In a wheelchair, the top of the rear wheel is slanted toward the seating system or mobility frame. Wheel camber can improve side-to-side wheelchair stability.

Suggested Reading

Aging with a disability. Available at http://www.jik.com/awdrtcawd.html *See:* www.agingwithdisability.org (Ranchos Los Amigos).

Barral JP, Mercier P. *Visceral Manipulation.* Seattle: Eastland Press; 1988.

Barton A, Barton M. *The Management of Pressure Sores.* London: Faber and Faber; 1981.

Bergen A, Presperin J, Tallman T. *Positioning for Function: Wheelchairs and Other Assistive Technologies.* Valhalla, NY: Valhalla Rehabilitation Publications, Ltd.; 1990.

Campbell S, VanderLinden D, Palisano R. *Physical Therapy for Children.* St. Louis, MO: Saunders/Elsevier; 2000.

Engstrom, B. *Ergonomics Wheelchairs and Positioning.* Hasselby, Sweden: Bromma Tryck AB; 1993.

Hotchkiss, R. *Independence through Mobility: A Guide to the Manufacture of the ATI-Hotchkiss Wheelchair.* Washington, DC: Appropriate Technology International, 1985.

Ride Safe. Rehabilitation Engineering Research Center on Wheelchair Transportation Safety from the University of Michigan Health System, University of Michigan Transportation Research Institute. 2005. Available at: www.travelsafer.org.

Trefler E, Hobson D, Taylor SJ, Monahan L, Shaw CG. *Seating and Mobility for Persons with Physical Disabilities.* Tucson, AZ: Therapy Skill Builders; 1993.

Ward D. *Prescriptive Seating for Wheeled Mobility.* Ft. Lauderdale, FL: HealthWealth International; 1994.

Werner D. *Disabled Village Children.* Palo Alto, CA: Hesperian Foundation: 1987.

Werner D. *Nothing About Us Without Us.* Palo Alto, CA; Healthwrights; 1998.

Zacharow D. *Posture: Sitting, Standing, Chair Design and Exercise.* Springfield: Charles Thomas; 1988.

Pope P. *Severe and Complex Neurological Disability: Managemnt of the Physical Condition.* St. Louis, MO: Elsevier; 2007.

2008 ISO Standards from RESNA (Inderdisciplinary Association for the Advancement of Rehabilitation and Assistive Technologies)

> RESNA Technical Standards Board
> 1700 N. Moore St., Ste. 1540
> Arlington, VA 22209-1903
> Email: publications@resna.org
> Internet: www.resna.org

> World Health Organization
> Who Library Database
> Internet: http://www.who.int/publications/en/

APPENDIX A
SEATING ASSESSMENT FORM (LONG FORM)

Name: _____ Date: _____

Disability: _____ Date of Birth: _____

Age: _____

Gathering Information
A. Reasons for Seating Assessment

_____

_____

_____

B. Health Issues Related to the Person's Disability
1. Person's diagnosis/disability _____
2. Breathing problems _____
3. Heart and circulatory problems _____
4. Seizures _____
5. Bladder/bowel control _____
6. Nutrition/digestion _____
7. Medications _____
8. Surgeries _____
9. Orthopedic concerns _____
10. Orthotic intervention _____
11. Skin condition _____
12. Sensation _____
13. Pain _____
14. Seeing _____
15. Hearing _____
16. Cognitive/perceptual/behavioral status _____

_____

C. Environments
Note smallest doorways, ramp incline, stairs, turning space, table/bed/toilet heights.

Dimensions / Place	Smallest door width	Ramp incline length/ height	Number of stairs	Smallest turning space	Table height		Bed height	Toilet height	Other
					Top surface	Leg clearance			
Home									
School									
Work									
Recreation									
Other									

D. Transportation

How will the seating/mobility system be transported? Can it collapse or be taken apart for transport? What extra supports are needed for safety during transport?

Car _____

Van _____

Schoolbus _____

Public transportation _____

Other _____

E. Assessment of Present Mobility System

Type of mobility system _____

Age and condition _____

Seat width _____

Back height _____

Special supports/straps _____

Other equipment used with seating/mobility system _____

_____

Equipment used in the past: pros/cons _____

_____

F. Funding Issues

Funding source _____

Guidelines/criteria _____

Documentation required _____

Physical Assessment: Posture, Movement, and Function

A. Posture in Present Seating/Mobility System

1. Pelvis/low back _____

2. Trunk _____

	Left	Right
3. Hips and legs	_____	_____
4. Knees	_____	_____
5. Ankles and feet	_____	_____
6. Head and neck	_____	_____
7. Shoulder girdles	_____	_____
8. Arms	_____	_____

Drawing/photo of total body resting posture

B. Functional Skills in Present Seating/Mobility System:

Note ability and assistance needed:

1. **Walking**: Able to walk?_____ Assistance needed?_____
   Assistive device? _____ Braces? _____ Distance? _____

2. **Transfers**   Surface Height   **Amount of Assistance**
   To & from bed _____
   To & from toilet _____
   To & from bathtub _____
   To & from car _____
   Ability to adjust or remove seating/mobility components _____
   _____

3. **Wheelchair Propulsion**
   Self-propel? _____ Axle position _____
   Posture and movement _____
   _____
   Power wheelchair? _____ Control, switches _____
   Posture and movement _____
   Attendant-operated? _____ Handle height _____

Are the following activities done in the seating system? If so, are they independently performed?
Describe changes in posture and movement, and space necessary to do activities.

4. **Dressing** _____
   _____

5. **Bathing** _____

6. **Toileting** _____

7. **Eating** _____
   _____

8. **Communicating** _____
   _____
   _____

9. **Tabletop activities** _____
   _____
   _____

10. **Work/vocational/homemaking activities** _____
   _____
   _____

C. Joint and Muscular Flexibility Assessed Lying on Back or Side

Note percentage of flexibility, and practical, comfortable flexibility of person's habitual posture.
The posture (i.e., rolled backward) under the body part (i.e., pelvis) is the person's habitual posture.

0% = Totally fixed. 100% = Totally flexible.

Person's Habitual Posture	How Flexible?	Comments
Pelvis/Low Back		
Rolled backward (posterior tilt)	_____	_____
Rolled forward (anterior tilt)	_____	_____
Tilted to the side (lateral pelvic tilt)	_____	_____
Turned (rotated)	_____	_____
Trunk		
Curved forward (kyphosis)	_____	_____
Curved to one side (scoliosis)	_____	_____
Rotated forward on one side (rotated)	_____	_____
Arched backward (extended)	_____	_____

	Left	Right	Comments
Hips			
Bending up separately (flexion)	_____	_____	_____
Moved to midline (adducted)	_____	_____	_____
Turned in (internally rotated)	_____	_____	_____
Spread open (abducted)	_____	_____	_____
Turned out (externally rotated)	_____	_____	_____
Knees			
Bent (flexed)	_____	_____	_____
Straight (extended)	_____	_____	_____
Ankles/Feet			
Bent up (dorsiflexed)	_____	_____	_____
Bent down (plantarflexed)	_____	_____	_____
Turned in (inverted)	_____	_____	_____
Turned out (everted)	_____	_____	_____
Head and Neck	_____	_____	_____
Shoulder Girdles			
Shrugged upwards (elevated)	_____	_____	_____
Pulled forward and turned in (protracted and internally rotated)	_____	_____	_____
Pulled backward and turned out (retracted and externally rotated)	_____	_____	_____
Arms			
Stiffly bent (flexed)	_____	_____	_____
Stiffly straight (extended)	_____	_____	_____

D. Balance and Postural Control in Sitting

Good _____

Fair _____

Poor _____

E. Assessment in Sitting: Flexibility and Postural Support

1. Pelvis/Low Back

a. Neutral pelvis _____

b. Active pelvic control _____

	How Flexible?	Comments
c. Rolled backward (posterior tilt)	_____	_____
d. Stiffening and sliding forward (thrust)	_____	_____
e. Rolled forward (anterior tilt)	_____	_____
f. Tilted to the side (lateral pelvic tilt)	_____	_____
g. Turned (rotated)	_____	_____

Hand simulation: Where, direction and amount of support, least amount of support.

_____

_____

_____

2. Trunk

a. Neutral trunk _____

b. Active trunk control _____

	How Flexible?	Comments
c. Curved forward (kyphosis)	_____	_____
d. Curved to one side (scoliosis)	_____	_____
e. Rotated forward on one side (rotated)	_____	_____
f. Arched backwards (extended)	_____	_____

Hand simulation: Posture of spine over pelvis. Where, direction and amount of support, least amount of support, amount and shape of contact surface.

_____

_____

_____

3. Hips and Legs

	Left	Right	Comments
a. Neutral hips	_____	_____	_____
b. Active hip control	_____	_____	_____

	How Flexible?		Comments
c. Moved to midline (adducted)	_____	_____	_____
d. Turned in (internally rotated)	_____	_____	_____
e. Spread open (abducted)	_____	_____	_____
f. Turned out (externally rotated)	_____	_____	_____
g. Turned, same side (windswept)	_____	_____	_____
h. Legs moving constantly	_____	_____	_____

Hand simulation: Where, direction and amount of support, least amount of support.

_____

_____

_____

4. **Knees**	Left	Right	Comments
a. Neutral knees	_____	_____	_____
b. Active knee control	_____	_____	_____
	How Flexible?		
c. Bent (flexed)	_____	_____	_____
d. Straightened (extended)	_____	_____	_____

Hand simulation: Where, direction and amount of support, least amount of support.

_____
_____
_____

5. **Ankles/Feet**	Left	Right	Comments
a. Neutral ankles	_____	_____	_____
b. Active ankle control	_____	_____	_____

Hand simulation: Where, direction and amount of support, least amount of support.

_____
_____
_____

6. **Head and Neck**
a. Neutral head _____
b. Active head control _____

Hand simulation: Posture of spine over pelvis. Head in relation to gravity. Where support is needed. Least amount of support. Amount and shape of contact surface.

_____
_____
_____

7. **Shoulder Girdles**	Left	Right	Comments
a. Neutral shoulder girdles	_____	_____	_____
b. Active arm control	_____	_____	_____
	How Flexible?		
c. Shrugged upwards (elevated)	_____	_____	_____
d. Pulled forward and turned in (protracted and internally rotated)	_____	_____	_____
e. Pulled backward and turned out (retracted and externally rotated)	_____	_____	_____

Hand simulation: Where, direction and amount of support.

_____
_____
_____

8. **Arms**	Left	Right
a. Neutral arms	_____	_____
b. Active arm control	_____	_____

Hand simulation: Where, direction and amount of support, least amount of support.

_____
_____
_____

F. Effect of Gravity in Sitting

	Relax	Pull Against	Head Control
Backwards tilt (optimal amount)	_____	_____	_____
Forwards tilt	_____	_____	_____
Tilting needed for better breathing, pressure relief?	_____	_____	_____

G. Pressure: Wiggle Test/Pressure Measuring

Put your fingers under concerning bony prominences and assess if whether:
1. You can wiggle your fingers.
2. Your fingers are pinched but you can pull your fingers out easily.
3. Fingers are pinched and it is difficult to pull your fingers out.

Sacrum _____   Coccyx _____   Ischial tuberosities _____

Greater trochanters _____   Other _____

Objectives

A. Person's Postural & Functional Objectives	B. Seating System Objectives
Pelvis	
Trunk	
Hips and legs	
Knees	
Ankles and feet	
Head and neck	
Shoulder girdles	
Arms	

C. Mobility and Other Objectives

_____
_____
_____
_____
_____
_____
_____
_____
_____
_____

Seating and Mobility Components
A. Seating System Components

Lower back support _____
Upper back support _____
Seat cushion _____

Seat-to-lower back support angle _____
Lower back support-to-upper back support angle _____
Leg-to-seat surface angle _____
Foot support-to-leg angle _____
Tilt of the seating system _____

Pelvic supports _____
  Anterior (front) _____
  Lateral (side) _____
  Inferior (bottom) _____

Trunk supports _____
  Anterior (front) _____
  Lateral (side) _____

Upper leg support _____
  Medial (middle) _____
  Lateral (side) _____
  Superior (top) _____

Lower leg supports _____
  Anterior (front) _____
  Posterior (behind) _____

Ankle/foot supports _____
  Anterior/circumferential (front) _____
  Posterior (behind) _____
  Medial/lateral (sides) _____
  Posterior (behind) _____

Head/neck supports _____
  Posterior (behind) _____
  Lateral (side) _____
  Anterior (front) _____

Shoulder girdle supports _____

Arm supports _____

B. Additional Components

Laptray _____

  Grasping bars: horizontal, vertical _____

Wedges (scapulae, arms) _____

Blocks (elbows) _____

Troughs (legs, arms) _____

Straps _____

Adjustability of components and angles _____

C. Wheelchair Considerations

Seat surface height at front edge _____

Width of seating/mobility system _____

Forward/backward position of
  seating system within mobility system _____

Cushion covering _____

Seating system removable from mobility system _____

Wheelchair foldability _____

Push handle height _____

Tilt or recline _____

Measurements in Sitting

Left   Right

1. Seat surface (the contact point of the buttocks) to:
   a. PSIS
   b. Elbows
   c. Bottom of ribs
   d. Inferior angle of scapula
   e. Top of evaluator's hands
   f. Spine of scapula
   g. Occipital shelf
   h. Top of head
2. Back of body to:
   a. Front of ribs (trunk depth)
   b. PSIS (pelvis to trunk offset)
   c. Back of head (trunk to head offset)
3. Leg length
   (where hips touch flat surface to back of knees)
4. IT to back of knee
5. Height of thigh
6. Back of knee to heel (or weight-bearing area)
7. Foot length
8. Trunk width
9. Shoulder width
10. Hip width (greatest width)
11. Outer knee width (relaxed, with knees apart)
12. Inner knee width
13. Ankle width
    a. Inner width
    b. Outer width
14. Ankle circumference
15. Head width
16. Head circumference

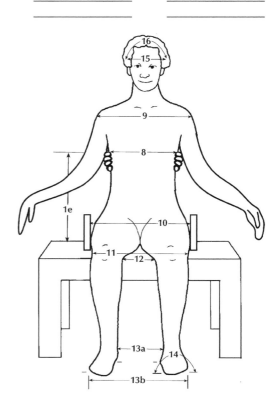

APPENDIX B
SEATING ASSESSMENT FORM (SHORT FORM)

Name: _____ Date: _____ Age: _____

Disability: _____ Date of Birth:_____

Gathering Information
A. Reasons for Seating Assessment _____
_____
_____

B. Health Issues Related to the Person's Disability _____
_____
_____

C. Environments
Note smallest doorways, ramp incline, stairs, turning space, table/bed/toilet heights at home, school, work, and so on.

Dimensions / Place	Smallest door width	Ramp incline length/ height	Number of stairs	Smallest turning space	Table height		Bed height	Toilet height	Other
					Top surface	Leg clearance			
Home									
School									
Work									
Recreation									
Other									

D. Transportation
How will the seating/mobility system be transported? Can it collapse or be taken apart for transport? What extra supports are needed for safety during transport? _____
_____
_____

E. Assessment of Present Mobility System _____
_____
_____
_____

F. Funding Issues _____
_____
_____

Physical Assessment: Posture, Movement, and Function
A. Posture in Present Seating/Mobility System

1. Pelvis/low back _____
2. Trunk _____

	Left	Right
3. Hips and legs	_____	_____
4. Knees	_____	_____
5. Ankles and feet	_____	_____
6. Head and neck	_____	_____
7. Shoulder girdles	_____	_____
8. Arms	_____	_____

B. Functional Skills in Present Seating/Mobility System
Note ability and assistance needed:

1. **Walking**: Able to walk?_____ Assistance needed?_____
   Assistive device? _____ Braces? _____ Distance? _____

2. **Transfers**   Surface Height   Amount of Assistance

   To and from bed_____
   To and from toilet _____
   To and from bathtub _____
   To and from car _____
   Ability to adjust or remove seating/mobility components_____
   _____

3. **Wheelchair Propulsion**
   Self-propel? _____ Axle position _____
   Posture and movement _____
   Power wheelchair? _____ Control, switches _____
   Posture and movement _____
   Attendant-operated? _____ Handle height _____

Are the following activities done in the seating system? If so, are they independently performed? Describe changes in posture and movement, and space necessary to do activities.

4. **Dressing** _____
   _____

5. **Bathing**_____

6. **Toileting** _____

7. **Eating**_____
   _____

8. **Communicating** _____
   _____

9. **Tabletop activities** _____
   _____

10. **Work/vocational/homemaking activities** _____
    _____

344

C. Joint and Muscular Flexibility Assessed Lying on Back or Side

Note percentage of flexibility. Note practical flexibility.

0% = Totally fixed. 100% = Totally flexible.

	Posture	How Practically Flexible?
Pelvis/Low Back		
Trunk		
Head/Neck		
	Left	Right
Hips		
Knees		
Ankles/Feet		
Shoulder Girdles		
Arms		

D. Balance and Postural Control in Sitting

Good _____

Fair _____

Poor _____

E. Assessment in Sitting: Flexibility and Postural Support

	Posture	How Flexible?	Hand Support

1. Pelvis/Low Back

2. Trunk

3. Hips and Legs

4. Knees

5. Ankles/Feet

6. Head and Neck

7. Shoulder Girdles

8. Arms

F. Effect of Gravity in Sitting

_____
_____
_____

G. Pressure: Wiggle Test/Pressure Measuring
Put your fingers under concerning boney prominences and assess whether:
   1. You can wiggle your fingers.
   2. Your fingers are pinched but you can pull your fingers out.
   3. Fingers are pinched and you can not pull your fingers out.
   Sacrum _____   Coccyx _____   Ischial tuberosities _____
   Greater trochanters _____   Other _____

Objectives

A. Person's Postural & Functional Objectives	B. Seating System Objectives
Pelvis	
Trunk	
Hips and legs	
Knees	
Ankles and feet	
Head and neck	
Shoulder girdles	
Arms	

C. Mobility and Other Objectives _____

_____

_____

_____

Seating and Mobility Components

A. Seating System Components

Lower back support _____

Upper back support _____

Seat cushion _____

Seat-to-lower back support angle _____

Lower back support-to-upper back support angle _____

Leg-to-seat surface angle _____

Foot support-to-leg angle _____

Tilt of the seating system _____

Pelvic supports _____

   Anterior (front) _____

   Lateral (side) _____

Trunk supports _____

   Anterior (front) _____

   Lateral (side) _____

Upper leg support _____

   Medial (middle) _____

   Lateral (side) _____

   Superior (top) _____

Lower leg supports _____

   Anterior _____

   Posterior _____

Ankle/foot supports _____

Head/neck supports _____

Shoulder girdle supports _____

Arm supports _____

Laptray _____

Wedges (scapulae, arms) _____

Troughs (legs, arms) _____

Straps _____

Adjustability of components and angles _____

B. Wheelchair Considerations

Seat height _____

Width of seating/mobility system _____

Position of seating system within mobility system _____

Cushion covering _____

Seating system removable from mobility system _____

Wheelchair foldability _____

Measurements in Sitting

Left   Right

1. Seat surface (the contact point of the buttocks) to:
   a. PSIS
   b. Elbows
   c. Bottom of ribs
   d. Inferior angle of scapula
   e. Top of evaluator's hands
   f. Spine of scapula
   g. Occipital shelf
   h. Top of head
2. Back of body to:
   a. Front of ribs (trunk depth)
   b. PSIS (pelvis to trunk offset)
   c. Back of head (trunk to head offset)
3. Leg length
   (where hips touch flat surface to back of knees)
4. IT to back of knee
5. Height of thigh
6. Back of knee to heel (or weight-bearing area)
7. Foot length
8. Trunk width
9. Shoulder width
10. Hip width (greatest width)
11. Outer knee width (relaxed, with knees apart)
12. Inner knee width
13. Ankle width
    a. Inner width
    b. Outer width
14. Ankle circumference
15. Head width
16. Head circumference

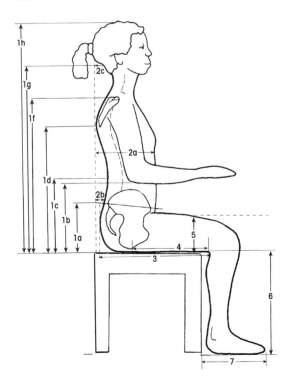

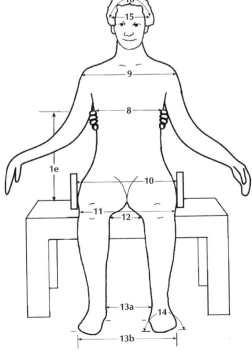

APPENDIX C
MEASUREMENT OF SEATING COMPONENTS

This form has been adapted from one used by Jamie Noon. You can use it as a template from which to design the seating/mobility system. Please note that the seating components are represented by capital letters. The underlined numbers under the components refer to the numbers in the person's measurement form. For instance, D. Height of the lower back support = 1a (height of the PSIS).

A. **Height of head support**: This refers to 1g, the measurement from the seat surface to the occipital shelf. The height of the head support will depend on the type of head support chosen (in this example, a sub-occipital support).

B. **Height of back support**: The height depends on the degree of trunk control and balance (see page 123). Remember, if the person has:
- Poor trunk control, the height can be to the spine of the scapula: 1f.
- Fair trunk control, the height can be to 0.5-1" (1.27-2.54 cm) below the inferior angle of the scapula: 1d.
- Good trunk control, the height can come to the last two floating ribs (ribs 11 and 12): 1c.

C. **Depth of lower back support**: 2b., pelvis to trunk offset measured from the back of the body to the PSIS.

D. **Height of lower back support**: 1a., seat surface to PSIS.

E. **Position of posterior head support**: 2c. This will be in relation to the back support. Sometimes the number will be positive (head forward of back support), and sometimes the number will be negative (head behind back support).

F. **Height of lateral trunk supports**: 1e. Left and right measurements may be different, especially if you are utilizing a 3-point control system for scoliosis.

G. **Length of pre-ischial shelf**: 4-thickness of soft foam and space behind the knee. (This means subtract for the thickness of soft foam and space behind the knee).

H. **Seat depth**: 3 (back of buttocks to back of knee) + C (depth of lower back support) + back support depth. Of course, if a lower back support is not used, do not add C.

I. **Lateral position of the lateral trunk supports**: 8. During the fitting, it is helpful to place these from a vertical reference line in the center of the back support. This is especially important if the person has scoliosis such that one trunk support is much more lateral than the other trunk support.

J. **Lateral pelvic supports**: 10. During the fitting, it is helpful to place these from a reference line in the center of the seat cushion. This is important especially if the person has a pelvis that is off-center due to a fixed pelvic/spinal/hip deformity. The height will be the height of the thighs: 5.

K. **Lateral upper leg supports**: 11. During the fitting, it is helpful to place these from a reference line in the center of the seat cushion. This is important especially if the person has hips and legs that are windswept or one is adducted/abducted. The height will be the height of the thighs: 5.

L. Width of seat: (<u>11</u> + width of K) dictates the width of the chair. So, if a person has spinal, pelvic and hip deformities which necessitate a wider back support or seat cushion, the seat cushion width will need to be the distance between the 2 widest parts of the body.

M. Depth of foot support: <u>7</u> + 10 cm. Please add extra room for cases where one foot is further forward than the other or if an anterior or posterior foot support is used.

N. Depth of laptray cut-out: <u>2a</u> + 5 cm.

O. Width of laptray: P + 20 cm.

P. Width of laptray cutout: <u>8</u> + 6 cm.

Q. Depth of laptray: N + 30 cm.

R.-V. Medial upper leg support
R. Rear and V. front width (<u>12</u>). The width will depend on your assessment of thigh location during hand simulation, and the type of medial upper leg supports. If the hips are flexible and comfortable at 5-7°of hip abduction, the front edge of medial upper leg support is typically wider towards the knees, due to the natural shape of the thighs. The rear width will depend on the length of the medial upper leg support.

S. Height (<u>5</u>) will be the height of the thighs.

T. and U. Length: The length can be the distance from the front of the femur to approximately one-third up the distance of the femur. If the tissue is thin over the femoral condyles, the boney prominences at the sides of the front edges of the femur, it is helpful to shape the support to relieve excessive pressure in these areas. In this template, the medial upper leg support extends over the edge of the seat surface.

Name: _____

Date: _____

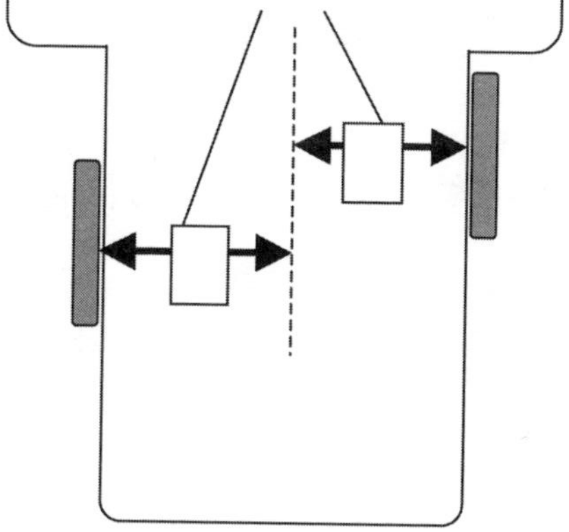

O. Laptray width: P + 20 cm

P. Width of the laptray cutout: 8 + 6 cm

Q. Depth of the laptray: N + 30 cm

N. Depth of the laptray cutout: 2a + 5 cm

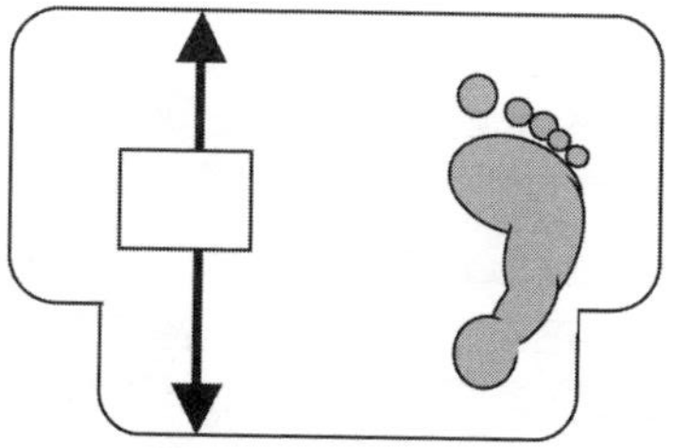

M. Depth of foot supports: 7 + 10 cm

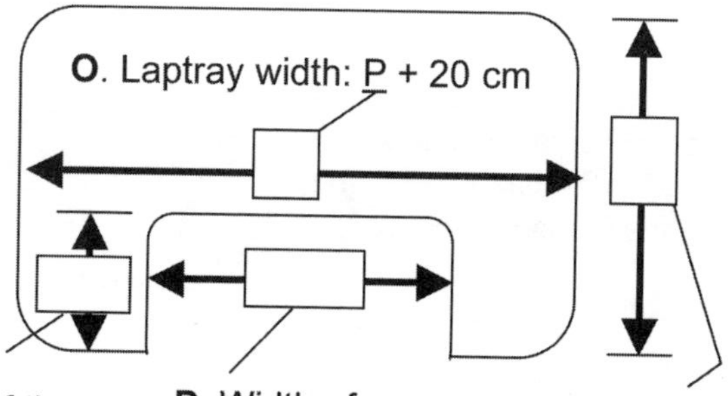

Medial upper leg support

R. Width at rear
S. Height: 5
T. Length: edge of seat surface to inner thigh
U. Length: edge of seat surface to front of femur
V. Front width: 12

Medial upper leg support

Edge of seat surface

R.

S.

T.

U.

V.

Special Measurements

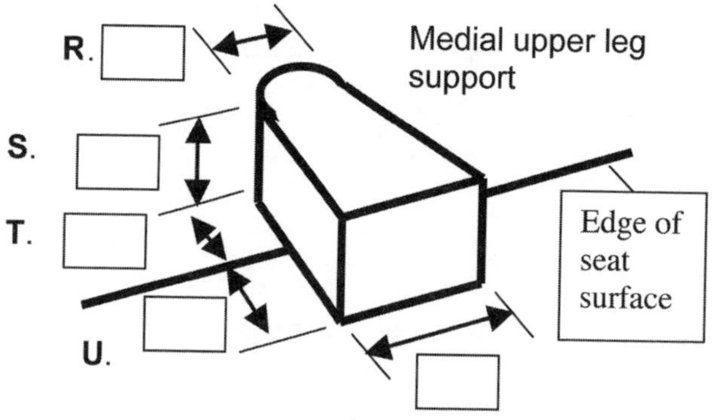

Note: This is a seat design for a person who requires postural support. If a pressure-relief cushion is needed, see pages 225-31.

I. Lateral trunk supports measure from midline: 8

J. Lateral pelvic supports— measure to midline: 10

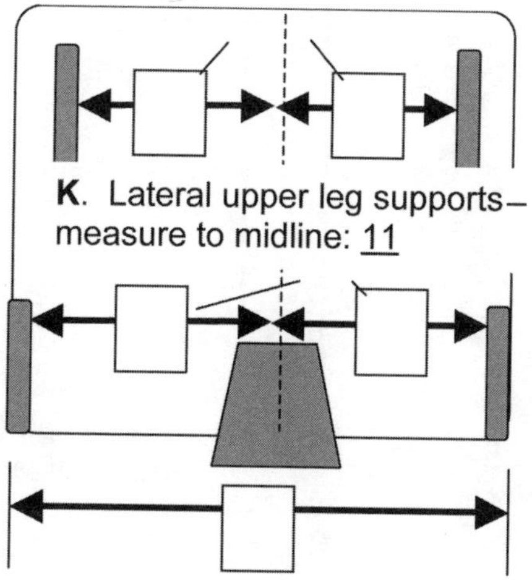

K. Lateral upper leg supports— measure to midline: 11

L. Width of the seat: 11 + width of **K**

Name:

Date:

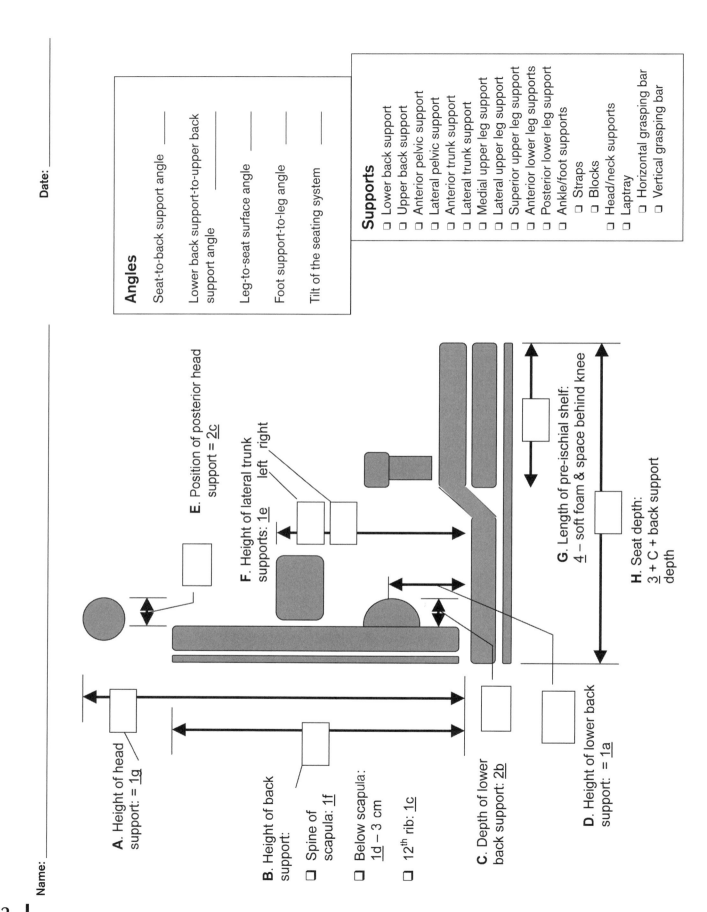

Angles

Seat-to-back support angle _____

Lower back support-to-upper back support angle _____

Leg-to-seat surface angle _____

Foot support-to-leg angle _____

Tilt of the seating system _____

Supports

☐ Lower back support
☐ Upper back support
☐ Anterior pelvic support
☐ Lateral pelvic support
☐ Anterior trunk support
☐ Lateral trunk support
☐ Medial upper leg support
☐ Lateral upper leg support
☐ Superior upper leg support
☐ Anterior lower leg supports
☐ Posterior lower leg support
☐ Ankle/foot supports
  ☐ Straps
  ☐ Blocks
☐ Head/neck supports
☐ Laptray
  ☐ Horizontal grasping bar
  ☐ Vertical grasping bar

A. Height of head support: = <u>1g</u>

B. Height of back support:

☐ Spine of scapula: <u>1f</u>

☐ Below scapula: <u>1d</u> – 3 cm

☐ 12th rib: <u>1c</u>

C. Depth of lower back support: <u>2b</u>

D. Height of lower back support: = <u>1a</u>

E. Position of posterior head support = <u>2c</u>

F. Height of lateral trunk supports: <u>1e</u>   left   right

G. Length of pre-ischial shelf: <u>4</u> – soft foam & space behind knee

H. Seat depth: <u>3</u> + C + back support depth

APPENDIX D
SEATING ASSESSMENT FORM (LONG FORM)

Name: Aaron Johnson-Benning   **Date:** September 28, 1994

Disability: Spastic quadriplegia and blindness from hypoxic encephalopathy at 3 years of age

Age: 14 years

Gathering Information

A. Reasons for Seating Assessment

1. Be able to wheel independently inside home and school. 2. Support his posture to improve function; feeding, using communication Unicorn board, drawing, using Braille write, dressing (shirt). 3. Be comfortable. 4. Be able to transfer with assistance easily (stand-pivot).

B. Health Issues Related to the Person's Disability

1. Person's diagnosis/disability _Spastic quadriplegia, (R)side more involved_
2. Breathing problems _significant asthma, hospitalized many times_
3. Heart and circulatory problems _cold feet_
4. Seizures _N/A_
5. Bladder/bowel control _Able to control bladder and bowel_
6. Nutrition/digestion _Now WNL—had gastro-esophageal reflux until '89 underwent Nissan fundal plication_
7. Medications _Corticosteroids as necessary for asthma_
8. Surgeries _Bilateral adductor releases, TAL, derotation osteotomy, 2° (R)hip subluxation_
9. Orthopedic concerns _Probably osteoporotic from heavy corticosteroid doses_
10. Orthotic intervention _Bilateral ankle/foot orthoses_
11. Skin condition _No skin abnormalities or redness_
12. Sensation _Increased sensitivity to touch on feet and head, otherwise normal_
13. Pain _Occasional discomfort around (R)hip_
14. Seeing _Unable to see_
15. Hearing _WNL_
16. Cognitive/perceptual/behavioral status _Cognition is WNL, Perceptual problems with memory; proprioception; spatial awareness; has great fear of falling_

C. Environments:

Note smallest doorways, ramp incline, stairs, turning space, table/bed/toilet heights.

Dimensions / Place	Smallest door width	Ramp incline length/height	Number of stairs	Smallest turning space	Table Height Top surface	Table Height Leg clearance	Bed height	Toilet height	Other
Home	27"	None	2	24"	30"	28"	26"	15"	—
School	32"	12"/1'	None	30"	28"	26"	N/A	15"	—
Work	N/A								
Recreation	N/A								
Other	N/A								

D. Transportation

How will the seating/mobility system be transported? Can it collapse or be taken apart for transport? What extra supports are needed for safety during transport?

Car _N/A_
Van _Family van has lift. Must remove seating system and fold wheelchair._
Schoolbus _Has lift and wheelchair tie downs – no need to fold wheelchair._
Public Transportation _N/A_
Other _N/A_

E. Assessment of Present Mobility System

Type of Mobility System _Lightweight wheelchair with sling seat and sling back_
Age and condition _4 years old – good condition_
Seat width _Seat width – 14"_
Back height _Back height – 14"_
Special supports/straps _Seatbelt_
Other equipment used with seating/mobility system _Laptray; Uses computer and Braille writer at school_
Equipment used in the past – pros/cons _N/A_

F. Funding Issues

Funding source _Private health insurance_
Guidelines/criteria _Needs to be medically justifiable_
Documentation required _Specific seating evaluation, justification letter_

Physical Assessment: Posture, Movement, and Function

A. Posture in Present Seating/Mobility System

1. Pelvis/Low Back _Rolled backward (post. pelvic tilt), Tilted down on(R) Rotated forward on(R)_
2. Trunk _Curved forward (kyphosis) and curved to the(R)(convex)_

	Left	Right
3. Hips and Legs	Neutral	Moved and turned in (add, IR)
4. Knees	Extends(L)foot off foot support	Flexed to 90°
5. Ankles and Feet	Turns in (invert), orthoses	Turns in (invert), orthoses
6. Head and Neck	Good head control, tends to rotate head to(L)	
7. Shoulder Girdles	Shrugs, good active control	Can maintain neutral, but tends to retract
8. Arms	Good control	and abduc

Drawing/photo of total body resting posture

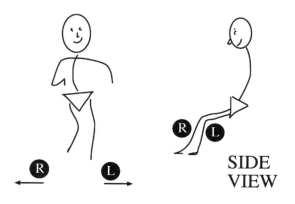

SIDE VIEW

B. Functional Skills in Present Seating/Mobility System:

Note ability and assistance needed:

1. **Walking**: Able to walk? _____Yes_____ Assistance needed? _Max Assist of 1 person_
   Assistive device? _____N/A_____ Braces? _Bilateral AFO's_ Distance? _10 feet_

2. **Transfers:**

	Surface Height	Amount of Assistance
To & from bed	26"	Lifted and carried
To & from toilet	15"	Max assist for stand-pivot transfer
To & from bathtub	bench = 17"	Max assist for stand-pivot transfer
To & from car	Now, lifted and carried to front seat of van.	

   Ability to adjust or remove seating/mobility components _Able to fasten and unfasten seatbelt_ _with push-button_

3. **Wheelchair Propulsion**
   Self-propel? _Yes propels with only (L) hand, so goes in circles_ Axle position _Behind his shoulders_
   Posture and movement _Leans trunk to (R), (R) leg flexes up, (L) knee stiffens and extends, leans trunk forward_
   Power wheelchair? _N/A_ Control, switches _N/A_
   Posture and movement _N/A_
   Attendant operated? _Yes_ Handle height _36"_

Are the below activities done in seating system? If so, are they independently performed? Describe changes in posture and movement, and space necessary to do activities.

4. **Dressing** _Puts shirt on/off with sitting in seating system – Assists mother. Needs to bend trunk forward and rotate trunk to (R)_

5. **Bathing** _Not done in seating system – transfers to bench_

6. **Toileting** _Not done in seating system – transfers to bench_

7. **Eating** _Able to feed self. (R) arm and leg flex when eating. (L) leg tends to extend off footplate when eating._

8. **Communicating** _Speaks. Using Unicorn board with tactile overlays to access computer_

9. **Tabletop Activities** _Needs tabletop close to trunk. Draws. Operates Braille writer with (L) hand._

10. **Work/Vocational/Homemaking Activities** _N/A_

Max. = Maximum   (R) = Right   (L) = Left   WNL = Within normal limits

N/A = Not applicable   post. = posterior   TAL = Tendon Achilles Lengthening

IR = Internal rotation   Add = Adduction   (I) = Independently

C. Joint and Muscular Flexibility Assessed Lying on Back or Side

* Note percentage of flexibility and practical, comfortable flexibility of person's habitual posture. The posture (ie. rolled backward) under the body part (ie. pelvis) is the person's habitual posture.

0%= Totally fixed. 100%= Totally flexible

Person's Habitual Posture	How Flexible?	Comments
Pelvis/Low Back		
Rolled backward (posterior tilt)	50%	
Rolled forward (anterior tilt)		
Tilted to the side (lateral pelvic tilt)	100%	Down on (R)
Turned (rotated)		
Trunk		
Curved forward (kyphosis)	100%	
Curved to one side (scoliosis)	100%	Convex on (R)
Rotated forward on one side (rotated)	75%	(L) forward
Arched backward (extended)		

Hips	Left	Right	Comments
Bending up separately (flexion)	0-90°	0-90°	
Moved to midline (adducted)	100%	100%	
Turned in (internally rotated)	100%	100%	
Spread open (abducted)			
Turned out (externally rotated)			

Knees
- Bent (flexed)   straightens to 90°
- Straight (extended)   bends to 90°

Ankles/Feet			
Bent up (dorsiflexed)			
Bent down (plantarflexed)	100%	100%	
Turned in (inverted)	100%	100%	
Turned out (everted)			

Head and Neck

Shoulder Girdles			
Shrugged upwards (elevated)	50%		
Pulled forward and turned in (protracted and internally rotated)		100%	
Pulled backward and turned out (retracted and externally rotated)			

Arms			
Stiffly bent (flexed)		100%	
Stiffly straight (extended)		100%	

356

D. Balance and Postural Control in Sitting
Good _____
Fair ___X_____
Poor _____

E. Assessment in Sitting - Flexibility and Postural Support
1. Pelvis/Low Back
a. Neutral pelvis _____

b. Active pelvic control _____

	How Flexible?	Comments
c. Rolled backward (posterior tilt)	50%	
d. Stiffening & sliding forward (thrust)		
e. Rolled forward (anterior tilt)		
f. Tilted to the side (lateral pelvic tilt)	100%	Down to (R)
g. Turned (rotated)		

Hand simulation - Where, direction and amount of support, least amount of support?
Behind pelvis – below PSIS, over sacrum. (R) side pelvis, snug and close to side thigh. In front of pelvis – over thighs – minimal force at a 90° angle to seat cushion.

2. Trunk
a. Neutral trunk _____

b. Active trunk control _Able to move (curve) forward and backward, to sides if pelvis supported._

	How Flexible?	Comments
c. Curved forward (kyphosis)	50%	at T12
d. Curved to one side (scoliosis)	100%	
e. Rotated forward on one side (rotated)	75%	
f. Arched backwards (extended)		

Hand simulation - Posture of spine over pelvis. Where, direction and amount of support, least amount of support, amount and shape of contact surface?
Behind trunk – support curving to contact back up to the lower ribs. His neutral trunk is with his head slightly forward of pelvis (hip joint)

3. Hips and Legs

	Left	Right	Comments
a. Neutral hips	yes	not (l)	
b. Active hip control	yes	no	

	How Flexible?	Comments
c. Moved to midline (adducted)	100%	
d. Turned in (internally rotated)	100%	
e. Spread open (abducted)		
f. Turned out (externally rotated)		
g. Turned - same side (windswept)		
h. Legs moving constantly		

Hand simulation - Where, direction and amount of support, least amount of support?
Minimal support pressing against the inner part of the R knee prevents (R) hip from excessively turning and moving in. Also prevents (R) side of pelvis from rotating forward.

4. **Knees**

	Left	Right	Comments
a. Neutral knees	not(I)	not(I)	
b. Active knee control	no	no	Can extend (L) knee,
	How Flexible?		difficulty flexing (L) knee
c. Bent (flexed)		100%	
d. Straightened (extended)		100%	

Hand simulation - Where, direction and amount of support, least amount of support?

(R) knee – likes to flex further under seat when reaching forward with arm.

(L) knee – needs moderate support at ankles to prevent involuntary knee extension

5. **Ankles/Feet**

	Left	Right	Comments
a. Neutral ankles	yes	yes	
b. Active ankle control			

Hand simulation - Where, direction and amount of support, least amount of support?

Ankles and feet are controlled within ankle/foot orthoses which are always worn.

6. **Head and Neck**

a. Neutral head _____

b. Active head control good control

Hand simulation - Posture of spine over pelvis. Head in relation to gravity. Where support is needed. Least amount of support. Amount and shape of contact surface?

Head is better aligned (not forward & rotated to (L)) when the pelvis is neutral, trunk is erect – so that shoulder girdle and upper trunk is slghtly froward of pelvis (hip joint).

7. **Shoulder Girdles**

	Left	Right	Comments
a. Neutral shoulder girdles			
b. Active arm control	good		
	How Flexible?		
c. Shrugged upwards (elevated)	50%		
d. Pulled forward and turned in (protracted and internally rotated)		100%	
e. Pulled backward and turned out (retracted and externally rotated)			

Hand simulation - Where, direction and amount of support?

(R) elbow and forearm – if supported underneath such that the elbow is flexed to 90° and positioned under the shoulder, the (R) side of trunk does not curve and lean so much to the (R)

8. **Arms**

	Left	Right
a. Neutral arms		Able to maintain
b. Active arm control	Good	

Hand simulation - Where, direction and amount of support, least amount of support?

See above – shoulder girdles

F. Effect of Gravity in Sitting

	Relax	Pull Against	Head Control
Backwards Tilt (optimal amount)	_____	X _____	_____
Forwards Tilt	_____	X _____	_____
Tilting needed for better breathing, pressure relief?	_____	_____	_____

G. Pressure: Wiggle Test/Pressure Measuring

Put your fingers under concerning boney prominences and assess if:

1. You can wiggle your fingers.
2. Your fingers are pinched but you can pull your fingers out easily.
3. Fingers are pinched and it is difficult to pull your fingers out.

Sacrum _____   Coccyx _____   Ischial tuberosities _____

Greater trochanters _____   Other _____

Objectives

A. Person's Postural & Functional Objectives

Pelvis
- Needs stable base of support
- Needs space for ischial tuberosities
- (R) side of pelvis needs support snug and close to the thigh
- Moderate support below PSIS and behind sacrum keeps pelvis in neutral
- Support over tops of thighs stabilizes pelvis and thighs

Trunk
Needs support from behind (sacrum to lower rib cage), in fixed, kyphotic neutral posture

Needs option of extension and lateral movement

Hips and Legs Need to be supported in 90° flexion so that the pelvis is in neutral

(R) hip needs to be supported in neutral to prevent excessive abduction/adduction. Support at (R) knee

Knees (R) knee needs to flex past 90° for reaching forward with arms

(L) knee extension needs to be prevented with support just below L ankle

Ankles and Feet

Supported by orthoses. Ankles are in 90° dorsiflexion

Head and Neck The posture of the head and neck are affected by the pelvis and trunk.

No direct support is needed.

Shoulder Girdles
(L) shoulder needs to be free to function

Arms (R) forearm and elbow should be supported underneath to prevent excessive abduction and trunk leaning

B. Seating System Objectives

- Seat Cushion provides stable base of support and allows space for ischial tuberosities
- (R) lateral upper leg support needs to be snug and close to the thigh to prevent obliquity
- Lower back support should be contoured and shaped to the sacrum and supporting the pelvis below the PSIS to prevent posterior pelvic tilt

- Upper Back Support contours to the shape of the fixed kyphotic spine
- Lower Back Support to Upper Back Support Angle needs to allow thoracic extension

- Seat-to-Lower Back Support Angle is 90° to support pelvis in neutral
- Middle (medial) upper leg support prevents excessive adduction and pressure of (R) knee

Leg-to-seat surface angle is 90° to allow arm and trunk function
(L) ankle/foot support needs to prevent (L) knee extension

Foot support-to-leg angle needs to support ankles in 90°
Back support height allow freedom of movement for shoulder girdles

Arm supports and laptray will support (R) forearm and elbow to prevent excessive abduction and trunk leaning

C. Mobility and Other Objectives

Aaron needs to be able to propel wheelchair so that it goes straight (one-arm drive mechanism)
Aaron needs to manipulate as many aspects of the seating/mobility system for transfers, ie. seat-
belt, foot support, brakes.

Seating and Mobility Components

A. Seating System Components

Lower back support _Contoured support behind pevlvis and sacrum_
Upper back support _Firm but contoured to the shape of Aaron's back. Extends to 1" under the shoulder blades_
Seat cushion _Anti-thrust seat_

Seat-to-lower back support angle _90°_
Lower back support-to-upper back support angle _Angled backwards slightly_
Leg-to-seat surface angle _90°, but allowing more flexion of knees_
Foot support-to-leg angle _90°_
Tilt of the seating system _0° in relation to gravity_

Pelvic supports _____
  Anterior (front) _Positioning belt set at 90° to the seat cushion_
  Lateral (side) _Hip block on (R) side of pelvis_
  Inferior (bottom) _____

Trunk supports _____
  Anterior (front) _____
  Lateral (side) _____

Upper leg support _____
  Medial (middle) _Wedge shaped block on a flip-down bracket with a push button that Aaron can control_
  Lateral (side) _____
  Superior (top) _____

Lower leg supports _Swing-away, fip-up foot supports for transfers_
  Anterior (front) _____
  Posterior (behind) _____

Ankle/foot supports _____
  Anterior/Circumferential (front) _(L) ankle strap set at 45° to foot support_
  Posterior (behind) _____
  Medial/ Lateral (sides) _____
  Posterior (behind) _____

Head/neck supports _____
  Posterior (behind) _____
  Lateral (side) _____
  Anterior (front) _____

Shoulder girdle supports _____

Arm supports _Desk-length, height adjustable armrests_

B. Additional Components

Laptray __yes__

Grasping bars –horizontal, vertical _____

Wedges (scapulae, arms) _____

Blocks (elbows) _____

Troughs (legs, arms) _____

Straps _____

Adjustability of components and angles _____

C. Wheelchair Considerations

Seat surface height at front edge __Low as possible to Aaron to stand from wheelchair, but high enough for to access dining room table__

Width of seating/mobility system __Narrow as possible__

Forward/backward position of seating system within mobility system __Seating system set far enough back in the wheelchair so that his shoulders are in line with the rear axle.__

Cushion covering __washable and well ventilated__

Seating system removable from mobility system __does not need to remove__

Wheelchair foldability __does not need to fold__

Push handle height __36"__

Tilt or recline __upright-no tilt__

*Needs one-arm drive mechanism

Contributors

Adrienne Falk Bergen, PT, ATP, is a pediatric physical therapist and assistive technology practitioner, who specializes in seating and wheeled mobility. She has practiced, written, and taught in this field for the last forty years, helping therapists and suppliers improve their skills in the field. She was the first president of NRRTS, and worked with RESNA to create the first certification for rehabilitation technology suppliers. In retirement, Adrienne moved to Florida where she has continued to work as a volunteer and to serve on committees to support continued development in the field. Adrienne is a wife, mother, and grandmother.

Jamie Noon has spent twenty-three years involved in seating/mobility services and developing innovative seating designs in the U.S. and abroad, after studying the fine arts. In the mid-1990s, he worked as a seating/mobility clinician at the Rehabilitation Engineering Center at Packard Children's Hospital at Stanford. He has provided seating/mobility clinical and technical training in Russia, Bangladesh, Sri Lanka, Nicaragua, Mexico, Tanzania, Kenya, Ethiopia, China, Phillipines, Vietnam, and Colombia. Jamie is a contributor to the development of International Wheelchair Guidelines for developing countries coordinated by the World Health Organization.

Jessica Presperin-Pedersen, MBA, OTR/L, ATP has been an occupational therapist since 1979, and began developing her expertise in wheelchairs and seating a year later. She has worked at major rehabilitation centers, outpatient clinics, schools, private practices and residences for individuals with developmental disabilities. She was one of the founding instructors for the occupational therapy program at Governors State University. Jessica enjoys sharing her experiences through writing and teaching throughout the world.

Betsy McKone, BA, OTR, ATP has worked in the field of seating and mobility for over twenty years, first as a seating clinician at the Rehabilitation Engineering Center at Packard Children's Hospital at Stanford and more recently as a rehab technology supplier for ATG Rehab, in Mountain View, California.

Cindy D. Smith, PT, ATP, graduated from the University of Vermont in 1978 with a BS in physical therapy. She has worked in the outpatient department at Craig Hospital since 1990, specializing in people with spinal cord injuries. She is currently the outpatient therapy coordinator and is an integral member of both the Skin Clinic and Seating/Positioning Clinic. She obtained her ATP certification through RESNA, and is currently working on her DPT through the University of Colorado.

Mark Richter, PhD, is the director of MAX mobility, an assistive technology R&D company, and an adjunct assistant professor in the Department of Biomedical Engineering at Vanderbilt University. Mark earned his PhD in mechanical engineering from Stanford University, with an emphasis in rehabilitation engineering, and has been active in the field since 1995. Dr. Richter's research interests include wheelchair design, propulsion technique, wheelchair setup, adaptive exercise equipment, and recreational technologies. He has taught several project-based courses where student teams designed assistive devices for clients with disabilities.

Brenda Canning, OTR/L, has been an occupational therapist since 1984 and has worked primarily in adult rehabilitation. She has been at the Rehabilitation Institute of Chicago for the last eight years, working exclusively in the area of seating and mobility for adults with a wide variety of disabilities. Her most challenging work has been with clients having longstanding disabilities (several years to several decades), a large percentage having spinal cord injuries. She has lectured at the International Seating Symposium as well other continuing education courses for allied health professionals, and has authored and co-authored articles on seating and wheeled mobility.

Index